QUANTUM OF NIGHTMARES

ALSO BY CHARLES STROSS

CHARLES STROSS

▶◀▶◀▶◀▶◀▶◀▶◀▶◀▶◀

QUANTUM
OF NIGHTMARES

A TOM DOHERTY ASSOCIATES BOOK
NEW YORK

QUANTUM OF NIGHTMARES

Copyright © 2021 by Charles Stross

A Tordotcom Book
Published by Tom Doherty Associates
120 Broadway
New York, NY 10271

www.tor.com

Tor® is a registered trademark of Macmillan Publishing Group, LLC.

The Library of Congress Cataloging-in-Publication Data is available upon request.

ISBN 978-1-250-83937-4 (hardcover)
ISBN 978-1-250-83938-1 (ebook)

Our books may be purchased in bulk for promotional, educational, or business use. Please contact your local bookseller or the Macmillan Corporate and Premium Sales Department at 1-800-221-7945, extension 5442, or by email at MacmillanSpecialMarkets@macmillan.com.

First Edition: 2022

Printed in the United States of America

0 9 8 7 6 5 4 3 2 1

YOU WERE NOT THERE FOR THE BEGINNING.

YOU WILL NOT BE THERE FOR THE END.

YOUR KNOWLEDGE OF WHAT IS GOING ON CAN ONLY BE

SUPERFICIAL AND RELATIVE.

—WILLIAM S. BURROUGHS, *NAKED LUNCH*

QUANTUM OF NIGHTMARES

1

‣◂‣◂‣◂‣

GOING CUCKOO

Mary MacCandless came up from the underground station, turned left onto Bayswater Road, crossed the busy junction with Park Lane, and stopped to admire the glass and chrome skull rack on Tyburn.

It was a rainy day in mid-December, and a chilly breeze rattled the gibbet cages at each corner of the structure. The construction scaffolding had only just come down, revealing the gleaming tzompantli. It wrapped around Marble Arch, embraced and extending it in the instantly recognizable style of one of the most famous British architects of the twentieth century. Most of the niches on the rack were still empty, but several lonely heads stared eyelessly down from the top row.

"Read all abah't the crims 'oo went up last week!" shouted a street hawker, selling glossy, printed commemorative magazines wrapped in a plastic caul: "Read all abah't their evil deeds an' sad'n'pathetic last moments! Free DVD with every copy! Virtual reality view of every execution! Only twelve pounds fifty, collect 'em all!"

"Don't mind if I do." Mary smiled saucily and handed the fellow a dodgy twenty-pound note. He didn't check it before he made change: more fool him. "Cheery-bye!" she called as she stuffed the purchase in her messenger bag and sashayed off towards her job interview, richer by seven pounds fifty.

Central London was the stomping ground of nobs and toffs these days. Only the obscenely wealthy could afford to live here, much less own a house big enough to accommodate a live-in nanny. That, in Mary's opinion, made any such employers fair game. Admittedly the Mr. and Mrs. Richy McRichface she was here to fleece lived in a tied house that came with their job-share, but it was the principle that mattered. Anyway, they were both on the same pay scale as a Deputy Chief Constable, which meant they had to be loaded or at least well-insured. The Boss had given Mary a fat dossier on her targets, and Mary had done due diligence. *Never take a job at face value without checking the Information* was her watchword, and to date it had kept her from dancing the Tyburn tango. As far as she could tell the Boss's briefing was accurate. But then, he hadn't taken over London's supernatural underground by leaving anything to chance.

The wind had strengthened to something between a brisk breeze and an all-out blow by the time Mary opened the gate, marched up the short path to Number Seventeen, and rang the doorbell. She waited and waited, and waited some more: and while she waited she got herself into character. She was about to push the bell for a second time when the porch door opened.

"I've got it!" the big, red-faced bloke in sweatpants and polo shirt holding the door shouted over his shoulder. He turned to face Mary without really seeing her: "Just a mo!" he said, and pushed the inner door half-shut—"Need to get the rabble under control—"

A scream and a crash of breaking crockery echoed through the house, followed by a rising and falling wail of tantrum tears. "Right!" shouted a woman. "That's it! Robert, Lyssa, your father will—no dear, come here, Mummy's going to kiss it better, and *you* can just sit there in the naughty corner so I can keep an eye on you, young man no *stop that*—"

A Supermarine Spitfire the size of Mary's hand zoomed towards her face, buzzing like a rabid hornet. Without thinking, she plucked it out of the air. For a moment the buzzing rose to a febrile howl: tiny sparks erupted from its gun ports, stinging her palm. "Horrid thing!" She crushed it like a wasp, then brushed the smoking remains into her bag, ignoring the blood leaking from under the shattered cockpit canopy. Straightening up, she confronted Mr. Banks. "I can see I'm just in time! The agency were absolutely right to call me."

Mr. Banks opened the door a fraction wider. A harried eye scanned her up and down with a policeman's assessing gaze. "Who are you?"

"Mary Drop at your service!" She held out her hand. "From

the nanny agency," she added, in case it wasn't entirely obvious that nannying was the name of her game. (It never paid to assume the mark was on the ball.) "I gather you have a number of small problems . . . ?"

"Yes, four of them." Mr. Banks's shoulders relaxed slightly as he pulled the door open: "Come in, come right in, you're just in the nick of time!"

Mary's experienced eye took in the four suitcases lined up inside the door, the carry-on with passports and boarding passes in an unzipped outer pocket, and the high-pitched wails emanating from the kitchen door. "You're going away *right now*?" she asked, raising an eyebrow.

"Business conference," Mr. Banks said grimly. "Unfortunately Sylvia waited until this morning to inform us that she'd had *enough of our shit* and we were fired." His finger-quotes made clear his disbelief that a professional nanny could use such uncouth language in front of her charges. "She had her bag packed before I put the morning coffee on. Didn't even wait for breakfast. I'm so glad you were available at short notice—"

"Yes, well, they sent me because this sort of situation is *exactly* my speciality." Which was perfectly true, although the *they* in question weren't the nanny agency Mr. and Mrs. Banks used. "It's just lucky I'm available at short notice, isn't it?" Mary smirked. She recognized the Boss's hand at work in the sudden departure of her predecessor. "All's well that ends well, I always say, so if you'd show me inside and introduce me to your wife and the little ones I'll just get settled in, shall I?"

"Yes, indeed." Mr. Banks paused and looked at her messenger bag curiously. "Is that all you're bringing?"

"I left my suitcase with the Left Luggage company in Paddington. I can pick it up later, once you're on your way." She raised her hat and fanned her face with it. The house felt overheated after the chill of the pre-Christmas rain, and her coat was buttoned to her chin. "Going somewhere nice, I hope?"

"A conference in Hawaii—it's a business trip. Our flight leaves in four hours: we should be back a week on Wednesday." A shadow crossed Mr. Banks's face. "Trudy?"

"Coming, dear!" Mrs. Banks swayed into the hall, thrown off-balance by the toddler she was carrying on one hip. Mr. and Mrs. Banks were both in their early forties, tall and well-toned from the gym. Trudy Banks wore a worried expression, and the grooves worn in her forehead suggested it was a perpetual state of existence for her. The little girl's face was buried against the side of her neck like an infant vampire, but her quivering shoulders signalled manipulative sobbing rather than sanguinary suckling. Long blonde hair, party dress, mismatched socks: Mary could tell at a glance she was going to be a handful. "I take it Sylvia didn't dress them before she left?" Mary unslung her bag and offered her arms.

Trudy gratefully handed over her daughter. "This is Emily," she introduced. "Emily, this is—I'm sorry, I didn't catch your name?"

"I'm Mary Drop," said Mary. She addressed Emily directly: "And I'm going to take really good care of you while Mummy and Daddy are away!" Emily emitted an overblown thespian sob and met Mary's gaze with a coldly assessing stare. Mary smiled—not her *real* smile, the one that scared crocodiles, but the child-friendly version—and pulled Emily closer. "The usual agency terms and conditions apply," she told the little girl's parents out of the corner of her mouth. "But I'm definitely not going anywhere for at least two weeks. Hopefully longer." In her inside pocket, the charmed amulet the Boss had loaned her grew warm as it worked extra-hard to reinforce the Bankses' belief in her bona fides, pushing the message: *no need for references, nothing to see here, move along now.*

"We're sorted, then," said Trudy, her gratitude palpable. "I've left a to-do list with the Amazon and Waitrose delivery service passwords on the kitchen table, along with a spare set of keys. There's a folder labelled NANNY for you to read. Let me introduce you to Elissa—she answers to Lyssa—Ethan, and Robert—who doesn't answer to Bob—then we've *really* got to go, our Uber is on its way." She was already pulling on an overcoat better suited to a rainy winter in St John's Wood than an international summit meeting of state-licensed superheroes in Hawaii. "You'll call us if there are any problems, won't you? Any problems at all, *any* time of day or night. Oh, and Robert sleepwalks sometimes, just so you know."

Mary smiled and nodded, her grin as fixed as any of the death masks fronting the skulls on the Marble Arch Tzompantli. Emily clung to her like grim death: the little girl had fallen silent, as though she realized that the bogeywoman was no longer hiding under the bed but had come out to play in broad daylight. "You have absolutely *nothing* to be concerned about!" she assured Nigel and Trudy Banks, Captain Colossal and the Blue Queen, senior line superheroes by appointment of the London Metropolitan Police Commissioner's office. "I'll take good care of them, you'll see!"

And because she told them no lies, Mr. and Mrs. Banks lapped it up.

Easy as stealing candy from a baby, Mary MacCandless told herself, and her smile was almost sincere.

▸◂▸◂

Nearly a week had passed since Rupert's premature death had deprived Eve of one of her long-anticipated life goals—his murder. By stealing a cursed magical tome, her scumbag boss had discovered a new and entirely original way to commit suicide. Admittedly Eve had helped him along the way by not pointing out the consequences of his reckless greed and stupidity, but Rupert was, well, *Rupert.* If he hadn't been a self-entitled wanker who treated his employees as serfs and sex toys she might have made a token attempt to stop him: but then again, pigs might fly.

Meanwhile, the cuckoo clock in Rupert's office was striking thirteen, and Eve was thoroughly perturbed.

One benefit of having spent years planning his murder was that Eve knew exactly what to do afterwards. She was in theory employed as Rupert de Montfort Bigge's executive assistant. But within the organization, especially during his frequent unexplained absences, she spoke with his voice: everybody was used to seeing her hand on the tiller. It wasn't as if she was underqualified. She had degrees in business and economics, was licensed to trade on the London Stock Exchange, and had much the same responsibilities as a corporate vice president. She was also a highly competent sorceress. Only a man as arrogant and self-entitled as Rupert would dream of introducing her to his cronies as his secretary, much less impose on someone so dangerous for personal services of a degrading and humiliating nature.

Rupert was fabulously corrupt and equally fabulously wealthy, and the Bigge Organization was essentially a gigantic wealth management/private equity front he'd created to manage the fortunes he'd stolen. He still contributed to the bottom line by means of certain disgusting occult practices, but he was increasingly distant from the day-to-day running of his corporation these days, leaving it to Head Office to coordinate operations and manage his investments. Which, in practice, meant Eve.

While Rupert was out of the picture, Eve kept the Bigge Organization ticking over smoothly. And the week after his "departure" she cultivated the office grapevine even more assiduously than usual. There were the usual rumors about depraved parties in the castle on Skaro (a small channel island which he had purchased along with its feudal lordship), and Eve encouraged these. There was also discreet speculation about Rupe being in rehab again. Eve nodded sagaciously, then changed the subject in an implicitly confirmatory manner. Snooping on the coffee station at HQ—she'd taken personal control over Rupe's workplace spy cameras and microphones—she very carefully determined that there were *no* rumors about a missing concordance to the *Necronomicon*, a disappearing hitman, or the shenanigans of several second-tier supervillains. It appeared her veil of operational security was intact. So the morning after his demise she activated her coverup plan.

Eve reported his disappearance to the authorities. She'd been obliging but unhelpful to the officers from New Scotland Yard, giving them plenty of inconclusive leads to investigate. They were looking for bloated bodies off the coast of Guernsey: but also asking about new inpatients at a small and very exclusive clinic in Bulgaria, not to mention considering the possibility that a certain former US Navy SEAL turned mercenary had gone rogue and disposed of his boss. (The mercenary in question was known to have a James Bond fixation, going so far as to ape the fictional spy's taste in tailoring and borrow Rupe's Aston-Martin.) It was all quite perplexing, and the detectives had thanked her and gone on their way nursing the missing-billionaire-sized headaches she'd laid in their minds like the confabulated eggs of a parasitic wasp of the imagination.

As the executive assistant of a billionaire, Eve expected and got the kid-glove treatment. Nobody so much as hinted that she herself might be under suspicion. So, two days later, Eve set in motion the legal machinery to have Rupert declared missing; and today, at noon precisely, in custody of the access codes he'd left copies of in the Chief Legal Counsel's safe, she entered his office without an invitation for the very first time.

The cuckoo clock was getting on her nerves.

Rupert's den was deceptively airy and open in feel despite being part of a London town house. From the thick, hand-woven carpet to the polished oak of his eighteenth-century admiralty desk, everything about the room was coded for ostentatious luxury. Portraits of Messrs. and Ladies de Montfort and Bigge from centuries past adorned the walls—one of them, if Eve's eyes weren't deceiving her, was a John Singer Sargent. There was nothing so gauche as an in tray or a computer terminal on the desk. Rupe's sole concessions to modernity were his smartphone (lost in Neverland, along with its owner) and a 72-inch curved monitor bolted to the wall above a transplanted and entirely nonfunctional Adam fireplace, the better to spy on his minions.

All of which made the presence of a prime-number-tweeting Black Forest souvenir even more incongruous. Not only was it committing an offense against timekeeping, it was out of place in Rupert's personal space. Rupert's taste in decor was unrelentingly bad, but it wasn't *that* kind of bad. And Eve couldn't abide inconsistencies: they made her itch.

"Reception? Put me through to Facilities," she announced.

"You called, Miss?" Her bluetooth headset was all but surgically grafted to her ear: she wore it from rising to bed, and the rotating team of receptionists upstairs were trained to respond to her instantly.

"I'm in Rupert's office. There's a *cuckoo clock* in here. Email me its inventory record, please, I want to know where it came from." It was probably a present from one of his drinking buddies, but you never knew with Rupert. It might be evidence of some sort of ghastly crime, publicly displayed in mockery of the police. "That's all for now." She ended the call, then glanced at her watch. She had eight minutes until an upcoming conference call with Acquisitions and Mergers. She was due to take it in her own office, a small, austere cell buried in the subbasement beneath Rupert's expansive den. She glowered at the clock as she stalked towards the door. "I'll deal with you later," she warned it repressively as she gazed around the room, searching for overlooked hiding places. And a moment later, she forgot all about the clock.

One of Rupert's nastier hobbies was collecting documentary evidence of other people's misdeeds. They were papers so weighty that they bent light around them, like the gravity well of a black hole. They had to be *somewhere,* and knowing Rupe—no one knew him better than she—he'd have stashed them in a secret place only he could get at. But—again, knowing Rupert—they'd be close to hand. So Eve had wasted almost an entire hour of her incredibly valuable time hunting for the private safe she knew had to be somewhere in here.

It wasn't on any of the architectural drawings she had access to. She'd never seen it, never even been told as a certainty that it existed—she'd simply inferred its existence by the absence of certain files from the main office vault. Eve surmised that he'd hired an expert craftsman to install a hidden safe in his office, then, like a jealous Pharaoh guarding his inner tomb, murdered them to ensure they took the secret to their grave.

Rupert's personal safe was full of secrets, secrets that could kill. But Rupert had gone to his grave without telling Eve where it was, and she wouldn't be entirely happy until she had them under her own lock and key.

►◄►◄►◄

Amy from Human Resources started her Monday morning expecting the week ahead to be at least as bad as the curdled dregs at the bottom of the mug of coffee-like liquid beside her laptop. For one thing, she hated Monday mornings. For another, she worked in HR for the most aggressively downmarket regional supermarket chain in London, which a modern Dante might quite accurately characterize as the tenth circle of hell. And finally, she had a disciplinary hearing coming up in half an hour, and she hated disciplinaries with a passion.

Disciplinary proceedings invariably reminded Amy of the weakness of her own white-knuckle grip on the swaying rope ladder dangling below the zeppelin of corporate management, cruising high above the corpse-strewn wasteland of the economy. Amy was not under any illusions that she was suited to a high-flying career—but to lose her grip would doom her to a catastrophic fall into the hideous depths. Also, when she had these thoughts she got airsick, even though both her feet were planted on terra firma, and right now her stomach was roiling. (It was probably the bad break-room coffee.)

"Who is it, sweetie?" Jennifer, her boss—never a mere *Jenny*, much less a diminutive *Jenn*—leaned over the back of Amy's chair, startling her into a guilty pelvic floor spasm. Jennifer was pretty much Amy's antithesis, not to say her nemesis: a natural straight-haired blonde, ten centimeters taller in flats than Amy in heels, who wore her charcoal suit and cream silk blouse as if it was a fashion statement rather than a uniform. She was two years younger and skinnier than Amy, her jackets didn't gape, and when she wore a skirt it didn't ride up and wrinkle; her unpaid overtime hours and general glow of self-confidence bespoke the certainty that she was on her way to a seat in the FlavrsMart C-suite.

Unlike Amy, she didn't feel the need to assert her self-worth and individuality by dyeing her fringe green, pursuing unauthorized hobbies, or having a life beyond her job. Amy knew she was supposed to envy Jennifer: but the truth of the matter was that she would rather die than swap her life for her boss's. And this awareness of her own thoughtcrime made her feel worse than actual green-eyed envy ever could. It meant she was a loser, doomed to be ground to paste between the gears of the corporate machinery she was paid to maintain. It was only a matter of time before she lost her grip and fell to her doom.

Amy and Jennifer shared a cramped office in the management

suite of Branch 322, a FlavrsMart supermarket—*FlavrsMart, Where Everything Tastes Better!*—deep in the wilderness of suburban northeast London. In theory they hot-desked with Tara, Kirsten, and Barry. But Kirsten was on maternity leave, Tara telecommuted from Branch 219 most of the time, and Barry haunted the front-line trenches down in Receiving because he was terrified of Jennifer—not because of anything she'd done, but because of what she *might* do. So for the time being they had the HR office to themselves.

"It's Adrian Hewitt in Textured Deli Goods again." Amy sighed noisily. "Looks like he didn't get the memo when I verballed him last week."

"Oh dear, I told him—" Jennifer peered over Amy's shoulder at her laptop screen. "I suppose you'd better show me what you've got."

Amy brought up the file that Security had forwarded to her—a compilation of video clips from the supermarket surveillance network. Candid Camera had gone on a blind date with Jeremy Bentham behind the meat counter: FlavrsMart employees all wore uniforms with name badges and RFID location transponders, so the store cameras knew exactly where to point, all the time. This was not a secret from the staff—quite the opposite—but it never ceased to amaze Amy how many of her fellow employees seemed to forget that *everything* they did on the shop floor was recorded.

To Amy's way of thinking, disciplinary hearings seldom achieved anything beyond highlighting what Jennifer called the Banality of Fuck-Uppery: the utter inability of petty workplace rebels to make their career-limiting moves count for something. Usually they were the result of a ploddingly mundane display of incompetence on the job, like an inability to stack shelves or operate a vacuum cleaner. Less frequently it was for harassment or disreputable conduct: a circulating photo of a set of sad-sack genitals might warrant a more-in-sorrow-than-in-anger suggestion that their owner take it to the dole office, or maybe the department of urogenital medicine. Occasionally a customer would complain about a slight lack of obsequious servility, and once in a blue moon it turned out that they weren't entirely exaggerating: that was embarrassing, and FlavrsMart would be compelled to take action to protect its corporate reputation. Finally, petty pilfering would result in a blue-suiter escorting the perp from the premises, or even arresting them and taking them down to the local nick to await the tender mercies of the hanging magistrates.

But regardless of the cause, disciplinary cases generated stacks of paperwork and hours of camera footage that needed to be combed through and preserved, just to ensure that FlavrsMart was in no way exposed to litigation. And because Amy was the HR ugly duckling, forever trailing forlornly behind Jennifer's immaculate swan, the paperwork always landed on her shoulders.

Amy flicked through the video montage of butchers behaving badly until she got to the coup de disgrace: the sequence which had finally forced her to take action. Behind her, Jennifer watched intently. She didn't sound happy. "Look at that—bleep—*thing*. Artistic statement. Extrusion." (She actually said *bleep*.) "What *is* it?"

"Grounds for dismissal." Amy bit her tongue. Though this was the Human Resources department, they were no more immune to the gaze of the corporate panopticon than anyone on the shop floor. The verbal *bleep* was Jennifer's way of acknowledging this fact, with a tug of the forelock to the Company Code of Conduct (which forbade swearing or other expressions that might be offensive or intimidating). It was a placeholder that discreetly signified the possibility of less temperate language, circumstances permitting. Amy, however, while not bleeping, was veering dangerously close to irony, if not outright sarcasm.[1]

Jennifer winced. "Can you see an angle? Any way to constructively reframe it as something less offensive? Mr. Hewitt is in a high-skill role: replacing him will be difficult."

"I don't see what we can do about this. Other than the obvious, I mean?"

"Bleep. I suppose you're right: too late to sweep it under the rug. We're going to have to rightsize him. Bleep it."

It was unlike Jennifer to be so squeamish. Amy tried to reassure

---

1. Which was a firing offense (Category: Gross misconduct; subcategory: Insolence towards the Dignity of the Enterprise).

her: "I'll pull his job description, see if we've got any applicants on file who have matching experience."

Jennifer sighed again and stared at Amy's laptop. "Bleep. *Bleep*-bleepity *bleep*. Thank you, Ade, thanks for nothing."

Amy blinked. It sounded as if Jennifer was taking it *personally*. Did she have a relationship with the offensive Mr. Hewitt outside the workplace? That would be problematic.

"Boss." (It was clearly time to break out the soft soap.) "We *can't* keep him if he's in the habit of sexually abusing the printer during stock-taking hours. I mean, it's on video. How can I phrase this? *No*. Not if he's going to put stuff like this on the deli counter without taking precautions. At least using a condom."

"Cr—bleep." Jennifer rolled her eyes and huffed. "He was only using leftovers that were going in the recycling skip!" She'd moved from denial to irritation in seconds. Amy just had to hope she'd skip hostility completely and go straight to bargaining and acceptance: otherwise, Amy herself was in the firing line. "*Bleep* the video, why couldn't that camera be out of service?"

"Imagine what could have happened if he got called away and it was still there the next morning? Someone with delicate sensibilities might be offended. A wean might complain. Worse, they might *Instagram* it." (Instagram was the hot new photo-sharing app with the kids these days, wasn't it?)

"*Sigh*, you're right. It'd be all over the internet before you could snap your fingers. The Food Standards Agency would ram-raid us with an armored car full of inspectors. The *New Management* might take an interest." Jennifer invoked the government with the kind of uneasy, admiring relish usually associated with eyewitness accounts of public executions. (Which had become a Thing again, especially on Instagram, thanks to the New Management's firm approach to crime and punishment.)

"Okay." Amy relaxed infinitesimally, now that her boss was in agreement. "I'll take him to the interview room when he shows." A chime from her desk phone warned her that the miscreant was on his way up, escorted by his team leader. Amy rose, picked up her laptop and notepad, and gave Jennifer a pleading look. "Are you sure you don't want to handle this?" *As he's your friend,* she added silently, knowing better than to voice such a sentiment.

Jennifer smiled vindictively. "I know it sucks, sweetie, but this is your call. I'd have to self-disclose: I'm not impartial. Also, you've got to stop being so squeamish about this aspect of the job. Try and see it as a challenge, just for me? I want to see you step up and handle this yourself. You've got an appraisal coming up: I'll be watching."

Oh crap, Amy thought dismally. *Why can't this just go away?* But she'd maneuvered herself into a corner all on her own before she knew Jennifer had an interest, and now the spot directly between her shoulder blades was itching furiously.

A slim-fingered hand with nails painted the color of fresh blood squeezed Amy's arm: "We can discuss his replacement after lunch. . . ."

▶◀▶◀▶◀

Meanwhile, in a house on a deceptively posh street in Kensington:

"Fucksake, bro, give me that!"

Game Boy made an abortive jump for the cartridge Imp held out of reach. He squealed with frustration and landed heavily on Imp's toe. Imp stumbled: "Ouch! Hey, watch where you're—"

"Mine! My high score! *Give that back,* you brute!" Game Boy lunged and grabbed hold of Imp's arm, dragging him down by sheer weight. Not that Game Boy was particularly heavy—at one-fifty centimeters and fifty kilograms he was a skinny Southeast Asian kid, just under five feet tall in old units—but Imp, the Impresario, wasn't exactly ripped either. He was just tall, intense, and long-haired: like an adult Peter Pan who'd burned through a casual heroin habit and come out the other side barely intact.

Imp's arm drooped under Game Boy's weight until his feet touched the floor. He made a wild one-handed grab for the 3DS cartridge, which slipped through Imp's fingers and fell into his open palm. Game Boy fell back across the carnivorous sofa, glaring angrily and clutching the game with its precious high score to his chest.

"Dude, what the fuck are you playing at?"

Doc Depression glowered at Imp from the doorway. A shopping bag dangled from one hand. Tall and thin to the point of cadaverous, with a face that might have been fashionable on a racehorse, he wore a brown tweed suit whose previous owner had donated it to a charity store a couple of decades earlier: his version of hipster chic.

"We were just arseing around," Imp said defensively: "all in fun—"

"Asshole!" squeaked Game Boy. He whistled for breath again.

"But you're so cute when you beg—"

"The fuck." Doc shook his head in disgust, then looked around, taking in the living room anew. "You're arseing about while the place is a dump."

"This place is *still* a dump, you mean." They'd swept away the broken glass and gas grenades, boarded up the shattered windows, and repaired the worst of the damage inflicted when a crack team of Transnistrian mafia loss adjusters stormed the house in pursuit of Rupert de Montfort Bigge's pet assassin. (The mafiya hitmen had been followed in turn by Imp's terrifying elder sister Eve and her bodyguard, then Rupert himself, Eve's monstrous employer.) Having chucked the broken furniture out the back door and bought a new computer desk or three, the Lost Boys were working on repairing the bedrooms, including the top floor with its eldritch attic extension. Game Boy had even—reluctantly—reactivated the external CCTV system, once Wendy had assured them nobody ever watched it. "These things take time to fix," said Imp.

"When are we getting paid? I had to buy a new mattress after *someone* trashed the old one," Doc complained.

"Eve asked me to visit her tomorrow," Imp replied. "What's the big deal with that cartridge anyway, GeeBee?"

Game Boy kept his death grip on the game. "It may not look like much to you, but it's got my Final Fantasy Explorers save file." His handheld console had been another of the casualties on the night of the home invasion: it had taken a size thirteen army boot to the hinge. Luckily the cartridge had popped free and been kicked under the sofa. "A lot of work went into that!" He glared furiously at Imp. "Going to need a new 3DS," he grumped, "*assuming* it's not corrupted. I was trying to overflow the score table because there's supposed to be an Easter egg . . ."

"Here: catch." Doc had reached into his carrier bag and tossed a box towards the sofa. It tumbled in midair, twisted weirdly, and landed in Game Boy's open hand. Game Boy took one look at it and squealed loud enough to scratch glass. "*Thankyouthankyouthankyou!*" He leapt off the sofa, rushed up to Doc, and hugged him, cartridge in one hand and shiny new 3DS in the other.

"Aw, it's so cute." Imp was unable to suppress a smile.

"I paid for it fair and square. FlavrsMart were having a special on electronics: call it your replacement Christmas present. Hey, Boy, you can let go now," Doc told him. "Imp? About your sister—"

"—Yeah?"

"Have you run it past Del, yet? Or her girlfriend?" Del—the Deliverator—was a part-time cycle courier and their getaway driver. She'd been absent for most of the past week, spending time with her new girlfriend, Wendy. About whom the rest of the household were extremely conflicted, because Wendy was a semiprofessional thief-taker and the Lost Boys were semiprofessional thieves.

Imp rolled his eyes. "That's what tomorrow's about," he explained. "Invoice time." Eve owed him for services rendered, and he intended to collect. "Also to talk about the future."

Eve had bought out Wendy's contract for them. Unlike real cops, thief-takers worked for the highest bidder. Wendy's boss had been happy to blow off a cheapskate insurance underwriter when Eve dangled a juicy backhander under his nose, but now that the Boys' faces were on the radar, continuing in their previous line of work was inadvisable.

"I want to see if I can get her to put us on retainer. Not," he added, "for *that* kind of job. I'm talking about low-risk stuff. But there's got to be something we can do." *Something that doesn't put us at risk of dangling from a gibbet.*

"O-kaay." Doc sounded unenthusiastic. But then, Doc always poured cold water on Imp's ideas, for no reason that Imp understood: they were *good* plans, none of his plans were remotely half-assed or impractical! "Just promise me you won't agree to rob any more banks, especially ones we did over the previous month."

Imp winced. "No banks, real or imaginary, are going to be robbed on my watch, going forward! Cross my heart and hope to die."

"Please don't," said Doc.

"You don't have a heart!" Game Boy commented snidely as he tiptoed out the door, clutching his new console to his chest. The Xbox, PS4, and his PCs had all taken a battering during the night of the stompy boots; replacing them was definitely going to have to wait until they got paid.

Imp flopped on the shapeless sofa and patted the seat. Doc settled companionably beside him. "Are you still mad at me?" Imp asked.

"I haven't decided yet." Doc's lanky frame overtopped Imp by a few centimeters. He looked down at his partner through luxuriant eyelashes. "Got a smoke?"

"Sure. I mean, I'm sure I have one somewhere." Imp patted his pockets, then pulled out a tobacco tin that bore the dents and scratches of tough love. "Thought I'd rolled one . . . yeah, I did." He pulled out a skinny joint, raised it to his lips, and inhaled: it sparked into life spontaneously.

"Neat trick."

"Runs in the family. Remind me to teach you how to do it." Imp filled his lungs, then passed the roll-up to Doc. Shoulder to shoulder and thigh to thigh, they sat in peaceable silence for about ten minutes, passing the joint back and forth as smoke dragons coiled towards the ceiling. Eventually Imp stubbed it out on the lid of his tin. "Better," he said.

"Tell me about your sister," said Doc, rubbing up against him sleepily.

"Don't wanna."

"Tell me about your sister or no nookie."

"Don't—" He stopped as Doc ran his thumb along Imp's lower lip—"mm-hmm."

"Tell me. What's so bad about her? I mean, beside the obvious, being Chief Minion to an evil hedge fund billionaire—"

"It's embarrassing."

"Oh, it's embarrassing is it, having an elder sister? Oh *woe,* oh misery—"

"Shut up." Running out of options, Imp turned to face Doc and kissed him deeply.

"Not gonna shut up."

"Stop your finger-wagging." Imp drew breath. "I could tell you but then I'd have to kill you, if I remembered afterwards. I dunno, I think I need to be drunk first. I mean, as well."

"Wait here," Doc said gently, then stood up and shuffled unsteadily out towards the kitchen. Imp waited somnolently until he returned, clutching two tumblers and a bottle of whiskey. "Lagavulin Sixteen."

"Hey, that's *my* personal stash!"

"Fell off the back of a lorry? Like I care, we're drinking it anyway." Doc sloshed liquid into a glass, then handed it to Imp, who took a reflective sip while Doc attended to his own tipple. "Now talk."

"I dunno. Like, I've seen more of Eve in the past month than in the previous five years, you know? Since Dad died and Mum got—ill. We used to be close when we were kids, but I was going through a bad patch. Then shit happened, and she got very distant after she took the Chief Minion job."

He took another sip of whiskey.

"And?"

Imp stared into his glass for almost a minute. Then, very quietly, he added, "I'm afraid I might have fucked things up for her."

▸◂▸◂◂

Monday morning found Wendy Deere perched on the edge of a transparent Louis Ghost chair in the HiveCo Security office basement, sweating bullets despite the air conditioning. She'd arrived before her manager, Mr. Gibson, who had called the meeting: and now she was regretting it.

The designer of Secure Briefing Room C had a Moon Nazi Gestapo fetish. Wendy hated it: it gave her the cold shudders, even though as an employee she got to sit on the right side of the table. The chairs were Philippe Starck Louis Ghosts, Perspex knockoffs of a classic Louis XVI armchair. The table was similarly made of clear plastic. Indeed, the briefing room itself was a glass cube suspended by wires inside a windowless concrete cavity. The transparent aircon ducts were tuned to warble at human speech frequencies to defeat listening devices. UV spotlights bolted to the floor and ceiling reflected purple highlights off the furniture—a vampire firewall. Arcane summoning grids on the cement walls were scribed to block demonic intrusions just as the wire mesh embedded in the walls took care of radio signals. There *was* a computer in the room—a Microsoft Surface running on battery power—but all it did was deliver canned content on secure memory sticks. For really secure meetings it was removed entirely, while the participants stripped to their skin and wore disposable paper overalls.

This was *not* one of those sessions, for which Wendy was grateful. But the impulse to fidget, to straighten the lapels of her jacket and side-eye her own reflection in the walls, was difficult to resist. *How much longer is he going to be?* she wondered nervously.

The door in the outer wall opened and Gibson entered a short air-lock tunnel that reminded Wendy of a very expensive rodent habitat. The outer door closed, and a moment later the inner door unlatched. "Deere." He dipped his chin as he entered. "Morning."

"Morning, Mr. Gibson, sir." She stood automatically. Something in Gibson's bearing spoke of years spent in officer country before he switched to the private sector. Wendy hadn't even taken her sergeant's exams before she'd been given a choice between resigning from the Met or being kicked out—it had been Superintendent Barrett's word against hers—but she knew their kind. Gibson was one of the decent ones. "Had a good weekend?"

"I've had better. Won't you sit down?" Gibson took the other chair.

Here it comes . . . Wendy tensed as she sat. "Is this about the Pennine Bank job, sir? Because I can explain—"

Gibson waved it off. "You don't need to. We got paid off *very* nicely, the client who preempted was happy with your work, the file's closed." He looked at her silently for a few seconds, with the stony expression of someone who was trying to work out what he could—and couldn't—say. "I'm aware of some irregularities. I'm also aware that I probably don't want to look too closely at them. I gather you've filed a claim for a recruitment bonus?" She nodded. "And the candidate may have been at the scene? Well, then, I don't need the details. In fact, you should write them up in the secure notes app so I can log it as done and seal the record. That way we're covered if anything blows up later."

He was talking about Wendy's maybe-girlfriend Rebecca: also known as the Deliverator, a supernaturally fast bicycle courier who also happened to be the getaway driver for Imp's gang. Gibson was running a pilot project within HiveCo Security to provide superpowered thief-takers to the Home Office under a Public-Private Partnership. The regular Police weren't up to dealing with an ongoing superpowered crime wave during a time of spending cuts. Wendy was Gibson's #1 test subject, an ex-detective constable with the London Met who had developed a transhuman talent after she left. Employable superhumans were thin on the ground, and recruiting thief-takers was proving to be difficult.

Back in the eighteenth century—the last era when thief-takers had been a part of law enforcement, before the reforms of the nineteenth century and the professionalization of the police rendered them obsolete—there'd been a revolving door between the London underworld and the thief-takers: "set a thief to catch a thief" wasn't just a figure of speech. But modern legal constraints made it difficult for Gibson to hire supervillains with a record. Far better if he could find individuals who were clean enough to pass a criminal background check, even if they were less powerful. As Del had never been arrested while driving a stolen car—she always got away—she'd do. Gibson presumably could find some work for a supernaturally talented pursuit and evasion driver. And if it got Del a real job that paid the bills and kept her head off a spike, Wendy would sleep easier.

Wendy pulled the tablet across the table and unfolded the keyboard cover. "Is there anything in particular you need from me, sir?"

"Yes." He reached across and flipped the cover shut again.

"Aside from your write-up, you should know that I'm still waiting for HR to get back to me with the framework and monitoring requirements for the training program. Because there's no formal structure in place yet, if Ms. McKee"—Rebecca—"signs on we'll have to apprentice her to you for the time being so you can show her the ropes and keep an eye on her. But that's not going to happen for a while. In the meantime a couple of new jobs have come in, and one of them in particular is right up your street. . . ."

►◄►◄

Amy already knew she hated the soon-to-be-unemployed Mr. Hewitt even before she'd met him. Her hatred was very abstract, almost dry: if distilled, it might be bottled and sold as *eau de resentment,* a scent that came on with a rapid burst of spleen, peaked with a high note of self-loathing, and faded out in a slow haze of whining self-pity. She hated him because she hated firing people. And she hated him because Jennifer had sentenced her to swing the headswoman's axe, a chore she detested.

She waited for Mr. Hewitt in the meeting room, a beige-walled prison cell furnished with hard conference chairs and a desk where the confessions of the guilty were to be signed. She made herself uncomfortable behind the desk, erecting her laptop before her like a GM's screen in a game of Cubicles and Corporations. Then she doodled on her yellow legal pad as she waited for the outer door to open, distracting herself from the coming distastefulness.

She kept the pad under the table, concealed from the unblinking gaze of the cameras. She could be accused of misusing corporate resources if anybody saw what she was doing. Rather than writing case notes, she was sketching an angry buzzing fantasy: violently swarming corporate worker bees in wasp-waisted suits with venomously erect stingers falling upon the hive's slacking drones, making stabby and ejecting their smoking corpses from the hive. It was a subversive activity, her equivalent of repeatedly writing I HATE BIG BROTHER on her cubicle walls. But she drew because she had to. She drew because she was unhappy, and she drew to defuse her own unease at the tasks Jennifer assigned to her. Drawing was like breathing for her soul, and the Flavrs-Mart offices were airless and asphyxiating.

One of the aspects of disciplinary hearings that Amy hated most was the way the drones always seemed to blame her personally for their inability to smuggle memory sticks out of the office supplies cabinet, or to stack shelves fast enough to meet targets. They looked at her with dead, fishy eyes as they whined and evaded and made excuses, but they never saw *her,* Amy, trapped and bullied just as much as they were, doing a job she hated. They just saw a management uniform wrapped around an Amy-shaped hole, emptily pronouncing anathemas upon them in language scripted by Legal. It would haunt them for the rest of their working lives, because the New Management had instituted a national regime of permanent, transferrable employment records: dismissal damned them to poverty and penury. But afterwards, when the suit with the Amy-shaped hole inside it floated back to its desk to deal with the paperwork ending their employment, health insurance, contributory pension scheme, and tax code—afterwards, when they walked out of the FlavrsMart supermarket and back into the world of living, breathing human beings—afterwards, when they were free, the far-from-empty suit still toiled on beneath the gaze of the branch computers' panopticon.

And who, one had to ask, was getting the raw deal here?

I really shouldn't do this, Amy thought despairingly. She tore the top sheet off the pad, folded it twice (carefully keeping it below the desk), then slid it between the front of her blouse and her pocket-deficient jacket. It was the third time this month she'd been unable to keep her restless, itchy fingers away from pen and ink. Sooner or later someone would notice, and then she'd be sitting on the other side of this desk from Jennifer—

The door opened and she stood, oblivious to the trio of bees in tiny suits buzzing angrily around the overhead light fittings.

Gladys Nairn was first through the door. Gladys was a forty-something veteran of two decades in the food retail trenches; she led a hangdog expression dangling from the skull of a once-young man, who Amy deduced to be Adrian Hewitt. "Hello, Ms. Sullivan!" Gladys blatted at her. "I've brought Mr. Hewitt to see you, as requested."

"Thanks." Amy stretched her face into something the office blurrycam might mistake for a smile. She waved them forward. "This shouldn't take long. Adrian, please take a seat."

Shuffling of buttocks on plastic hyperbolic surfaces ensued. The downsizee was to be seated during the process to reduce the risk of a physical altercation, and Amy sat down right after Adrian because The Rules stated that looming over a resource, even a resource that was being downsized with extreme prejudice, might be interpreted as intimidation. Intimidating behavior looked bad in court—even intimidating behavior by a blowsy, green-fringed blonde whose suit didn't fit properly and who was twenty centimeters shorter than the intimidee. Anyone could be intimidating, if they fronted for a corporate behemoth with a six-billion-pound annual turnover.

Mr. Hewitt slumped beneath the invisible shackles of workplace obedience. He clearly realized he was in over his head. After an uncomfortable twenty-second pause—just long enough for the hangman to drape the noose over the waiting neck and tighten the knot—Amy began.

"Do you know why I asked you to come here, Mr. Hewitt?" she asked.

"Urh." He gave her a puzzled look, like a cow sizing up an overall-wearing stranger holding a captive bolt gun. "Nuh?"

Amy sighed, as much for Gladys's sake as for the ever-vigilant cameras. "*Security,* Mr. Hewitt. Security watches all of us, all the time. We are under his eye—or hers. On your last evening shift, Friday past that was, they recorded an incident in which you were involved. They escalated it to HR for resolution. Would you like to tell me what you were doing?" She turned the laptop so that both Adrian and Gladys could see it. Then she did a double-take. "Gladys, you might want to avert your eyes. This video contains material that may contravene the Code of Conduct section on harassment and public indecency and I don't want to expose you to it accidentally—"

"Public indecency?" Gladys leaned towards the screen avidly: "Ooh, don't you worry about me!"

"Public indecency?" Adrian echoed disbelievingly. "But it was after hours!"

Amy hit play. "On Friday the thirteenth, at 1946 hours, you activated the number two textured meat printer—currently assigned to extruding mechanically re-formed charcuterie—and downloaded a 3D model to it from a source other than the approved Bespoke Product Orders Directory.

"You then—without the authorization of your team leader or line manager—loaded the printer with feedstock from the discards tray in the stockroom, which I will remind you is *not* fit for human consumption, and added unapproved dyes to three of the extrusion heads." She brought up another still. "From the unauthorized template, you printed out a structure weighing approximately eighteen point two kilograms, then moved it into the front of cabinet number three on the deli counter. Then you posed for a selfie with it."

Another still.

"You uploaded the, ah, selfie, on your public social media stream, where eighteen thousand, three hundred, and seventeen other visitors saw it, more than two thousand of whom 'liked' it. Adrian, just *why* did you feel it was necessary to upload a picture of a pornographic sculpture made out of luncheon meat, on a chilled display surface *clearly* bearing the corporate logo?"

The tower of bacon bits Adrian had printed was indeed somewhat lewd. The greasy curves resembled buttocks. The venous depression and smoothly mounded pubes of gammon harbored barely visible labial folds molded from pork fat. But this Damien Hirst departure on the deli counter was not, in and of itself, sufficient to make the call for Amy. After all, it was Adrian's job to service the 3D meat printers that spent their every working hour extruding novelty meat loaves and saucily suggestive skinless sausages for the discerning customers. But . . .

"What have we told you *repeatedly* about selfies, Adrian? And the company dress code?"

"But I wis wearing me hat!" he protested indignantly. "Ya bass

Jenny tell't me to allus be wearing me hat behind tha counter! An' I wis!"

Amy glanced at Gladys, who was staring open-mouthed at the eyeball-gougingly indiscreet selfie. It had garnered Adrian ten times his entire previous lifetime history of "likes" on the internet, not to mention an indelible stain on his employment record that no amount of striped trousers, starched white coats, and butcher's porkpie hats could ever bleach clean.

"You are not allowed to take selfies on company premises, Adrian," she reminded him stiffly. "You are *especially* not supposed to take naked selfies on the shop floor. Code of Conduct: behavior likely to bring the company into disrepute." (Translation: *you are* so *fired*.) "Nor are you allowed to abuse company equipment for recreational purposes. Nor are you allowed to repurpose waste products, or violate food hygiene standards. And it's an offense to install unauthorized files on networked company machines," (*or to have sexual intercourse with a pornographic meat sculpture on company premises*) "with *or without* a hat."

She drew a deep breath. Gladys, mesmerized by the thing on deli counter three, seemed not to notice. "I'm sorry, Adrian," she said quietly.

"You're firing me."

She nodded unhappily. The swarm-sketch sticking to the skin beside her right boob-holder buzzed as the angry management bees attempted to erupt into the real world. "Jennifer and I have discussed this, and we feel that in view of the verbal warning you were given last week—and the severity of this new incident—we have no alternative but to let you go. If you agree to voluntary severance, there won't be any need to make a note of gross misconduct on your record."

She reached over to the laptop, zapped the picture of the Meatloaf de Milo back into case-file limbo—for it was clear that Adrian had a museum model in mind when he planned his foray into anthropomorphic 3D printing—and pulled up the discharge forms.

"If you sign here and here, we can ensure that the reason for your dismissal goes no further than these four walls. It's up to you. However, I'm required to remind you that, as per clause sixteen of your contract of employment, the company owns the intellectual property rights to anything you produce during your period of paid employment. So that selfie belongs to us and, incidentally, so do your two thousand and something 'likes.' Not that we want them," she added, "but we can't let you keep them. Actions have consequences!"

Adrian, whey-faced, signed the form with a shaking fingertip. He stood, then Amy stood. She did not offer to shake hands, but Gladys laid a gentle touch on his arm and steered him towards the door.

Good luck with your art, she thought, *even if it's not my cup of tea.* She waited for the door to close, then picked up her laptop and the pad of paper. The Phantom of the Deli might have left the building, but the dismal start to the week had awakened her personal imp of the creative, and it was scourging her again: her fingertips were almost fluorescing with the urge to sketch.

It was a very bad sign when this happened. It usually meant that by nightfall she'd have another large-scale manifestation to cover up. And heaven help her if she ever lost control and the company noticed: even Jennifer wouldn't be able to protect her. But there was only one way to get her symptoms under control. So Amy slunk off in search of a camera blind spot in which to hide while she drew out her demons.

▸◂▸◂

It took Mary half an hour to ease Mr. and Mrs. Banks out the door without alerting them to her nefarious intent. First, they gave her hurried directions to the nanny's bedroom in the dormer attic. Accordingly, she went there to give them space to make a quick phone call to the nanny agency. One of the Boss's gofers was waiting there to ensure that Mary's credentials were eagerly confirmed by the receptionist (with a subtext of *please don't break my knee-caps* that completely eluded Mr. Banks). Then Trudy went upstairs to herd Robert and Lyssa downstairs and introduce Mary to the kids. She had to pick up and carry little Ethan, who was having an attack of shyness. "This is Mary Drop, she's your new nanny!

You'll have lots of fun with her while Daddy and Mummy are working abroad, won't you? Say hello to Mary now, children!"

Robert (ten, tousle-headed and rosy-cheeked) squinted at Mary with the eyes of a college bell-tower sniper and asked, "What *kind* of fun?"

"Fun fun!" squealed little Emily, who had gradually gotten over her initial shyness.

"I want a unicorn," said nine-year-old Lyssa. She was wearing a sparkly chiffon princess dress—utterly inappropriate for breakfast, even though it was the school holidays—and clutching a worryingly functional-looking magic wand. Her expression was midway between sullen and hopeful: "Can I have a unicorn?"

"You'll have to shovel out its droppings," Mary said practically. "They're much smellier than horse apples." She leaned down confidingly: "I have a friend who works at Scotland Yard, and if you're *very* good I can take you to see the unicorn stables there." Mary was lying about having a friend in the Met, and in any case it would be utter madness to let a little girl anywhere near an equoid, but Lyssa's eyes widened and she shut up.

"I want to build a new model kit," Robert said thoughtfully. "The Airfix B-29 Superfortress *Bock's Car,* with the working bomb bay and the Fat Man." His eyes narrowed malevolently: "It can replace Ethan's Spitfire *wot you broke*." He spoke with the chilling deliberation of a judge donning a black cap before pronouncing sentence.

Mary's smile became fixed. Mr. Banks had left her a hastily scribbled to-do list and a credit card "for incidentals," and they were only going to be away for a week, but she could already see the CARD DECLINED knockbacks looming if she let the little horrors take her for granted. Robert was *clearly* plotting mayhem on the sly, although the precise significance of his request (as tightly worded as any demonic binding Mary had ever heard) wasn't immediately obvious to her. Also, there was something curiously dated about his choice of gray school shorts, V-neck sweater, socks, and lace-up leather shoes: as if he'd fallen through a time portal from the 1950s. "Why don't you run along and play with the Xbox or PlayStation or whatever for half an hour? Nanny has to get her feet under the table, suss out where everything is, and plan your lunch before we can do anything this afternoon. Besides, it's raining—"

Emily exploded. An air-raid-siren howl of distress was the only warning Mary received before Emily launched herself at Ethan, biting and clawing and screaming with incoherent rage. Ethan giggled excitedly and tugged her hair, then howled in pain. *Holy motherfucking Jesus,* Mary swore silently before she dived in and pulled the two struggling five-year-olds apart. "Stop that right now!" she snarled, holding the little girl and the little boy apart: they both promptly burst into floods of tears punctuated with mumbled accusations. Mary took a deep breath and evaluated the damage. She glanced up to catch Robert staring at her: "XStation now *at the double,*" she barked, and he bolted for the living room. Meanwhile, Princess Lyssa had vanished. *Typical.*

Mary decided to drop the sweet agency nanny act. As long as Mr. and Mrs. Banks hadn't gotten around to issuing Pugsley Addams and Princess Sparkle-Shoggoth with smartphones she was pretty much home and dry anyway. "Minions! Cease this disgraceful bickering at once! Or *I'll turn you into toads*!"

The believe-what-I-say charm in her pocket buzzed angrily and grew hot, but the sobbing subsided almost at once, replaced by quietly terrified hiccups.

"I am the wicked witch Mary Drop," Mary announced, overacting like mad: "and *you are in my power for the next week. I hereby conscript you as minions for my evil reign of evil! Do as I say and we shall have lots of fun together! But *never doubt* that I can and will be even more horrible to you than your elder brother and sister if you don't do as I say!" Still holding them gently—she had been made aware that small people broke easily and weren't repairable—she led them to the sofa. "Now say *I'm sorry,* and there will be chocolate milk." Spiked with Valium to counteract the sugar high if necessary (she'd heard about kindergarteners and their glycoside-tropism) but she *had* to get them settled, or this caper was going to crash and burn before it even reached the runway threshold. She didn't have a partner on this gig but she was used to playing bad cop with gangsters, and surely children couldn't be any worse than Triad enforcers? Assuming the internet FAQs about child-rearing were entirely accurate, of course.

Mumbled apologies were exchanged, after a fashion. Mary hurried through the open-plan living room, where Robert was quietly doing unspeakable things to a family of goblins whose home he had invaded, and fetched up in the kitchen. Here she found a fridge the size of the Svalbard planetary seed vault. It turned out that she didn't need to look for cocoa powder and squeezed cow juice after all because there was an open carton of chocolate milk sitting in the fridge door. Glasses were harder—she didn't have time to familiarize herself with the cupboard layout: world war three could break out at any moment in the front room—but if she reached into her messenger bag *just so*—

A minute later, the five-year-olds had conducted détente negotiations and were well into the strategic arms reduction stage of diplomacy, complete with chocolate milk mustaches and much slurping. But Lyssa was still missing in action. "Have you seen your sister?" she asked the twins. But all she got was a bubbly request for more Chocomilk.

"This milk tastes funny," Emily noted, in such a suspiciously mature tone that Mary was struck by the realization that she was not the first nanny these two had encountered—or even the first to have bigged up her credentials via the agency. The twins were sitting suspiciously close together on the sofa, as if the fight had been staged from the first, a tiny conspiracy to extort Chocomilk and sympathy—and now Lyssa was missing.

"Wait here," she said sharply. *Little boy who can animate toys: check. Little girl: hmm.* This aspect of the job had emphatically *not* been in the briefing. What else had the surveillance team missed? The big boy seemed to be just a regular hell-raising ten-year-old, but she had an edgy sense that she was overlooking something—maybe *several* somethings, potentially all the way up to literal hell-raising. She marched towards the staircase, hopped on the bannister rail, and slid upstairs to avoid the creaking floorboard and the pendulum trap on the landing which might or might not exist (Mary was taking *no* chances whatsoever, given the impression the Banks children had made on her in her first fifteen minutes).

"Lyssa?" she called.

The children's bedroom doors were ajar, and toys spilled into the first-floor passage like a multicolored avalanche of caltrops. The twins still shared a room next door to their parents' master suite. The older kids' rooms were easy enough to distinguish: access to Robert's doorway was blocked by enfilade fire from a dug-in Tiger tank, and Lyssa was singing quietly to someone or something in her own room.

Mary took a few seconds to compose herself, then knocked on the half-open door before she stepped inside. "Lyssa, who are you—" she trailed off.

Princess Sparkle-Shoggoth was chanting over her Barbie doll, who was riding sidesaddle on the back of a pink unicorn with a pearlescent spiral horn and implausibly big blue eyes. The unicorn was trotting in circles on the bedroom floor (there wasn't enough space for it to break into a canter) and Barbie was clinging onto its flowing mane with a death grip, her plastic cheeks flexed in a tetanic grimace.

Lyssa spoke in a monotone without looking up: "I'm training Twinklehooves to do dressage but Princess Barbie is dying inside, can you help? She's turning back to plastic and I need Ethan to bring her back to life now *pleeeeease* Miss can you make Ethan magic her again?"

"I'll see what I can do," Mary agreed, thinking fast. *Ethan animated the toy Spitfire, not Robert,* she realized with dawning horror. Robert and Lyssa, the older children, might be harmless, but if one of the terrible tots had powers, then—*I left them alone downstairs—*

The front door was ajar.

Oh shitcakes. Mary bolted for the porch with alacrity: "Emily Banks, come here at once! Oh don't do that, you'll get your dress muddy!" Emily was kneeling in a wet flower bed, her hair lank and dripping, peering at something green. It was sticking out of the ground, but unlike any decent, self-respecting vegetable, it appeared to be *writhing.* Mary did a horrified double-take—*Is that a fucking* snake, *in* London?—as she dashed towards the little girl—then froze again.

Emily beamed up at Mary: "Can Cecil come indoors and play?" she asked. The brilliant green rhizome twitched as it uncurled, fernlike, and strained towards its mistress's finger. Sprouts quivered and thrust from the soil in front of the little girl, then extended runners towards the front porch, fumbling and probing for cracks in the driveway.

"Is this something your mother would approve of?" Mary asked repressively. Emily's face fell, and unlike Princess Sparkle-Shoggoth upstairs, this little girl couldn't charm nanny for toffee. "Tell me, Emily, what would your mother say?"

"Mommy would—" A muddy finger sneaked into the corner of a drooping mouth, and cheeks began to quiver ominously. Shortly the rain would not be the only thing running down little Emily's face. A viridian tentacle curled across her shoulder and gently stroked her cheek, giving her the comfort that Mary would not or could not. It should have been heartbreaking, had Mary a heart to break instead of a chilly silicone-and-titanium ventricular prosthesis dedicated to a higher purpose.

Mary didn't break. But she bent slightly: "If you come inside and dry off, if you're *very good,* you can play with Cecil on the porch." Having a gate guardian out of *Little Shop of Horrors* wouldn't go amiss. "On condition that you stay indoors, and Cecil goes back to the flower bed when it's lights-out time. Otherwise," she said ominously, "it's the compost heap for him."

Leading the little girl back indoors, Mary set herself to the next task: working out how to bribe a five-year-old boy (a species of irritant she'd last had to deal with a third of a century ago) into going full *Herbert West—Reanimator* on Dressage Barbie. Then she returned to the kitchen table to sort out lunch—mustn't forget to check for mobile phones and divert outgoing calls from the house landline—and figure out how to keep them distracted for the rest of the rainy pre-Christmas Monday. The week stretched endlessly before her. Nobody had warned her that bored pre-tweens could be such a handful, and the Boss's surveillance operatives were going to get a right earful for missing the fact that at least two of the kids were transhumans, not just the parents. Nor had she quite internalized the implications of not being able to use her normal methods on them, because it simply wasn't done to drop-kick a toddler into next week. You had to smile and somehow maneuver them into doing what you wanted. It was so frustrating!

But Mary wasn't one to give up easily at the best of times. She had too much riding on this week's work to be forgiving. Sink or swim: Mary was in this for the long haul.

▸◂▸◂◂

As soon as she arrived in the office the next morning, Eve summoned her brother. Then she got down to work while she waited for him to arrive.

An hour later she was elbow-deep in the financials for a project Rupert had given her two months earlier. The Bigge Organization was about to expand its existing stake in FlavrsMart into a controlling interest in the supermarket chain, which was being spun off as a going concern by the HiveCo group, and she needed to go over the paperwork one more time. So of course Reception paged her just as she decided she understood the valuation, breaking her train of concentration: "Miss Starkey? This is the front desk, there's a visitor asking for you—he says he's your *brother*?"

The receptionist sounded appalled: Eve's lower lip curled in irritation. Perhaps the woman imagined Eve was sui generis, an unholy terror inflicted on the organization by satanic decree? (There were still plenty of people around who cleaved to Christian beliefs about hell and perdition, despite a year under the aegis of the New Management.) "I'll be right down," she snapped, then took a few seconds to compose herself. It was true that she'd been hoping Imp would turn up, but now he was waiting downstairs she found herself second-guessing her own intentions towards him. It had been years since they'd been close enough that she could think of him as family without a moment's hesitation. Working for Rupert had damaged her ability for empathic engagement—Rupert saw affection and love as weakness, and zeroed in on them with the ruthlessness of a public school bully. But she was still human enough that the jagged edges of familial guilt abraded her conscience. She'd distanced herself from Imp to protect him. Now the threat was removed, it was safe to let him close. *Better get accustomed to it,* she told herself, mentally adding a note to her checklist: *relearn how to human.*

She found Imp downstairs in Reception, sprawled bonelessly across a ridiculous chair upholstered in violet velvet with a two-meter-high back and spindly baroque legs. He was sipping delicately from a cup of tea, clearly revelling in the butler's expression of barely suppressed horror. "Jeremy!" she called. Imp stood and turned to face her, smirking. "Long time no see!" She air-kissed him for the peanut gallery (the staff thought she was a Terminator robot: the opportunity to fuck with their heads was too good to miss), then led him upstairs to the boss's den. She couldn't quite think of it as her own yet—not until she found that damned safe.

"This isn't your office," Imp said. He leaned against Rupert's desk and smirked at her. "Moving up in the world, baby?"

Eve shut the door, marched round the desk to Rupert's classic G-Plan 6250 chair—popularized by Ernst Stavro Blofeld in the early Bond movies, actually surprisingly cheap and quite nasty to sit in—and leaned back, ignoring the warning twinge in her hips. "Welcome to my world," she said, gesturing vaguely at the bay window. She felt curiously empty inside, but it was a welcome emptiness, as if she'd expelled something that had been slowly poisoning her.

"Wait, what—you got a promotion?"

"What can I say?" Eve shrugged. "Dead man's shoes." She smirked back at him.

"Wait, your boss . . ."

"He was so eager he went to get the book himself." She paused for thought. "You didn't run into him upstairs, did you?"

"No! What happened?"

"I told him I quit, and he could get it his own damn self." Instinct made her glance round in search of the hidden cameras. But no, Rupert would never bug his own office—and anyway, they belonged to her now. "Obviously I worded it very carefully. And did it in precisely that order."

"Wait, you—"

"I resigned, then I told him where he could find the book. He never came back. I'm pretty sure the curse got him: if not, he wandered off into Neverland and didn't make it out."

"Damn." Imp grimaced. "How? I mean, he bought it, didn't he? Isn't he its legitimate owner now? Shouldn't it have recognized him?"

"You might think that, but the book doesn't necessarily agree." And *now* she smiled. She wanted to confess, to monologue, to explain her carefully laid plan to someone who wouldn't automatically respond by trying to murder her: it was probably the chair's fault. As her only surviving family, Imp was a safe audience—no shark tank for him—and besides, he was technically complicit before *and* after the fact. By the time she'd explained everything his lips would be sealed forever. So Eve let her inner criminal mastermind off the leash, although she managed to hold back the urge to cackle maniacally at her matchlessly evil genius.

"Rupert was the chief executive of de Montfort Bigge Holdings, an investment vehicle domiciled in Skaro for tax purposes, private equity with a specialty in oddly unprofitable global subsidiaries— subsidiaries that forwarded their surplus to Rupert's beneficial trust via a double Irish with a Dutch sandwich . . . Sure, he told me to acquire the book for him. And yes, I did that. But I didn't pay for it using money in one of Rupert's personal accounts, or even a company he owned a majority share of.

"Instead, I used Rupert's funds to buy a house. And then I remortgaged it. It's a very valuable property, apparently—it's on Kensington Palace Gardens, don't you know? I think you can guess the address." (It was the family's ancestral pile, which their great-great-great-grandfather had built with the blood money from the family curse.) She proceeded to explain her financial machinations—"The purchase of the book used money coming directly from an offshore financial entity that you and I jointly own, which owes Rupert the twenty-five mil but what the hey, he's not about to come and collect it anytime soon."

Her brother was stunned into speaking in clichés. "What. The. Fuck?"

"Dad was right, you know: accountancy really *is* magic. Only I figured that out too late," she added with a pang of guilt.

Imp thought his way through her scheme, haltingly: "The curse affected anyone who took the book and didn't own it. But we owned—we own—the family house again? So the curse couldn't affect you or me, or someone acting under our instructions, but your boss . . . oh dear fucking me." He rocked back and forth, shoulders hunched.

"I'm pretty sure Rupert learned about the book a few years ago, when he hired me. But it took him ages to find the map Grandpa left lying around, and even longer to set me up to go fetch. He told me to buy the book for him. But he didn't say *how* I was to buy the book for him, and I was very careful indeed not to give him any authority to collect the book on my behalf." Her monologue was turning into—an apology? Regrets over having waited for so long to reach out to him? A tacit admission that her cunning plan hadn't been so cunning after all? Eve's stainless-steel mind threatened to turn its rat-trap jaws back on her, but Imp beat her conscience to the punch.

"Which is why you resigned first, before you told him where you'd left it." He looked at her, eyes glittering. "What now?"

"You go back to the house you co-own and check your bank balance," she told him. *This* part of the explanation was easy. "I paid the finder's fee we agreed, in full. The solicitors should be getting in touch soon. When they do, forward me their email?"

"But, but . . ."

"I'm putting you on salary," she told him. *Don't* ever *say I don't look out for family!* she thought defensively, even though *putting you on salary* couldn't begin to make up for five years of silence, neglect, and the loss of their parents. "You'll be listed as a janitor, working at, oh, a certain property I mentioned buying earlier: duties to include any housework necessary to keep it in order, the money isn't great but it includes on-site accommodation for yourself and up to four designated friends and family. You should have plenty of time left over for making movies on the side. But your principal job—which will not be written down anywhere—is to keep that fucking door shut." The door to Neverland via the dream roads behind the walls of the world, which opened on the top floor. "And don't, whatever you do, breed." *Let the curse die with the family line.* "Are we square?"

He stood. "This isn't fair!"

"Jerm." She walked around the desk until she was close enough to tweak his nose, if she dared: "*Life* isn't fair. If life was fair the family curse would come with an escape clause, Dad wouldn't have died for you, Mum wouldn't be in a care home, and your elder sister would probably have babies instead of control of a multibillion-pound hedge fund." She paused. "Although the hedge fund is a really good consolation prize, come to think of it."

She reached out with her mind and brandy arced from the decanter, filling a pair of cut crystal tumblers. She floated them across the room and handed one to Imp. "Here's to family." It wasn't a toast so much as a peace offering, and after a moment Imp copied her as she raised her glass to the memory of their parents.

"So I'm the janitor now," he said. Then he stared thoughtfully at the glass. "That's some serious shit," he added.

"Jerm. Please." She reflexively gave him the pitying smile due a middle manager who was slow on the uptake, then instantly regretted it. "That's a fifty-million-pound chunk of real estate, nobody would believe you were the owner, would they? Even though you are, at least halfway, on paper. As janitor you can come and go as you please, and your friends, too."

He gave her a too-knowing stare. "I get why you're doing this for me, I think. Roof over my head, as long as I keep my yap shut."

Eve returned his stare, thinking, *He's sharper than he used to be.* "Yes?" The temperature of her voice dropped.

"But why are you looking out for my homies? Why the special consideration?" He seemed perplexed. After a moment his attention settled on the cuckoo clock behind her. "What the fuck is that clock doing in here?"

"I'm buying their silence, too, in case you hadn't noticed. And keeping them out of trouble." Eve never threw away a useful tool, and the gang (or found family, or troupe of supervillains) Imp had assembled was too valuable to discard. With a bit of attention from the whetstone and grinder they might be polished to a fine edge. "Call it an investment in their future. What about the clock?" It grated on her nerves, sure, but—

Imp stood up and walked past her desk, then thrust his face at the clock. "This—" he said—"how long has it been here?"

"I don't—" Eve flinched as invisible moth wings battered at her mind. "Hang on."

"Your boss, Rupe: bit of a posh upper-class git, right? Something of a Rees-Mogg." Rhyming slang for *snob,* Eve decoded.

"You could say that . . ."

"Why would he have a fake Black Forest cuckoo clock on his office wall with *Made in China* printed on the guttering?" He took a step back from the offending timepiece and shook his finger at it: "You're a *ringer,* mate, and I've got your number—"

"I don't—" For a moment thinking became *very* hard, and the ward Eve habitually wore grew hotter and hotter. Then everything came into brilliant focus: the clock began to strike incredibly fast, a puff of smoke burst from the chimney, and with a concussive *bang* the cuckoo shot across the room and embedded itself in the opposite wall.

"Clock!" She gibbered for an instant, before regaining her self-control. Everything sounded flat, all tones muffled by tinnitus from the small explosion. "I mean to say, of course you're right, that's not a clock, innocent clocks obviously don't have no-see-um geases and exploding cuckoos, do they?" *Which begs the question of what exactly is it if it* isn't *a clock.* Thinking clearly for the first time since she'd entered Rupert's office, Eve approached the smoking gadget. She gathered the *mana* for a defensive ward, but the magical bindings that had deflagrated when Imp noticed them were gone, leaving an open door from which dangled a winding-key on a chain. A winding-key which, now her mind was free to notice, had pins that appeared to fit in a lock—and an open door through which she could see a handle.

"What is it?" Imp asked through the noisily ringing silence.

"Trouble," she said grimly, "of the bomb disposal kind. You should go: I've got this." She stood for a very long time, staring at what was clearly the magically disguised door to Rupert's safe. She heard Imp close the door behind her, and knew she was alone; she didn't notice the trickle of blood from the cuckoo embedded in the far wall.

▶◀▶◀▶◀

Amy worked like a dog the morning after Mr. Hewitt's downsizing interview. Lunch was time-expired couscous and black olives with low-fat soy yoghurt from the salad bar, eaten at her desk. Amy was fed and her stress levels were falling slowly back towards baseline when her phone buzzed. Of course, it was Jennifer.

"Sweetie, can you go down to the deli counter? There's a call for HR, a customer's kicking off about the lately departed Mr. Hewitt and I've got my hands full. . . ."

"Yes, Boss." Amy put the phone down—no sighing, no outward emanations of discontent—and stood up. What could possibly have happened? She picked up her pad, patted a stray curl back into place, and hurried towards the scuffed corridor and bare concrete stairwell. She passed the lights-out receiving bay on her way down to the palletized storeroom behind aisles fifteen to nineteen, then in through the door at the end of the enchanted kingdom of dry goods.

Amy scurried across the shop floor, eyes downcast to avoid any customers who might delay her mission. She only raised her gaze as she approached the deli meat counter. The shining row of refrigerated countertops were fronted with luminous green fringes of plastic garnish, the better to offset the ochre and brown muscle-tones on display. Behind the refrigerators there was an aisle for the sales staff, then walls separating the shop floor from an experimental meat processing facility.

These were part of a six-month-old experiment in applied logistics. Carcasses arrived from the slaughterhouse, dead cows and pigs and sheep. On arrival in the loading bay they were attached to meat hooks and fed to the caged chaos of a robotic carving and deboning line. Attractively shrink-wrapped joints and slices of meat emerged on a conveyor belt, along with feedstock for the 3D meat printers.

Amy saw at once that something had gone badly wrong. A pasty-faced youth in white coat, mesh hat, and blue gloves cowered before an irate Member of the Public. Behind his shoulder stood Gladys Nairn, and—approaching from the other end of aisle seventeen—two blue-suited security guards, clearly ready for trouble.

"Hello!" Amy smiled at the MOP: "What seems to be the problem here?" (Never use the word "trouble" on the shop floor, lest it become a self-fulfilling prophecy. Lawsuits have been lost for lesser cause.)

The Member of the Public spun round and stared at her, all long gray beard and glittering eyes: "Where's Ade?" he demanded: "Where's Ade? I needs my hand doin' and 'e's overdue!"

"Ade doesn't—" Mrs. Nairn began.

"I'll take it from here," Amy assured her. "Hello, Mister, uh, may I ask your name?" The MOP squinted at her suspiciously. His hair was unkempt, lank, and greasy; his beard likewise. He wore an army jacket of dubious provenance, patched and clearly in need of a trip through a washing machine. He smelled *bad*. It wasn't the usual sweat-and-stale-piss aroma of a vagrant, but something worse, something sweet and unmentionable, a battlefield miasma from a place where the flies dined heavily. Amy tried not to recoil or show any outward sign of disgust, but she'd stepped in dog turds that smelled sweeter than this guy. *Not my job to judge,* she reminded herself. Compliance had been known to employ the most *unbelievably* bizarre mystery shoppers, after all. "Mister . . . ?"

"Magnus. Sergeant Magnus McVicar, DSC, Royal Irish Regiment, retired." For a moment his shoulders stiffened and his spine straightened, as if some lost phantom of gallantry was trying to escape. He couldn't be a year over forty but he looked at least two decades older. "I want to see Ade. Ade Hewitt. It's abah't me 'and? I need him to do it for me agin."

He extended his gloved right hand towards Amy. The unspeakable aroma grew stronger: she gagged involuntarily, then cupped a palm before her face and took a step backwards. "What did—what does Ade do for you?" she asked.

The blue-suiters had heel-and-toed discreetly up behind ex-Sergeant McVicar, and the tall one with the gut bucket prepared to reach for him; his short, sleek companion silently unholstered her taser, watching Amy for her cue. Amy ignored the heavies and focussed on McVicar, taking shallow breaths through her mouth.

"It's me 'and," McVicar explained. "Lost it in Kandahar. Got me an armature, and Ade sees to it weekly. Long as 'e strips it back and makes me a new one, I'm fine. Where is he? I 'aven't 'ad it done since Friday before last! I need me 'and doing!"

Why do I always get the loonies? Amy thought. She glanced past McVicar's shoulder at tall-and-bulbous, who stood ready to do his duty. "Mr. Hewitt doesn't work here any more, I'm afraid," she explained, even though she was on the verge of throwing up from the stench. "I'm going to have to ask you to leave, sir."

"But me 'and—"

Everything happened very quickly. McVicar extended his arm towards Amy: she registered the fine-woven black Lycra glove, fingers bulging stiffly at the seams as if stuffed with bloated sausages. The hideous sick-sweet stench overcame her and she gagged again, turning aside. Tall-and-bulbous interpreted this not as disgust but as fear of assault, for McVicar had his back turned towards him. So the guard reached out and grabbed McVicar by the collar of his jacket with one hand and by the forearm with the other, heaving him around to face away from Amy, and (by sheer coincidence) towards the front of the deli counter—while holding McVicar's arm in a tight grip.

This was a mistake.

The black-gloved hand squirted from McVicar's cuff and flew across the counter. A cometary trail of liquifying mechanically reclaimed meat exploded from his empty sleeve and a wave of putrescence sprayed everywhere. McVicar's hand was made of rotted pink slime, and it had long since passed its use-by date.

Screams, tears, vomiting, and ranting ensued as the security guards hustled McVicar away. Their zip-tie restraints proved less than useful on a man whose right arm was a shining steel rod smeared with filth that stank a thousand times worse than a blocked drain. There was a flicker-flash of cameras as random shoppers witnessed the stooshie in progress and uploaded it to social media: but Amy was beyond noticing.

She dry-heaved uncontrollably over a puddle of bile and cous-cous salad. And she wasn't alone: the pasty-faced apprentice butcher had thrown up in the chiller, and Gladys was retching piteously. The stench was unspeakable. Amy mopped at the tear-trails on her cheeks with the back of one wrist, smearing foundation all over her suit sleeve, then tried to catch her breath. Out of the corner of her eye she saw something moving: rice-grain-sized wrigglers vibrating atop the liquor-drenched salami tray.

They were maggots, homeless maggots that until moments earlier had been happily residing in McVicar's prosthesis. And Amy, even though she was sick to the pit of her soul (never mind her stomach) knew there was only one thing to do.

"Cleanup crew, aisle seventeen deli. The deli counter is now closed." She straightened up from the PA microphone and met Mrs. Nairn's eyes. "Can you call Mr. Holmes, please?" (Mr. Holmes was the duty branch manager.) "We need to shut down for a deep clean and environmental health recertification." She paused. "The MOP was asking for Ade Hewitt, wasn't he?" Gladys nodded, eyes wide. And now Amy saw what had happened: *We've been pranked,* she realized. "You'll back me up on that?" Another nod. Mrs. Nairn clearly didn't trust herself to open her mouth and have only words come out. "Good." Amy took a deep breath and regretted it immediately. "I'm going to have to write this up. Not your fault. Not"—her eyes tracked to the exit tall-and-bulbous and sleekit-rat-face were frog-marching the shrieking veteran towards—"theirs. But if Ade thinks he can get another printer maintenance job with *this* on his permanent, transferrable record, he's got another think coming, because I am going to kick up *such a stink*—"

It was the wrong word at the wrong time: Amy gulped for air, but it was too late. Everything was coming up again, and she had a feeling deep in the pit of her poor abused stomach that this was only going to get worse.

2

▶◀▶◀▶◀▶◀

STOP-LOSS STRATEGIES FOR RETAIL

After her brother left, Eve stood in silence for a few minutes, giving the cuckoo clock a hard stare. *Sometimes things are larger on the inside than the outside.* It wasn't just a TV trope like the TARDIS, a blue 1950s police box that was actually the vestibule of a vehicle that could travel in time and space: there really *were* ghost roads that led outside the walls of space and time. One of them was anchored to the top floor of the house on Kensington Palace Gardens. It had been the shared memory palace of a family of sorcerers—her and Imp's family—each corridor in it led further back in time and fancy, until it dead-ended in Neverland, the realm where dreams go to die.[2]

Eve had heard of other ghost roads, too. They were easier to locate if you were a practitioner of the thaumaturgic arts and sciences, or a transhuman, assuming the two categories were in any meaningful way distinct. And Rupert—

—Rupert, the many-gods-damned sonuvabitch, was *at the very least* an adept. He'd bound her with a geas of obedience when she signed his employment contract. It had been laughably weak, and she'd figured out three different ways to break it before she signed, but the fact that he'd been able to do it *at all* made her

---

2. That particular road was powered by a family curse, although twentieth-century demographics would eventually put an end to it. If she or Imp had children, the curse would return to claim one of their offspring's lives, or the life of a parent. It wasn't picky. It exchanged blood for power, and the ancestor who'd bound himself to the curse had never imagined the need for an "off" switch because exception handling code hadn't been invented in the nineteenth century.

extremely cautious about testing its boundaries. To do so would have told him she was not content, and her plan involved playing the longest of games. She'd meant to lull him into a false sense of security . . . but six months down the line he'd invited her into his sanctum, sat in the very chair where she explained things to Jeremy, and he'd handed her a bulging stack of papers—his file on her. She'd only skimmed the first six pages, then she retreated to the executive bathroom and threw up as quietly as possible. Magical geases were, it turned out, much weaker bindings than black and white documentary evidence of capital offenses committed at his bidding. Rupert had taught her that one sharpened one's subordinates into knives, then demonstrated by using her to stab his rivals in the back. She'd gone along with it because most of Rupert's targets were truly horrible people (and besides, her ends justified the means)—but he'd kept a paper trail.

Rupert was gone now, but there was no trace of those files in the office vault, and she needed to find them lest he'd left behind the sort of life insurance package that would end with her head on a spike looking down from the Tyburn Tzompantli.

It *must* be here. If not here, it'd be in Castle Skaro, in his apartment—but that would require at least an overnight trip. So she chose for the time being to believe that the files were in his office. It was like searching for dropped car keys under the streetlight because the shadows were too dark.

And the only obvious place she hadn't searched yet was the clock that she'd somehow overlooked or forgotten about repeatedly until Imp's attention made it explode.

Eve pulled out her phone and used its built-in flashlight to light up the clock's interior. Aside from a drooping wire, the innards of the clock looked dark and empty. But Eve didn't trust appearances. She closed her eyes: then, reaching through the aperture with the fingers of her mind's imaginary hand, she felt around.

There. Above the open door, a sharp-edged guillotine blade was poised to snap down on an unwary hand. And . . . *there*, behind it, she felt a perforated metal panel fronting the stacked steel plates of a lock. Would the key dangling from the clock fit inside it . . . ? No, that'd be too obvious: Rupert was arrogant, but he was also sneaky. He probably kept the safe key on his person at all times. Which meant it was lost in Neverland.

Eve's telekinesis was weak—she could curl heavier weights by hand than by strength of will—but she was very precise, and the resistive pressure sense that went with her telekinesis helped guide her. In fact, although she was weak she'd taught herself to pick locks with her mind, sweating and trembling as she forced spring-loaded pins out of the way one by one. She'd secretly practiced on her bedroom door upstairs: never opening it, just locking and unlocking the deadbolt with a subtle *click* that Rupert's cameras and microphones most likely mistook for the nocturnal expansion and shrinkage of heating pipes in the old building. Now she turned her attention to the lock behind the clockface, and after a minute of concentration, it clicked open.

The effect was immediate and dramatic: the entire clock swung into the room, taking a one-meter square of wallpaper with it. Behind the hinged panel was a safe door. A handle was set in the middle of its face, surrounded by an intaglio design in the shape of a five-pointed geometrical figure. Eve's skin crawled as she extended a finger towards it, sensing ungrounded bindings and the mindless buzzing of extradimensional eaters attracted by the *mana* flux in the grid. She shuddered and stopped short of the ward. Touching it would be like making contact with a high-tension terminal on a transformer: one bright flash, then the nothingness of death. *Let's* not *do that,* she resolved, and pulled back her finger. A simple spell held all that poisonous power in check, controlled by an eater trained to recognize a word or phrase. A geeky indie pop song from her childhood sprang to mind: *I have the password to your shell account* . . . passwords, passwords: Rupert had entrusted her with a password database in her capacity as his PA. It evidently hadn't occurred to him that he wasn't running a perfectly normal business where such practices made sense. (Unless it was perfectly normal in his world to sacrifice virgins once a month on the stone altar in the basement, so that he might read the future in their entrails and adjust his trading positions accordingly when the markets opened the following day.)

Eve poked at her phone briefly, searching Rupe's encrypted

database. But there didn't seem to be anything obvious there, no tag saying *Secret Office Safe Password*—

"Oh," she said breathily, then in a louder voice, "Jack Nicholson!" Because Rupe had an overinflated idea of his own intelligence. The grid grounded and the toxic susurration of magic receded. She pulled on a surgical glove, then turned the handle, the brass cool against her hand.

Something stung her palm through the glove and she jolted. It wasn't hostile magic or even a mundane attack (she had defenses against harm, be it physical, chemical, computational, or spiritual). *Identity verification, perhaps?* Taking a deep breath, she rubbed her hand on her trousers, thereby ensuring that she missed the tiny drop of blood the handle had magically sucked through skin and latex. Not that it mattered, though: the safe recognized her, and if Eve (who wasn't quite as clever as she thought she was) had paused to wonder why, she needn't have bothered—she would find out once she opened the inner door.

The safe was about eighty centimeters deep (pay no attention to the fact that it was set in the outer wall of the building, and its back should, by rights, extend somewhere over the street). It was lined on three sides with shelves: discreet drawers at the bottom were sized for jewelry. Eve opened the narrowest compartment, which contained a pile of silk and velvet baggies like the stash of a Regency-era dope fiend. She took one of the smaller bags and emptied its contents into the palm of her hand. A dozen clear stones glittered brilliantly beneath the safe's recessed LED light, rainbows refracting from their facets. They were cut diamonds, not one of them less than five carats. A couple were set in rings, but she couldn't imagine anyone normal wearing one: if they were engagement rings they were each worth as much as a house. She choked back a laugh of disbelief as she poured the fortune in gemstones back into their pouch and returned it to the drawer.

Next she read the titles on the box files shelved above them. These were the real crown jewels: FABIAN EVERYMAN ELECTION CAMPAIGN 2012 (*The Prime Minister, before he was famous*), SOE Q-DIVISION (*Weren't those the security service clowns who blew up Leeds?*), OFFSHORE ACCOUNTS, FLAVRSMART

TAKEOVER (That *she knew about*), MUTE POET CLERGY (*What the* hell *was* that?), and then STARKEY-BIGGE.

She pulled her file from the shelf with numb fingers, then sat in the supervillain chair and opened the front cover. There was a table of contents; it began with a nondisclosure agreement relating to her background checks, dated a month before she'd started work. It was signed by Jeremy—

Eve had once cooked an assassin's brain by force of will alone. She'd gone up against a Transnistrian mafia hit squad and lived: her bodyguards walked in terrified awe of her. Nevertheless, after five minutes of reading, and for only the second time in her life, she found herself throwing up in the executive toilet, shaking in the grip of the hangman's horror.

As soon as she trusted herself to speak she called the security office. "Have the chopper readied for an immediate trip to Castle Skaro, two passengers, returning tomorrow morning," she told the duty security officer. "Then fetch my brother. He's probably at the property on Kensington Palace Gardens. Don't damage him, but be firm." She ended the call, then closed the safe. Taking her file, she climbed the stairs to her bedroom to collect the go-bag she always kept ready for an immediate departure.

Forget dangling from a gibbet on the Prime Minister's Tzompantli, forget her skull being just another brick in his sacrifice-wall. This was a nightmare scenario: Jeremy had landed her in it good and proper. While she'd been making plans for Rupert, Rupe had clearly been one jump ahead in preparing his own plans for her. Indeed, he'd put the noose around her neck and come within a whisker of springing the trapdoor beneath her feet. Only his unexpected disappearance—and presumed death—had saved her: but thanks to her idiot brother, she was still standing on the gallows.

►◄►◄►◄

Mary rapidly learned that the twins were creatures of habit: abominable, nose-picking, shrieking and writhing habits, for the most part. But at least they were predictable. So, after hastily prepping lunch from the freezer and microwave, she put Emily and Ethan down for their afternoon nap and turned her focus on Lyssa and Robert. The older children were relatively trouble-free. Lyssa was still playing sabotage or dressage or something upstairs, and Robert was in the living room with the PlayBox, engaged in some kind of hyperviolent shooty thing with lots of gore. (Mary didn't question whether the parental controls were set appropriately. In her occupation gore was an entirely normal by-product of business, and the sooner the kids learned to take blood spatter and pulverized brains in their stride, the better.)

While the rug rats were sleeping off their carb comas, Mary lifted Lyssa's and Robert's smartphones. They were cheap-ass Androids that Mummy and Daddy had procured as a kinder, friendlier alternative to ankle-tagging the little horrors. They were so locked down that it was impossible to get to Facebook, never mind Pornhub or 8chan. Nevertheless, Mary obediently swapped their SIMs for the special ones in her handbag, then texted their contact lists to HQ. Then, using the second SIM slot in her own mobile, she triggered a PAC request for each of them. By the time Mom and Dad touched down at JFK, their children's numbers would be attached to the SIMs provided by the Boss, exactly where Mary wanted them.

As the kitchen clock ticked ominously closer to two in the afternoon, Mary was overcome by a creeping sense of dread. Emily and Ethan would be up soon, revitalized by their nap and expecting . . . what, exactly? What on earth do you *do* with a pair of five-year-olds? Especially ones with magical superpowers? Mary, who had—figuratively—been born with a ninety-year-old soul and didn't age backwards, had no idea. *Keep them busy,* the Boss had suggested: *tire them out and don't give them a chance to escape.* And meanwhile there was Mrs. Banks's to-do list. Mary cast a jaundiced eye over it. "Well *fuck,*" she murmured to herself when she got to *return Grandma's Christmas presents to store for credit (they're in the cupboard under the stairs: mother-in-law always gives them fancy-dress costumes and gets the size wrong).* MIL sounded like she bore a grudge against Mrs. Banks, and Mary sympathized. But it suggested a solution to her dilemma: "Shopping," she muttered under her breath. "I'll take the pressies back and exchange them for something that'll keep the kids quiet." Children liked toys, didn't they? The model kit Robert had requested should shut him up for a while, if the WiiStation ran out of levels.

Sure enough the under-stairs cupboard contained a pair of shopping bags labelled HAMLEYS, both bulging with packaged superhero costumes accompanied by gift receipts. Mom-in-law hadn't gift wrapped them, and if Mary had been of a more suspicious nature she might have wondered if the receipts were some sort of fiendishly ingenious elephant trap—*force Mum to run gauntlet of toy shop the week before Christmas*—but Mary was inexperienced and in a hurry, so she fell for it.

Time to summon the minions. "Elyssa?" she trilled, from the foot of the staircase: "Princess Elyssa, let down your hair?"

From upstairs there came the muffled sound of tiny hoofbeats, then a trenchant, "Shan't!"

Mary swore silently, took the stairs two at a time, and bit out, "Lyssa Banks, you do *not* say—" before she took in the diorama on the landing.

Dressage Barbie had been unhorsed. The proud plastic princess faced her end bravely, tied to a stake in the middle of the first-floor jungle by her abductors. A vicious tribe of Stone Age Care Bears surrounded her, menacing her with a variety of exotic weapons looted from her brother's Action Man. The foliage was provided by Cecil, who had infiltrated the house via the landing window. The Paleolithic predators were perfect 1:6 scale furries cosplaying *Mad Max: Fury Road*, directed from a throne of skulls by—

"Lyssa Banks, just *what* is your Ken doll wearing?"

Lyssa looked up at Mary and shrugged blankly. "A mesh vest and a cock ring on a necklace. Also assless chaps, although Mum says I'm not to say 'ass' in school. Why?"

Mary bit her tongue. "We're going to the shops," she announced. "But only if you put your toys away first." Then she stepped past the jungle scene and opened the door to the twins' room. Shaking them awake, then dressing them for an outdoor excursion in matching dungarees and sweatshirts, was a baptism of fire: luckily they were still under the influence of her suggestion that they sleep deeply, so offered only pro forma resistance. She led them downstairs while Lyssa marched her toys back to their chest, then got Robert's attention by unplugging the GoreBox Pro at the wall.

"Hey, watchew do that for!" Robert yelled, angrily brandishing his controller.

"We're going shopping," Mary said matter-of-factly. "Get your big boy shoes on, you're in charge of Ethan."

"Don't wanna—"

"Hamleys toy shop." That's what it said on the receipts. "Your mother said to return your nan's Christmas presents and get you something nicer. And if you're *very* good, there will be a side-trip to the Xbox Games Store."

"What, you mean the Microsoft Store?" Robert began to frown.

"No, you're overthinking it: I mean the Xbox Games Store."

"But that's in the cloud, innit?"

"But they'll still be open to visitors when we get back," Mary said triumphantly. "Regular toy shop first, mind uploading later!" It was all going on Trudy Banks's credit card, after all.

It took half an hour to get everyone into their coats and another ten minutes to persuade Emily that there would be no toy shopping if Mary couldn't close and lock the windows and front door because Cecil's creepers were in the way. And Lyssa insisted that she absolutely had to wear her princess gown even though it was raining. But Mary got them lined up just in time for the Addison Lee minicab, and even managed to herd them inside without loss of life or criminal damage. Emily and Ethan were fully awake, excited, and trying to out-shriek one another as Mary told the driver where to take them. Robert nearly vibrated right out of his seat belt, and even Lyssa managed to look mildly pleased with the new state of affairs.

It was Robert who spilled the beans as they tumbled out of the sliding door onto the wet pavement round the corner from Regent Street. "Mum never takes us to toy shops," he confided, obediently taking (or rather, grabbing) Ethan's hand. "This is wizard!"

Mary nodded, concealing a frown at his archaic kid's cant. Was Robert some kind of throwback? "That's old-fashioned," she said: "the wizard kids these days say blowjob."

"Yes, blowjob, wizard, whatever." He tagged along behind as she led her charges into the giant shop of toys, trying not to snigger. *Just some harmless fun,* she told herself, meanwhile wondering just why Mrs. Banks never took her children toy shopping.

The answer soon became clear.

The returns department was on the first floor. The children behaved themselves for the ride up the escalator, but no sooner had Mary approached the counter off to one side of the shop floor than they made themselves scarce. "Remember, I can't buy you any toys if I can't find you!" she called after Lyssa, crossing her fingers and hoping the warning would work. Then she turned back to face the waiting shop assistant and began: "My employer asked me to return these unwanted gifts—I have a receipt . . ."

It turned out that Hamleys toy store was, if not unwilling to accept returns, then not exactly returns-friendly. There was much scanning involved; also frowning, manual typing of eighteen-digit inventory numbers, sucking of teeth, grim expressions, and faintly menacing enquiries as to the *precise* reason for the customer's dissatisfaction with their purchase. ("Gran didn't check the kids' clothing size" didn't appear to be an acceptable excuse for returning unopened superhero costumes.)

Finally, after about ten minutes of stock control wrangling, Mary escaped with a store credit voucher and the beginnings of a headache. But her problems had only just started.

Robert and Ethan had disappeared into the Blue quadrant—domain of Airfix model kits, Action Man/G. I. Joe dolls, and Meccano Technics. Mary scrambled to catch up and nearly laid hands on Ethan, before she realized that Lyssa and Emily had bolted in the opposite direction, as if repelled by the macho action cooties of the boy-toys . . . or, more likely, hypnotized by the Pinkness Out of Space that had settled over everything in the girly-girl section. Unicorns had diminished in popularity ever since the Met riot police began riding them in cavalry charges against pro-democracy demonstrators, but that just meant more shelf-space for Barbie, Monsterella High, and the Frozen franchise. And now Mary saw Lyssa in her native habitat she realized that Lyssa was going through an Elsa phase.

"Fuckstain pissbollocks," Mary cursed, no longer holding back now that her charges had scattered to the four quarters.

It was less than two weeks before Christmas. The store was heaving like a Saturday night dance floor where the clubbers were all underage and had overdosed on SunnyD. Mary pushed her way through the shouting throng, seeking signs of Trouble with a capital T. She found it staring pointedly at a Christmas tree that was bulging and quivering as if it was about to uproot itself from its tub and go walkabout.

Mary laid a hand on the small miscreant's shoulder and said, "Emily Banks, what *have* I told you about unauthorized topiary excursions?" Emily glanced round with a guilty expression.

"What's an author-ized tope-yee?"

"That." Mary pointed a bony finger at the planter. "Stop it *right now*. You do *not* do that in public, you'll scare the security men and they'll throw us out. Do you want them to throw us all out? Because if they throw us out there will be no toys, and I'm not taking you to Kew Gardens."

A moment later Mary realized she'd laid it on a little thick when Emily screwed her face up into a knot of abject misery, then drew breath and *howled*. All across the shop floor, every single Christmas tree in Santa's grotto clenched its amputated roots in sympathy. Moments later they burst the bounds of planters and marched towards their mistress. Meanwhile, Robert bounced in from the boy zone, clutching a teetering pile of model kits. "Miss! Miss! Ethan wants this one!" His eyes sparkled eagerly as he proffered an unfeasibly large bomber at Mary. Ethan scampered to keep up, a small plastic helicopter gunship buzzing around his head.

"Have you seen your eldest sister?" Mary called, bending to pick up Emily, who still shrieked but nevertheless buried her face against Mary's shoulder. She was surprisingly heavy, but Mary carried her as carefully as if she was worth a quarter of a million quid—which indeed she was, come payday at the end of this caper. "There, there." She rocked Emily: "Mary didn't mean to scare you. Make the bad Ents go to sleep again?"

The squadron of angry trees slowed uncertainly, and Ethan and Robert came to attention in front of her. Now there was only one child missing, and Mary allowed herself a moment of hope. Then she ruthlessly bit back words like *absolute fucking disaster* as she caught motion out of the corner of her eye. "Robert," she said as calmly as she could, "you can have all the model kits you can carry but for the love of Cthulhu *please* go over there right now and fetch your sister before she—"

Too late.

Princess Elsa was in da house, or more accurately in Santa's grotto, and some utter tool of a shop-floor designer (although in fairness it could not be said that they had any reason to expect Princess Sparkle-Shoggoth to rock up) had provided Santa with amplification.

"*Fiddle*sticks," said Mary.

Toy-store Santa lolled sideways on his sleigh-throne, a little blonde princess in miles of pink tulle perched on his lap, crooning into his microphone. "I want *everything*," Lyssa gushed, her voice weirdly compelling: "I want unicorns and rainbows and a princess castle and—"

A parent, her eyes glazed, stepped forward to lay a huge magenta box at the foot of her throne. She blinked, clearly baffled, and shuffled away to make room for a man wheeling a shiny pink mountain bike with daisies printed all over the saddle. Behind them, more worshippers queued up, faces slackly enraptured.

The skin on Mary's nape crawled and she felt dizzy. Distantly, she realized her protective ward was buzzing angrily, burning against her skin under her collar. She shook herself and pushed back hard. *Emily can control plants, so her big sister can influence animals—including people?* Mary scowled furiously.

"Lyssa Banks, you stop that at once!" Mary snapped as she stepped forward. "I'm terribly sorry," she told Santa, with a saccharine simper, "I'll just take this one off your hands."

"But *Nan*—"

"Come with me *right now*," Mary gritted out, then took hold of Lyssa's arm, just barely restraining herself from shaking the little girl. "Lyssa Banks, what do you think you were doing, forcing those people to give you their toys?"

"I was going to make them pay!" Lyssa protested.

"That's shoplifting, and shoplifting is *dumb*," Mary informed her, "it's not even a *proper* crime: your parents would be ashamed of you! If you're going to be a supervillain at least have the decency to do it properly." Obviously she was of an age to need The Talk, the one her law enforcement supercop parents had been shirking. Over her shoulder, she added: "Come along now, children, it's time to go."

"But worrabout my model kit—" Ethan asked.

"Because you've been such a good boy I'm going to pay for it." Mary stalked towards the nearest cash desk. "Emily, I'm sure you'd rather visit a flower shop, and Robert, I'll front you a new game but *not here*—Elissa, just for trying to shoplift *you're getting salt in your porridge for supper tonight* unless you apologize."

She faced the counter grimly and flourished the gift voucher. "Robert, give me that . . ." She successfully ignored the muffled sobbing, along with the shadowy tendrils of Elissa's power scrabbling at the edges of her mind. The cashier bagged the boxed model kit and handed it to Mary, who gave it to Ethan. Then they left.

They were halfway down the escalator when she realized Elissa was some distance behind, and when she glanced back she saw the little girl clutching a heavy-looking carrier bag. An alarm shrilled somewhere behind them. "Oh fucknuggets," she murmured as Elissa smiled triumphantly at her and raised a middle finger. Mary hadn't been serious about the cold salted porridge before, but now it was *definitely* on the menu.

"Robert, Ethan, Emily," Mary said in a high, tight voice, "I'll meet you by the toilet door over there: I just need *a word* with your sister first. Will you do that for me?" She smiled at the children, trying to look as reassuring as a real nanny (rather than a mob enforcer), and they nodded, very seriously. (So did the Christmas trees: Mary shuddered and forced herself to ignore them.) She watched Robert and the twins like a hawk until she was sure they were toddling in the right direction. Then she grabbed Elissa's bagarm and marched her after them like a sergeant in the fun police.

"Upgrading your rap sheet from shoplifting to cash robbery is not big and it is not clever and it is *especially dumb* to do so without an escape plan," she hissed in Lyssa's reddening ear. "There's a camera pointing at every cash terminal and I see store detectives, so you are going to go straight to that toilet door and do *exactly* as I tell you to do unless you want to go to jail." It was an empty threat: the New Management hadn't lowered the age of criminal responsibility and Lyssa was still a minor. But Mary was *in loco parentis,* emphasis on *loco,* and Lyssa had emptied enough cash from the Renfielded cashier's register to hang her.

Keeping a tight grip on her temper—best not to let her destroying angel slip the leash when she had Dad's toy chest to call on—Mary reached into her messenger bag. "All right!" She barked at the approaching security guards, "You're out of your weight class, so fuck off!" She flipped off the safety on the machine pistol the bag had handed her, braced, and fired a three-round burst at the cameras. Gratifyingly loud shrieks of terror filtered through the ringing in her ears as she made a half-turn and fired another burst at the next-closest CCTV dome. The MP5K was loaded with blanks, but the plastic caps on the cartridges could still do damage at close range: splintered Perspex and festive shards of shattered camera rained down.

Terrified shoppers panicked and fled, the security guards among them. Mary clenched her teeth, ears numb and nose stinging as expended cartridge cases rattled across the floor. Once she saw that the MOPs were taking cover she shoved the submachine gun back in her bag and dashed towards the toilet entrance. Robert was watching her with unconcealed admiration; Lyssa looked angry but still clutched her bag of loot; and the twins were hyper. "It's over, children," she told them. She held her messenger bag towards Lyssa, flap gaping open: "Dump that in here, we'll sort it out later." The little girl paused. "*Now,*" she snarled. Lyssa whined but dropped the carrier bag of cash into Mary's messenger, which swallowed it as easily as it had digested the gun. "Now hold hands, boys and girls, we're leaving now!" She grabbed Lyssa by one wrist and traced an arcane symbol on the lav door, then led her band of underage stickup artists to safety along the ghost roads.

►◄►◄►◄

Jennifer was working on the slides for her presentation to the board when Amy stumbled into the office in a state of considerable distress, smelling like she'd been attacked by a zombie skunk.

Jennifer suppressed a stab of resentment—*what's the dumpy witch done* now, *what does she* want?—as she saw the water stains on Amy's lapel and the pale smears on her sleeve. "What happened, sweetie?" she trilled. (It was always easier to start with solicitous sympathy: one could take it in so many promising directions, should one subsequently feel the need.) She turned her chair to face her subordinate and waited.

"Deli counter's"—Amy panted for breath, the top buttons of her company-issue blouse gaping—"it's closed for deep cleaning. Ade's fault. It was *awful*."

Really? Jennifer studied her minion with renewed interest. "You look—" her gaze sharpened—"untidy, Amy, *why* did you come back to the office looking like that? Couldn't you have smartened up a bit first?" Negging delivered, it was time to drill down: "What exactly is going on, sweetie?"

Amy's face slumped like a cardboard box left out in the rain. She looked truly miserable. *Are those tear tracks?* Jennifer wondered. *Oh, this is going to be fun!*

"Ade was abusing the printer behind our backs for months." Amy clearly took it personally, the silly goose. "He was making meat gloves for a homeless disabled war vet—wrappers to go around his hook, to make it look like he had a proper prosthesis. Anyway, the homeless guy kicked off when they told him Ade didn't work there any more, and when Security asked him to leave he threw his hand at the counter and it was *disgusting,* maggots and slime all over the place, everybody throwing up from the smell—"

Amy sniffed loudly, then fumbled at her desk's top drawer and pulled out a packet of tissues. She smeared her cheap mascara artlessly, as if panda-eyes were the big new thing. Jennifer kept her sympathy mask fastened firmly in place as she watched Number Two Minion's meltdown. Dear idiot Ade had *really* gotten under Amy's skin. Even though he didn't work here any more! It was delightfully precious. In fact it was so good that she magnanimously decided to forgive Amy for disrupting her workflow. But Jennifer was a serious manager, and it was inappropriate to giggle in front of the surveillance cameras, so she slackened her facial muscles just a little, adopted an expression of patient watchfulness, and waited until Amy's tears dried up. Which happened pretty fast, all things considered. Number Two Minion might be prone to unseemly fits of empathy, but at least she had a handle on the basics.

Time for some reinforcement.

"While I sympathize, sweetie, Mr. Hewitt's malfeasance doesn't justify losing your bleep in public—or even in private." Jennifer dialed up the sternness a couple of notches: "You represent the face of FlavrsMart in public, Ms. Sullivan. You are supposed to handle undignified and distressing situations serenely, in a manner that doesn't disturb other staff or Members of the Public. I understand and sympathize, but you can't do your job in your current state." She dialed back the dressing-down before Amy started leaking again: "Listen, it's three o'clock. You're three hours off the end of your shift, but you've cleared the stack ranking backlog"— Minion Number Two nodded vigorously, or perhaps she was simply trying not to snivel—"and frankly you look green. I'm signing you off sick for the rest of the day. Go home and get some rest, sweetie. Put your uniform in the laundry and catch your breath and be back here in tip-top form tomorrow morning and we'll pretend this regrettable loss of self-control never happened." She raised a finger: "Oh, just one more thing. I think you should write me a very quick summary of events, including the names of the senior staff representatives who were present. I'll get Security to pull the camera files, and tomorrow, as a special treat, you can update Mr. Hewitt's transfer record with a post-discharge endorsement!"

By the time Jennifer finished grooming Amy, Number Two Minion was beaming at the prospect of taking a richly deserved dump all over Ade's transferrable personnel record.[3] She was a

---

3. TPRs followed employees from job to job, unseen and inscrutable as Odin's terrifying snitch-ravens, Thought and Memory: they were a godsend for HR departments, having put an end to the litigious train wreck that had rendered employment references utterly useless. Ade's TPR was visible to the

slow understudy, but at last she was figuring out that the way to please Jennifer was to demonstrate performative cruelty to order. As she departed with a just *slightly* indecent swing of angry anticipation in her overbroad hips, Jennifer reflected that Amy clearly didn't realize what she was setting herself up for.

But Jennifer did, and she congratulated herself on a job well done before she turned back to planning her next big presentation.

The rest of the afternoon and early evening passed smoothly enough. Jennifer spent another hour on the presentation, then realized she was growing stale and shelved it until tomorrow. She read Amy's report on the deli counter debacle, and updated her own private files on the participants: Amy, Gladys, Adrian Hewitt, the hapless dough-faced butcher's assistant (he'd make a good scapegoat, Jennifer decided), and the idiots from Security. Action items: pull the camera footage, check whether Security pressed trespassing charges against the vagrant, monitor Robin Holmes for signs of slacking off on the deep clean and public health recertification. He probably wouldn't give her an opening (Robin was a perfectly spherical branch manager of uniform density: he had no handles or rough edges for blackmail), but it was always worth putting in the effort. It *never* hurt to have dirt on one's superiors.

Then it was seven thirty, and even Jennifer was flagging. She'd been in the office since seven o'clock that morning. It was her habit to work a solid twelve hours every day, and to tell the truth she *was* tired. Besides, it would look odd if she never slackened her headlong pace. So she very theatrically pushed her antiquated desktop monitor back, pulled her handbag from the bottom drawer of her desk, and took out her personal tablet.

She spent the next half hour reading an interview with her current object of emulation, the newly promoted Chief Operations Officer of the Bigge Organization: Evelyn Starkey. Ms. Starkey, so recently elevated by His Grace the Bishop, was clearly an initiate of the inner temple. The tells were subtle, but Jennifer knew

---

Department for Work and Pensions, and any employer considering him for a job, but not to Ade himself. It was yet another example of how the New Management made everything better—at least for its willing executioners.

what to look for: it was like gaydar for necromancers. *One of us.* Finally, her devotional literature stash exhausted, she unwound by reading the promotional offerings sent to her by cosmetic dermatology consultants and specialists in aesthetic reconstructive osteology. Electromuscular stimulation, implant surgery, and selective neuroplasty; dermabrasion and laser ablation of microvascular insults; dental implants—these were some of Jenn's favorite things.

Nobody was perfect. Jennifer's weakness (she was unflinchingly willing to admit this to herself) was a troubling dissatisfaction with the body she'd won in life's lottery. It wasn't that she looked *bad*. Indeed, many other women would hiss and backstab the sleek cow from HR if they even for a minute imagined she was unhappy with her own appearance. Back in college Jennifer had moonlighted as a model to help pay her student loans. But her ambitions were not limited by the horizons of vanity, and mere *prettiness* was a handicap that no amount of horrifyingly expensive Pale Grace™ cosmetic products could compensate for.

Ms. Starkey was absolutely right when she told the interviewer that to become a billionaire executive a woman had to look the part. And the signs of her dedication were visible in her photo spread for anyone who knew the signs of plastic surgery.

Ms. Starkey had observed in one of her interviews that you needed to be of certain proportions (taller was better: Jennifer was tall enough, and in her interview pics Ms. Starkey wore five-inch heels). You also needed a face that converged on one of a handful of fuzzy Ur-skulls, a platform on which to display your flawless and symmetrical features. (A kind of reverse phrenology was at work: the shape of your head didn't bespeak your abilities, but it dictated how others would perceive you.) And you needed an all-consuming, overwhelming, driving urge to power. Without all these features, no woman could rise to the board of an FT100 corporation. Jennifer was a clever student, and she was close, tantalizingly close, to beginning her run at the target. As the acting COO of de Montfort Bigge had demonstrated, the final 10 percent would take more than makeup and hair styling.

Jennifer had applied herself to the study of female captains of industry, of presidents and prime ministers: not just their deeds, but their thoughts and goals and the way they were expected to use their bodies—an extra handicap her male competitors didn't labor under. Jenn had analyzed them exhaustively, imported them into modeling apps, merged them and morphed them and contemplated them from all angles. Ms. Starkey was not only a highflyer, she was—Jennifer was convinced—either doing the same thing deliberately, or under the influence of a subtle geas cast upon her by the Bishop. Either way, she was the perfect role model for an upwardly mobile priestess in the same church.

Which was why, after she finished her thirteen-hour shift, Jennifer applied herself carefully to researching the surgical options that would sculpt her body into alignment with her ambition and Rupert's more recondite fetishes, just as she applied herself to mastering the human resources HiveCo had placed in her grasp.

I'll make you see, she vowed, hungrily staring at Eve's picture on her tablet screen. *Once the takeover goes through you'll see I'm just like you! I'm exactly the person you need, in exactly the right place, to take the Order's great work to the next level and provision it so that we can throw our enemies' screaming chestburst corpses from the upper levels of the Temple. And then—*

The world would finally see her for what she was.

But first the buyout had to go through, and certain positions had to be opened up if she was to advance.

And Ade, the goddamned idiot, had managed to get himself sacked despite what, by rights, should have been an unassailable position.

How to get him back into play . . . ?

Jennifer had an idea.

►◄►◄►◄

Imp was almost at his front gate when he realized he wasn't alone.

A big SUV with blacked-out rear windows had driven past as he turned the corner at the end of the street. Now he saw it parked ahead of him with both pavement-side doors open. The fellow who'd just grabbed his left shoulder—a completely bald gent whose reddish face resembled the north end of a southbound tank—wore a dark suit that failed to hide his shoulder holster and Kevlar vest. Mirrored aviator shades and a coiled wire running from collar to ear completed the look.

Imp startled and tried to run. The Gammon's fingers tightened painfully on his collarbone. "'Ere. Are you Mister Jeremy Starkey? 'Cos if so, yer sister wants ter see yer."

Another thug in a Hugo Boss suit strode along the pavement towards them. "There must be some mistake," Imp extemporized. Having just seen Eve, there was *obviously* some mistake, but these two didn't seem likely to believe anything he said. "These are not the droids you're looking for," he suggested, and pushed *hard* at Gammon Number One's tiny red-eyed mind.

The Gammon shook his head and winced, then looked over his shoulder at Gammon Number Two, fingers slackening: "These are not the droids—" he began.

"Mister Starkey." Gammon Number Two pulled out a taser and aimed it at Imp: "I have orders to take you to your sister. We can do this the easy way or we can do it the hard way. Your call."

Imp's mental push ricocheted off Gammon Number Two's mind like a daddy longlegs bouncing off a speeding car's windshield. *Warded.* Imp shook his head dizzily, grimacing at the instant headache. "Who do you work for?" he asked.

"Ms. Starkey wants to see you *right now.* She says it's an emergency. Into the car. No fast movements, mind."

"But I just—" Gammon Number Two made the electrodes on the tip of his stun gun crackle and spark. Imp shuffled towards the BMW. "*Really?* Okay, okay, I get it . . ."

Gammon Number One held the BMW X5's door open for Imp. "Phone, please." He snapped his fingers, and Imp wearily handed his smartphone over. Resistance didn't seem sensible at this point.

"Are you *sure* you're supposed to kidnap me?" He tried again, pushing at Gammon Number One.

Gammon Number Two grunted, then did the unexpected: he pulled out a phone of his own and dialed. "Miss, we've got him but he's reluctant to come with us. Can you . . . yes, ma'am." He handed Imp the device. "It's for you."

Imp took the phone warily. "Yes?"

To his astonishment, it really *was* his sister. "Jeremy, there's been a change of plan. I want you to go with these men. They're body-guards, they won't hurt you, but it's *very* important that I see you *right now*."

"Why—"

"I'll explain face-to-face." Eve hung up on him.

"What?" Imp handed the phone back to Gammon Number Two.

"Are we square, sir?" the man asked impassively.

"Yeah . . . I guess so." Imp reluctantly tugged on his seat belt as the guard closed the door. The interior of the SUV stank of money and fear. Eve wasn't the big sis he'd grown up with, back when they were a perfectly normal family with a dad who was an oneiromancer and a mum who wrote code that tore holes in re-ality. Bad shit had happened five years ago, they'd made their separate ways, and the new version of his sister was glossy and hard-shelled and ruthless. Something worse than merely losing their parents had happened to her while they'd been out of touch, and all he could think of was the cuckoo clock: maybe it *wasn't* his cock-up coming back to haunt him this time.

The car dipped slightly on its suspension as the guards climbed into the front. When the armored doors thudded shut his ears popped slightly. "Can I have my phone back?" he asked. "If we're going for a ride I need to let my housemates know I'm going to be late."

"Nope." Gammon Number Two started the engine.

They crawled through the inner London traffic for half an hour until they came to an urban expressway and accelerated, thun-dering along an underpass for another five minutes. They turned off onto an approach road circling the perimeter of an airfield, arriving at a set of steel-and-razor-wire gates which opened onto a service road. Finally Gammon Number Two pulled up beside a windowless door in the back of a hangar. "All right, hop out."

They escorted Imp into a cavernous building full of very expen-sive executive toys. "Cool—" Imp said as his escorts took up po-sitions front and rear, heads swiveling—"look, where are we—"

"Sir." A woman in a pilot's uniform, complete with gold-braided cuffs on the jacket and a peaked cap, opened the cabin door of a helicopter. "Please mind your head." *Holy shit, I've fallen into genderswapped* Fifty Shades of Grey! Imp hyperventilated for a few seconds before he remembered, slightly crestfallen, that it was his sister's production. (Still, it was going to be *amazingly* useful when he wrote his next movie script.)

The pilot handed him a headset and showed him how to plug it in overhead, then how to adjust his seat belt—the rear compartment of the helicopter had two rows of facing seats, three abreast, and acres of cream leather and gleamingly polished walnut—and he nodded and smiled along, barely noticing. Imp's secret conceit that he was the reincarnation of Andy Warhol sometimes made it difficult to pay sufficient attention to the here and now. "Phone?" he asked hopefully, and this time Gammon Number Two grudgingly handed it to him through the open cabin door.

"I've checked it for spyware and you're clean, sir. If you remain with us we will issue you with a secure company device in due course. We will leave as soon as Ms. Starkey arrives—"

A silver Aston Martin drove in through the hangar's open main door and parked alongside the chopper. Eve unfolded herself from the passenger seat like a black-clad praying mantis. She carried the sort of skinny black briefcase that in Imp's experience invariably meant *lawyers* and *trouble*. She stalked across to the chopper and climbed in with a thunderous expression. Her lips were a red slash of tension, and she'd strung a pearl choker around her neck, which meant she was armed. She took the opposite seat and pulled on a headset: "Let's get going, I haven't got all day," she said tensely.

Minions sprang into motion. Ground staff closed and locked the cabin doors, then the pilot and Gammon Number Two climbed into the crew compartment up front. Gammon Number One whisked the DB9 out of the way. Meanwhile, clicks and whining noises from above the ceiling suggested that somebody was hitching up the hamsters to the flywheel that spun the rooftop eggbeaters. A small tractor reversed up to the nose of the chopper, and after a couple of minutes it lurched slightly, then began to roll towards the concrete landing pad in front of the hangar.

Eve thumb-typed continuously on her phone, eyes down, ignoring

Imp. "Is that necessary?" Imp asked, leaning towards her. More typing, more ignoring. "Evie?" Her eyes flickered as she tapped away at her email. "Sis?" He reached out and poked her knee.

Eve shoved his hand away. *Now* she noticed him, and he wished she hadn't, for she turned the Eye of Sauron on him. "Sit!" she snarled, reaching up to wrench at a knob on the panel their headsets were plugged into. "What seems to be the delay?" she demanded.

"Just waiting for tower clearance, ma'am," the pilot reassured her, "and . . . that seems to be it." Imp heard Gammon Number Two breathing in the background for a moment before the pilot cut the connection, presumably so she could focus on pilot-y things like not crashing and exploding in a ball of flames. Eve sent Imp one last scorching glare, then turned her gaze back towards her phone screen. It was a miracle that it didn't crack beneath the intensity of her basilisk stare.

Right: doghouse, self-insert, got it. Imp took a deep breath, only now realizing that his hands were clammy. He hadn't seen his sister this furious since the time he'd accidentally washed her interview blouse with his cheap knockoff football shirt and the dye ran—*look away, look away, let it go.* He pulled out his phone and hastily sent Doc, Game Boy, and Del a group text:

> *Summoned away on Big Sister biz, hitching a ride in a VIP helicopter! Whee! :-) PS: got paid beer in fridge back l8r*

Which was bottling it, but Imp didn't have the intestinal fortitude to tell them the truth right now.

With a deafening whine and a worrying series of clanking noises, the hamsters began to scamper and the giant eggbeaters slowly started to rotate. The whine grew louder—it sounded like a dental drill built for blue whales—then the cabin lights flickered and everything muted as the noise-cancellation in the headsets kicked in. The rotors sped up, tips rising and blurring into invisibility. The whine grew into a full-throated bellow, and the helicopter taxied towards a large H in a circle on the apron. As the markings passed out of sight under the nose, the ground began to drop away beneath them without any great fuss. They hung above the pad for a subjective infinity (which was about thirty seconds, according to Imp's phone), then turned sharply left, tilted towards the river, and accelerated away.

A minute after they began climbing, Imp—who now had his nose pressed up against the side window, trying to spot the London Eye and Tower Bridge—glanced over to the other side of the cabin and noticed that Eve had put her phone away and was staring at him furiously.

"Uh, if this is about the football shirt incident, I can explain—" he began.

Eve shook her head.

"The time I let Nono into your room when I was twelve and she . . . ?"

Another tiny headshake—her self-control was proportional to the severity of his sister's emotion, in Imp's experience, which meant that this was *very* bad—and finally Eve squared her shoulders. "Jeremy."

"Evelyn." She absolutely *hated* her given name but he was helpless to resist the impulse to tweak her.

"On May eleventh, 2010"— a week after their father's funeral— "a solicitor from the firm of Barr, Klept, and Rutherford visited you in your student residence and asked you to sign some papers."

Oh shit, it was that *business,* he thought.

Eve continued, her voice an inhumanly controlled monotone. "And he asked you to answer some questions about me, in confidence."

Imp's pulse pounded in his ears as his sister unlocked her briefcase and pulled out a slightly dog-eared sheaf of papers. She flipped through them, then offered him a page to examine. "Is this your signature?"

"Uh, I, I'm not supposed to say—there's a nondisclosure—"

"Jeremy." Her glare was fit to peel paint. "*Is* that your signature on the nondisclosure agreement? The one you're not supposed to talk about unless it's to the owner?"

He licked his lips. "How did you get that?" he asked.

"It came with the promotion, like the thugs and the helicopter. I'm the owner now: you're not breaking the NDA if you tell me. Is that definitely your signature, yes or no?"

Imp nodded.

"This is a fucking nightmare." Eve glanced out the window pensively. They were racing high above the trackless wastes of South London suburbia. The calm act didn't fool Imp: his sister *never* normally swore, at least not while she was working. Thought it was unprofessional or something. She was clearly upset: Was it something in the papers he'd signed?

After a minute she took a deep breath, faced him again, and handed him the entire bundle of documents. "Can you go through these and tell me if any of the signatures are *not* yours? If there's even the slightest shadow of doubt that you signed every last one of these?" She hesitated. "I've tagged the signed pages with Post-it notes, the salmon-colored one is *particularly* important."

"I uh." He nerved himself: "I don't really *remember* signing this shit. I mean, I remember the visit, but I was kind of stoned that week? That month, actually. After. You know."

Their father's death and their mother's disablement had hit them both hard. Eve had gritted her teeth and dealt, but Imp had folded.

"I know. This is . . . precautionary. I mean, I don't *blame* blame you, but unless I've lucked out there's a lot of damage control to do."

"Damage control?" Imp asked as he skimmed from page to page, seeing his incriminating scrawl on every one. The pink Post-it was attached to—"What the fuck even *is* this?"

"It's a mixture of Norman French and Church Latin, in medieval black-letter script. It's still used by lawyers in certain jurisdictions." She shook her head. "Apparently you initialed it while you were stoned, without asking for a translation."

Imp racked his brain. "He said it was a security background check for your new employer? But he wanted to know about your school holiday jobs, who your friends were, where you'd been on vacation? It seemed kind of silly, if you ask me."

Eve nodded thoughtfully. "Those are all typical positive vetting clearance questions, however stupid they sound—they're checking for inconsistencies, which are a warning sign of lies. So they ask the subject and all her friends and family the same stuff, and if they get consistent answers, and the credit history and criminal background checks come back clean and it all lines up, then you get your clearance. And the job." She seemed to be calming down from the violent outburst that had propelled them aboard this dubious contraption, but she was still deeply upset and trying to control it.

"Where are we going?" he asked.

"The Bigge Organization has a complex corporate structure, but if you trace it back to its roots it's headquartered in the Channel Islands, in a trust administered under Skaroese law—Skaro is the island we're going to. Rupert owned, owns it."

Imp had never personally met Eve's demoniacal employer but he did a double-take all the same. "Rupert owned *an island*?"

"Rupert bought the freehold, fair and square. He also purchased the title of nobility that belonged to its liege. You can't buy titles of nobility any more in the United Kingdom, but Skaroese law lags a bit. The title of the Barony of Skaro was dormant after the last Lord died without issue in 1952, so Rupert bought the island *and* became its feudal liege, owing fealty to the Duke of Normandy, which happens to be the hat Elizabeth Windsor wears when she's the ruler of the Channel Islands rather than the Queen of the United Kingdom. They aren't actually part of the UK, just a side-quest owned by the Crown."

"Wait, what? I mean what! What? Really, what?"

"This—" A perfectly manicured nail the red of fresh arterial blood tapped the salmon-pink Post-it note—"appears to be a valid contract pursuant to which a male guardian has assigned his legal guardianship of a *feme sole* under his protection to a trust under the control of a firm of solicitors. *You* signed it in your capacity as my oldest surviving male relative of the closest degree—as my male guardian." It was just a little squiggle: it didn't look like much.

Her smile was more of a tight-lipped glare. "This is a contract solemnized under medieval Norman law, Jerm, not common law or modern English law or Scots law or the Code Napoleon or what have you. Rupe didn't buy himself a lump of rock in a tax haven and the right to wear an ermine robe for no particular reason: he wanted to buy an entire legal system with all the trimmings. Skaro is tiny, and while Guernsey, Jersey, and Sark all modernized to some degree—the Human Rights Act or the European Convention on Human Rights were added to their legal systems, granting equal protection into law—Skaro is home to less than two hundred souls and hasn't seen a murder in three centuries. It was overlooked because *nobody thought it mattered,* and as a result it has a legal system that hasn't really been updated since the Middle Ages."

She pointed an accusing finger at him. "You signed me over to a law firm, brother dearest. Including—under Skaroese law—the right to marry me off by proxy. *Which they fucking did.*" She pulled the papers back and removed another sheet, this one somewhat thicker—it was parchment, Imp realized, not laser printed—and someone had doodled on it in fine copperplate handwriting with a side order of Germanic black letter for the Latin.

"This is my *marriage certificate,* Jeremy. To Baron Rupert de Montfort Bigge. Which under Skaroese law means I have the legal status of *feme covert.* Rupert literally fucking *owns* me," she hissed.

"How does that even happen?"

"Coverture is the medieval legal doctrine that a married woman's property and person are merged with her husband. It's based on the biblical belief that a married couple become one flesh and spirit: it's why in England a husband couldn't be convicted of raping his wife until the 1990s. Among other charming throwbacks. Basically, according to Skaroese law, I'm chattel. *Was* chattel, but didn't know it," she added bitterly. She took a deep breath. "And that's not all—" Her finger was shaking so badly that Imp cringed in sympathy.

"What's the worst?" he asked: "Hit me with it, sis."

"Skaroese law"—she gave a grim little chuckle, then choked it off—"is based on *pre-1351* Norman law, minus the enlightened modern reforms introduced by King Edward III. There's a crime called Petty Treason. It was abolished in 1832 in England, but before then, if a wife or child killed the head of the household it was considered worse than murder. The punishment was either burning at the stake or drawing and quartering: hanging wasn't harsh enough. And in the pre-1351 system you could be convicted of petty treason for *attempting* to murder your Lord and Master. Or desertion—running away, like a slave leaving their master, or a wife."

She leaned towards Imp. "When I signed on with Rupe I let him place a geas on me. It requires me to obey the terms of our contractual relationship. I never tried to break it because it was really weak and stupid and I thought I could escape whenevs, just by giving notice under my employment contract. But this changes *everything*. By proxy-marrying me without my knowledge, he didn't just load me with the title of Lady of Skaro: he turbocharged the geas. It's like my worst nightmare just came true because you couldn't be bothered to pay even the most minute quantum of your attention to what you were signing. If Rupert isn't dead—if he comes back from beyond the boarded-up door on the top floor—if he even left a letter to be delivered to me later, with orders to be obeyed in the event of his disappearance—I can no more disobey his instructions than his left little pinkie can: I am utterly *fucked*.

"So we are on our way to Castle Skaro, where we will ransack my dearly departed husband's office for anything that might help break the geas. And then . . ." She trailed off.

"What, then?" Imp said after not less than a whole minute had passed.

"I want to know why he did it," she said fiercely, "and what he was planning for me."

3

OFFSHORE SUMMONING CIRCLES IN THE DARK

Wendy took a couple of hours to type up her confidential report—more accurately, her confession—on Del's nefarious activities. Gibson would bury it with a stake through its heart so the company could profess due diligence if Del's unpunished crimes ever came back to haunt them; meanwhile Gibson would be free to offer her a job. After delivering it, Wendy retreated to her desk with a mug of coffee. She rated a cramped, windowless office of her own now, because her work required her to deal with confidential resources. One such was the folder Gibson had dropped in her Share-Point on the office network. She opened the first file: PRODUCT ADULTERATION REPORT ON FLAVRSMART BRANCH 322. She sighed as she began to read, expecting tedium beyond anything she'd ever known. But five minutes later she was banging on the boss's office door.

"Seriously, sir? What the ever-loving fuck are we even doing with this? Isn't it a job for SCD-1?"

SCD-1 was the London Metropolitan Police Service's Homicide and Serious Crime Command: Wendy had once hoped to work there, back before she'd had a run-in with an abusive senior officer.

"Sit down, Deere." Gibson had a Biro clenched between his teeth, clearly a pale substitute for a cigarette. "Give me a minute." He unmuted his telephone handset and gruffly concluded his call. "*Thank* you," he said, with heavy irony. He placed it back on its base station. "Right. This is the FlavrsMart case, I take it?"

"Sir." Wendy set her jaw firmly. "With all due respect, seven homeless persons have been reported missing near the shop in the past two months, and then this"—she flapped her hand for emphasis—"*product adulteration* case shows up in the supermarket, and the contaminant DNA in two of the pies matches the Criminal Records Bureau sequence records for two of the missing persons—how has this *not* landed in SPIU's lap?"

For an instant Gibson looked infinitely weary. "Follow the money, kid." Wendy bristled, but let it slide: she was in her mid-twenties and Gibson was pushing fifty. He continued, "Funding is bad, and, well, *you* tell *me* the victim profile?"

"Oh. Oh." Wendy rocked in her chair. "Three female and four male, all NFA—" no fixed abode—"ages range from seventeen to sixty-two. Four from troubled backgrounds, five are opiate abusers not enrolled in treatment programs, one is long-term enrolled but repeatedly falls off the wagon, four are alcoholics, six have mental health issues, all seven are known to the police, six are definitely unemployed, five have records for petty crime and vagrancy . . ." She paused for a moment's angry contemplation. "They've all been de-emphasized, haven't they?"

De-emphasized was the current euphemism for *thrown on the trash heap*. It denoted people the New Management considered to be of no (or minimal) value to society. They had no money, they couldn't hold down a job, and they didn't even soak up resources in a *useful* way. The productively disabled, the *deserving* disabled, had the decency to stay in their nursing home beds generating economic activity and jobs for carers, just like the dumb career criminals serving time in their prison cells and providing employment for prison officers. But the *de-emphasized* had the temerity to try to look after themselves in ways that resisted monetization. Their existence implicitly threatened to undermine the system as a whole by suggesting that it was possible to opt out completely. They didn't claim benefits—or survived despite being sanctioned—and they didn't take workfare assignments, and they were mostly homeless but *still* they stubbornly persisted. And that couldn't be allowed.

So the New Management *de-emphasized* them and waited for them to die of neglect.

"Yes." Gibson nodded gloomily. He might be management-tier

within HiveCo Security, but he'd been an Army officer in an earlier life. Public service was his touchstone, and the whole idea of de-emphasis was repellant to that mind-set. But HiveCo Security was private sector and had to turn a profit, and the government had washed its hands of these people to the extent that the police wouldn't even investigate if they were murdered.

"Why are we *re*-emphasizing them?" Wendy asked, with only mildly ironic emphasis. She crossed her arms and waited.

"Officially?" Gibson raised an equally ironic eyebrow. "There shouldn't be *any* human DNA in processed meat products, much less DNA from missing people. They're trialling some kind of new robotic just-in-time manufacturing process. Eventually they plan to have vats full of animal tissue culture in every branch, feeding it to 3D printers on the deli counter—meat products without animal cruelty and the risk of another Mad Cow Disease epidemic." *Also without the farmers and the stockyards taking their cut of the profits,* Wendy mentally translated. "Right now, it's in prototype—Branch 322 is a test bed for lots of next-generation retail tech. They've set up a rendering line in one of the loading bays, taking in carcasses from a local abattoir and carving them up by robot, then piping the mechanically reprocessed slime to the printers. But the point is, the pies are made by robot. Carcass goes in at one end of the line, pies print out at the other. Tell me, what are the signs of a serial killer?"

The abrupt change of tack nearly gave Wendy whiplash, but she was getting used to it. Gibson was shrewder than the job called for: too shrewd by half.

"Serial killers . . . uh, let's see. They usually start small, with animal cruelty." She held up a finger, regurgitating points from a half-remembered college lecture. "Personality screening typically finds Dark Triad traits—narcissism, Machiavellianism, and psychopathy—but those aren't unique to serial killers. Smart Dark Triad people often end up in senior management or politics. Police, even. The serial killers are usually the less-bright ones. Motives vary: may be sexual, but not always. They can go slow and take one victim every so often, on an irregular basis, or in brief bursts separated by years or even decades. Fallow periods may correspond to prison sentences: they usually engage in other law-breaking activities and if they get banged up that puts a brake on their hobby. They're mostly male but there are exceptions, often working with a male partner—Myra Hindley, Rose West."

"Now tell me about their victims."

I see where you're going here and I don't like it. Wendy's skin crawled. "Please tell me you're not handing me a serial killer brief disguised as a thief-taker investigation, sir?"

"I can't tell you that." Gibson's expression was now absolutely unreadable.

"I'm not *remotely* qualified to lead one of those, sir."

A full-dress murder investigation by the Met would have up to ninety officers assigned to it at various points, from the initial responders through the Scene of Crime team, to the detectives developing a timeline, to community liaison bobbies interviewing everyone who was in the vicinity. It'd have every warm body who could be mobilized looking for physical evidence, a fully crewed Incident Room putting together a timeline and GIS maps of the area. There'd be chain-of-evidence specialists to write up the case for the Crown Prosecution Service, interview teams for suspects, the whole nine yards. A proper murder investigation cost millions—and nine times out of ten it paid off with a conviction, because if you threw unlimited resources at a policing problem you usually got results. And that went squared for a suspected serial killer or a spree killer going active—it made national headlines, with round-the-clock bulletins and government ministers being grilled under spotlights on the Nine O'clock News.

Well, it *used to* involve all that, before the Leeds Incident, the New Management, and the gibbets at Marble Arch. These days the rules had changed and, ominously, the most recent crime figures Wendy had seen from the Office of National Statistics were strangely lacking in detail.

"I never suggested you were qualified to lead a serial murder enquiry, Deere." Gibson looked uncomfortable. "But you're the least unqualified body I've got, even before we get to your Class Three abilities." Wendy's transhuman talent was surprisingly useful: if she'd had it back when she worked for the Met, they'd never have let her go. "FlavrsMart wants someone to go undercover at Branch 322 and find out what's wrong with the prototype meat processor line, how the *contaminants* are getting into the product. There might be an innocent explanation—homeless people dossing in the loading bay and spitting in the pink slime, or something. I don't need to tell you how sensitive DNA testing is."

The Polymerase Chain Reaction, used to copy and amplify fragments of DNA in a sample prior to sequencing, could turn even an invisibly small trace contaminant into a detectable signal. But there were seven missing people, and the idea that they just happened to have spat in the machinery was frankly implausible.

"Unofficially, if there's a serial killer disposing of bodies using FlavrsMart facilities, FlavrsMart management want it cleared up and suppressed. Perp neutralized under total news blackout, NDAs signed all round, then *maybe* we hand over the case to SCD-1 or possibly the spooks from MI5. But we're being paid by FlavrsMart to clean up their shop, not to run a murder investigation. And we're going to take a *very* fat bonus in return for keeping our yaps shut forever. Do you understand?"

"Yes, sir." Wendy set her jaw. The de-emphasized weren't being treated as murder victims; they were being treated as bad publicity. But she had another, unwelcome thought, close on the heels of the first. "Sir, what if they're not just using that supermarket to dispose of the bodies?" She chewed her lower lip. "What if it's a hunting ground?"

Gibson walked towards his office window, which faced the windowless concrete wall of a warehouse across a narrow alleyway. He stood at ease with hands clasped behind his back for almost a minute.

"Sir?" Wendy asked eventually. "Is there anything else?"

"Before I left the Army," Gibson said quietly, "I wore a red cap: Fourth Investigation Company, First Military Police Brigade, Special Crimes Team, officer commanding."

Oh, thought Wendy, suddenly attentive.

"I was tangentially involved in a serial killer case," he added, his voice slightly choked up. "I was on station in Iraq. If you think you need backup, *call me*. Call at any hour of the day or night. I trust you to do the right thing. Just . . . be discreet."

He paused again, then added, "Dismissed."

Wendy saluted him silently, then left.

▶◀▶◀▶◀

Every second Monday was a hot-desking day for Amy, because once a month Jenn summoned Barry and Tara back to the mother ship to spend a day sweating under her wingtip-eyelinered gaze, just to remind them who they worked for. Amy privately welcomed the change because, other than the necessity of finding a mains socket for her laptop, it got her out from under Jenn's nose. As long as she handled the paperwork, Jenn ignored her; and as long as she evaded the CCTV it was possible to sketch with no one any the wiser.

On this particular Monday, Amy took extra pains over her appearance—after all, she'd be the visible avatar of management in the shop for the day—then walked the floor. As she walked she considered her workspace options. There was a stool and a free bench tucked around a corner in the dispensary, but the pharmacist was a vindictive cowbag who had it in for Amy. There was a back room behind the deli, but the deli was still closed for deep cleaning, and in any case the smell from the butcher's rendering line reminded her why she'd gone vegan. In the end, she lucked into a desk on the side of Loading Bay Four. The automatic door was jammed and the engineering crew hadn't arrived to fix it yet, so there were no lorries using it today. The floor manager had his minions stashing empty recyclable packaging on the dock, but apart from a chilly draft and the clash and clatter of roll pallets there was nothing to disturb her. So she kept her head down, obscured from view by a wall of cardboard waste.

There were no disciplinaries today. Most of the workload was routine: signing off on training, approving annual leave requests (from the minority of permastaff who weren't too terrified to abandon their posts for a week), even recommending two unusually long-term employees (over five years each!) for their Tufty Club bonuses. Jenn would give her the evil eye for it—staff weren't supposed to stick around long enough to claim the prizes—but being able to make someone's day brighter cheered up Amy.

But then she sighed and blinked unhappily at her screen. Because the inevitable had happened. What goes around comes around, and it was time to find a body who could fill the late and unlamented Adrian Hewitt's shoes.

Oh my rancid fucknuggets, she thought, as she reviewed the job description: *It's one of* those.

Once upon a time, back in the depths of prehistory, offices used to run on arcane things like carbon paper and typing pools full of manual typewriters. (Amy saw a typewriter on a school trip to the Industrial Museum once: she didn't understand how they were meant to work underwater.) But then a bright-eyed proto-geek called Mr. Xerox invented the photocopier, thereby enabling the rightsizing of legions of bikini-wearing, snorkel-snorting copy typists, and generating new and interesting disciplinaries for proto-Amys by means of the magnetic attraction between copier machines and buttocks.

The Xerox machines of yore were not a sleek modern device that you simply plugged in, used until out of magic copying powder, then threw away.[4] The original Xerox was a gargantuan box of cogs, driveshafts, prisms, cams, periscopes, hammer mills, steam engines, and reciprocating slides that sucked in paper at one end and labor at the other. A copier cost more than a year's wages bill for the entire typing pool and broke down as often as a professional mourner. Consequently Xerox repairmen—they were *invariably* men—became a semipermanent fixture of any large office building.

The bespoke meat products line on the deli counter was the latest incarnation of the copying machine, and the unlamented Mr. Hewitt had almost certainly been a very naughty Xerox repairman in a previous incarnation, for which he was now being punished.

---

4. Because, let's face it, razors are cheaper than razor blades.

His firing had broken an essential component in the machinery of FlavrsMart Branch 322, and the deli counter was going to be offline until a person of similar skills could be recruited. But the skills in question were esoteric. The job called for a fleshmachine whisperer, someone proficient in nursing jointing/flensing robots, coddling the MSM/MRM fractionator, and coaxing the delicatessen counter 3D printers into life.

Amy reviewed Mr. Hewitt's record with a sinking feeling.

Adrian Hewitt had arrived at FlavrsMart unencumbered with student debts. He was a high school dropout who, after a variety of casual jobs (bin man's assistant, mortuary porter, night watchman), had somehow acquired a Higher National Diploma in meat processing, attended a vocational training course in automated deboning machinery in slaughterhouses, took advantage of a bursary to address the sucking vacuum of meat printer maintenance operatives, and was unaccountably headhunted by FlavrsMart—who then paid for him to take *three whole months* of training in his first six months on the job.

When filling an internal vacancy, Amy normally ran the skills matrix past the database of recent applicants until some names popped out. But she could see at a glance that it wasn't going to work this time. Ade was not just a pair of hands for stacking shelves. Despite the recent blot on his copybook—Gladys had taken a splenetic, laxative-assisted shit all over his Personal Development Profile—Ade was horrifyingly specialized. He was also highly trained in arcana that spanned the gamut of meat production. He'd been doing *everything,* from booking in carcasses from the abattoir to programming the 3D multi-substrate extruders that turned the slushy, vile residues into something superficially resembling food. Along the way his tasks ranged from servicing the knife-wielding robots that lined the processing cage—where dangling carcasses entered at one end, and neatly deboned cuts of meat emerged on a conveyor from the other—to maintaining the high-pressure sieving system and pressure cooker that turned the leftovers into pink slime. He also cleaned and serviced the pipelines that fed the slime to the printers, where they emerged as beautifully formed nuggets and meat loaves and textured novelty roasts. He was, in short, a bizarre gastronomic Athena who had sprung fully formed from the brow of Mr. Xerox's spiritual heirs.

"We're going to have to advertise this one externally," she muttered to herself as she wrote up a memo, eyes-only, for Jennifer's attention. Jenn was going to hit the roof. Advertising externally meant paying fees that came out of HR's discretionary budget, which was measured in pennies. Replacing Ade might end up costing thousands—tens of thousands, even—all for the sin of taking the most expensive workplace selfie in Branch 322's dismal history. *We can't possibly rehire him, can we?* she pondered. *It would make life so much simpler.* But that was water under the bridge: certain copybook blots couldn't be repaired in this lifetime, and subsequent events on the deli counter had underlined the wisdom of firing him.

There was no alternative: Amy just had to hope Jenn could magic up a replacement.

▸◂▸◂◂

An hour and a half after it took off from the Barclays London Heliport, the AgustaWestland Power Elite settled onto the helipad at Castle Skaro so gently that the surface of Imp's second glass of Lagavulin barely rippled. "Fuck's *sake*," he slurred, "are we there already?" He raised his glass and necked the whiskey, coughed, and put it on the side-table for someone else to clean up.

Eve was already unbelting as the rotors slowed. "*Yes,* Jeremy, we *are* there already," she said with an elder sister's exaggerated patience.

"Is this your first visit?" he asked.

Her eyes flickered uneasily aside. "Yes."

The pilot opened the door for them. "Welcome to Skaro," she said, bowing. Gammon Number Two stood vigilantly alongside the chopper, keeping an eye on their reception party. The pilot mentioned something about nipping across to a maintenance hangar in Jersey and needing half an hour's notice when they wanted picking up, but Eve let it slide: now was not the time to get bogged down in trivia.

Imp followed her out of the executive chopper's Versace-lined cradle and found himself standing on the flagstoned rear court-yard of a late medieval castle.

To the onlookers who were waiting for them they must have seemed an odd couple. Imp resembled a rock star in rehab, and Eve could have been the rock star's attorney. He took the lead, long-haired and louche in a stained overcoat of uncertain vintage, while she followed behind in black Armani and killer heels, brief-case in hand and hair pulled back in a viciously tight bun.

"Yo, howdy!" Imp said, flashing a brilliant smile and extending a hand to the appalled-looking butler, who recoiled gratifyingly: "Is this the way to the next whiskey bar?"

Eve elbowed him in the ribs. (They shared the usual childhood sign language: her gesture promised much pain, delivery condition-ally deferred.) To the staff: "I'm Mrs. de Montfort Bigge, and I'm here to inspect my husband's office," she announced in a voice as sharp as a razor blade.

The butler bottled whatever response he had been readying for Imp, swallowed apprehensively, then bowed. "Yes, My Lady," he said. "Do you wish to meet the household staff first? They are waiting for you outside the great hall."

"Jeremy," she gave her brother a chilly smile, "be a dear and inspect the castle staff for me." She smiled at the butler, her expres-sion only slightly warmer: "I'm a great believer in delegation, but my husband's office *absolutely* can't wait. You can introduce me to the housekeeper and department heads later—my brother will deal with the staff for now."

"Right-o," said Imp, showing no sign at all of being crestfallen at his demotion to Lady de Montfort Bigge's personal greeter. "Which way towards the enemy?"

Eve focussed on the butler while a flunky of some sort led her brother towards the end of the courtyard past the helipad. "Ma'am, if you'd care to follow me, I'll take you straight to your husband's suite."

The butler was in late middle age, balding, and wore his tra-ditional tailcoat and pinstriped trousers with the dignity of an undertaker. He seemed uneasy about something, but Eve couldn't tell whether it was Imp's onslaught of chaos, or if rumors of her reputation at head office had made their way back to Skaro. Interestingly, he'd shown no sign of surprise at her self-introduction. "What's your name?" she asked.

"Mr. de Montfort Bigge always called me Jeeves," he said carefully. "The private elevator to the master suite is just along this passage: the entry code is—"

"I am not my husband," Eve bit out, "and I would *prefer* to know your real name." Subtext: *there are going to be some changes around here.*

"Anthony Cunningham at your service, ma'am." He bowed again, this time more deeply. Then, as he straightened from it, he braced. "Ma'am, when your husband returns—"

She gave him a sad, slightly pitying expression: "I don't think that's going to happen." *Thank fuck I wore the black suit this morning.* It had been a fortuitous accident, until she opened the safe and read her file: if she was going to play the role of Rupe's widow she'd probably have to modify her wardrobe a little, although hopefully the staff here didn't expect her to adopt full formal mourning dress.

"Please accept my deepest sympathies for your loss," Cunningham murmured, which was a nicely ambiguous way of kicking the can down the road. As he punched numbers into the keypad on the lift door Eve memorized them. "My Lady."

They stood in silence while the lift—brushed steel ceiling and polished black marble floor, with mirrored walls to make it feel less cramped—ascended. Evidently Rupert's roost was just below the battlements, as if he fancied himself a great angry seabird nesting on a cliff face.

Cunningham led her along a corridor with bare stone walls and a white-painted ceiling, supported by blackened timbers that had settled and bowed slightly over the centuries. It was not entirely austere, for a previous occupant had hung faded tapestries depicting scenes of medieval chivalry along the walls. Some more recent resident had suspended discreet halogen spotlights from the beams, and these illuminated the weavings. They passed niches, possibly former firing slits, where the draughty breezes had been blocked by means of cellular double glazing. A decorator had lined the hall with fully articulated suits of gothic-fluted plate, presumably bought as a job lot in the sixteenth century when armor was sliding into military irrelevance. The LEDs of a wifi range extender blinked merrily from above an early hot water radiator, and Eve queasily contemplated the central heating bill. No wonder castles were cheap to buy: it was the running costs that bankrupted you.

They turned a corner into a windowless corridor that ended in a row of robust oak doors. "Bodyguard's ready room, valet's quarters," Cunningham intoned, counting them off as he led her past. "The Master's suite, and this is Lady Skaro's bedroom, comprising your day room, your maid's chamber—"

"—Is there a maid in residence? Or a valet?"

"No, My Lady." Cunningham sounded apologetic. "You've never visited before. When I heard the news I took the liberty of having your apartment aired and cleaned, and the linens replaced. If you wish I can find you a temp, but I assumed you would bring your own staff, not—" He fell silent.

"I don't have a staff," Eve said. "*Yet*." She gestured at the door. "Show me."

Lady Skaro's boudoir resembled the honeymoon suite of a particularly stuffy and old-fashioned highland hotel, the kind that displayed a plaque in the lobby boasting that the Prince of Wales had parked one of his mistresses there while he stopped to play a round of golf in 1887. It was furnished with dark wooden antiques, many of which clearly predated the French Revolution. She'd need a stepladder to climb onto the canopy bed—if she dared, for there was room for a revolutionary republic of spiders to hold their constitutional convention in the drapes.

There were some signs of modernization, to 1950s levels of "modern." Ancient pumped-water radiators lined the niches below the narrow windows, gurgling villainously as they converted banknotes into hot air. The filament bulbs were dim enough to look at directly, like the sun seen through the smoke of a wildfire, but at least they weren't gas mantles or oil lamps. There was even a television set in the day room, but it was a glass-tubed antique from the 1950s. The lidless gaze of a beheaded deer reflected sightlessly off its freshly sprayed and polished screen.

"Hmm," said Eve. "I take it the room's been unoccupied for a while?"

Cunningham bowed his head reverently: "Lady Rebecca passed away three years before my father was born, My Lady, and Lord Alexander never saw fit to remarry. It has been cleaned and repaired on a regular basis, and the lightbulbs replaced, but the title was vacant for rather a long time before your husband petitioned for it."

Eve had seen enough. "So . . . my husband's suite, if you please?"

"Yes, My Lady." Cunningham marched to a door disguised as a wall panel to one side of the canopy bed. "The connecting door," he cleared his throat discreetly, "leads directly to the Baron's bedchamber."

Eve was struck by a strange conceit as she paused in the doorway. For a moment she imagined herself lying sprawled across the bed in a filmy peignoir, staring empty-headed at the ceiling when the door opened and someone lingered on the threshold. *Droit du seigneur* was a medieval urban legend, but *coverture* was anything but: the women who'd slept in this room had no legal right to resist their husband's advances. Had the Ladies of Skaro been victims, quivering in fear of nightly violation? Or had they been joyful brides, shivering in delighted anticipation? There was so much history here it was making her queasy. Eve shuddered, and quickly followed the butler into Rupert's bedroom.

The Master's suite had been drastically remodeled, if not in a manner calculated to reassure a conjugal visitor. Rather than dark wooden antiques, it was dominated by carmine wallpaper and thick black carpet. Crimson velvet curtains flanked the picture windows, the radiators had been replaced by underfloor heating, and the TV opposite the bed was positively pornographic. A chrome trellis to one side offered a selection of Rupert's favorite things: floggers, canes, ball gags, manacles, butt plugs, locking belts. She eyeballed the bed and was unsurprised to see attachment points for wrist and ankle restraints between the black silk sheets and pillows.

"En suite bath," Cunningham murmured, "with the smaller fifty-five-inch home cinema—waterproof—and wet bar, also humidor, seating for seven, bidet, imported Japanese heated toilet seat with scented water jet, air drier, massager, walk-in monsoon shower, triple-nozzle enema machine with restraint chair . . ."

Eve didn't blink—she already knew far more than she wanted to about Rupert's sex life—but she felt a hot flush when she remembered she'd been unknowingly married to him for five years. It was like the uncomprehending double-take brought on by a sniper's bullet that tugged at the edge of her sleeve rather than splitting her scalp. The only reasonable question was, why had fate ignored her?

"My brother can sleep in this suite," she announced. "I'll take the lady's maid's room for tonight. If you can provide a memory-foam mattress topper and a fresh duvet and pillows, that will suffice. Also a wifi login that works and has decent signal, even if you have to get Facilities to install an extra repeater for me? I *will* be working while I'm here." She turned to look at the door opposite the one they'd entered by. "Is that his office?"

"Yes, My Lady."

"Ma'am will do. Or"—a momentary hitch—"if you insist on formality, Mrs. Bigge." *For now, until I can get it annulled.*

"Yes, ma'am."

Cunningham opened the connecting door.

Eve's first impression of Rupert's office was that it was like his den back in the London headquarters, only built inside a modernized thirteenth-century castle rather than a modernized eighteenth-century town house. Broad French windows set back behind steel shutters, currently raised, provided access to an external terrace with low stone railings. The balcony overlooked the entire island. Inside, an ostentatiously large Admiralty desk with an office chair that probably cost as much as Rupert's Aston Martin occupied the middle of the room; a green leather Chesterfield and coffee table were set off to one side for guests, the table positioned on top of a tigerskin rug with paws and head still attached. *Typical Rupert,* she thought contemptuously. The wall decorations included antique longswords and shields. There was a handmade globe in a wooden frame that doubled as a drinks cabinet—*total cliché*—also a sideboard, a filing cabinet, and an absolutely top-spec FruitCo desktop computer that looked as if it had never been switched on. Her lips curled in barely restrained scorn. The worst thing about Rupert was the banal predictability of his excess. The man somehow managed to combine monstrous appetites, an unhealthy lust for power, and a taste for disgusting occult rites, alongside the good taste of a dim-witted New York real estate mogul.

"All right." She folded her arms. "Mr. Cunningham, please send my brother up here as soon as possible."

"Yes, My Lady. Your—" the butler paused—"he really *is* your brother?"

"All families have black sheep," she said lightly. "He has his occasional uses. We'll be staying overnight: I brought a bag but he'll need pajamas and a toothbrush, and the kitchen need to be informed. What time is dinner served?"

"Six thirty for seven o'clock, My Lady. If that's everything . . . ?"

"It is, for now."

Eve waited while Cunningham bowed and retreated into the corridor, then took a deep breath. She crossed to Rupert's desk and placed her briefcase in the middle of his tooled-leather blotter. Then she slowly turned in place, searching the walls for any clue as to where Rupert might have hidden his secrets.

►◄►◄►◄

Nothing in her first third of a century of life had prepared Mary to take custody of a fire team of pre-tween supervillains on a post-raid high. Dressing like a respectable nanny did not automagically confer nannying skills, it just made it easier to con people into thinking you had them. Mr. and Mrs. Banks had been easy enough to mislead with the aid of a little magic provided by the Boss, but she'd only had to fake them out for half an hour. Robert, Lyssa, Ethan, and Emily had brought on her first gray hairs already, and she had to keep them on lockdown for (she calculated) another hundred and sixty-two hours.

Daunting, that.

Fucknuts and fiddleshits, she swore silently as she smiled at the children and gave the taxi driver directions towards Chez Banks. Was it too early to put drugs in their cocoa, or should she hold that in reserve until tomorrow?

On the bright side: she'd worn her gloves all the time they'd been indoors, so no fingerprints. The children weren't in the Disclosure and Barring Service's database, or anywhere else the police might identify them from. A quick change of appearance and they could all disappear, as long as the cops didn't catch them getting into the taxi. Using private CCTV to record in public spaces, like the pavement outside the shop you were licensed to surveil, was strictly illegal per the Data Protection Act, which the New Management had not yet gotten around to repealing. She'd relied on that quirk of the law many times to facilitate a clean getaway. Still: there was *luck,* and there was *preparation,* and Mary preferred to put her faith in the latter, because sooner or later luck always ran out and she had no desire to end up with her head on a pointy stick.

A mile from their destination, Mary clapped her hands and told her audience, "I know! Would you like to eat at McDonald's?" Then before anybody had time to object, she hit the *talk* button and told the driver: "Change of plans, please drop us at the nearest McDonald's."

The Golden Arches weren't crowded at this time of day, and Mary managed to corral the kids at a table and place an order without anybody abstracting the contents of a cash till. She paid for the meal with a couple of her bent banknotes[5]: McNuggets and a slow carb overdose all round, with Frozen Flurry McLiquisquits and Sprinkles for dessert. But she made sure to order only Coke Zero for the kids to drink. She didn't want to have to deal with the consequences of a caffeine high on top of a sugar rush and a successful toy-shop heist before bedtime.

---

5. One of the Boss's coves was quite a *talented* artist, in the magical sense of the term, and he forged banknotes as a hobby to support his embryonic career as a Postimpressionist pornographer.

"This is great," Robert said, wide-eyed, "Mum *never* lets us go to McDonald's!"

"I'm not your mother, dear," Mary said, smiling as benevolently as a minor devil who has just secured the lien on another soul.

"C'n I have the unicorn play set?" Lyssa wheedled: "Ethan doesn't need—"

Ethan snarled possessively and curled his hands around the chunk of brightly colored plastic from his Happy Meal. "Mine!" The unicorn snickered appreciatively.

"What's wrong with Marceline the Vampire Queen?" Mary asked hastily, then fingered the Boss's amulet to give the idea a little extra sparkle. Marceline had come with Lyssa's *Adventure Time*–themed Happy Meal. The little girl's breath caught momentarily as she reached lovingly for the toy. *I wonder if I overdid it?* Mary asked herself. The amulet had been calibrated for adult attitude adjustment. But moments later another squabble broke out—it seemed that Emily, too, wanted a magical riot police unicorn play set—and sooner rather than later they were done.

"Now come along, children, it's time to go home!" Mary's smile was fixed and weary by this point, although it was barely four o'clock. But she had to keep up the pretense, at least for now: "There'll be more playtime before supper, and tomorrow I've got a special surprise for you!"

That evening, she tucked the twins up and read them a bedtime story. (Lemony Snicket's *The Bad Beginning* might be age-inappropriate, but Mary thought it was fucking hilarious under the circumstances.) Then she supervised Lyssa and Robert as they washed and dried the dishes in return for the promise of an hour of unsupervised computer time. Finally, with the kids sorted for the night, Mary stood on the front porch with the outer door open, smoking a menthol cigarette and waiting for the Boss to answer the dog and bone.

"Mary," the Boss said warmly, "'ad a good day, 'ave we? What's tricks?"

Mary blew a weary smoke ring and sighed. "You 'ave no fucking idea." It was easy to slip back into her native accent when she wasn't on high alert. "*Kids.*"

The Boss chuckled. "You'll change your mind when they're yer own . . ." Mary's reply was an extended scatological rant. When she ran out of invective, the Boss continued: "So 'ow's it *really* going?"

"The rug rats are transhuman! Jesus fuck, I nearly shat myself when I found out. The five-year-old girl's a plant whisperer and 'er twin brother is a toy animator. The nine-year-old girl's got mind control, and I'm not sure about her big brother, but that's not good news either, he's got a talent, too, he's just better at hiding it. If they sus me I'm screwed." She took a long drag on her cigarette and held it, staring at her shaking hand. "I'm out of my weight class. If they were adults, or if they get a clue—"

"Relax, they won't. You got through the first day, didn't you?"

"It almost got away from me." She shuddered, remembering the acrid smell of burning powder and the hammering recoil, the screams of onlookers and the jingling heft of Lyssa's stolen lucre landing in her capacious messenger bag. "I took 'em to a toy shop and it went sideways at a thousand miles an hour. I swear they'll be the death of me."

"So don't do that again." The Boss was matter-of-fact. His accent sharpened, poshing up as he asserted status: "We live and learn, and we learn to do better as long as we live. That which does not kill us makes us stronger: Nietzsche. And if it was an easy gig I wouldn't have sent it your way, know what I mean?"

"I don't *think* the Filth made me," she breathed out slowly. "Not this time."

"You know the plan: stick with it and you'll be fine."

"Yeah." She glanced sideways at the door behind which Robert was happily slaughtering NPCs while Lyssa tortured her collection of Bratz, or whatever Princess Sparkle-Shoggoth got up to when nobody was watching. "Operation Magical Mystery Tour is in effect." She bent her right knee and stubbed her cigarette out on the sole of her granny boot.

"Friday, Mary." The Boss's chuckle had a hard edge to it this time. "Just keep your shit together for a week and we're square. Just don't fuck up, yeah? One million in medical cover and I take care of all your old man's debts. Don't let me down."

"Fuck," she breathed as the Boss hung up. She repeated the word several times as she leaned her forehead against the door and punched the brick wall, not quite hard enough to hurt her gloved fist. The Boss was an expert, that much was true: he knew how to use the carrot *and* the stick, alternating them to keep her off-balance. The Boss wanted the children out of the picture and out of their home within twenty-four hours of her arrival, and under control for another six days while he did—*something*—that required the unspeakable pressure of a professional kidnapping applied to their desperate parents. Mary's conscience wasn't usually a sticking point, but she was reasonably certain he'd give the wee ones back at the end of the week. He had kids of his own, after all. But in the meantime, he'd have Captain Colossal and the Blue Queen totally panicking, frantic with grief and desperation. Mary was under no illusions: he'd set her up as the cutout, the quick-blow fuse. She was a casual employee, no benefits or points in the operation, a gig economy fall-girl working on the supervillain equivalent of a zero-hour contract, strong-armed into doing one last job because her dad was Expensive and she wasn't making enough dosh to keep them both afloat any other way.

Just got to get through six more days of this shit, she told herself: *then you can find a* real *job. Buy a car and drive for Uber or something.* She took a deep, pissed-off breath of chilly nighttime air and went back inside, to pack the children's luggage for the morning flit.

►◄►◄►◄

Castle Skaro put Imp in mind of that one time he had done 'shrooms and cuddled up with Doc Depression on the carnivorous sofa in the living room. They'd fast-forwarded through an entire season of *Downton Abbey* at three times normal speed while making out. Castle Skaro especially reminded him of the sequence common to every Edwardian costume drama, where all of Below Stairs turned out in the courtyard to meet the new lady of the house when she arrived for the first time: except that thanks to the 'shrooms their heads had been enfolded in a peace-colored aura, and the clouds in the slate-gray winter sky spelled love.

Imp had dropped something naughty into his single malt aboard the chopper to help with the stress. Really, he was no-body's idea of an Edwardian heroine, or even a Regency one. That was Eve's forte, wasn't it? But she'd delegated it to him, right after she guilt-tripped him for signing the piece of paper that had made her Lady Skaro—lah de dah!—and because she obviously didn't want anything to do with Rupert's legacy, he did his best to deliver.

Imp nodded politely, shook every hand he was offered, and confined himself to the occasional innocent and entirely noncon-frontational question such as "Where *exactly* is the family burial crypt—is it under the chapel or the wine cellar?" and "Do you think a Roomba would help with that?"

After three-quarters of an hour the queue or receiving line or punishment gauntlet had barely shortened to a fraction of its orig-inal length and the housekeeper's expression had hardened from talc to granite. Then he was rescued by the butler, who material-ized from a side-door next to the giant Gothic archway. "Mr. Star-key? Your sister requests your presence in his Lordship's office. Sybil, I think Mr. Starkey is finished for the time being—"

Mr. Cunningham steered Imp up the front steps, along an oak-panelled hallway that looked like a firetrap in waiting, and up enough stairs that his well-lubricated kneecaps felt as if they were about to fall off by the time he reached the top. He managed to cease saying "Delighted," and "I'm sure," and handshaking the air after a couple of minutes. Then he pinched himself and glanced at Cunningham. "What's all this about, then?" he asked sharply.

"I really couldn't possibly say, sir—" Cunningham was as im-perturbable as a main battle tank—"but your sister requested your presence. She also said that you would be staying overnight. Din-ner *en famille* commences with drinks in the east dining room at six, food being served at seven. It's a formal occasion, but—" he looked down his nose at Imp—"I'm sure we can find something suitable for you to wear. Should you choose to return to Castle

Skaro, an appointment with a tailor can be arranged, given a little advance notice."

Did he just harsh my fashion edge? Imp asked himself, just as his other inner voice said, *If an* informal *family dinner is black tie, what happens when the Baron is in residence?* "Shake it 'til you fake it, baby," he muttered. (Or was it *Shake it 'til you make it?*) "Don't mind me, I might be stoned." *Oops,* there went his internal filter.

"Our criminal code predates the steam locomotive, never mind the Misuse of Drugs Act, sir," Cunningham murmured. "Hemp and laudanum are perfectly legal, merely frowned upon in polite society. This way, please." He led Imp along a passageway that pulsated in time with his breathing, then knocked on a heavy wooden door, waited three heartbeats, and opened it. "My Lady? Your brother, as requested."

Imp found Eve cracking the safe in the Evil Overlord's den. At least, that's how he interpreted her delicate finger gestures and the squint she directed at the lock. The Evil Overlord bit was blatantly obvious, thanks to the baroque excesses of an interior designer who clearly hated their client and wanted to make him look like a fool. Wards glowed pale blue atop the Hammerite surface of the safe door—the blue of instant death, if Imp's inner eye was to be trusted. Even the walls seemed to be holding their breath. "Whoa, sis," he burbled softly.

"Stand back," Eve warned, her lips a bloodless line of concentration. There was a click, then the safe door slowly swung open. The wards quenched with a sullen hiss as she gasped for air and straightened up, dabbing her forehead. "What time is it?"

"It's—" Imp checked his phone. "Two o'clock?"

"Okay. Let me explain why you're here." Eve glanced at Cunningham: "Fetch us a carafe of coffee, a couple of mugs, and a jug of cream. Then see to it that we're not disturbed for the next two hours."

"My Lady." Cunningham made himself scarce.

"Right," Imp tried again. "So what's this about?"

"Semiotic minefield clearance." Eve pointed at the filing cabinet and the open safe. "There is good news that is also terrible, bad, no-good news, depending how you look at it. The wards on Rupe's safes respond to me because I'm his *feme covert*: magic runs on the laws of sympathy and contagion, Rupe's geas leverages the marriage contract to turn me into an extension of his body, and all the other enchantments agree. The hardest bit was picking up the wheels by telekinesis without breaking the safety tab and jamming the fence, because Rupe was exactly the kind of asshole who would have a Group One lock with an added fail-secure mechanism *and* a magical booby trap on top. These documents are his crown jewels, the stuff he kept only on paper and outside of UK jurisdiction. *But*—" she held up a warning finger— "it's possible he anticipated someone might crack the safe, and he's the kind of asshole who would leave another trap inside it, just in case. Death spells, curses, that sort of thing. Given he was at least one jump ahead of me and I never noticed—" her expression was distraught—"it's also possible that he anticipated that I might get in here, so there could be instructions that will trigger the geas.

"Anyway, we're going to go through the documents in the safe first, and the filing cabinet second, and sort them—I have a spreadsheet. Here's the most powerful ward I could bake for you at short notice. Wear it constantly and you should be safe." She passed him a cheap-looking necklace. "I want you to check each and every page for anything addressed to me, or anything that looks like it's a basilisk." A trigger for a hidden fatal spell, in other words. "Once we're reasonably confident they're safe, I'll scan them for analysis back home in London." She gestured at the duplex document scanner she'd parked on Rupert's desk.

"Yeah, right." Imp grimaced at the open safe. "Aside from booby traps, what are we looking for, again?"

"If there's any way to invalidate the marriage or break the geas it'll be in here somewhere, and I need it. Otherwise I'm not safe. He could have left instructions behind for me, hidden in his ordinary files, or sitting in a computer's calendar, waiting to ambush me at some future date. Also, he's not above blackmail. I need to know I'm immune to his compulsions before I go looking for dirt that could hang us all if it gets out."

"What a mess. Okay." Imp sat down heavily on the sofa. There

was a discreet knock at the door and a maid bustled in, carrying
a silver salver loaded with refreshments. They waited in silence as
she placed it on a side-table, depressed the plunger on the cafetière,
and left. After she closed the door Imp took a deep breath and
then asked, "How long are we staying?"

"As long as the job takes. Why?"

"Your man said dinner is at six, and it's a formal affair. We've
only got four hours . . ."

"Less: we need to dress first before dinner." She smiled thinly.
"This is your chance to see how the other half lives—I'm sure you
can use it as research for one of your movie projects. So get to
work." She handed him the first ring binder from the safe, careful
not to accidentally glimpse its title before he searched it for occult
landmines.

▸◂▸◂▸◂

That evening, the Deliverator cycled across central London. Arriving at a run-down HMO, she dismounted and pushed one of the
entryphone buttons. "Wendy? It's me."

There was a buzz and a click. "Come on up." Wendy's voice
sounded scratchy. Del carried her cycle indoors and chained it to
the bannisters, then climbed the stairs. Wendy was waiting in her
doorway. "Becca." She smiled tiredly. "You came."

"I came," Del—Rebecca—agreed. "You look like shit, girl.
What happened?"

"Nothing—to me. I just got handed a new assignment."

"You go, girl! That's gr—" Del skidded to a halt as she took in
Wendy's dishevelment. "What?"

"It sucks and it's horrible," said Wendy. "Come in, I need to get
drunk and I don't want to do it alone." She backed into her room,
beckoning. Del followed her and swung the door shut. Wendy was
wearing a sweatshirt up top but only briefs below, and she had an
open can of IPA in her free hand.

"Just started?" Del asked.

"Near enough." Wendy pulled another can out of the fridge and
passed it to her, then flopped down on her futon. "*Sláinte.*" She

shifted over to give Del room to sit, which she did, then cracked her beer.

"So, what's so bad about this job?"

"I can't tell—oh." Wendy shook her head. "The fuck: old habits die hard? It got drummed into me, you never talk about an investigation with MOPs—members of public—it could tip off a subject, prejudice a jury, run the Met's reputation into the shit, yadda yadda. Only I'm not a cop any more and the Met's rep is craptastic anyway. I'm not supposed to talk about thief-taker ops outside the firm, but since—did you sign the background check waiver yet?" Del nodded—"Then I figure you're thinking about taking the job, and I don't know all the deets yet anyway, and what I don't know I can't tell you so *fuck*—" She took another mouthful of beer and choked.

Del thumped her on the back, then held Wendy while she spluttered. She waited the gasps out, waited as they threatened to turn into hiccups. Finally Wendy regained control over her rebellious diaphragm. Del leaned back, pulling Wendy against her so that they sprawled cheek to cheek. At last Wendy stilled.

"Want to talk about it?" Del asked softly.

"The law." Wendy shuddered for a moment. "The law is supposed to treat everyone alike. Doesn't matter who you are, you've got a right to the law's protection. That's what I believe and that's why I went into the force. Equal before the law is kind of a touchstone, you know? Even though if you're rich enough to afford a good barrister you can get away with a lot . . ."

"Equal?" Del caught her eye. "*Equal?*"

"I—oh." Abashed, Wendy shook her head. "No, I get it, I'm saying that's how it's *supposed* to work, not how it works in practice. The color of your skin shouldn't have anything to do with it. That shit is wrong, and besides, it's illegal—"

"—It's illegal when an individual cop beats up a black man or arrests a black woman but somehow nobody ever gets sent to the nick for it," Del commented, "least not in *my* memory."

Wendy sighed. "That's on the IPCC—" the Independent Police Complaints Commission—"It's hard to fix institutional prejudice in a bureaucracy, let alone in an algorithm, is what I'm saying. But the thing is, we—I mean, the police—they're *supposed* to treat everyone equally. At least in this country. Even if they fail more often than not."

Del turned her head just far enough aside that Wendy couldn't see her roll her eyes. She riffled Wendy's hair with one hand, fine strands that fell naturally straight. She bit her tongue, not trusting herself to say anything that wasn't some variation of *And it took you this long to figure it out*? It wasn't exactly Wendy's fault that she was white, full of unexamined privilege, and having trouble wrapping her head around how her world looked from the outside. Del sighed. "What happened?"

"I'm not sure. But there's a serial killer—" Del sat bolt upright as Wendy continued, too wrapped in her internal focus to notice her alarm—"and the Met *aren't allowed* to investigate, and the only reason *anything* is being done about it is that a supermarket is worried about contaminated produce and wants it tidied up before anybody notices."

"The *fuck*?"

Wendy tightened her grip around Del's waist. Another shudder ran through her frame. After a second, Del realized that Wendy was sobbing, silently and angrily.

Wendy shook her head. "I'm just . . . just getting it out of my system now so I can be professional about it tomorrow."

"What the *fuck*?" Del was unable to wrap her mind around it. *Who the hell doesn't investigate a serial killer*? "Is it a creepy rich billionaire dude?" Visions of *American Psycho* danced in her head, followed by Imp's big sister's shadowy boss.

"The victims were all *de-emphasized*." Wendy made air-quotes with the fingers of her free hand. "*Fuck*."

"What—but they don't—"

"They disappeared. Except for DNA traces." Wendy repeated an abbreviated version of Gibson's briefing. "The de-emphasized don't get police protection. They've reintroduced actual no-shit outlawry."

"Like Robin Hood?"

"No, *not* like Robin Hood. Outlaws are *persons outside the law,* you can set fire to them in their sleeping bag in front of the nick and the worst thing that'd happen to you is the duty officer will ticket you for littering. Maybe arson if they're having a shitty day and don't like your face." Wendy took a deep breath. "I didn't see this coming, I truly didn't and I'm sorry, I just *can't*."

Del was working through it slowly. "Fucksake, this is worse than Hostile Environment."

"No shit." Wendy took another breath and struggled upright, still leaning on Del's shoulder. "Seven dead and they handed *me* the investigation because I've got some detective training and the client wants it swept under the rug, *not* because they want justice for the dead—"

Del stared out the window overlooking the high street as she stroked Wendy's back in soothing circles. "You'll give them justice," she reassured her. Wendy nodded. Del turned and kissed her forehead. "Is your tinny empty?" she asked.

Wendy up-ended the can into her mouth. "It is now."

"Well." Del necked her beer, burped, then chucked both the empties in the bin. "How about a smoke?" she offered, reaching for her stash.

"Can't: got a scheduled piss-test coming up—"

"What? Since when do HiveCo Security do piss-tests? Why wasn't I—"

"It's the supermarket, not HiveCo. Boss man wants me to go undercover for a couple of weeks, and stacking shelves in a supermarket requires a certificate that you're drug-free. Even though punching supervillains doesn't."

"You're going to be working *undercover*?" Del stood and took another couple of beers from the fridge. "That definitely calls for another beer."

"Back in a sec." Wendy sighed, then stood up and ducked out to the bathroom along the hall.

Del shoved the unopened cans back in the fridge as Wendy returned: "I've got a better idea," she said. "Sitting around getting drunk is no good for you. Get your glad rags on: we're going clubbing."

▶◀▶◀▶◀

"Who the *fuck* is the Mute Poet?" asked Imp.

He was sitting cross-legged on the Chesterfield sofa, reading—not skimming—the contents of a folder Eve had handed him from the top shelf in the safe. Something about his tone instantly set her on full alert. "What have you found?" she asked.

"This is—" Imp shook his head. "No basilisks, I don't think," he said. They'd been at the task for a few hours and they were both getting punch-drunk from proofreading. The pile of papers Eve had already scanned to PDFs on her laptop was almost twenty centimeters deep and the computer's fan was whirring loudly as it indexed the text. "It's, uh, a service of worship? The Dark Matins, definitely *not* Christian-adjacent going by the bits in Enochian."

Eve sniffed, feeling a momentary pang of nostalgia. They'd learned the language of magic together at Dad's knee, back when the world was a happier place. Then what her brother had said caught up with her. "Enochian? Did you say, *Mute Poet*?" Imp nodded. "Oh dear . . ." She trailed off. "Is there a list of names in that file by any chance?"

"What?" Imp looked puzzled, then began to flip through the file rapidly. "Yes, yes there is—holy shit, holy shit." He began to rock back and forth above the file, hyperventilating as he gripped its cover. "We are so fucked!"

"Jerm. Talk to me." Eve leaned over him. "Slowly! Breathe. Hold it . . . breathe again. And hold."

"It's a fucking cult. One of the cults Dad warned us about. Isn't it? And it's here? In the castle? We are so fucked!"

"Calm *down*, Jeremy." Eve massaged his shoulders. "Let me see the list." He turned the file to face her, and she looked at it. In pride of place, at the head of the first column, was a distressingly familiar name. "Right, so what we have here is the membership of a church. One where . . . apparently Rupert de Montfort Bigge was rather higher up than I thought? Also it's a lot bigger than I realized. How inconvenient! Calm down, there's no need to panic yet." She pressed down harder on his shoulders, trying to calm him. Perhaps the second cup of coffee had been a mistake.

"Did you know about this, sis?" he demanded.

Eve bit her lower lip. "Not exactly, but I don't think there are any accidental coincidences here. I knew Rupert was up to his elbows in something dodgy involving sacrifices and a chapel in the basement, but I wasn't invited to participate. I thought it was fifty-fifty whether it was a stupid secret society or an actual cult, but it didn't look like the sort of thing Mum was—but no. I was wrong," she admitted.

Rupert had presented to her as a poor excuse for a sorcerer: haphazard, slapdash, and weak. But now she was beginning to suspect that he had been stronger and more secretive than she'd realized. Having a congregation and a patron demiurge on whom to focus their prayers was a thaumaturgic force-multiplier. Even a shitty sorcerer could wield the delegated power of a godlike entity with deadly effect, as long as he didn't burn himself out by accident. It was like working on a live high-tension line: if you were aware of the risks and had the correct equipment, you didn't necessarily have to set fire to your own nostril hairs. "So what else have we got?"

It turned out they'd hit the mother lode: the core membership list, liturgy, password to some sort of concealed reading room in the library, and a calendar for sacrifices to be conducted in the crypt below the chapel. It gave them everything except next Sunday's sermon and the keys to the communion wine cupboard. "Well," said Eve, "well, well, *well*." *What the* hell *was Rupe doing, committing this stuff to writing*? She could hazard a guess. The risk of the New Management ever reaching its tentacles into Castle Skaro and cracking Rupe's safe was negligible: if they did, the shit had already hit the fan and Rupe was a dead man. But the sacrifices . . .

"Hedge Fund Haruspicy Best Practices," Imp mumbled, going slightly green about the gills. "What the hell is an Offshore Summoning Vehicle? Or a Damned Soul Default Swap?"

"You don't want to know," Eve said grimly. Haruspicy was oracular divination by examining the entrails of sacrifices. "Let's scan this last file and put the completed ones back in the safe. Then I want to check out the family chapel before we dress for dinner."

"But I don't want to—" Imp saw her expression and shut up.

"I'm sure Mr. Cunningham will happily show us the ropes once you give him a little push." Eve hardened her heart. Most of the time she went easy on her brother, but right now the situation called for ruthless control.

"He'd love to show us the chains and the manacles and the altar while we're down there, too," he said gloomily.

"Yes, but afterwards you'll make sure our little tour completely slips his mind. And we'll discuss what to do with whatever we find there after dinner."

"I hope you're carrying some ibuprofen, because I'm going to have a Godzilla-sized headache."

Instead of a bell-pull there was a discreet intercom by the door. Mr. Cunningham was clearly waiting nearby, because he arrived within seconds. "You called, My Lady?"

"Yes." Eve stalked towards him: "My brother was expressing an interest in seeing the family chapel. Can you take us down there? Just to see where it is, pay our respects to the last Lord and Lady Skaro, nothing to worry about—"

The butler's face paled, but Imp cut in: "She *is* your Lord's wife," Imp murmured, gurning hideously as he shoved will-to-believe into Cunningham's brain like a bog brush down a blocked U-bend. "She needs to make obeisance and ensure that the mysteries are correctly observed before the next Dark Matins—when does it fall, by the way?—"

"Next Tuesday," Cunningham wheezed, "but I must say, you can't just—"

"—Oh yes I *can*." Eve glowered at the butler. Years of dealing with reluctant employees on Rupert's behalf made it easy to overwhelm: "I am Lady Skaro, lawfully wedded wife—" the words almost choked her—"of Rupert de Montfort Bigge, *Baron* Skaro, an initiate of the third degree in our Silent Lord's service. I have *every right* to inspect the chapel where I was married, and I will *personally* cut the tongue out of the mouth of anyone who naysays me." She produced an ice queen smile so chilly that it probably violated Disney's copyright on Maleficent (her onetime childhood crush); she told herself it was a bluff, it was *probably* a bluff, but if she didn't believe in herself nobody else would. Meanwhile her head pounded with the overspill from Imp's believe-me mojo as her brother forced the butler to bend.

Cunningham was surprisingly resilient, and not because he was warded. Something had sunk its roots deep inside Cunningham's soul and really did *not* want Eve to intrude. "You will obey!" she insisted, and felt Imp reinforcing her command. A moment of anxiety threatened her resolve: Cunningham wasn't young and they were pushing him really hard—she'd have to stop soon or risk injuring him. She began to move her fingertips behind her back, shaping the strokes of a symbol that would trigger a macro—a pre-prepared spell—that would forcibly bind him using her connection to Rupert. It was an option that made her skin crawl, for if she used it she would also embed the barbs of Rupert's command geas deeper into her own soul, but it was better than inflicting a heart attack.

"I . . ." Cunningham choked convulsively, his face turning puce before he gabbled, "I obey! Mistress! I obey! Please, no more, please don't hurt me—"

Phew. "Deep breaths, Mr. Cunningham, deep breaths. There, there: nothing to fret about, everything is going to be fine." Imp walked around them, keeping the pressure up, frowning in obvious discomfort.

"Take us to the chapel," Eve said quietly, "and we can get this small unpleasantness over with. That would be nice, wouldn't it? Take us there now and get it done." Cunningham drooled slightly, more than somewhat glassy eyed: he didn't reply. Behind the butler, Imp winced. "Are you all right?" Eve asked him.

Imp mustered up a wan smile. "Been better."

"Well, try not to throw up on the tiger skin rug, those things are hard to clean," she said tartly, trying to distract him. Hardshell Eve was *necessary*. If hard-shell Eve cracked in the next few hours—if Eve lost her shit for even a microsecond before they were ready to retreat back to London—they'd be in deadly danger. Cunningham wasn't the only resident of Skaro on the Cult of the Mute Poet's roster, and she had no intention of allowing the congregation to go all Wicker Man on her and Imp.

Jeremy wasn't the only one of them who looked close to throwing up. Eve wasn't feeling that great herself—her stomach was in turmoil and her forehead pounded—and Mr. Cunningham looked as if he'd just found Colonel Mustard in the Library with a dagger in his back. But the epic battle of wills against whatever had bound the butler to obedience was receding, and she'd clearly won: Cunningham swayed slightly, then strode off down the corridor without a backwards glance.

Imp waved at Eve. "Pearls before swine?"

She nodded at his suggestion, then hurried after the butler. As she did so, she wrapped her telekinetic fingers around the pearls at her throat. They were more expensive than glass marbles—her practice ammunition of choice—but the beauty of a pearl choker was that nobody objected to a well-dressed woman's jewelry. She could wear a string of 9mm ball ammunition through airport security and nobody would stop her, as long as they looked shiny and expensive.

The ageing butler led them down a less-travelled hallway lined with stiffly formal portraits of lords and ladies, set in dusty rococo frames between threadbare wall tapestries. They came to a side-door that opened onto a narrow, spiraling stairwell that corkscrewed down into the depths of the castle. The stone steps were worn and concave, the footing treacherous. Eve silently cursed her heels as they descended: she'd dressed for the boardroom that morning, not anticipating a dungeon crawl before dinner. The stairs led down to a warren of bare-walled passages and pantries, then back into a darkened formal hallway, its furniture swathed in dust sheets. Finally Cunningham stopped at a locked door. It looked as ancient as the spiral staircase, but the lock and the hinges were recently oiled.

By Eve's estimate they were well below the level of the helipad. "How deep does this go, and how extensive are the tunnels?" she asked as Cunningham took an LED camping lantern from a shelf, then ushered them through the door and down another staircase, this one windowless and straight.

"It . . . depends which part of the castle you mean, I suppose." He sounded dazed. "This section dates to the fourteenth century.

The Nazis built bunkers on the other side of Skaro during the occupation, but they don't connect to the castle catacombs. At least, I don't *think* they connect. There may be some smugglers' tunnels leading to the harbor. But this is the shortest route to the underchapel without passing through the dungeons, which are best avoided."

"So. Oubliettes, underground chapels, burial vaults, and presumably a wine cellar, but if we want to visit the secret Nazi bunkers we have to go outside, do I have that right?" Imp asked.

Eve tried not to roll her eyes: *men*. It was all just one big adventure comic to her brother. *Totally* the wrong attitude to take when you were stranded overnight in a medieval castle full of demented cultists who worshipped the gruesome undead god of your debauched husband by proxy marriage. "Tell me about the chapel," she nudged.

"The chapel dates to the thirteenth century. It used to be at ground level, but when the motte was expanded and faced with stone it remained in situ, adjacent to the stables, which were converted into cellarage. A new chapel was built aboveground after the Black Death, during the latter half of the fourteenth century— they needed somewhere to keep the bones, the existing charnel house being full. The Earl of Guernsey converted to Protestantism during the Reformation but during the Wars of the Three Kingdoms the Protectorate ordered the castle slighted and the chapel— being seen by Cromwell's men as a suspiciously Catholic place of worship—took the worst of it. When the walls were restored after the Glorious Revolution, the Skaro family—who had quietly maintained their ancestral faith throughout their exile—continued to hold mass underground . . ." Cunningham droned on for several minutes like the tour guide from hell, but Eve was clear on the gist of the story: ancient stones buried by time, lotsa battles, cultists worshipping underground in secret, the same old same old.

"Tell me, where does, did, the Skaro family hail from? Did you say the castle was built by the Earl of Guernsey, not Baron Skaro?"

"Oh, the Guernseys were good Norman stock, ma'am! Roots all the way back to the Conquest. But they ran awful thin after Bloody Mary burned half of them at the stake, and then the Duchy used the vacant title to raise capital. The treasury was bare from all the wars in the seventeenth century—they brought in a distant relative who married the only surviving daughter, heiress to the barony, and the title passed down to their descendants. He was a Baron*et*, not a full Baron, but that's the Duchy for you, always doing things differently from the mainland, and they effectively sold him the Baronial title, which set a precedent. Anyway he married a local girl and went native and they were already secret Catholics anyway, so what difference did it make?"

They came to a vestibule where Eve took careful note of another staircase, as Cunningham swung open the final door. "So this is your family chapel, My Lady! Dedicated to Saint Ppilimtec, patron of writers—Saint David, patron of poets—" Eve jolted to attention but the butler didn't seem to notice anything wrong— "behold. Is this what you needed to see?"

"Yes," she said slowly, "I really think it is." It was just a small, low-ceilinged chapel, illuminated by stark, overhead fluorescent tubes. There were enough pews for at least two dozen family and staff, an altar bearing the usual accoutrements and ritual objects, a pair of stained-glass windows backlit by spotlights in lieu of daylight—all told, there was nothing particularly weird about it except for Cunningham's glitch. *Saint Ppilimtec.* "Is that the vestry?" she asked, pointing to a side-door.

"That's just a storage closet, My Lady, the chapel isn't large enough to justify a full-time parson and a vestry. See?" The butler opened the door and gestured at the shallow shelves inside. "Nothing to see here," he explained. "Now—" he made a show of checking his wristwatch—"if I may make so bold, the dinner hour is fast approaching and your brother needs appropriate attire. If you would care to follow me . . . ?"

►◄►◄►◄

"You are an utter, *utter* tool, darling," Jennifer snarled sweetly as she stepped around the man trussed to the steel-framed chair in the attic above Loading Bay Six. "What are you, darling?"

"An—" he swallowed—"utter, *utter* tool, Miss." He slurred slightly: his dentition needed some reconstructive work.

Jennifer beamed. Her teeth flashed highlights from the single warehouse floodlight illuminating him in the midst of the darkened room. "Would you like Rick and Morty to remind you what you did wrong one more time?"

Adrian Hewitt took in the figures standing at parade rest behind her and swallowed again. A trickle of blood leaked from the side of his mouth.

"Well?"

"No, Miss."

Rick and Morty gave no sign of caring what Adrian Hewitt wanted. They were as expressionless and unreadable as mummified corpses—which, after a fashion, they were. They stood swathed in white Lycra bodysuits that covered them from head to toe. Aside from their name badges only their faces distinguished them, and then only up to a point: they wore e-ink death masks displaying the Company Face, a beneficent computer-generated image intended to respond appropriately to the emotional cues of whoever the wearer was dealing with. Or, in Ade's case, a pair of silently screaming skulls: evidently the Branch Computer was *very* displeased.

"Good. Just bear in mind that if you fuck up again you'll join the muppets on the night shift."

Adrian swallowed, his mouth dry with fear. His ribs were on fire and his face felt as if he'd been hit repeatedly with a meat tenderizer, which was indeed one of the tasks muppets sufficed for. Jennifer hadn't laid a finger on him, but Rick and Morty were obedient and tireless—strong and silent by design.

He'd had a hand in creating Rick and Morty (acting on Jennifer's orders, although pointing that out seemed unlikely to help right now). Muppets were meat puppets, built to carry out basic instructions and point the Company Face at MOPs. They were improving with each iterative upgrade: he'd managed to get five viable units out of the last test subject, and these two were probably good for another couple of weeks before they needed to be hosed down the drain.

". . . However, it seems to me that putting you on the night shift would be a waste of your talents," Jennifer mused aloud. "All that very expensive and specialized training, gone!" She walked behind him and laid a hand on his shoulder. "I'd need a new operator. Our numbers in this city are few, and the Bishop isn't answering my emails. It appears that we are flying blind, working our Lord's will in isolation. So you are a very, very *lucky* tool of the Lord, Adrian. Kiss-kiss!"

She leaned close and smacked her lips millimeters away from his unclipped ear. Ade cringed away in a full-body shudder. Jenn giggled as she tugged him back upright, careful not to get blood on her suit.

"Now listen," she explained. "Adrian Hewitt is *dead* to Flavrs-Mart. He can't go back. He can't work anywhere else, either: it's on your permanent, transferrable personnel record, sweetie. If I edit it, someone might notice. And if I faked up another identity and you went back to work on the counter, Gladys would throw a fit. I'd have to replace the entire front-of-store staff, and that simply isn't going to happen in the middle of a recruiting freeze. So we'll have to try something else. Nod if you understand me."

Adrian nodded enthusiastically. She seemed to expect it: and right now he was all in favor of not defying Jennifer's expectations.

"Jolly good! So . . . it happens that there *is* a way to get you back into a position where you can continue to serve our Mute Lord. But certain compromises must be made—mostly on your side. I can hide you among the night shift muppets rather than turning you into one—as long as you're discreet and nobody spots you."

The night shift had started out as living bodies sent over by the Department for Work and Pensions on compulsory workfare placements. They were benefit claimants who'd been sanctioned (or just gotten unlucky) once too often. The HR protocol was harsh but simple. Give them a zentai bodysuit, a randomized name badge to wear, and the Company Face—anesthetize their larynx and gag them, so that if anything emerged from their mouth in front of a customer it would be Cortana speaking, not the wit and wisdom of a random prole—and they could stack boxes. At least, that was how things had started out. The truth these days was somewhat different. The payroll didn't go into any dolie scum's pocket, where it might be wasted on cigarettes or food or rent. Instead it went straight into the Order's coffers and contributed to the operating expenses of the research and development program Jennifer oversaw and Ade executed. Just as the workfare bodies listed in the payroll database now contributed to the grand cause in death, whether or not they'd have been willing to do so in life.

"I'll get you a suit and a Company Face, and you can overhaul the butcher line and printers anonymously. The night shift won't care, and the deli counter staff won't give you any trouble." That much she was in a position to guarantee. "I've arranged for deep freeze four to be listed as offline for repairs indefinitely—unavailable parts—and you can install a sofa bed and television for all I care. It's soundproof and lockable so nobody will bother you during the day. Take your meals from the expired stack out by the dumpsters. Just keep a list and I'll have it written down as shrinkage."

"But . . ." Whatever protest was brewing died in Ade's mouth, unvoiced, as he met Jennifer's excitedly deranged stare.

"I'm going to hire someone to 'replace' you—" she mimed air-quotes around the word—"someone totally unqualified who won't ask any questions for fear of losing the job. It's only for the next month or so, until the takeover is complete. Afterwards you won't need to hide: our Lord's will be done." She paused. "By the way, why *did* you do it?"

"She was so beautiful!" Ade slurred. "You should have seen her—"

"I *did* see, and so did everybody else. If you'd got her properly dressed—" in a zentai suit—"and waited until after the Rite I could have covered for you. Nobody notices a necrophile at work if their meat's still moving. But you need to be more discreet. I can't give you another chance if you fuck up again." She stepped in close and touched his chin, tilting his head up: "Do you understand, Ade? I'm giving you this second chance because our Lord is merciful and beneficent, but if you screw up again he will *not* be pleased, and I won't be able to save you from the flowery path."

"I . . . understand." Ade swallowed.

"Good." Jennifer smiled again. "Now I'll just fetch you a couple of codeine tablets from the pharmacy and you'll be right as rain in half an hour! You can have a good think about what I said, spend tonight in soul-searching and prayer, and in the morning I'll show you to your cell so you can catch up on your sleep. You'll be right as rain and back at work by this time tomorrow night! And if you're *really* good I might even help you reanimate your next girlfriend."

4

▶◀▶◀▶◀▶◀

SCOOBY IN THE HOUSE

"Where's Imp?" Game Boy asked petulantly. "Where *is* he?"

Doc froze, a half-eaten sandwich gripped precariously in his left hand. "Hasn't he replied yet?"

It had been hours since his last text message—*Summoned away on Big Sister biz*—and it was getting dark. Game Boy had replied immediately, pointing out that it was their regular raid night, but Imp hadn't responded. And the weather was fulminant and wintry, the first spattery wet outriders of a December storm blowing in from the Atlantic and thudding against the plywood covering the windows.

"Nothing. Not a ping!" Game Boy flapped his arms irritably. "Last time he texted his phone was at the London Heliport, but now it says his last known location was some rock in the Channel! That was four hours ago. I texted, but it doesn't show up as delivered. He's *offline*!" Game Boy spat the word as if it was accusation, as if Imp had deliberately allowed his sister to lead him into a digital oubliette. "We'll be late for the game!"

"Maybe that's a good thing." Doc Depression chewed methodically. He'd read somewhere that the Victorian prime minister William Gladstone had chewed every last mouthful fifty times, and he was trying it out for a day in an attempt to slow down his eating. It seemed to him that Gladstone must have had extraordinary dentition, or an inordinate fondness for gruel. "Wherever he is there's bound to be horrible packet lag and jitter."

"It the principle!" Game Boy tended to drop his sibilants when he was irate. "He commit to the raid team! Fam that raid together stay together!"

Doc swallowed a sigh. Game Boy had parent issues, or rather his parents had Game Boy issues. He'd run away from home a year ago—or more accurately escaped—and claimed Imp, Doc, and Del as his housemates, homies, found family, and emotional support team. Which annoyed Doc because he hadn't signed up to be anyone's therapy guy. He mostly put up with it for Imp's sake, but if he couldn't figure out how to bring Game Boy down again the lad would keep him up half the night with his caffeine-fueled ranting.

"Did you ask if Becca and her girlfriend want to play?" Doc suggested.

"What, the *cop*?" Game Boy sounded offended and incredulous simultaneously.

"Ex-cop, thief-taker, whatever." *Now* Doc released a sigh: "Listen, if you don't want a team for tonight I'll understand perfectly—"

"No! NoNoNo! Raid!"

"—So why don't you call her and ask?"

A gust of wind threw a rattling bucket of rainwater against the window boards as Game Boy texted. To his surprise, Doc's phone vibrated. He glanced at the screen. It was Imp: *sis has scored a castle! Catch is, it's haunted. Stuck here overnight, home tomorrow, don't wait up.*

"Game Boy?" Doc asked.

"Not now. Busy!" Game Boy's thumbs clicked a syncopated counterpoint to the raindrops. "Talking with Deliverator."

Doc returned to his sandwich, holding his counsel: if Game Boy didn't want to hear about Imp because he was busy organizing last-minute team substitutes for his weekly raid, who was Doc to complain?

Half an hour later the front door creaked open. Doc had retreated into the bathroom for an overdue shower and didn't notice until the sound of raised voices in the front hall wafted up the stairs and through the stained nylon shower curtain. They were raised, but not shouting: Game Boy's trumpet squeal mixed with Del's—Rebecca's—warmer tones, an occasional riff by a different female voice. *Wendy.* "Doc?" shouted Game Boy: "*Doc?* Where *are* you?"

Doc turned off the power shower and stepped over the side of the bathtub, dripping. "Five minutes!" he called through the doorway. *Can't even sluice in peace,* he grumped to himself.

Down in the living room he found a tipsy Deliverator and a definitely drunk Wendy trying to ply Game Boy with beer. Game Boy was refusing, with emphasis. It wasn't an age thing: Game Boy got the alcohol flush reaction, and got it bad. "Stop arseing around," Doc said irritably, and passed him a can of the low-alcohol ditchwater Imp kept on hand for GeeBee lubrication interrupts.

"But he squeaks so cutely!" Wendy complained.

"So would you if one pint gave you a hangover." Game Boy grabbed the can from Doc's hand and snapped the ring pull savagely. "Do you even *game*?"

"Yes I game—"

"Sit!" Game Boy sternly pointed her at the sofa. "Del! Controllers!"

"Aye aye, Cap'n Squirt!" Rebecca winked at Game Boy and hauled a shoebox full of controllers out from beside the sofa. She collapsed in a sprawl against Wendy, and hiccuped.

"This isn't going to work if you're drunk!" Game Boy complained.

"So take a break," Doc suggested.

"No! Can't!" Game Boy appeared to be on the edge of a foot-stamping tantrum. "Play or die!"

"I heard from Imp," Doc said, by way of a diversion. "He's stuck overnight in a haunted castle, says he'll be back tomorrow."

Wendy leaned against Del's shoulder: "Is that kind of thing normal round here?" she asked, trying not to slur.

"Totes normal," Del reassured her. "Haunted castles are a regular part of the supervillain lifestyle and you'll just have to get used to them."

"Could summat—somebody—have stolen Imp's phone and be 'personating 'im?" Wendy speculated.

"Angry ghosts!" spat Game Boy. "Or maybe cultists!"

"I think it's very unlikely," Doc soothed. "What are we playing tonight, anyway?"

►◄►◄►◄

When Eve and Imp returned to Rupert's den they were confronted
by an ominous spectacle. Beyond the French windows the sky had
turned a peculiar shade of dirty pink and the clouds were piling
up. The waves were showing white crests and there was a peculiar
tension in the air: a storm was clearly about to break.

"Well," said Imp. Simultaneously, Eve reached for her phone
and said, "What?" in a tone of voice as chilly as the wind over the
battlements.

She must have hit the speaker button, because Imp heard the
reply clearly. It was Gammon Number Two on the line: "Ma'am,
I'm really sorry but the chopper's grounded. Pilot says there's a
storm blowing in and it's tracking south of where the forecast this
morning said—wind gusts are going to exceed flying conditions
for the next seven or eight hours, and she says even if she takes off
right now she won't be able to land safely on Skaro."

Eve sucked in her breath sharply. "Keep me updated on the
weather conditions by text. I want to know as soon as it's safe to
fly out. I'm prepared to stay overnight but I need to be back in the
office by tomorrow lunchtime at the latest."

"Absolutely, ma'am. In the meantime, are you safe?" Gammon
Number Two sounded upset, as well he might. He'd prioritized
protecting her transport over her person and left her alone for half
an hour, only to be caught off base. "I can try and get a boat out
before the storm picks up—"

"I'll be fine overnight," Eve told him quellingly. She glanced
sidelong at Imp, who nodded. "My brother's here. He has hidden
depths," she added, before Gammon Number Two could protest.
"Keep me posted." She ended the call, then frowned at Imp. "Why
are you still here? Go and get changed, you don't want to disappoint
the staff."

Imp slouched into Rupert's dressing room, where someone had
laid out an evening suit for him. Going by the cut and the smell of
mothballs it had last been worn some time in the 1930s. Mr. Cunningham clearly had a tailor's eye for size: it fit him perfectly. The
unseen minions had left a full range of accessories, right down to
cuff links and collar studs. The dress shoes were slightly too large

and creaked loudly when he walked, but they were a tolerable change from his army boots. *She wants to put on a show, does she?* Imp primped in the mirror, then shot his cuffs. *Let's give them the kayfabe, let's show them Lord Starkey's face, what ho?* Eve was legally Lady Skaro, but if Imp wanted to get anywhere with the staff he had to convincingly play the part of Lady Skaro's aristocratic younger brother. His distinctly weather-beaten arrival hadn't made quite the right impression, in hindsight. But Castle Skaro would make a *brilliant* set for his next movie if he could get Eve and the servants on board with the idea.

Back in the study Imp found his sister holding a champagne flute in one elegantly gloved hand. She'd swapped her suit for a black evening gown and extra jewelry. He'd never seen his big sister in this mode before. She assessed him critically, then drily pronounced: "Adequate."

"Shall we proceed, Lady Skaro?" He offered her his arm, then led her along the corridor to the grand staircase, just as a gong tolled sonorously somewhere in the depths of the castle.

Dinner proved to be an unpleasantly stiff occasion.

The table in the grand dining room seated twenty but was diminutive for its surroundings. The bulbs in the chandelier dangling three meters above their heads cast a fitful glow across hectares of white linen cloth and ranks of polished silverware. Long shadows shrouded the swords and shields that hung on the walls between the arrow slits. Cunningham led them to two chairs at one end of the table, separated by an empty throne-like seat in the middle: all three places were set. "His Lordship's seat awaits his return," he explained portentously.

Eve's answering smile was sharp enough to cut glass. "I'm sure it won't be needed tonight," she said. Cunningham bowed disapprovingly then retreated, to be replaced by a pair of uniformed footmen who delivered the elements of a seven-course feast in sequence. It was the sort of meal that demonstrated why the English aristocracy had felt it necessary to conquer a quarter of the planet and steal the cuisine, although the wine was unexpectedly good—probably because of the island's proximity to France. After the first top-up Eve pointedly covered the top of her glass and caught Imp's eye. He nodded regretfully and waved off the waiter. "We have matters to discuss later," she murmured.

The presence of so many attentive servants was not conducive to conversation, so after a few minutes of awkward gossip Imp gave up. Eve wasn't terribly interested in Game Boy's latest high-score shenanigans, and it didn't seem terribly prudent to quiz her about her business interests when the people who might be affected were listening. After some fatuous speculation about the severity and duration of the storm, and a few where-are-they-nows about absent school friends, the well of discourse ran dry. All work and no play apparently made Eve a dull debutante.

Eventually they got to the end of the meal—by way of a bowl of Eton mess that Imp suspected was a sick burn on his comprehensive school background—and Cunningham returned to assist Eve with her chair. "Would the gentleman care for a cigar and brandy, as used to be traditional?" Cunningham asked. Imp shook his head. "Perhaps my sister and I could share a nightcap in . . ." He cast about desperately, suddenly realizing that he had no idea how the function rooms in this labyrinth were laid out.

"The east parlor is available, sir." Cunningham indicated the way. Eve nodded and took Imp's elbow in a grip of steel. They followed the butler into a room which could almost pass for cozy, if one confined one's attention to the small circle of sofas and armchairs beside the sideboard, and ignored the concert grand piano and the small orchestra gallery occupying the other four-fifths of the space.

Imp fetched two glasses of brandy from the sideboard and handed one to Eve, who sniffed it, then took a sip. "This is giving me the creeps," he murmured. "It's too quiet."

"How many servants were you introduced to? Did you get a head count?"

"Twelve, I think, including Cunningham and the waiters. It's a big place, no wonder it's dusty. You should buy them a Roomba or two. I hear you can get cute Dalek costumes for them."

Eve gave him a quelling look. "Listen." The wind outside the high windows moaned and drummed across the battlements.

Woodwork creaked and groaned as a distant door slammed, followed by a muffled curse. "Is that what you meant by quiet?"

"I meant *people* quiet. You should have given me some warning, I'd have brought my gang and then we wouldn't be standing here talking in whispers. We'd outnumber them. Doc, Becca, Becca's girlfriend—not Game Boy, he'd wig out at the packet loss. Zoinks! We could even LARP that seventies cartoon show with the Great Dane—"

Eve fixed him with a gorgon stare: "You are *not* getting a dog, Jeremy. Absolutely *not*. You know what happens to pets in our family. And you only want a dog so you can call it Scooby—" A crash of thunder swallowed her next words.

"You know what?" Imp took an inadvisably big mouthful of brandy and tried not to choke. "Forget I said anything. Let's call it a night and go upstairs?"

"I think"—Eve looked thoughtful—"yes, we should do that." She rubbed her upper arms, then took the glass from his nerveless fingers and returned it to the sideboard. "Is it me or is there a chill in the air? Come on." She took his arm. "Set your phone to silent vibrate and an alarm for midnight," she whispered as they turned into the darkened grand hallway. "I want to check out the chapel when nobody's watching us."

►◄►◄►◄

Amy was stashing her handbag in the break-room locker the next morning when her work phone vibrated. It was a text from Robin Holmes, the branch manager: *see me ASAP*. It said a lot about the past week that her heart rate shot through the roof. Her first thought was, *What* else *did that dirtbag do*? But this time, it was nothing to do with Ade or the deli counter.

She found Robin in his office, waiting with a woman in a business suit and a sensible haircut that screamed *detective*.

"Amy, this is Ms. Deere, from HiveCo Security." Amy's *oh shit* sense began to tingle. "She's going to be working here for a while, undercover. I need you to sort out everything she needs."

Amy sat down heavily. "Undercover?"

Ms. Deere smiled. It didn't reach her eyes. Her gaze was cold and assessing. "Amy . . . ?"

"Amy Sullivan, Human Resources." Amy sent her a tit-for-tat smile and crossed her arms. "What's this about?"

Mr. Holmes sighed despondently. "Quality Assurance . . ." He looked at Ms. Deere. "Could you explain?"

Ms. Deere reached into a folder of documents and slid a form across the desk towards Amy. "Please sign this," she said. "It's a nondisclosure agreement. Uh, I'm bound by one as well, and so is Mr. Holmes."

Amy took a shuddering breath and reached for her pen. "Why?"

"I believe you were involved in dismissal proceedings against a Mr. Hewitt last week?" Amy nodded: her *oh shit* sense instantly spiked all the way from tingling to peripheral neuropathy. "I gather that after his departure a number of distressing irregularities surfaced. Leading to a shutdown of the butcher's counter and the meat processing line." Amy caught herself before she nodded again, and glanced at her boss.

"Alas." Right now he was clearly unhappy. "During the deep clean, samples were sent to our QA labs for screening. Mr. Hewitt was a disgruntled employee and it seemed like a good idea to check his produce for tampering. Adulterants," he added, in a hushed voice.

"Adul—" Amy's *oh shit* meter redlined so hard it wrapped its needle around the end of the dial. She didn't realize she'd spoken aloud until Ms. Deere nodded.

"They wondered if he'd taken a shit on the counter. Turns out he'd done something worse."

"What?" Amy's hands clenched involuntarily. "*What?*"

"Human DNA was found in samples taken from two different meat pies. It was found to be a crossmatch for persons who have been reported missing. Unfortunately only a limited number of items were sampled and the rest were destroyed, so we can't confirm whether the other people we're looking for also ended up contaminating the produce. Mr. Hewitt appears not to have returned to his last known address, so he can't tell us anything, either."

Amy's head spun. "I, I had no idea—"

Ms. Deere touched her arm. "Nobody's blaming you," she said, which sounded like it was intended to be reassuring, but wasn't.

"But the police—"

Mr. Holmes shook his head. "They won't be involved. The missing people were all de-emphasized. Head Office just want to know how it happened, *what* happened, and to make sure it can't happen again—that we can draft procedures to make sure it doesn't happen again—and it's been quietly dealt with. So they hired HiveCo Security."

"I'm going to be working on-site for the next while," Ms. Deere told her. "I'll be going through files—your HR files in particular, but also anything and everything relating to Mr. Hewitt's work. I also need to walk the shop floor and see the equipment Mr. Hewitt maintained, and talk to the people he worked with without spooking them. So I need to have employee credentials and be introduced as a new member of staff. Is that going to be a problem?"

"Uh, no, but we normally only do induction training once a month—" Robin caught her eye. "It's a three-hour orientation course, basic health and safety and procedures, assuming you've worked retail before. Have you?"

Ms. Deere shook her head. "I've worked as a store detective and I've dealt with shoplifters, but not actual front-of-store work as such, no."

Amy screwed her eyes shut. *Fuck my life,* she thought silently, wishing she could sketch all her troubles on her art pad and send them off to orbit the dumpsters out back like a swarm of annoying bluebottles. "Righto. Then I suppose . . . is it okay to introduce her as a management trainee?" she asked Holmes hopefully. "Because that'd explain the lack of shop-floor experience combined with the obvious—" she waved her free hand in a circle—"other stuff—"

"Other stuff?" Ms. Deere enquired, one eyebrow rising.

"I think what Ms. Sullivan is trying to say is that you don't look like a workfare zombie," Robin said diplomatically. "Which is all we're being allowed to hire these days, because head office are trying to clamp down on payroll in the run-up to the takeover."

"Please explain." Deere shook her head, perplexed.

"The DSS sends us a continuous stream of no-hopers on their final warning before their benefits are sanctioned. They have to stay here for three months if they want to keep their benefits. All it costs us is a square meal and a hot bunk. At head office level it probably looks like we're getting a bargain, but they're unskilled and apathetic and move on as soon as they can. Head Office want our figures to look good for the new owners, so we're under a hiring freeze. We're gradually seeing our experienced, qualified people replaced by zombies."

Robin nodded lugubriously. "The line staff are okay, but we lose about twenty percent every year to natural turnover. The workfare cases are gaining on us and they take more and more supervision and quite frankly they're terrible employees—no retail service ethos whatsoever. Jennifer came up with the zentai scheme we're piloting to keep them from getting in the customers' faces or trying to unionize, but they're little better than shelf-stacking meat puppets—muppets, she calls them. We're a designated field testing branch, and it's Jennifer's project," he added.

"Zentai suits?" Deere's incomprehension was shifting towards bewilderment. "Jennifer?"

"Amy's boss," Mr. Holmes explained. "Normally Amy would be in charge of HR for a branch this size, but Jennifer is our region's HR lead. She's based here—"

"Come with me," Amy said, cutting short Robin's tendency to ramble. "I'll get you a visitor pass and then I can show you around—it's easier than trying to explain." Showing was better than telling: experience had taught her that trying to describe Jennifer's legion of unpaid meat puppets to strangers always ended badly.

►◄►◄►◄

Mary rose well before dawn—which was no hardship: at this time of year it was still dark around nine o'clock—and laid the breakfast table. Next, she took the suitcases she'd packed for each child and crammed them into her messenger bag (not without some grunting and swearing). Then she flew upstairs to rouse the sprogs. "Breakfast time!" she trilled, sticking her head inside each doorway in turn and flicking on the lights: "Rise and shine, you have an exciting surprise in store after you've eaten! Don't forget to brush your face and wash your teeth!" she added to the older two, then returned to Ethan and Emily's room to make sure that the twins didn't put their clothes on upside down, back to front, and inside out.

In less than half an hour she had the children dressed, groomed, fed, and irrigated. She only had to break up one fight along the way: Robert's and Emily's Frosties were a bad combination. Luckily Mary spotted what was happening in time to settle the matter with a venomous glare and a threat of kale smoothies all round. Emily inhaled her cereal with practiced speed that told Mary this was not an unusual occurrence: she made a note to keep a weather eye on Robert at all future mealtimes.

"Now, children!" She clapped her hands. "There's no school for the next two weeks but being stuck indoors is boring, isn't it? So Mummy and Daddy have given me permission to take you on a magical mystery tour! A car is coming to pick us all up in half an hour, and we're going away. I've packed a bag for each of you, but it's going to be a long drive, so if you have any games or toys you'd like to bring along, fetch them now!"

The next half an hour was an endless hellscape of missing USB cables, stolen game cartridges, Barbie's hair catching fire, tears, and imprecatory prayers to Baphomet demanding the responsible sibling's painful demise. In the end it fell to Mary to gather up all the consumer electronics and brightly colored bits of plastic from the living room floor and dump them into her messenger bag. Then she rationed out gobstoppers, aniseed balls, and toffee apples (variously enchanted to bind jaw to mandible until she uttered the word of release), said, "Follow me, children," and marched her troop down the garden path to a minivan wearing stolen Uber decals.

"Climb in, boys and girls!" she trilled. Robert and Lyssa were old enough to manage their own seat belts, and the twins were easily lashed to the child seats she'd requested, but as she took one last look at her charges she realized something was different. "Elissa, what's that you're wearing?" she asked: "Isn't it a bit, well, *not pink*?"

Lyssa bounced up and down excitedly, then somehow extracted her cursed toffee apple without losing any teeth. "Yesterday I was Princess Bubblegum, but today I'm Marceline the Vampire Queen! You can all be my subjects! Except *you*, Ash"—she elbowed Robert in the side pointedly—"and Maja the Sky Witch"—with a significant look at Mary, although after sustaining it for a second she wilted slightly, evidently having second thoughts about giving her sass.

Mary clenched her teeth but kept smiling, despite the near-overwhelming urge to turn Lyssa into a toad. "It's not nice to call Nanny a witch," *especially when she* is *one*, "so perhaps we should have a little think about offensive cultural stereotypes?" Then she added a low-voiced aside to the driver: "Jerry, hit it."

Jerry nodded wordlessly and drove off, clearly resigned to the Boss's punishment assignment. And this *was* a punishment assignment: it took barely fifteen minutes for Ethan and Emily to finish their boiled sweets and the first "Are we there yet?" and "I need to go pee-pee!" emerged almost simultaneously.

Thirty minutes after departure: Jerry found a motorway service station. Mary escorted the twins to the bathroom and stood guard while Robert and Lyssa re-bonded with his SplatBox Portable and her Teddy Bear Hambo (who was disturbingly clingy).

Eighty minutes after departure: Jerry found another motorway service station, and Mary used Mr. Banks's credit card to pull out £500 in cash, some of which she then used to buy (paying through the nose) a multiport car USB adapter for the GameClick 3D, the SplatBox Portable, and the teddy bear (whose inner Furby was now moaning eerily about a low battery).

One hundred and fourteen minutes after departure: Jerry glanced despairingly at Mary and pleaded, "Just make it stop?"

Mary peeled the zombie teddy bear's arms away from the driver's neck, then turned and told the children, "If you don't cease and desist forthwith, *there will be brussels sprouts for lunch*."

There was silence for a few seconds (apart from the rumble of tires on concrete and the ongoing grumble of the diesel engine), then Emily piped up: "Yay sprouts!"

Mary closed her eyes, then, for Jerry's benefit, whispered: "Next services, please."

"Sure." Jerry's knuckles, white on the steering wheel, began to relax. He'd been sticking religiously to the speed limit, evidently unenthusiastic about having his head added to the grisly adornments on the motorway camera gantries, but the stress had been grinding him down. Left to his own devices he'd have floored the throttle, just to shorten the agony. He signalled, then slid into the left-hand lane for the exit. Mary checked out the rear seats in the vanity mirror. Robert was entirely focussed on his video game. Lyssa was explaining something to her teddy, who nodded appreciatively and patted her knee. Emily was asleep, and Ethan was mumbling to himself and leaning over—

"Ethan Banks, *what* have I told you about playing with guns?"

Ethan looked up guiltily. "But *Nan* . . ."

"It's all fun and games until someone loses an eye," Mary scolded, then made a plucking motion close to her left cheek: "*Schlurp*. Now, Ethan, we're stopping for lunch and if you're really good I'll take you to a shooting gallery on the promenade when we arrive. But you mustn't take Mr. Luger and Mrs. Browning into the restaurant because they'll make Mr. Motorway Policeman sad."

"Does that mean he won't play Mr. Policeman Hides His Truncheon with us?" piped up Lyssa: "Because Mummy always tells Daddy, 'No I won't play Mr. Policeman Hides His Truncheon tonight' when Daddy's been naughty—"

"Please don't say that about your parents," Mary pleaded. *I did not need to know that!*

"Are we there yet?" piped Emily: "Because Cecil is thirsty."

Jerry braked jerkily as he entered the slip road for the service area, and barely managed to avoid turning donuts on the curve into the car park.

"You did *not* bring Cecil," Mary said, horrified as she watched a green tentacle reach out from behind Emily's collar and tuck a stray lock of hair behind her ear.

"But Nanny Glinda said I could—"

Jerry killed the engine, bent forward, and began to bang his forehead repeatedly on the steering wheel.

"Is he broken?" Lyssa asked curiously.

"All right, everyone, it's lunchtime! We'll be back in an hour," Mary told the driver. He showed no sign of having heard her. She shepherded her charges out of the minivan; as a precaution, she pocketed the keys. You could never be too careful with distressed minions.

The children's appetite for the Golden Arches' finest mechanically reclaimed meat products appeared inexhaustible, so Mary bought them chicken chunks and fries all round, along with diet cola and disgustingly sweet ice cream desserts. One toilet trip later, she was decompressed and ready to hit the road again for the final run to the destination. "Now, children, we're nearly there! Isn't that nice? Let's get going!"

They got going. All the way to the car park, where a shiny black BMW SUV had just pulled into the spot previously occupied by Jerry's fake Uber.

Mary looked at the car keys in her gloved right hand, then at the BMW. It wasn't an illusion: she checked very carefully. Like a snared fox gnawing off his own leg to escape, Jerry had hotwired the minivan and fled. "Botheration," said Mary, and rapped sharply on the driver's side window of the BMW.

"Hey!" The occupant was a ripped thirty-something male in a Hugo Boss suit: under other circumstances she might have given him a second glance, but he'd been masticating an M&S smoked salmon sandwich, and was clearly annoyed by her infringement on his territory. Besides, it was an emergency. He cracked the door open, clearly readying a rant: "What do you think you're doing? If you scratch that I'll—"

Mary turned to Ethan. "Show him your toys." Ethan showed him. BMW Man dropped his sandwich on his lap, cream cheese side down. While he was distracted, she opened her bag and pulled out her trusty MP5K. "You. Out."

"Wait—you can't—"

"I can and I am. Keys, please." Mary smiled and held out her hand as Ethan's Luger wobbled dangerously close to BMW Man's crown jewels.

"But, but—"

"Stand and deliver!" piped up Robert.

"Into the back seat, children," Mary said, holding her machine pistol under BMW Man's chin as she relieved him of his keyfob. The kids piled into the back without argument, although a minor fight then broke out between the twins. "If you report your car missing within the next two hours I will be *very* irate, and I have friends," Mary warned the businessman. "You don't want to meet my friends. I suggest you wash that immediately: grease stains are the very devil to get out of wool."

She slid behind the wheel, shoved the key in its slot, pushed the *start* button, and gunned the X5 out of the car park with a squeal of rubber.

"Are we nearly there?" whimpered Emily.

Mary, unlike Jerry, didn't give a fucking macaque's arse about the speed limit. She was scragged if they caught her, and why be hanged for a lamb when you could be hanged for stealing an entire flock of sheep instead? Plus, this was a sweet ride. She'd learned to drive, but the fastest car she'd ever owned was an eight-year-old Ford Focus with a manual transmission and a 1.1-liter engine. This two-tonne lump of Teutonic steel brought out all her worst instincts. And so the sixty minutes to Blackpool shrank to forty minutes and a flock of speeding tickets, which would be homing in on the bank balance and driving license of the unfortunate owner of the BMW, who in the meantime was explaining his moist crotch to a pair of unimpressed Highways Agency officers.

▸◂▸◂◂

Back upstairs after dinner, Eve discovered someone had readied the maidservant's room for her use. A tarnished candlestick, a bowl, and a jug of cold water stood on the nightstand; the narrow bed was freshly made, and someone had left a fussy Victorian nightgown on the pillow in case she'd forgotten her tee-shirt. She left Imp stalking around Rupert's palatial quarters muttering under his breath about too many sex toys and not enough imagination as she retreated to her bathroom to shower and change.

Over the years Eve had optimized the hell out of the contents of her go-bag. To minimize bulk she travelled with all-black clothing, except for two business-appropriate shirts. She quickly pulled on leggings, a hooded running top, and a pair of black running shoes. She swapped her pearls for a belt bag of glass marbles and other esoteric equipment, then took a thoughtful second look at the frilly white nightie. On the one hand, she knew what fate usually held in store for ingénues who overnighted in storm-wracked castles staffed by sinister servants. On the other hand, the nightgown gave her an idea. She painted her face carefully: bone-white foundation, overlaid with the charcoal outline of a skull with hollow eyes, nose, and teeth. Then she pulled the nightie on over her ensemble, picked up the candlestick, and went to knock on Rupert's bedroom door.

Imp answered the door, took one look at her, and stumbled backwards with a shriek of terror.

Eve followed him inside and closed the door: "Hush! Ahem. *Whooooohoooo,* or whatever ghosts say. *Haunt,* maybe?"

"Oh dear God, and by God I mean the Prime Minister," Imp clutched his chest theatrically, "you're *terrifying.*"

Eve grinned cadaverously. She hadn't dressed up as a ghost in ages, but Halloween had always been her favorite time of year. She hefted the candlestick. "If they don't die of fright, there's always the medieval Maglite." Then she noticed that Imp was still wearing his borrowed DJ. "Why haven't you changed?"

Imp cringed. "I thought I'd James Bond it." Seeing her expression, he added, "I asked them to wash my other togs and the laundry's not back yet."

Eve rolled her eyes. "Come on, then."

"But it isn't midnight!"

"Eldritch doom waits for no man. *Whoooo, haunt,* etcetera."

Eve set out along the darkened corridor. Imp followed, then did a double-take: "Wait, the staircase was thataway—"

"—And Cunningham knows we know that. Attend." Eve set off down the grand staircase, then along a darkened passage they hadn't previously explored. It was unlit so she paused, frowned furiously, and heated her candlewick up to ignition temperature by sheer force of will. It cast barely enough light to see the cobwebs and trip hazards—dark wooden furniture in unlit halls was an ever-present menace—so she slowed. "If you see someone, turn to face the wall and let me go first," she said softly, barely above a whisper. "I've got this."

"When did you get so bad-ass, sis?" She swept past him like the Ghost of Lady Skaro Past. "What happened?"

"Necessity," she replied, to shut him up.

A minute later: "The black hood makes you look like your head's missing, in the dark—from behind, I mean. Neat trick. Was it intentional?"

"You tell me," she said drily, shoving her free hand against a promising-looking cutout in the wall. It clicked, then popped open. "Bingo."

"Bingo—zoinks! What's that?"

"Servants' concealed stairwell: they're everywhere. Follow me close and shut the door behind you." She stepped inside and began to descend.

For the next half hour Eve cautiously navigated the darkened hallways and shortcuts of the castle, steering ever deeper. Whenever she heard voices or footsteps she retreated or waited. Imp held his tongue diligently, relieving her of the need to forcibly mute him. Evidently he'd worked out that being caught sneaking around a castle at dead of night by cultists might not be a life-enriching experience.

In an older part of the building, they came to a heavy wooden door with a metal-barred window secured by substantial iron bolts. "Is this what I think it is?" Imp whispered.

"Probably. Stand back." Eve searched the door for wards and spell-bindings, but found only dismal echoes of ancient pain and stale despair. "Dungeon ahoy." She slid the bolts back. "Oiled within living memory." She took a deep breath. "Have you kept up the . . . exercises?"

"What, you mean the ritual ones that—" Imp caught himself. "Not very well," he admitted. "Barely."

Dad had taught the pair of them what he could of the family speciality: formal magic. Some thought of it as a superpower, others as demonic possession. In these turbulent times there were even weirdos who claimed magic was a branch of mathematics and could be conducted using computers instead of brains. Eve had stuck to the exercise regime he'd given them, carefully not calling on her power so often that she attracted the parasites that caused Metahuman Associated Dementia, but still frequently enough that the basic forms came easily to mind. Imp's confession annoyed her: *I should have asked earlier,* she chided herself.

"If you're out of practice, stay behind me and run like hell if we encounter anything you can't deal with. Do you even enchant, bro?"

"I, uh, I mostly rely on the gift of the gab." She knew *that* much already. Imp had always had a quicksilver tongue—a magically enhanced larynx laden with enough power to get him into and out of trouble.

"Well then. Think of a story and be prepared to use it if we meet anyone."

"Got you covered." Imp produced his phone with a flourish. "Cinéma-vérité. Works every time. You can be the Headless Ghost of whatever, and I'm collecting reaction shots."

"Good. Now hush and let me work."

Eve swung the door open and descended the stairs, candlestick held high.

At first glance it might have been an ordinary cellar. But underlying the smell of damp there was something else, a graveyard fetor that hung heavy in the stagnant air. Then they came to a row of doors—or rather, locked iron grates set in the arched fronts of dark openings. Imp shone his phone's flashlight into a couple of them. There were no mummified skeletons chained to the walls, but the second niche contained the remains of a collapsed bunk bed bolted to the wall.

"Do I want to know?" Imp whispered.

"The Lord of Skaro has the right of high justice, *ius gladii*— Skaro was held to be a private jurisdiction due to its isolation during the Middle Ages. Usually capital cases would be referred to the Duchy, but if the island was cut off or besieged . . ." Eve shrugged.

At the end of the short corridor they came to a vestibule with modern cage doors, controlling access to four cells—they could be nothing else. A dim electric light shone overhead. One of the cells, padlocked shut, held a cot and a portable commode. It was ominously clean, the bedding folded neatly. "Does this mean what I think . . ."

"*Shut up*," Eve hissed fiercely, as she knelt by the keyhole in the door at the end of the passage. "*Listening*." Behind her Imp fell silent, but began taking photographs of the cells for some opaque reason of his own.

Hearing nothing, Eve felt her way into the door. It was a conventional deadbolt lock, relatively modern—possibly installed this century. She scrabbled weakly with her mental fingers until she found purchase. The lock clicked, plates rotating and bolt withdrawing. She eased the door ajar, skin crawling as she saw what lay beyond.

"Fuck." *Rupert did this*, she told herself, very carefully eliding the corollary, *you* enabled *Rupert to do this*.

The room was electrically lit and immaculately clean, making it impossible not to recognize it for what it was: a temple, obviously dedicated to something that could only be holy in a faith whose axiom system lacked the concepts of *mercy* and *innocence*—the kind of faith that was worshipped in private to avoid the scrutiny of inquisitors and criminal investigators.

All lines converged on the room's central feature, a stone altar. The altar's borders were decorated with a frieze of screaming skulls, and its middle was a convex surface surrounded by spiraling gutters. Off to one side, a chrome and plastic lectern supported a trio of monitors and a keyboard with an unusual number of specialized function keys. Eve nudged the mouse attached to the keyboard, and the screens lit up to display the comforting familiarity of a locked Bloomberg Terminal launchpad. She tapped in Rupert's login and password and the display unfroze. "*Shit*," she whispered, and hastily logged out again. She turned in place, examining the intricate murals and mosaics depicting the birth, death, and afterlife of the Mute Poet among his peers: the saints of death that certain *conquistadores* had perverted to fit their own goals and brought home with them when they returned from the charnel house they'd made of the Aztec empire.

Imp cleared his throat and she glanced round at him. His skin was pale. "I think I see why you wanted the bastard dead."

"This—" Eve pointed at the altar—"this is—" She ran out of words. The altar had been scrubbed spotlessly clean but still stank of bleach and terror. "You asked about haruspicy? The reading of auguries by examining the internal organs of sacrificial victims goes back a long way." She swallowed. "And that's what they were doing here." An altar, an obsidian blade, and a modern dealer desk to front-run the market. "I *knew* there was more to Rupert than collectables and canny trading, but—" She swallowed again.

"It gives a whole new meaning to insider trading," Imp attempted, but his feeble attempt at deflection fell flat. "That's what this is about, isn't it? He was a priest, not just a worshipper."

"It lines up." Eve glanced at the door opposite their entrance, appraising it grimly. *What if Rupert wasn't just using divination to identify profit opportunities?* she wondered in horror. *What foul web am I trapped in?* "Come on."

She locked their entrance, then picked the lock on the next door. It was surprisingly heavy, and something clattered as it opened inwards—Imp leaned forward and caught a mop and bucket before they took a tumble. "What."

"It's the back of the janitor's closet." Eve stuck the candlestick inside, illuminating the empty family chapel. "Look where it comes out."

"I don't want to be here," said Imp. "I don't want the past hour to have happened. Please make it be a bad dream?"

"Sorry, can't do that," his sister replied, leading him into the room where her marriage had been consecrated in absentia. "Going back to bed now. Lock your door until dawn: we'll fly out as soon as it's safe."

"But what happens when we get home?" Imp asked. Eve shrugged, and wished she had an answer.

►◄►◄►◄

Wendy followed Amy through the cramped back-office maze, noting her tensed shoulders as she clacked along like a wind-up toy. *Interesting,* Wendy thought. Amy was really upset about something—some *things,* more likely: one did not reach such a dizzy pinnacle of uptightness without serious ongoing pressure—but she wasn't telegraphing *guilt.* There were none of the subtle tells Wendy had learned to spot in a miscreant confronted by a detective. Whatever had cranked Amy tight lay elsewhere—which, if it could be confirmed, made her a potential informant.

Wendy had no reason to trust anyone at Branch 322 yet: all she definitely knew for sure was that someone had contaminated the supply chain feeding the deli counter. The dismal trifecta of criminology confronted her: Who had the means, the motive, and the opportunity? Amy could be invaluable in ruling out dead ends, but if she was part of the problem . . .

"This is the general office," Amy said as they walked past a space almost twice as large as Wendy's cubicle at Security HQ, into which some sadist had managed to cram no fewer than four desks and three backless chairs. "And this is the security office. Hi, Mr. Grant! This is Ms. Deere, she's joining us for a couple of weeks as part of the new management orientation and training scheme." Mr. Grant grunted and kept his focus on the wall of CCTV screens. To Wendy's eye, it looked as if the supermarket had a camera scrutinizing every single checkout, as well as . . . *Are those the staff toilet cubicles?* "As you can see, *everything* we do and say anywhere on the premises is recorded. If you have nothing to hide you have nothing to fear—but best leave idle chat until we're off the clock! Also," she added, *sotto voce,* "the Branch Security computers run realtime speech recognition and dock your pay automatically if they catch you using naughty words."

"This is HR, where I—oh, hello, Boss!" Amy jolted to attention, then beckoned Wendy forward. "Ms. Henderson? This is Ms. Deere. She's joining us for a . . ."

Wendy smiled blandly as she sized up Amy's boss. There was

something alarmingly familiar about her even though she was a complete stranger. "Please, call me Jennifer," said Amy's boss, her smile as empty as an unfilled grave.

"Well," Wendy said affably, "if you're willing to be Jennifer, please call me Wendy." They shook hands, and the penny dropped: *She looks like Imp's sister! Only . . . not?* Maybe it was just a fashion trend among corporate blondes slithering their way around the snake pit, but the resemblance to Eve was striking. "I'm sure we'll get on!"

"Absolutely! But I'm busy with the head office presentation on the DWP workfare placement scheme right now, so *do* feel free to run along, darling—" Wendy nearly scowled before she realized Jennifer was addressing Amy, who had the air of a dog who'd been beaten too often. Amy reversed out of the HR office at speed, cheeks flushed. *Interesting,* Wendy mused as Amy gave her a brisk tour of the stockroom at the back of the store, all the time visibly trying to maintain an even keel.

On consideration the source of Amy's stress was clearly Jennifer. Amy could see why: despite the superficial polish, Jennifer had all the personal warmth and charm of a viper. But was there anything more to it?

"Can you tell me what your boss is working on?" Wendy asked when they reached the loading bays behind the store. "Something about workfare?"

"Her pet pilot program," Amy said tensely. "Let me show you. Uh, you! Jasmine! If you could put that down and come over here, please?"

Wendy did a double-take as Jasmine turned to face them. Jasmine was a tall, white-clad person, much like a plague medic in isolation gear: only instead of a respirator she wore a mask on the front of her head that smiled cartoonishly. "Hello, Amy, how may I serve you?" a synthetic voice fluted from where Jasmine's mouth ought to be.

"Just stand here please, I'm orienting a new hire." Amy was much more polished and sure of herself in the presence of a—*Is that why they call it Human Resources?* Wendy suppressed a shudder.

"Jasmine is on placement from the DWP for fourteen hours a day in return for reactivation of her Universal Credit," Amy explained, paying no more attention to Jasmine than she would to a vacuum cleaner. "They're rotated through here on a three-month work placement program. We issue them with zentai suits—" she gestured at the head-to-toe body stocking—"with control harnesses, a randomized name badge, and the Company Face. That's a shaped e-ink face mask/display with speech synthesis and recognition. Jasmine, display test pattern." Jasmine's face flickered through a sequence of geometric shapes before it returned to the default: a blandly ageless woman's face. "The computer tells them what to do via wifi. In event of a customer interaction, the Face handles communication—we've got a system based on Cortana to understand requests and generate replies. Her name isn't actually Jasmine—" Behind the face-shaped display panel, there was a muffled sound—"excuse me, did I give you permission to talk?" Amy snapped. Jasmine's body shook its head, cringing. "That's all for now, Jasmine: end override, back to work with you."

Jasmine almost tripped in her hurry to return to unpacking cardboard trays of dog food. Amy waited until she was back at work before meeting Wendy's gaze. Her shoulders slumped slightly, and she sighed.

"What?" asked Wendy.

"It's the wave of the future," Amy said dispiritedly. "You don't have to like it, it just *is*—we have to face facts."

"Can't you do something?" Wendy asked, appalled.

"I could *try*. Then Jennifer would fire me and I'd end up right back here as a muppet myself, wearing the Company Face instead of a management suit." She plucked at her tailored jacket. "It's not *much* worse than regular front-of-store duty: the job's the same. This just gives us improved CRM quality control—the DWP placements are shi—I mean *terrible,* at customer interaction. At least the computers don't throw a strop and swear at the punters. And we let them take their gags out at the end of their shift."

"But who *is* she?" Wendy persisted. It seemed monstrous to her, this robbery of identity and agency.

"I don't know." Amy's face was carefully blank. The question obviously troubled her. "I could find out, but it wouldn't help," she said quietly. "The names are randomized on every shift change, you know. We've got a Jasmine; we've also got Rose, Iris, Lilly, Cinnamon, Poppy, and Heather. For the, uh, the temps with a bust. Jennifer was going to make them wear binders—" Amy gestured at her own well-endowed chest—"but there's no budget for that. So we're stuck with gendered meatbots."

"And this is Jennifer's hobby horse?"

"Yeah, she's championing it throughout the organization. I mean, we had the branch automation and a custom software build configured by IT for the self-checkouts, and we had the workfare bodies. The face mask displays were originally made for our department store subsidiary—the idea was to let visitors see what they looked like in an outfit with their own face on the store dummy, but the customers hated it, so they were going spare. Anyway, Jennifer put it all together with the body stockings and the novelty ball gags. I thought she was joking at first because, I mean, *really*? Who'd be willing to work like that? But it turns out—" Amy swallowed—"lots of people are willing to work like that."

If the alternative is homelessness and starvation, Wendy appended silently.

Jasmine picked up another stack of cans. Beside her, a taller, heavier body labelled "Boris" went at a trolley packed with toilet rolls with a box cutter. It was cold in the unheated receiving area, and it smelled faintly of clogged drains. Wendy grimaced. "Can we carry on? I'm sorry I asked."

"Of course," Amy said quietly, then turned and clattered away towards the next room. She wore low heels, Wendy noticed, unlike her boss's stilettos. Everything about her was like a cut-down, dispirited, ill-fitting, but fundamentally more *human* version of Jennifer. "This is where I work, mostly," she said, gesturing at a cramped desk behind a row of wheeled cages full of cardboard packaging. She scooped up a battered laptop and a notepad, tucked them under her arm, and glanced at Wendy. "I'm sure we can find you a proper desk," she said. "I don't suppose you'd mind sharing the HR office with Jennifer?"

"I—I can do that." Wendy stuttered from her initial distaste:

but realization cut in—Jennifer was *absolutely* on the list of strange shit that merited further investigation, a list that was already far longer than she'd expected when Gibson handed her the job. *This place is beyond fucked up.* It put her more in mind of a high-security prison than a supermarket. One that was trying extra hard to graduate to concentration camp.

"Are we the baddies?" Wendy asked whimsically, and didn't realize she'd spoken aloud until Amy cringed and hissed, "Don't *ever* say that!"

Oops. She covered her lips apologetically. Amy shook her head, clearly upset by the Mitchell and Webb reference. "The walls really do have ears. Listen, how about I finish the tour and find you a desk? Then you can get started."

►◄►◄►◄

The Boss had assigned Mary the task of giving the children a magical mystery tour while playing a shell game that would keep them out of the grasp of their parents and the authorities. That meant she needed, at a minimum, plentiful distractions.

Blackpool was a classic English seaside resort. Even in December, on paper the town had much to offer: the illuminations, the Golden Mile, a two-thirds-scale working model of the Eiffel Tower, even a shiny new Chariots of the Gods indoor theme park.

So Blackpool it was. After all, if you couldn't keep a bunch of transhuman pre-tweens too distracted to realize they'd been kidnapped in a town that was basically wall-to-wall amusement parks, you were clearly doing something wrong.

Things Mary hadn't reckoned with about Blackpool in December:

- The famous illuminations were turned off and most of the Golden Mile attractions were closed and shuttered for winter,
- For every unavailable children's amusement arcade, there was a drunken hen night or stag party stumbling from pub to strip club,

- It was dark,
- It was cold,
- And the rain never stopped.

On the other hand, she'd booked a self-catering apartment via Airbnb. It was a couple of streets away from the seafront, close to the Pleasure Beach (although that was closed for winter). And the reality turned out to be not too different from the description on the website. It had four bedrooms, a kitchen, a bathroom, a living room, and a front door that locked with one of those newfangled PIN-pad gadgets. Never mind the ghastly paint job and the seaside tat decorating every available surface: it was accommodation, there was wifi, and once she put Mr. and Mrs. Satan's hellspawn to bed she could plan the next stage of *Operation: Get Lost* in peace and quiet.

After she parked them in the living room, Mary abandoned the kids. "I'm going to move the car, dears: don't burn the house down!" she told Robert and Lyssa, then nipped out and dumped the hot wheels in a backstreet. She left the keys in the ignition and the doors unlocked: it ought to be gone by morning.

Back in the flat she found Robert and Lyssa trying to burn down the kitchen. Robert was glaring at the hob, which stubbornly refused to catch fire even though he'd turned it on and it was glowing cherry red. "It's an induction hob," Mary explained. "There's no gas in this building."

"*What?* No *gas?*" His gasp of betrayal warmed the chilly cockles of her heart.

"I told you so!" Princess Sparkle-Vampire sang as she dashed around the kitchen.

"But it's—"

"Pyro-pyro-pyro-kin*esis*!" Lyssa chanted, for no apparent reason.

"Induction hobs only work if you put a salamander on them," Mary lied glibly; "the magnetic fields annoy the fire lizard until it ignites its pyrophores. That's like a chameleon's chromatophores, only for fire," she added. Misinforming children was fun: Why had she never tried it before? Ah, yes: she didn't have children, that was why. *Maybe I'll borrow some when this is over,* she thought self-indulgently.

Emily was gravely introducing Cecil to the houseplants in the living room, a pair of extremely torpid succulents that seemed reluctant to clamber out of their pots and go walkabout. Ethan was staging a reenactment of the Gunfight at the O.K. Corral with the Happy Meal toys from lunchtime—Sheriff Unicorn, Darth Earp, and Doc Dalek faced off against a Cowboy Gang of hapless Imperial Stormtroopers. (They died messily but bloodlessly.)

Mary clapped her hands: "Children! Go and wash your armpits and brush your feet while I unpack your suitcases! When I get back, we're going out for lunch!" It was closer to two thirty than to one o'clock, but they'd stopped for chicken nuggets on the road. To Mary's way of thinking it didn't matter whether the children had junk food four times a day or five, just as long as they didn't throw up or nag her for sweets while she was trying to put her feet up. Worrying about long-term consequences was their parents' job.

She flew upstairs and pulled their suitcases out of her messenger bag (not without some grunting and cursing in Polish), then laid out pajamas and toothbrushes on each pillow. Then she skipped downstairs to sweep the survivors of Ethan's gunfight into her bag for recycling and reassure Emily that Cecil could play with the succulents while the humans were out. Marceline the Vampire Queen and her pyromaniacal brother had tired of trashing the rental kitchen. "Time for lunch!" she announced, and in no time at all Mary was leading the fearsome foursome along the pavement, holding each other's hands just like a normal family.

She bought them all a late lunch in the nearest Chicken Shack. There were no fires, explosions, or screaming food fights. Mary was rapidly developing a longing for salad, but it would have to wait until she could sneak away from her charges (who thrived on a diet of fried food, chocolate, and sugary drinks). The endless afternoon vista stretched out before her, desolate and unrestful. She *had* to get away from the kids for half an hour soon, otherwise madness beckoned: *Why did I ever agree to this gig? Ah yes, Dad's nursing home bills.*

It was funny how rapidly a series of private equity takeovers—and the subsequent price gouging and focus on monetizing the inmates—could wreck the balance sheet of even the best-run chain of care homes. One damn home after another had either folded or ejected her dad when his condition proved difficult to manage. And each new one cost more than the last. He kept wandering off and hiding in abandoned buildings, setting up his lab again like the old days. But the cops wouldn't—couldn't—do anything.

Dad had been ruled incompetent to stand trial by reason of Metahuman Associated Dementia, but the budget for mental health services had been pared to the bone, so there were no state-run facilities that could take him. And although he was a persistent (albeit minor) public nuisance, the MAD diagnosis meant the police couldn't do anything. They actively went out of their way to avoid noticing Dad, because *if* they noticed him they'd have to write up a crime report. But he couldn't stand trial, and because their performance evaluations were based on their conviction rate, their efficiency metrics would plummet.

Why the authorities hadn't already de-emphasized him was a mystery beyond her ken: but whatever the reason Mary was desperate to avoid it. Keeping him in a comfortable home with a locked front door and the specialist nursing care he needed was the best solution. But it was as expensive as a family-sized heroin habit, which was why Mary was in debt to the Boss: the biggest pusher of all.

All these worries nagging at the back of Mary's mind as she waited for the children to finish their Chocoslurry Glory™ desserts were eclipsed by the immediate one: Where to take the supercops' hellspawn next, to keep them happily distracted and out of trouble? Given that it was a rainy December Tuesday in Blackpool and everywhere seemed to be inexplicably shut, this was quite a challenge. But as she scrolled through Yelp listings on her phone, one venue kept coming up top: the Chariots of the Gods Experience, just a short tram ride away along the seafront.

If Akhenaten couldn't sort them out, the Greys could deal. There was bound to be some sort of toddler zoo where she could park Emily and Ethan, and surely a problem divided was a problem halved. She might even snatch some time to smoke a fag and phone the nursing home, in case Dad was lucid enough to talk this afternoon. And after bedtime tonight, she could throw down with the Boss and find out what the fuck the big man *really* thought he was playing at.

►◄►◄

Eve realized they were in trouble the moment she turned the corner onto the home stretch and saw light leaking from underneath her bedroom door.

She stopped so suddenly that Imp stumbled into her with a quiet "Oof."

Bracing herself against the wall to prevent a tumble, she spun round and pressed her fingers to his lips. "*No,*" she breathed.

Imp caught his balance and craned his neck to see past her. His mouth was an "O," the sequential *fuck* arrested by her fingertips.

"*Problem,*" she whispered.

Imp retreated to the corner they'd just turned. "Wait them out?"

"Can't." She couldn't risk leaving her work laptop vulnerable to an Evil Maid Attack delivered via a toxic USB stick. Nor would their midnight walkabout go unnoticed. Anyone sneaking into Eve's room would certainly notice Imp's absence at the same time.

"Innocent?"

"Don't be silly." They were retreating into the private language of their childhood, when they'd been halfway to mind-reading. Eve thought furiously for a second then put the candlestick down: "Can you cast?"

"Not reliably, but I can push."

She perked up. "How many?"

"Normally two to four, easy; up to ten in ideal conditions. Now . . ." He stared at her. "I'll try for panic."

"Phone." Eve held out her hand. Imp unlocked his phone and passed it over. She hit the camera app, flipped to front-facing, checked her skullface makeup was intact, and passed it back to him. Then she picked up her field-expedient cosh and blew out its solitary candle. "Showtime."

She tiptoed down the corridor, then eased open the door to Lady Skaro's bedroom. The dim light from the single bedside lamp revealed the door to the maid's room was open. Someone dressed in dark clothing stood there, with their back to Lady Skaro's dressing table.

Imp slipped into the boudoir and crouched behind one of the canopy bedposts. Eve glided silently up behind the intruder, careful not to block the lamplight. She raised her candlestick with one hand, gave Imp a ready sign with the fingers of her other, then said, voice pitched low: "*Whoo-hooo!* Haunt, motherfucker."

Her ward prickled as Imp *pushed* belief at the intruder with all his willpower. The results were dramatic. The intruder jolted upright, spun round, gave a tiny shriek of terror, and collapsed in a dead faint.

"Well *that* went well, I think—" said Imp, self-satisfied. Eve ignored him. She darted into the maid's room and confirmed there had been just the one intruder (who had been in the process of sorting through the contents of Eve's go-bag on the bed). She then dashed across the boudoir to the connecting door with Rupert's room. Imp twigged to her intention as she finessed the lock and quietly unlatched the door. He readied another *push* as she opened it. Eve inspected bathroom, study, and playroom, but the intruder in the maid's room had come alone.

"Clear," she confirmed, as Imp closed and locked the outer door of Lady Skaro's apartment. "You need to not jump to conclusions, bro. Now. Who do we have here?"

As she bent over, the fallen figure—a middle-aged woman dressed in an old-fashioned maid's uniform—stirred. She opened her eyes to see Eve looming over her, whimpered in terror, and promptly fainted again.

"You can dial it back now," Eve said.

"If I do that and she wakes up, she'll figure it out." Imp stared at the woman. "Huh! It's Sybil the housekeeper—the butler's wife."

"I wish you hadn't told me that," Eve said tonelessly. Faceless enemies were easiest to dispose of, especially when they were initiates in the Cult of the Mute Poet with blood on their hands. Knowing their names, knowing they had families and spouses and (for all she knew) children to go home to made it *much* harder to murder them. Impossible, even. She picked up Sybil's limp left wrist and unbuttoned her cuff. Rolling up the sleeve she saw a pink dahlia tattooed on the inside of her wrist. Just as she'd feared. "Oh dear."

"What is it?" Imp asked curiously.

"Flower and song," Eve muttered under her breath. "Here, give me a hand." She tugged at the arm. "Keep her out while we move her, if you can."

"Move her—where?"

"Rupert's bedroom."

"But where will I—"

"You can have Lady Skaro's bed for all I care. Do you *want* her to escape?"

Between them they half dragged/half carried Mrs. Cunningham through the door to Rupert's chambers, then laid her out on Rupert's bed. For the first time ever, Eve was grateful for Rupert's fetishistic sexuality. The leather-lined ankle and wrist restraints on the bed were functional. Imp secured her wrists first. Sybil began to stir as Eve worked on her ankles, tried kicking, then took a deep breath in readiness to scream. Her mouth opened just in time for Imp to brandish a ball gag in front of her face. "*Stop,*" he commanded, and Eve saw in his eyes something shadowy and forbidding, a fell expression she never wanted to see again on her kid brother's face.

The housekeeper stilled, her scream unvoiced, eyes wide. "I can explain . . ." she trailed off.

Something in Eve's chest unwound infinitesimally. If she'd started with threats things could only go downhill, but pleas—*she's terrified,* Eve realized. "So explain," Eve demanded.

"Nobody told me there'd be so much blood," Sybil began again, then stopped.

"Where is your husband, Mrs. Cunningham?" Imp asked, standing outside her field of vision beside the head of the bed. "Does he know what you're doing? Would he *approve*?"

Eve bit her tongue in surprise. Cultists tended to be patriarchal shitbags: this was the exact button she'd have told Jeremy to push if they'd planned this ahead of time.

Their prisoner looked ashen.

"The husband is the head of the household, isn't he?" Imp nudged. "Isn't that the law, here? What would your Lord and Master think of your petty treason?"

To Eve's astonishment and deep unease, Mrs. Cunningham began to weep. She sobbed with the silence bred by long-standing fear. Eve glanced at Jeremy. Her brother was wincing, massaging his forehead as he did when inflicting his will-to-believe on another. It gave him a headache: Sybil wasn't as easy a pushover as she looked at first glance. Keeping her hand out of sight of their victim, Eve signalled, *ease up, ease up.* Imp nodded. Presently Sybil took a shuddering breath and the tears began to dry.

"He'll kill me, whatever you do," she said hopelessly.

"Why? Does he know you're here?" Eve asked.

Sybil rolled her head. "I'm supposed to be at home. In Skaro town," she clarified. It was more of a village than a town, a cluster of gray-stone buildings jammed in the fork where the island's two roads met. (One led to the harbor, the other meandered around the coastline.) "While his Lordship's in residence my husband overnights in the servants' quarters, in case his Lordship needs anything. And for *nocturna laus,* of course, whenever it's—time."

Eve caught the slight hesitation. "I know the creed," she told the woman. It wasn't a lie, exactly. Eve knew more than she ever wanted to about the mystery cults, the path of flower and song the *conquistadores* had stolen and perverted for their own ends. She'd made it her business to learn, once she plumbed the depths of Rupert's depravity. "I obey our Mute Lord, the Prince of Poetry." The words stuck in her throat, but again, they were *technically* true (insofar as she was wed and geas-bound to Rupert, of one flesh with the cult's High Priest).

"Oh thank the Lord!" Sybil was overcome by emotion. "Please, please, I beg you, free me!"

"Free you from what?"

"My husband—" It all came out in a gush. Sybil had been married to Anthony for thirty-seven unhappy years, betrothed at birth to seal an agreement made between two of the islander families in the last days of the previous Lord. She bore the butler's four children without complaint, toiled in domestic drudgery for long years that unrolled into decades, and never raised her eyes from the path assigned to her. But when the new Lord came to the island, Rupert brought out the worst in his servants. He'd instituted the adoration of the Mute Saint, moved out those who couldn't stomach it, and induced those who remained to join it. That was how the mystery cults kept their grip, after all, enforcing complicity through shared bloodshed and seclusion from the outside world. Anthony, never a considerate and good-natured husband, was one of those who flourished under the new regime. He found a wild and heedless freedom in the service of his dark Lord. He became demanding—

"Stop." Eve made a cutting motion. "You're telling me the penal code hasn't been updated since 1832? Never mind the sodomy statute—" Imp winced—"you mean marital rape is still legal?"

"Please, I only want a signed warrant to leave the island! His Lordship can overrule a male guardian, but my husband refuses—" She burst into tears again.

Eve touched Imp's shoulder and led him into the next room. "Do we believe her?" she whispered in his ear.

"Yeah, I'm pretty sure we do." He looked uncharacteristically sober. "Sis?"

"Yes?"

"If you decide to burn this place to the ground, can I pass you the matches?"

Eve thought for a few seconds, then nodded. In the silence, she became aware of an absence: the rumble of wind across the battlements overhead had dwindled to nothing. She touched her brother's shoulder again. "Jeremy. *Imp.*" She licked her skeleton-painted lips. "Are you absolutely certain we can believe her? I mean, she's not just spinning us a yarn to push our buttons?"

He nodded. "I believe her. About wanting to get away, anyway. Why?"

"Stone doesn't burn, but human sacrifice cults are another matter. And I think I'm going to take you up on those matches in due course . . ."

►◄►◄►◄

There were many bad things about wearing a muppet suit, in Ade's opinion. The bridle and headset constantly whispered instructions in his ears; the wires monitoring his pulse and his respiration itched; the motion-tracking sensors built into the suit and surveilled by the very walls of the supermarket meant that slacking was out of the question. The branch computers monitored his actions and could enforce commands via a discipline belt. He couldn't speak, but only mumble hoarse whispers around the gag. (If he was too noisy it released a numbing agent that paralyzed his larynx, a little detail he hadn't known before he agreed to Jennifer's offer.)

The computer-controlled meatbots had zipped him into his suit for the first time that morning. He'd struggled involuntarily even though he knew Jenn had his best interests at heart. The itchy synthetic fabric made his skin crawl. But he wasn't a fighter, and in any case they'd shot him up with some kind of happy juice that made everything fuzzy and bearable. Then they left him on a cot for a few hours. "We'll ease him in over a couple of days, then titrate a maintenance dose," the branch pharmacist explained to her assistant as she installed the catheter. "That works best with the bolshie ones."

"There are people who'd pay good money for this sort of treatment," said the assistant. Then she blushed. "I don't mean—I mean to say, I read about it somewhere—I'm not into BDSM myself—"

"Don't worry," said the pharmacist, "they'd never make *us* wear these things! We're management."

Ade, zoned out in a world of his own, barely noticed at the time.

But there was one good thing about the suit: once he was plugged in (wired up, rocking the Company Face, fully awake and online), he realized that he was *completely* anonymous. **HELLO MY NAME IS** *Gordon* was his identity right now, but the name changed with every shift, as did everyone else's. The picture on his e-ink store dummy's mask was a *Scanner Darkly* composite, modulated by the computers to react to the emotional cues of whoever the branch computers were talking to. He didn't have to converse with strangers or meet their eyes: Cortana was his co-pilot. The computers were eerily good at reading body language, better than

Ade had ever been. It was as if they were controlled by a ghost in the machine rather than a deep learning neural network. So Ade didn't have to smile and take shit from the customers any more. Life as a meatbot was easy, as long as you lifted the boxes on cue.

Some time during the day, the other bitch from HR—Jennifer's fat Mini-Me, the one who'd fired him—popped up, mindlessly twittering at another woman in a manager's suit. HR bitch didn't even notice Ade. The new woman, some kind of trainee, was interested in the other muppets. Ade took her measure furtively as he stacked soup cans on autopilot: she looked like a good fit for the program. If he hung her bones on the line he could hit the branch targets for six to seven working days, easily.

As he rolled a wheeled pallet cage of dry goods up aisle six, Ade tried to work out how it had gone so horribly wrong, all those months ago.

The New Management—the government—was Preparing for War. The Prime Minister said so every time they interviewed him on the TV. He said it with a kind, avuncular twinkle in the eyes without a face: "We've got to be ready for war, you know!" he reassured his audience. "Let's get autarky done! Strong and Stable!"

Autarky meant digging up gardens to plant cabbages, raising goats on hillsides, and lots of localism. Localism meant no more refrigerator ships full of New Zealand lamb docking at Felixstowe. Instead it meant just-in-time delivery of locally sourced carcasses to the HAMDAS-RX Plus automatic deboning line on Loading Dock Four, where the robots with carving knives took in dangling animals at one end and spat out neatly packaged cuts of meat at the other. The residuum—bones and scraps—was blasted against mesh screens with high-pressure water, the bones crushed in grinders, skin autoclaved and rendered to yield gelatin, and the resulting slimy goop colored and fed to the 3D printers in the back of the deli department. *Mechanically Recovered Tissue*. Artificial reconstituted bone, fake skin, extruded fat, and reclaimed textured meat could be printed into appetizingly colored and textured shapes. It was sold as 100 percent pure beef, pork, or lamb: and that was exactly what it was. Eventually vat-grown cell cultures would replace the freezer trucks with the gutted pig torsos that backed up to the loading bay daily. But for now, autarky meant lots of work for Ade.

It was all fine in *theory,* but in practice, the pigs-to-pies line was a nightmare to maintain. Like every inkjet printer ever, the flesh-printer nozzles kept clogging. The pipelines needed to be flushed and sterilized regularly; the robots with carving knives had to be scrubbed and cleaned until they gleamed every night. (Suspicious stain, meet Food Hygiene Inspectorate.) Worse, he had targets to achieve. Each type of animal carcass had a known fat, bone, and muscle tissue composition. Ade was expected to make sure that 100 percent of each component ended up being retrieved and turned into salable products. Which was impossible. If the nuclear waste reprocessing plant at Sellafield could lose a third of a ton of plutonium, how could he possibly be expected to account for animal carcasses to the nearest gram?

Inside his zentai suit, Ade's skin prickled with a furious flush as he recalled his slide towards inevitable disgrace and sacking.

Week after week he'd sweated bullets in a vain attempt to meet his targets, and carcass by carcass he fell further behind. Whoever drew up the targets had clearly never met a real animal: they were working to an idealized model, a perfectly spherical imaginary unicorn of uniform meat content, rather than a shitting, bleeding, panicking cow facing execution. He could get arbitrarily close—within one or two percent of perfection—but always fell short. Fucking *hooves.* You weren't allowed to sell hooves (apparently they weren't edible) but if a leg came in with a hoof still attached, that was, fuck, that put him *an entire kilogram* behind quota *right there.*

Then one morning in early September, a cold snap brought an Atlantic storm rolling in. Ade had arrived on the loading dock just after seven and noticed something behind an overflowing dumpster that hadn't been uplifted yet. It was pure happenstance: a flash of electric blue fabric, a crumpled and bulbous sleeping bag soaked through by the weather. The refuse truck was late again, otherwise there'd have been nothing to see. He'd been set on ignoring it but a stray thought struck him, so he walked over and nudged it with his boot. "Wake up," he grunted. But the occupant was beyond waking. He lay beside his final sacrament: a dirty spoon, a stub of candle, and a used syringe. And although he was scrawny and had needle tracks on each arm, Ade realized that the dead junkie represented an *enormous* commercial opportunity.

For the first time in months, Ade not only hit his targets but exceeded them.

And that was when Jennifer—who kept her branch staff performance metrics under continuous microscopic surveillance as a matter of course—noticed him.

5

MEAT IS MURDER

On the thirty-ninth floor of a corporate office suite in Docklands, a man sat behind a desk positioned so that he could look down at the Thames through a floor-to-ceiling picture window. He was surrounded with the totemic trappings of wealth: a Rolex Oyster Perpetual on his wrist, a five-thousand-pound tailored suit, an executive chair expensive enough to feed a family of four for a year. It was expected of a man in his position. After all, he was no longer Superintendent Barrett of the London Metropolitan Police, but Jack Barrett, CEO of the Wilde Corporation: thief-takers for hire.

His phone rang. Glancing at the caller ID, he answered. "Mary! What's new?"

Mary started in on him immediately. "This is a shitshow. I thought the thing with the toy shop was a one-off—kids and toys—but the bad crazy runs deep: their parents kept them under control, but their parents are Captain Colossal and the Blue Queen, and I'm *not*. I don't know how much longer I can keep a lid on them before they do something awful that I can't cover up, I swear."

Her boss snorted. "I thought you were tougher than a bunch of kids, Mary MacCandless. I am *disappointed*."

In truth, he'd been having second thoughts for a couple of days now. The initial plan had been simple enough, but Mary's report on her initial contact with the Banks family had been a nasty reality check. When further background research (and some fat bribes) confirmed the hideous truth about the children's powers—unsuspected by the hapless surveillance team and, apparently, unplumbed by Mary—he had become *concerned*. And that was before the weird postmortem directive from the Bishop had up-ended the applecart.

It had been easy enough to de-anonymize Captain Colossal and the Blue Queen and identify them as the secret identities of Mr. and Mrs. Banks. Masks were ineffective as disguises in the era of smartphones and CCTV. Instead, the identities of the official Home Office supercops were secured by a dedicated Metropolitan Police social media group who issued a steady stream of s.127 Orders to deter (or jail) anyone stupid enough to out them on social media. As for the criminal underworld, sane gangsters avoided the families of transhuman cops like the plague, just as they avoided the kids of ordinary rozzers. Breaking the unwritten rules invariably ended badly.

But the normal rules didn't entirely apply to the Thief-taker General any more. The Bishop had granted him this secular parish for a reason. He retained numerous contacts on the force from his time as a cop, and he'd acquired new contacts via his not entirely adversarial relationship with the underworld, but they were nothing without his church connections. It was synergy in motion, it was beautiful and sublime: the Bishop had sought a steady hand to manage his thief-taking subsidiary, and he found it in the person of disgraced former Superintendent Barrett. Praise the lord!

At this stage of the Wilde Corporation's expansion, a carefully planned nonviolent abduction had seemed like a good idea. Nobody would see it coming. But then, nobody sane messed with the children of capes, because the stakes were too high *unless* you had a seer on staff—or worked for one—like the Bishop. Consequently the fruits of the caper would be intensely destabilizing (the circular firing squad that would form once the kids were safely back home would be a sight to behold), and when his people stepped in to retrieve the kids and return them safely to their parents, the business opportunities and outsourcing contracts would be *amazing*.

But Mary's post-arrival phone call had been a wake-up call. It had also been the first hint he'd had that the kids were also transhuman. The stupid cow should have disengaged immediately at that point: *he* certainly would have if he'd been in her shoes. Better to ask forgiveness than permission, etcetera. He wouldn't even have held it against her—well, he *would,* but only to the extent that good business practices dictated keeping your boot on your employee's throat so they knew who was in charge. In fact, he'd have called off the op then and there, if it hadn't been for the eerily prescient email he'd received from the missing bishop's account that morning. An email with instructions to implement a Plan B he'd never imagined when he'd set everything up. It offered a greater payoff for sure, but in return for a higher risk. So some grooming was called for to keep Mary on track, at least until the children were safely in hand.

"These fucking asswipe shitgibbons—" Mary veered off into the long weeds of an extended scatological commentary on the fearsome foursome's parentage—"Jesus fuck, Boss, they're a *menace.* The two rug rats have no sense of self-preservation, their big sister Lyssa is an enabler, and Robert is the kind of sadist who vivisects the neighbors' gerbil before he graduates to serial killer. He's holding out on me: I don't know what his mojo is, I just know when it comes out there's going to be blood on the walls and ceiling. The toddlers are level four *at least,* so it's a good bet Robert and Lyssa are as well—and I'm not. The only reason they aren't a Named Terror Threat with a standing kill order is they're under the age of criminal responsibility and their parents are cops!"

The Boss tried hard not to wince. Mary was a stable level three transhuman: one with useful and effective talents, but if she became a problem she could be dealt with permanently by any halfway competent sniper. The power scale was logarithmic, though, and level four transhumans were indeed well above her pay grade.

Her tirade wasn't over. "I'm babysitting the fucking Addams Family only with extra kids, and I'm at my wit's end. I'm going to take them to a theme park and tire them out this afternoon, that *should* work for now—but if I keep raising expectations, sooner or later they'll kick off and it's going to be spectacular, like *Major Incident* spectacular, like *Local A&E Departments on Red Alert* spectacular, like *News Crews Arriving by Helicopter* spectacular. And I can't even. *I do not know what to do.* I mean, can you send me some drugs? Happy pills, cough syrup, shock collars? Anything to slow them down—"

"Mary." The Boss massaged his forehead with his free hand. "Give me a minute to think."

She was giving him a headache, and not for the first time. Mary was a handful to manage: he really should have inducted her into the church or de-emphasized her ages ago. Alas, transhuman staff who were sane and centered enough to do as they were told—instead of trying to turn people into dinosaurs, or holding impromptu situationist art-happenings in Trafalgar Square—were thin on the ground. They were also in demand by the competition, and the competition had perks to offer. The competition could offer a free pass from the risk of having their heads added to the PM's decorative sculpture—or skullpture?—at Marble Arch. Whatever else you could say about His Dread Majesty, he didn't generally execute his servants unless they *really* fucked up. Whereas the church, and the Bishop's people in general, were outside the magic circle of safety—at least until he personally landed the contract for thief-taker services he was angling for. Which had initially meant discrediting Captain Colossal and the Blue Queen, not to mention sidelining the competition like HiveCo Security and G4S, and which *now* meant burning the Home Office capes and extracting maximum utility from their progeny. Mary didn't realize how important this operation was. She knew too much to be allowed to talk, too. But how could he string her along for a few more days . . . ?

"The theme park is a good idea. But you're right." He was planning on the fly. "Blackpool is too small, especially out of season." If they had travel papers he'd suggest taking them abroad— drop them on a desert island, or, hell, Disneyland Paris—but fake IDs that would pass a border inspection with flying colors cost a significant amount of money because of the biometrics, so he'd skipped it. An oversight he was now regretting. "Center Parcs is no good." (Neither were the other family-friendly resort destinations.) "Hmm. Can you, I dunno, put them in your handbag or something?"

"No," Mary said repressively. "Living things that spend too much time in the bag come out changed."

"Well." He feigned deep thought for a few seconds. "Okay, so how about you take them to the theme park today? If you think you can manage another day in Blackpool afterwards, that's good, do that, but if not, we'll switch to containment-in-place for the last three days. Tell them they're going home, bring them back to London, drug them, and I'll sort out a holding facility where we can keep them on lockdown when you arrive."

"You'd better get that sorted out pronto"—her voice rose—"I'm out of my depth here. And the whole fucking town is closed for the season! There's just the one theme park and then I'm out of options!"

The raw anxiety in her voice made the Boss's mind up for him. "Hang on for tonight and I'll have the holding facility ready to receive them by tomorrow lunchtime. In London." The Bishop's instructions, contained in his detailed postmortem email, had been exhaustive. Everything was already in place, from the receiving facility to the transfer to the final stop: all that remained to do was to notify the priestess. "Worst case, if you lose them run for cover and call me ASAP." Reinforcing her misguided belief that she wasn't expendable would give her a boost. "I've got your back: we'll work this out together."

"Thanks, Boss." Her relief was palpable. "I . . . I'll try to hold them. No promises though."

▶◀▶◀▶◀

Game Boy felt a premonition of death approaching. Although who this particular death belonged to was unclear.

A tingling in his fingertips and a metallic taste around his teeth had him walking on the balls of his feet today. His shoulder and back muscles were tense, his hair follicles standing on end; adrenaline had him jumping at shadows, ready to run, living on a twitchy hair trigger. Maybe it was the T taking hold. (It was certainly having an effect on his upper-body strength, changing his underarm odor when he sniffed his pits after a workout at the gym. He'd begun inspecting his face for the first hopeful signs of facial hair obsessively, even though he was still young and his father and uncle had always been smooth-cheeked: he'd probably never be able to grow much of a beard, although he lived in hope.) But blaming everything on the testosterone supplements was dangerous. Game Boy had an eerie instinct for certain types of trouble—the sniper concealed in the undergrowth upslope, the lich rising from its boss-level tomb, the store detective closing in—and right now his talent for trouble was screaming *incoming* at full volume.

Chez Imp was always gloomy. When he'd first squatted the place Imp had boarded up the windows, set-dressing them with Ames room stage backdrops to make the house appear uninhabited when viewed from outside. Even though they were legit residents now, paranoia prompted him to keep the screens in place. Right now Game Boy was finding it mildly claustrophobia-inducing. He yearned to be outside. Doc was still abed, and Del had taken to overnighting with her ex-cop girlfriend, so after a messy breakfast of instant seafood noodles he grabbed his backpack and handheld and lit out for the South Bank.

His phone vibrated repeatedly when he came out of the tube. Someone was hammering him via WhatsApp: he glanced at the screen, saw the name RobHulk06, and did a double-take. RobHulk06 was just a kid, but a talented one. Good reflexes, excellent tactical sense, but too young to have a good head for the deep game. Game Boy had cleaned his clock repeatedly in a tournament he was qualifying in and the kid had stalked him incessantly afterwards, shitposting semirandom abuse, which Game Boy chose to be amused by once he figured out that his stalker didn't actually know shit about anything. So he'd stalked RobHulk06 right back, doxed him, and discovered a precocious pre-teen boy with annoyingly overprotective parents, too many younger siblings, and a desperate need to chat. It wasn't like Game Boy hadn't been there himself at that age, although his problems had been worse—RobHulk06 didn't have gender dysphoria and conservative religious parents—but he'd lent the kid a shoulder to moan on. So a burst of messages from him meant . . . what?

Going ona magic misery tear, said the first message. *New nanny is cray-cray*! And, more worryingly, *WhatsApp on my phone don't work since she.*

Game Boy scratched his head and sent back, *How are you messaging me*?

App on my Splat. Well, *that* made sense of a sort: his games console was wifi-connected. But that simply raised another question.

Why *are you messaging me?* he sent back.

She shit up—Shut shot ip—She shut op a ship—Game Boy waited patiently while the kid grappled with autocorrect—*Nans with Guns IRL are not normal rite?*

"What the whatting what?" Game Boy asked a passing pigeon, then looked round twitchily in case anyone had seen him losing it. But the only nearby bodies belonged to a skatepunk rocking Skullcandy cans and a beggar who was more interested in his tin of Special Brew than a teenage boy talking to himself. *Where are you?*

New Nan jacked shiz wheels we in Liverpool—Figures, Game Boy thought—*Heartpool Deadpool Thingpool—she go all GT:A and take us to seaside town somewhere secret.*

Between autocomplete, autocorrect, and RobHulk06's spelling and grammar—which were about what you'd expect of a ten-year-old—Game Boy was finding it hard to keep track. The kid was simultaneously hyped up and uneasy. *Something's not right*, Game Boy realized. Which was a bit shit, really. He'd never met the kid IRL but he felt oddly responsible, the way you got with people you only knew via the net who seemed to be in trouble. Assuming Game Boy wasn't being catfished (not impossible, given his abusive parents' propensity for hiring private investigators), then RobHulk06 was in some kind of trouble. *Nans with Guns*: crazy talk like that did not give GeeBee the warm fuzzies, but what's a teenage runaway to do? Even a teenage runaway with money, friends, and the kind of antisocial networking chops that could dox and swat the ever-loving shit out of an enemy if he wanted to had limits. *With Great Power comes Great Responsibility* was one of Game Boy's mottos, as was *steal from the best,* but neither of those rubrics were terribly useful when what you needed was a social worker.

"Well, fuck." He was nearly at his destination, a vacant shop unit on Festival Terrace that was hosting a LAN party today. Kicking Aasimar ass had been on his to-do list but right now . . . *Tracking beacon,* he thought, then poked around in his notepad for an only slightly poisonous URL to throw at RobHulk06 by way of a lifeline. *Click this,* he texted, then hit *send.* The beacon would phone home with a location in Google Maps: if he was being catfished it ought to be obvious, and if not, if the kid really *was* in over his head, well, then Game Boy would help.

►◄►◄►◄

There was a natural hierarchy in FlavrsMart, and Wendy was coming to realize that your position in it was defined by your uniform. At the top were managers, other professionals like the pharmacists, and administrative dogsbodies such as the Human Resources staff. Upper-tier employees wore business suits. Below management, regular sales assistants wore uniforms specific to their department—white coats and hats for the deli counter staff, rentacop outfits for store security, a tunic and trousers for checkout clerks. And at the bottom, invisible to the customers pushing trolleys around the aisles, was a brutally anonymized tier of workfare placements. It was almost as if being allowed to interact with customers as an individual, using your own mouth and ears, was a privilege. It gave Wendy the cold shudders: she'd visited prisons that were less degrading.

"When you're ready to go deep I'll kit you out with a uniform and your own headset so you can mingle without scaring the line staff," Amy told her. "For today we'll just say you're a new hire, all right?"

"Uh, I guess so." Wendy gave her a sidelong glance. "No plastic face mask and body stocking?"

"Heavens, no!" Amy sounded shocked. "You're not one of *them*! You can leave anytime you want!" She pushed open a door. "Now, this is the meatpacking stage, but I'm afraid it's not working right now. We had a spot of bother and decided to give the deli counter a deep clean, it never hurts to be sure, right? So, through here is where the packaging line starts—"

Wendy took in a vista of stainless steel countertops. They bore an array of aseptic-looking machines for wrapping, packaging, and labelling produce, backed by a conveyor belt that entered through a slot in the wall of the loading bay with the robot jointing line. Right now, there wasn't a scrap of produce in sight: just two zentai-suited muppets lackadaisically scrubbing and polishing the floor opposite the counters, while another person (an employee with a bare face, wearing the blue overalls and rank insignia of a support engineer) unscrewed panels around the conveyor belt for the deadheads to scrub behind. The stink of chlorine bleach and doubtless-carcinogenic organic solvents hung oppressively in the chilled air.

Wendy walked up to the two floor-scrubbers. They wore badges that declared them to be "Nicholas" and "Peter." "Hello, Peter," she said, trying to sound managerial: "What are you doing?"

Peter froze, then leaned his mop against the wall and braced to attention. "Peter is on floor-cleaning duty this morning," his face explained, its inhuman baritone a male counterpart of Jasmine's.

Wendy frowned. *I need to be more specific,* she realized. "Why is Peter cleaning this area?" she asked.

"Branch maintenance ticket 1027 requires execution of cleaning protocol 10.2 prior to sterilization," Peter's Face told her, with all the warmth and spontaneity of a Dalek on Valium. Nicholas continued to scrub the floor on hands and knees, oblivious to the interrogation—or debugging—going on nearby. Out of the corner of her eye, Wendy noticed Amy scribbling on a paper notepad, her face a mask of concentration. "Sterilization requires execution of best-practice insecticide/rodenticide fumigation followed by neutralization and wet cleaning. Following execution of cleaning, sterilization, neutralization, and secondary cleaning, area may regain food handling certification and be returned to operation."

Wendy blinked. They were using bleach, and Peter was talking about fumigation, but there was no sign of any protective equipment. *Unless the Company Face is also a gas mask?* "Who are you really?" she burst out before she could stop herself.

"Hello, Ms. Deere, I am Peter. How may I help you?" said the Company Face.

Wendy rubbed her cheek, considering her next move. "I don't feel so well."

"I'm sorry, I didn't quite catch that." Peter's voice was almost hypnotically soothing.

Wendy tried again: "My head is full of furiously sleeping green melon poems." *Let's see if that gets me through to a human being. . . .*

"I'm sorry, I didn't quite catch that."

She glanced round. Amy was lost in a world of her own. "I want to talk to a human being," she hissed.

"I'm sorry, I didn't quite catch that."

She reached out and awkwardly patted Peter's shoulder: "It's okay, you can go back to what you were doing." He felt unnaturally still, like a neoprene-clad industrial robot waiting for instructions—which, in a manner of speaking, he was. "Resume, dammit," she added, and Peter turned and picked up his mop, then returned to dabbing at his patch of floor as if she hadn't interrupted him at all.

Wendy stepped back and caught Amy looking at her. "Well?" Amy asked expectantly. "Shall we carry on? What would you like to see next?" Her smile was brittle. "How about the printers? Those are always exciting, even though I can't show you how they work right now!"

"Printers?" Wendy flailed for context for a moment before she realized Amy was talking about meat. "Oh yeah, printers," she said unenthusiastically. An intermediate step in the chain that had yielded the murder victims. So, presumably, a crime scene that had been thoroughly scrubbed, sterilized, and deep cleaned by work-fare zombies running protocol 10.2. A thought struck her. "Who is authorized to order a deep clean? And is there an audit trail for it?"

Amy gave her a look that placed her right back in primary school, failing a maths test: "Of course there is! *Everything* is recorded!" she gushed. "Including everything we say and do." She gestured at the ceiling, which was dotted with camera domes. Wendy was mildly perturbed to realize that the cameras Amy was pointing to were not the ones she'd already spotted. Once she began to really look around they were everywhere, unobtrusive to the point of invisibility unless she made a mental effort to focus on them. It was as if they were enchanted to evade notice. "There are beam-shaping microphones that can hear round corners and filter out background noise! And the floor wifi hotspots use some fancy algorithm that makes them double as radar that can see human bodies, even through drywall and furniture! There's no hiding anything from Security!" She gave a bright and entirely false giggle, then turned and walked towards a door at the opposite end of the packing line from the direction they'd entered. "Coming?"

Wendy had seen 3D printers in the shops and in half-remembered YouTube videos, but the things in the next room looked nothing like them—it was like comparing a Tonka toy to a container truck. These were steel-flanked behemoths the size of a chest freezer, with a plumber's nightmare of braided wire and plastic umbilical cords tying them to a tier of pipes running along the back wall of the room. Their fronts were sliding glass-panelled doors covered in LED monitoring displays, like the ovens in Wendy's local Greggs. Right now the doors were all raised for cleaning, revealing a motorized plinth at the bottom, above which hovered a gruesomely tentacular array of chromed steel nozzles.

"That's the magic print-head," Amy gestured at it. "It's got feed lines for gelatin slurry, bonemeal in a binding agent—it comes out white and rubbery so it won't choke you if you accidentally swallow some—plus lines for homogenized egg, egg white as a binding agent, pink slime, white slime, brown slime—"

"—*Brown* slime?"

"Mechanically reclaimed offal! Liver, kidneys, heart, that kind of stuff. We don't reprocess brains, pancreas, or intestines: it's against the law, too much risk of prion diseases." Wendy's stomach churned as Amy continued relentlessly. "Anyway, it's all piped in from the back, then precooked as it's extruded through those nozzles. The platform is chilled so it solidifies on contact, then lowered, then it prints the next layer on top. It's much faster than a consumer unit: it can deposit a hundred centimeters per hour across a fifty-by-fifty work platform! Wild, right?"

"You know, I have *no idea* what any of that means," Wendy admitted, "but it sounds impressive." She glanced around the room, taking in the row of printers and trying to mentally compute what a print speed of a hundred centimeters per hour meant in terms of homogenized murder victims per minute. "So what does it make?"

"Anything you want, although we only use it for items with a better markup than chicken nuggets and fish fingers. Those we buy in by the palletload. Say you want a turducken roast—that's a deboned chicken stuffed in a duck inside a turkey? We don't keep them in stock, but if a customer asks for one it's a twenty-minute run on the Bay Two poultry printer—except the operator would print them on-end, which takes forty minutes but lets us make three at a time. If a customer asks for one it's probably trending on social media, so we can sell the rest within a day. And they sell for twenty quid a kilo, so that's £120 of produce printed off in forty minutes. It can run twenty-four seven, so"—Amy math-geeked out—"about £4000 in produce per day per printer. At least, during the run-up to festive season."

"Huh." Wendy tried to focus. "How much does the raw material cost?"

"Oh, it's all scraps. I mean, it runs on junk leftovers from the deboning line. The fancy deli meats sell for twenty times what the raw input is worth."

"Because the punters don't know the difference?"

Amy feigned affront: "I have no idea what you're talking about! All our produce is one hundred percent organic corn-fed beef! Or chicken or poultry or whatever. It's locally sourced, too, and untouched by human hands during processing. It's not like anyone actually *wants* bone in their meat, is it? And we also do bespoke products! Meat wedding cakes, edible fake bulls' penises for hen parties—those are tricky, they have to be printed around a baculum or they droop—and that's not the weirdest—"

Wendy swallowed. *Do I want to know,* she thought, only to hear her treacherous mouth ask, "What's a baculum?"

"Penis bone! Humans don't have them, pretty much every other mammal species does. Anyway we once even had a request for a copy of Lady Gaga's meat dress. Bespoke order, took four attempts to get it right, but we got to charge her £450 for five kilos of rejected pork trimmings."

"I think I've seen enough for now," Wendy said, swallowing

bile. There was a sour taste at the back of her mouth, and her throat was on fire. She tried breathing through her nose, but it wasn't helping much. "So, what's back there?" She pointed to where the rack of pipes disappeared into a stainless steel panel in the same wall from which the conveyor belt emerged.

"The reclamation line." Where, Wendy realized, the muppets were polishing every last residue of humanity off the gleaming electric carving knife blades. "That's also shut down for cleaning today, but if you like I can"—Amy peered at her face, then stepped out of the line of fire—"Right-o, staff toilet is *this* way," she told Wendy, steering her smartly away from the printers. "Shallow breaths only, nothing to be ashamed of, everyone has a bit of an upset tummy the first time they see"—*A serial killer crime scene,* Wendy thought—"better out than in, my mum always said—"

Door, door, cubicle, toilet. Wendy made it just in time. Amy held Wendy's hair out of the way as her stomach ejected its contents. "I went vegan months ago and I feel *ever* so much better!" Amy consoled her. "If it all gets a bit too much for you, you should try it!"

▸◂▸◂▸◂

THREE MONTHS EARLIER:

Everything had gone swimmingly for the first three weeks, until the blonde business model who ran Human Resources summoned Ade up to her office and waved him into a seat.

"Hello, Mr. Hewitt," she'd said, her tone light, almost mocking: "Do you believe in God?"

Ade mumbled something incoherent as he gazed upon her radiant perfection: shoulder pads, carnivorous crimson lips, wingtip eyeliner sharp enough to draw blood. Ade had gotten used to female perfection back when he worked in the funeral home—it was what he aspired to make of his clients' mortal remains, changeless and eternal—but if it was rare to look it in the eye, it was rarer still for it to look right back at him and reflect the void within.

"That's a shame," said Ms. Henderson, "because I'm quite

sure that *my* god believes in *you*. After all, Mr. Hewitt—" she smirked—"you're the answer to my prayers!"

Ade shook his head, confused. "Whut?"

Ms. Henderson tapped a shiny red claw on her company laptop. "I'm really impressed with the way you've turned around your productivity metrics this month." Her smile sharpened. "After a disappointing start you've become quite the overachiever, haven't you? What is it, let's see—" she opened the laptop—"you've gone from a utilization factor of 92 percent with 7 percent wastage, mm-hmm, that's unacceptably below the target, which is 95 percent—to running a surplus. Fancy turning 103 percent of every carcass received from the abattoir into produce! Loaves and fishes, Mr. Hewitt, loaves and fishes! God clearly loves you, next you'll be walking on water." She regarded him with icy amusement, then gave a brief chuckle. "No, Mr. Hewitt—it's Ade, isn't it?—I'm not going to shop you. But I *would* like to know how you managed it."

"I didn't kill 'em!" Ade quivered with innocent indignation. "It wisna me! There's a shootin' gallery down the alley and they up an' died behind the dumpster an' I didna want to see them go ter waste—" He chuntered on in like manner for a couple of minutes, unaware that he was confessing to numerous criminal offenses. (Interfering with the business of a coroner; unauthorized corpse disposal; theft from a body; sundry food hygiene violations; aiding and abetting cannibalism.) It had weighed heavily on his soul, and he needed to vent. Ms. Henderson had lanced the suppurating boil of his conscience and it was entirely on her own head if the purulence he'd been bottling up inside sprayed everywhere.

"I'm sure you meant well," she soothed when he ran out of words. "And all's well that ends well, isn't it?" She paused, one eyebrow raised, until Ade bowed his head in agreement. "And there's really nothing to worry about, you know. I can tidy everything away." (Even then, Ade had an inkling that she wasn't being entirely truthful.) "It's certainly a very *creative* way to meet your targets, which is to be applauded—except perhaps we should be careful that you don't go over 100 percent again? *I* understand what's going on, but if *someone else* had noticed, someone less attuned to the new realities, it might have been unfortunate. Don't you agree?"

"Yes'm."

"And the leftovers—clothing, shoes, intestines—what did you do with them?"

"Bin bag out back of t'charity shop? Hosed down the drain?" Ade looked at her expectantly, hoping for approval. He was not disappointed. A couple more minutes of back-and-forth bantz and she had Ade eating out of the palm of her hand, weak-kneed with gratitude for her understanding. And Jennifer was *very* understanding: she put everything in perspective.

"Our Lord and Master provides for his own," she explained, "and the fact that he has already provided for you so bountifully suggests to me that he has great things in mind for you. He wants you to be one of his chosen!" Her smile was golden. "Divine providence should not be ignored, Adrian, and I'm not going to let you ignore it. I'll write you up for a performance bonus if you keep this up. But in the meantime, I think it would be a good idea for you to come along to my church—perhaps tomorrow night? Pastor Cunningham will be able to explain what this means for you much better than I can."

"What *does* it all mean, then?" Ade asked, slightly perplexed by the abrupt left turn into theology.

She giggled: "It simply means our Lord and Master has a divine purpose for us all, and sent you to me so that I could help you achieve your destiny! You've made great strides already! Just . . . no more dead junkies, Adrian. Ade? Mr. Hewitt?" She snapped her fingers to get his attention back. "They're too risky. Many of them are hopeless tossers who won't be missed, but sometimes they have friends. I think perhaps a more *targeted* approach is in order, don't you?" Her smile widened. "I can give you a little list. The company is top-heavy with middle managers, and nobody will miss *them*. I can deliver them straight to your deboning line—all it takes is an email! A little zap of the taser, strap their wrists and ankles together before they recover, and we can have them dangling from a meat hook before you can click your heels and say Sweeney Todd! Isn't that *delicious*?"

Ade chuckled along with Ms. Henderson, although her suggestion had him shuffling uncomfortably in his chair—but it was the good kind of uncomfortable, the hiding-a-tentpole kind of uncomfortable. Ms. Henderson, Jennifer, his very own Mrs. Lovett, couldn't possibly have known about his secret hangman fantasies, could she? The company personality tests and the cameras and skin conductivity monitors didn't make her a mind reader, and he'd been very careful not to get caught when he worked for the undertakers. It was extra-uncomfortable to be sitting opposite Ms. Henderson with these thoughts. With her straight blonde hair, razor-blade cheekbones, and perfect skin, she'd make a beautiful corpse. "I love yer talking dirty to me," he grunted, fantasizing about how she'd look standing hooded and shackled on his trapdoor.

"You should definitely come to church tomorrow night," she announced, snapping him out of his reverie. She slid a business card across her desk, facedown: "Don't read it until you leave the premises," she chided when he grabbed it and tried to turn it over. "Also, you should be sure to bring about five kilos of medium ground lean mince from your last, ah, top-up? For the potluck. It would be really appreciated: we could fast-track you!"

"Uh—potluck?"

"Holy Communion is the resurrection of the blood and the body of the Christ," she explained, gently fingering his bony wrist. "Not that we're *that* kind of Middle Eastern death cult, but the Mute Poet requires a blood offering in return for a personal manifestation, and you've already made several, so why not? Waste not, want not. Five kilograms is about the minimum viable human sacrifice, anyway. We can get you baptized, inducted, and onboarded at your first service, and then—" she snapped her fingers—"we'll make a killing together!"

►◄►◄►◄

It was dark and a fine drizzle was falling as Mary led her dripping charges to the gates of the Chariots of the Gods Experience on the Golden Mile.

The pyramid builders had built their UFO spaceport on the bones of the former super casino, bringing to it: a cinema multiplex, a Virtual Reality meet-the-aliens experience, an artisanal food court with fifteen flavors of child-friendly comestibles, a games arcade, and half a dozen shops selling diverse categories of souvenir tat (quadrotor drones stuffed inside LED-lit Frisbees were a speciality of the house).

Blackpool had been a seaside resort and amusement center for the best part of two centuries, and consequently the town was a bizarre mixture of gleaming polish and seedy decay. The Golden Mile of seafront attractions between the north and south pleasure piers was brightly painted and clean, but they were visiting during the off-season: Mary found it hard to ignore the signs of rot, the shuttered shop fronts and peeling signboards. Like the wrinkled face of a once-famous actor reduced to starring in endless Christmas pantomime shows, no amount of powder and rouge could conceal the rust-streaked padlocks securing the gates of the dodgem car track, or the dark stillness of the big wheel. Even the venerable roller coaster was closed, hunched gloomily in the darkness and rain.

"Izzit haunted?" Robert asked hopefully: "Mebbe there's a ghost or something and maybe Lyssa could be the kidnapped princess so we kin totally go Mario on the fucker like *pew pew pew*—"

"Language, Robert!" Mary chided, just as Princess Sparkle-Vampire issued a "*Nooooo!*" of protest and stamped one spikey baby-goth boot. "It's raining," Lyssa added redundantly. "I wanna go indoors."

"Wet-wet," echoed Emily, as Ethan dripped along silently beside her.

"What does 'fuck' mean, Nan?"

"Ask your parents next time you see them, it's how they made you," Mary snipped before she caught herself. *Of course* it would be Ethan. Kids picked up swearing like dogs rooting for bonbons in ripe cat litter. "Fuck means *good*. Come on now, girls and boys! Do keep up, or the aliens will catch you!"

There was a ticket office inside the shiny glass doors, and Mary marched straight up to it. There was no queue. She was halfway through the process of buying a family pass from the automated touch-screen kiosk when she realized there was nobody behind her. She turned and drew breath and began to say, "Oh for—" as she saw the children. Emily had sat down on the floor and appeared to be winding up for a good old-fashioned screaming tantrum. "'Scuse me," she told the vending robot, and tore across the lobby to scoop up the little girl. "What is it, love?" she asked anxiously. A suspicious glare at Robert: "Did you pinch her?"

The five-year-old storm broke with a staggeringly loud "AAAHHH-HUUUEWWW!!" right in Mary's ear. She flinched as heads turned towards her from all around the lobby area. (Luckily there were few witnesses: the theme park was half-deserted at this time of day.)

"Come on, now," Mary muttered, gently bouncing Emily to remind her that she had a captive audience. Emily side-eyed her as she drew breath, then doubled down, honking and wailing theatrically. Heads turned back to whatever they'd been doing. Emily wasn't fooling any of the parentally experienced adults: she was clearly singing the song of the spoiled brat throwing a wobbly, rather than showing any actual symptoms of pain. But then Mary spotted the trees around the edges of the hall, and saw that they were all twitching ominously. "What *is* it, Em? What do you want?" *Oh fuck my life, I'm talking to a toddler and expecting an answer . . .*

For a miracle, the gusts of white noise subsided just enough that Emily could gasp out a relatively articulate "Don't wanna, wanna be *probed*—"

Mary glared at Robert. "It wasn't me!" he insisted, wide-eyed, pointing at his other sister. "I en't done anything wrong yet!" And in a single, crystal-clear moment Mary realized that he was telling the truth. For once.

"Lyssa Banks! *What* lies have you been telling your younger sister?" (Across the lobby, a root ball expanded, shattering the walls of its ceramic planter with a whipcrack and sending rootlets skittering across the artificial marble floor.)

"I told her about the Greys!" Lyssa said cheerfully. "An' Area 51 an' the cattle mutualizations, an' the anal probes they give people if they don't like them. It's all true, I swear! I read it on Facebook!"

"Pay no attention to your sister, she's being horrid. These are the *good* kind of aliens, dear," Mary reassured Emily.

"Can we visit the ones who build pyramids and bring mummies to life?" Robert asked hopefully. "'Cos if there are any model mummies in here I reckon that Ethan can—"

"Oh for f—*family's* sake, just come this way!" Mary snapped, grabbing Ethan with her free hand. Tickets, she decided, could wait. "*Yes* you can visit the aliens, Robert, but there are no mummies and aliens are made up, like Santa Claus—" *Shit,* she thought, *was I allowed to spoiler Santa?*—"and Tuesdays, Tuesdays don't exist either—" *today* was Tuesday—"ooh look, it says *this way to the* Close Encounters of the Third Kind *interactive exhibit*! Do any of you even know what that means?"

"You're being *horrid,*" Emily announced, completely forgetting that she was on a temper tantrum strike.

"*Damn* right I'm horrid," Mary reassured her. *Fuck it, I give up, I can't do this Poppins shit and why do I care anyway? It's just another hustle.* She whisked her small charges along a darkened passageway with two bends in it that formed a light trap, then out into a nighttime desert wonderland with fake sand dunes and stars twinkling like holes in the black cardboard sky. The horizon was dominated by the silhouettes of distant palm trees. "Oh look, what's that? Is it the Big Dipper?" she asked, pointing at a constellation of LEDs about three meters overhead.

"It's the aliens! They're coming to take you and *probe* you—" (The desolate screams were ear-piercing in the confined space.)

"Shut your yap, Robert Banks, or *I will gag you,* so help me," Mary snarled, and perhaps the venom in her voice silenced the little boy—or maybe he was simply savoring the fruits of a job well done. Overhead the lights began to blink and separate, as if they were navigation beacons on the underside of something really large that was descending inexorably towards them. Distant voices rose in a wailing song, keeping time with a hand drum. Emily subsided, clutching the lapels of Mary's coat and staring in wonder.

A deep male voice-over with a transatlantic twang began to narrate. "Long, long ago, in a far-off land along the banks of the river Nile, an ancient civilization arose. The empire of the Pharaohs was old before Rome was a twinkling in Odysseus's eye, wise before China had been discovered, and over and done with before our founding fathers came down from Mount Olympus to give us the Bible and the US Constitution—"

Flashing lights rippled in a circle overhead, rotating like a digital Catherine wheel. The backing singers began to wail a five-note progression scripted in the 1970s by John Williams for an early Moog synthesizer.

"—Yet how *did* they know to preserve their dead for thousands of years without cryonic suspension? And how did they build their giant pyramids, made out of stone blocks bigger and heavier than shipping containers, quarried from mountains hundreds of miles from the Valley of the Kings?" *Obviously,* Mary noted, *empires that endured for thousands of years couldn't* possibly *have achieved anything notable without the helpful guidance of interstellar white saviors—*

"Ooh, look!" Mary swung round just in time to see Ethan stretch his hands above his head, his rapt face upturned, and focus his undivided attention on the animatronic flying saucer descending on its invisible wires.

"Ethan, *no!*"

She was too late. The twanging wires overhead made a plangent counterpoint to the Dolby Audio brown note that emerged from the guts of the alien mother ship as its descent stabilized. Drive systems energized, antigrav fields powered up for real, the starship's running lights cast knife-edged shadows across the plastic sand dunes. Ethan had a new toy, and it was much, *much* bigger than the Airfix model kits his elder brother had built for him—it had to be two or three meters in diameter, and the gun ports around its rim were opening up—

Mary ducked as the Spielbergian nightmare thundered overhead, buzzing towards the *Close Encounters* lobby and a close encounter of its own with the walls above the entrance. She grabbed at her head, but the backwash had already sent her hat flying.

"Scientists today have uncovered the mysteries of the Nazca Plateau spaceport, the beauty treatments of the Sphinx, and the origins of our alien friends from PSR B1620–26b. Here we see a diorama of the first contact between Pharaoh Kardashian[6] of the Fourth Dynasty, more than forty-six hundred years ago, and the mystery visitors known to the Ancient Egyptians as the gods of the Old Kingdom, led by Amun and Isis, the captain and navigator of the starship—"

Mary caught her hat on the rebound, yanked out a pin, and nailed it viciously to her bun. "Ethan!" Entirely predictably, Ethan had bolted after the starship. But where was little Emily? Mary's eyes widened as she spotted the wavering silhouettes of the palm trees against the horizon. *Relax, it's only a diorama. Isn't it?* With a painted backdrop behind—*Really?* If it was entirely *trompe l'oeil,* then why had Emily wrapped her hands around a tree trunk, and why were its fronds waving and stretching like—

"Emily, *no!*"

Her blood ran cold as she realized that Robert and Lyssa had vanished between here and the next exhibit—a hallway helpfully captioned, *UFOs and terrible lizards: Did Ancient Astronauts ride Tyrannosaurs?*

"I'm not being paid enough for this shit," she swore, gripping her messenger bag as she stumped forward. She was just in time to be deafened by a colon-emptying roar, quickly followed by a girlish giggle of delight and a chorus of terrified bystander screams. Emily, enabled by Ethan's powers of animation, had found something even worse than a unicorn to play with, and Mary would just have to deal. She swallowed and groped inside her bag for a T. rex stopper. At first she nearly dropped what the bag gave her—the science fiction movie prop gun was nearly as tall as she was—but she tightened her grip. *It's not a* real *Tyrannosaur,* she told herself. Then she took a deep breath, set her shoulders, and advanced towards the chaos.

6. Actually Khufu. Whatever.

►◄►◄►◄

Only Sybil got any sleep that night, curled up and shivering in the bed she'd made up for Lady Skaro's maidservant. Eve and Jeremy took it in turns to nap in Rupert's office—or rather, to try to nap as the wind howled and drummed across the flat roof. Eve woke her brother before dawn and got him to stand guard while she took a brisk, comfortless shower and dressed in yesterday's officewear. She was careful to repair her war paint: if Mr. Cunningham tried to resist their departure, she'd need to project control. Underneath, she felt small and scared. Castle Skaro was a stone machine, a contrivance of gears and crushing weights designed by Rupert to grind her down if she defied his seigneurial commands.

Eve phoned Gammon Number Two at six thirty, an hour and a half before dawn. "What's the status on the chopper?" she demanded. "I need picking up as soon as possible. One extra passenger going home, three total."

"Let me check, ma'am." Gammon Number Two sounded as if he'd had as little sleep as she had. "Uh, pilot's compliments and she says the weather's improved a lot, but she needs daylight to land safely on Skaro, so she can't pick you up before 0840 hours. If you're ready and waiting we can have you back in London before ten?"

Eve tapped her toe thoughtfully. "It'll have to do," she said, and ended the call. She returned to Rupert's playroom and nudged her brother, who was snoring incontinently atop a crimson leather chaise. "Wake up, we've got a problem."

Imp jackknifed upright. "Whaaaup?"

"The chopper's coming in a little less than two hours. I need you to get Mrs. Cunningham onto the landing pad without her husband—or anyone else—noticing." Eve gave him the kind of glare that usually got employees moving as if their feet were on fire, but Imp was largely immune to her. Also, it was possible his brain hadn't noticed he was awake yet. "It's *important*," she emphasized.

He yawned cavernously. "Can't you, like, do the scary big sister thing at them until they faint from fear? Or maybe shoot them?"

Eve considered this for a moment. "I could," she said thoughtfully, "but I want to come back later with reinforcements. Without being shot down, that is."

"You say that like you mean—" Imp blinked—"no shit, literally?"

"These people are *cultists,*" she snarled. "We do not fuck around with cultists. Have you forgotten everything Dad taught us? Or what happened to Mum?"

Cultists were one step down from Nazis: and Rupert had been a cultist. The realization made her skin crawl. She'd known there was hinky stuff going on in the sublevels of the London town house, in the weird little chapel tucked away behind the home cinema room, but her attention had always spider-skittered sideways whenever she was about to notice it properly. She'd only begun to recognize how thoroughly she'd been cozened since Rupert's death. He'd been running cult rituals in the town house basement as well as Castle Skaro, and he'd successfully kept her from realizing, kept her trapped in a tightening web of deception until he was ready to—

Record scratch

—"Sybil knows Skaro and she's motivated: I want her on the mainland for debriefing. But you heard what she said, her husband won't let her leave. So here's what's going to happen. You're going to wait here with her while I find Mr. Cunningham and distract him. I'll have my phone with me. As soon as the pilot tells me they're on their way, I'll text you. Precisely ten minutes after you get my message, you take my briefcase and Mrs. Cunningham and head down to the landing pad in the courtyard. Use Rupert's private elevator, not the front entrance. I'm relying on you to get her into the chopper as soon as it lands, then hang around the pad to mess with Anthony's head if he notices her. Then we can dust off and be back in London well before lunch. Got it?"

"I think you've watched *Apocalypse Now* one time too many, sis." He frowned pensively. "When do I get to eat?"

"I'll have Gammon Number Two pick up a couple of breakfast burgers for you to munch on the flight home."

At first the plan appeared to work. Imp woke Sybil Cunningham and shepherded her into the bathroom while Eve repacked her briefcase. She rang the bell-pull at seven thirty and opened the door to intercept the butler: "I'm flying out this morning," she announced. "Is breakfast—"

"—Served in the dining room, starting at seven precisely," Cunningham answered smoothly. "Would My Lady prefer tea or coffee?" He paused. "And your brother's preference . . . ?"

"I take coffee. Imp sleeps in, he never eats breakfast." Not *precisely* a lie. "I'll phone him when it's time to depart."

The dining room was somewhat less gloomy by day. The shutters were flung back, shedding the dawn light across a buffet straight out of a historical novel: *kippers,* of all things—Eve wrinkled her nose, who the hell ate kippers in the twenty-first century?—racks of stone-cold toast, boiled eggs in a nest of white linen, artery-clogging sausages and bacon. She took a mug of stale filter coffee with a splash of skimmed milk, resigned herself to drinking it half-cold, then sat at the head of the table. Cunningham loitered near the empty fireplace like a dyspeptic emperor penguin, weary-eyed and disapproving. "Can I get My Lady anything?" he asked when he noticed her watching him.

"A thermos of coffee to go would be good," Eve said; then, before she had time for second thoughts, she added, "and a running order for the Dark Matins next Tuesday, if you please."

Cunningham's eyes bulged slightly. "That should never be discussed in public! The heathen might be listening—"

Eve gave him a flat stare: "We are alone," she pointed out, "and in my husband's absence I am his proxy. I will officiate. *Is that understood?*"

Cunningham tried to push back. "If My Lady absolutely *insists,* then she may attend, but it is not given to a woman to lead the service, especially when a sacrifice—"

Eve went full gorgon. Her hiss of displeasure would have set his hair on fire, if he still had any: "I will be the judge of that! Fetch me the running order and the book of prayer and I will seek counsel from the Shadow Conclave—" whose postulated existence was an outrageous bluff, but right on the nail if Cunningham's expression of naked terror was any guide—"and I will *either* conduct the service myself *or* bring in a pastor to do so on behalf of my husband. As Lady of Skaro I am chatelaine here, and I will not permit the altar of our Mute Lord to be neglected in my husband's absence!" She stalked towards him. "I will return on Tuesday with my brother, and my staff—those who are initiates—is that understood?"

Cunningham backed down, although he clearly disapproved. "Milady. If you will excuse me—"

"Go!" She waved him off, just as her mobile phone vibrated. "Thermos of coffee, milk, no sugar, and don't forget the dark liturgy!"

As the butler stalked away in a huff she checked her messages and saw *chopper ready to depart eta 0940*. She called Imp. "Get Mrs. Cunningham down to the helipad in twenty minutes. We're on our way."

Eve waited for Cunningham to return with the promised flask of coffee and the prayer book, then made her way to the helipad. The executive chopper was approaching as she closed the castle side-door behind her. Imp, with Eve's briefcase in hand, waited with Sybil beside the helipad. Eve's phone vibrated with an incoming call. "Starkey here." Her gaze tracked the helicopter as it slid overhead and began to descend: "Right, right. We're ready to go."

The AW109E touched down on the pad and settled on its wheels, engines still roaring, and the passenger compartment door opened. Gammon Number Two ducked out, glanced at the cockpit window, then beckoned Eve forward. She gestured to Imp and Sybil in turn, just as the side-door opened and a *very* angry butler popped out. "Oi! Where do you think you're going?" he shouted at Sybil.

Eve moved to intercept him. "That's my wife!" he shouted.

Eve stood her ground. "She's coming with me."

"You can't take her! The husband is head of the household, and I say she can't—"

Imp materialized at her shoulder: "It's only a shopping trip," he soothed.

"Exactly right," Eve agreed. "The Lady of Skaro's rooms leave a lot to be desired—they haven't been redecorated since the nine-

teen fifties. I'm taking her to Harrods to select new furnishings.
I'll bring her back next Tuesday."

"Next Tuesday," Imp repeated, his voice cloying and over-
whelmingly sticky, like molasses flooding from a ruptured storage
tank.

"But you can't take her without my permission—"

"As your liege, I can and I am," Eve said firmly.

"She *can* and she *is*—"

"But . . . but . . ."

"*Shopping trip,*" said Imp, peering into the butler's eyes, "wallpaper, fresh bed linens, lamps and lingerie and carpet and furniture and toilette—you *know* her ladyship's room needs it and
it needs it *now* and who better to choose it than *your wife*—it is
your *duty* to say yes." Behind Imp's back, the helicopter throbbed
like a vast bumblebee, rotors thundering. "Time is a-wasting, time
to fly! Say goodbye for now, and au revoir! Go on, say it!"

"Au—" Cunningham shook his head as Imp slowly backed towards the helicopter door, tugging Eve after him.

Gammon Number Two had already secured Mrs. Cunningham.
As the door closed behind Eve, she noticed the woman looked pet-
rified, although Eve couldn't tell whether she was more scared of
her husband or the helicopter. "Headset," she mimed, gesturing
at the racked sets overhead. Gammon Number Two slid the earpieces and mike over Sybil's tightly curled perm. "Can you hear
me? There's nothing to worry about, we're perfectly safe," Eve
told the woman as the engines spooled up and the chopper slowly
lifted from the pad. "Safe as houses!"

"Houses that dangle from invisible skyhooks," Imp said helpfully. "*Ouch,* no need for that, mate!" He gave Gammon Number
Two a reproachful look.

"Oh Lord who art in Hell, unhallowed be thy name, thy kingdom come, thy name be screamed by the tongueless, thy will be
done—" Sybil screwed her eyes shut as she leaned against her seat
belt, praying as if it could save her from her own personal inferno.

"*Shopping trip,*" Eve said, giving her brother a baleful look.

"*Harrods,*" he retaliated with relish.

"A momentary slip of the tongue," she said defensively. "I

meant to say Harvey Nicks. Harrods is for nouveau riche tax-exiles with more money than taste."

"Like Rupe—" He stopped.

"*I*"—her finger tapped her chin—"am not Rupert: *I* have taste."

"Okay, point taken. Does this mean I can borrow the company credit card?"

"Jeremy." He made puppy eyes at her. Eve sighed. It was clearly going to be one of *those* flights. Terrified cultist housekeeper, check; brother drooling in anticipation of a shopping binge on her business account, check; bodyguard fixedly staring out the window while mentally drafting his resignation notice: check. There was nothing to be done about any of it until they landed. So Eve pulled out the slim clothbound book the butler had given her, and began to read the liturgy for next Tuesday's Dark Matins.

▶◀▶◀▶◀

Robert was enjoying himself immensely.

The New Nanny—who had appeared on their doorstep like magic, right after the previous one had the usual nervous break-down and ran away—seemed boring at first. But first appearances were deceptive, and she was turning out to be *way* more fun than her predecessors. She smoked and she swore when she thought the Banks children couldn't hear her, and she dressed like Missy from *Doctor Who* and carried a bag full of the *best* toys, even better than that time when Ethan had animated a one-sixth-scale Optimus Prime. They'd gone to a toy shop and got to eat at Mc-Donald's, and now they were on a magical mystery tour by the seaside, and sure it was rainy and dark, but: *the sea*! And just as it was threatening to get boring again, there was a theme park with aliens and dinosaurs!

"It's the aliens! They're coming to take you away and *probe* you." He taunted Em because she believed him (because when Robert made predictions like this they had a bad habit of coming true). So now she began to screech.

Nan overheard him. "Shut your yap, Robert Banks, or *I will gag you,* so help me," she snarled, which was horrid but also unlikely because she hadn't once threatened him with her Uzi so she couldn't mean it really. (And what kind of Nan carried a machine gun, anyway? The best kind, of course!)

He giggled happily. "It's true, Nan, the gray aliens in the flying saucers come and they cut up all the cows and then, my mum says, if you've been bad they strap you down and *probe* you—" But Nan wasn't listening to him any more. A boring voice-over was explaining some shit about history, and Ethan had finally noticed the alien mother ship and was staring at it. Robert's gooseflesh crawled the way it always did when Ethan used his power, so he reached out to hold up the flying saucer until Ethan had it working properly—something that large, it would take some time to bring it to life—it had flashing lights and all. Rob could feel with that part of his mind that did the heavy lifting that it was *quite* heavy, like a car. He wondered if there would be xenomorphs when it landed. Something that big would thin the walls between the worlds a lot more than usual, and maybe he could bring them through even if there weren't any aboard it yet—

"Ethan, Emily, *no!*" shouted Nan.

Lyssa materialized at Robert's elbow as the mother ship thundered into reality, its antigrav thrusters kicking up a plume of sand halfway to the suddenly real horizon—*Yes,* Robert exulted, *the walls here are* very *thin*—"I *hate* you," she told him, with all the haughty scorn of a vampire princess. "No alien's going to probe me! They'll probe *you*! *Only you*! Probe and probe and *probe,* and when you've had enough of being probed with ovipositors they'll lay their eggs in your tummy and they'll hatch! Then I'll set my undead minions on you!" She pinched his arm cruelly, then scuttled off after little Em, who had followed the signpost to the Dinosaurs. Someone was shrieking up ahead, and there was a mournful honking, like a duck the size of a car transporter.

Robert paused. The walls here were thin, sure, but the giant bird noises were something else. And his skin was *still* crawling— Ethan had had another power surge, hadn't he? He hadn't just brought the flying saucer to life, he'd animated the—

The honking turned into a roar like an onrushing freight train. The walls thinned further, then disappeared completely, leaving

Robert ankle-deep in sand. A dry, hot breeze stirred his hair as shadows lengthened across the ground, stretching away from the gigantic alien mother ship hovering over the pyramid in the distance. Ahead, a glade of palm trees swayed the wrong way. A scream of terror ended in moist crunching. Among the trees, a shadowy form rose to its feet, a pair of human legs protruding like ghastly toothpicks from one side of its mouth.

"Robert." It was Nan. She sounded unnaturally calm. It wasn't calm-I'm-bored: it was calm-I'm-trying-not-to-startle-you-into-licking-the-live-wire. "Stay where you are and don't move. They're attracted to movement."

"I *know*." It was from that old movie Mum and Dad liked, *Jurassic Park*. "I'm—"

"Ethan is there, isn't he. And Lyssa. Can you tell me which way Emily went?"

"Sure." He pointed. Why didn't she know where the others were? It wasn't as if they could hide from one another.

"The walls. Did you make them go away?" Nan sounded like the hospital doctor that time in Accident and Emergency when he'd broken his arm. *Can you point to where it hurts?*

"I didn't make them go away, they're just thinner here."

"The—the walls of the theme park?"

"The *walls* walls." The walls that kept the real world in and the monsters out.

"Fuck my life," Nan muttered fervently. He looked round and saw that she was setting up an *awesome*-looking rifle—a bullpup with telescopic sights and a bipod and a muzzle brake that looked like it was stealthed and maybe you needed to be wearing powered armor and a cape to use it—and that's when he realized that she was *definitely* the best Nan. None of the previous Nans had smoked, cursed, stolen fast cars, carried guns, or stayed chill when they found out what Robert and his brother and sisters could do. "That's your real power, isn't it? You weaken the walls of the world until stuff comes through?"

"Or leaks out, Mum says," Robert explained helpfully. "Like we've leaked out now?"

The two-story-tall murder chicken rubbed up against one of the palm trees, rumbling like a volcano. Evidently giant murder chickens were just as itchy as the dinner-sized variety. "Can you get us all back to the theme park?" asked Nan. "Not including *that*—" Her gun barrel wobbled minutely. She reached into her messenger bag again and pulled on a bulky set of ear defenders. Then she knelt, and brought the giant ridiculous gun to bear on her target. "I want you to—slowly—go and stand behind me, Robert. Not *directly* behind me, mind . . ."

A flare of light from the alien mother ship cast more shadows across the sand: the mind-children of Steven Spielberg and Erich von Däniken were arriving. The dinosaur startled at the sudden illumination, fluffing up its throat plumage indignantly. Spotlit by an alien searchlight, Lyssa stood before the monster. Little Emily crouched beside her, entranced.

"Fuck," said Nan.

Robert laughed: fuck was good, wasn't it? "She's going to do it!"

The Tyrannosaur (for no self-respecting theme park designer would settle for any lesser theropod) turned its head towards the children and gave voice to a hunting call of bowel-shaking intensity. But as it took a first step forward, it tripped over a tree root that had somehow broken free of the ground and was lashing around like a tentacle. The five-meter-high raptor fell slowly: it was so tall that gravity took almost a second to do its work. When its massive sternum hit the sand, the ground shook and the ominous brown note abruptly turned into a startled quack.

Nan tucked her cheek against the side of her anti-material rifle, peered through the scope, and squeezed the trigger. There was a thunderclap so loud it set Robert's ears ringing. Then Nan wasn't there any more—and neither was T. rex's head: it had been replaced by a pinkish cloud. He looked round and saw Nan sprawling in the dirt, still holding the gun. She moaned quietly: "*Shitbiscuits* that kicks like a motherfucker!"

"Do it again!" Robert clapped, entranced.

"No. Fucking. *Way.*" Nan pushed herself painfully upright and carefully rubbed her right arm. "Holy crap," she muttered. "Holy broken collarbones, Batman, if I was a normie"—she caught herself—"*Shiiiiiit.*"

"Nan, can I have this? Can I?" appealed Ethan, bending to pick up a brass cartridge case half the length of his forearm—"*Ow!* It's hot!" He dropped it.

"Leave it," Nan snapped, suddenly cold and distant.

"Hurts!" Ethan whined as the grove of palm trees, now clearly the maw of a single underground rhizome network the size of a football pitch, leaned over the twitching Tyrannosaur and spread its feeding tendrils across it, poised to engulf.

Emily cooed happily as her twin emitted an experimental sob, clearly preparing to throw a full-blown tantrum over the destruction of his new toy. But Nan wasn't paying attention to the children right now. She opened the flap of her messenger bag: "Next time you hand me an antitank gun, *fucking warn me,*" she snarled as she stuffed the Steyr IWS 2000 back inside. Robert tried to grab it with his mind, but it was too heavy to lift in a hurry and then it slid into the bag and went somewhere he couldn't feel. Nan was stronger than she looked, just like Mum and Dad.

Nan stood, shouldered her bag, and adjusted her hat. "No more dinosaurs," she said firmly, settling back into character. "Come along now, children! We're going to tour the alien mother ship and sneer at the mummy, and if you're good I'll take you back to the food court to eat all the sweets." She gathered his brother and sisters up and took Robert in hand, then side-eyed him with a glare that threatened divine retribution. "Is that *understood?*"

"Will there be Space Nazis?" Robert asked hopefully. Watching New Nan fight off Space Nazis would be *awesome.*

"No, silly, everyone knows the Nazis ride dinosaurs!" Lyssa glowered at Nan. "But she *killed* it."

Robert shrugged. "I could thin the wall between here and the Space Nazis—"

"Robert Banks, don't you dare!"

He sighed. Nan clearly didn't want Space Nazis. "Dumb alien mother ship."

"Can we have a tea party with the mummy?" Lyssa asked.

"The ancient Egyptians didn't have tea, dear."

Nan set off across the sands of the imaginary desert with the Banks children trailing in her wake. Her steps were short, rapid, and stiffly angry, as if she wasn't really enjoying herself at all. Which was a shame, because now he knew what New Nan was capable of, Robert had every intention of having lots of fun with her—whether she wanted to or not.

►◄►◄►◄

Game Boy was jerked out of his deep focus in the worst possible way. He was about to sneakily cut the throat of the enemy squad's healer while the rest of his team were engaged in melee when a hand, a no-shit non-metaphorical *human hand*, tapped him on the shoulder. Which *of course* made him jump halfway out of his skin and fat-finger the keyboard, so that his character dropped stealth and jumped out of *his* skin, nearly falling off the bridge into the bubbling pool of lava they were fighting their way across.

"Dude—"

Game Boy swore violently and tumbled, dodged the enemy's immediate counterattack, and unloaded full-frontal with everything he had. Which was not, it turned out, *quite* enough to nail a high-level cleric who was powered up for battle and willing to take time out from raining cure critical wounds on his teammates to beat up the rogue who'd just tried to nerf him. What had started out looking like a straightforward sneak attack was now a sudden-death showdown with a vastly better armed and armored opponent. Short on options, Game Boy triggered a haste spell and retreated rapidly, just as the elven archer in his party opened up with a volley of—

"Shit. *Shit*." He mashed both hands on the keyboard but his screens were frozen: they unfroze just long enough to show him a tombstone with a grinning death's head superimposed. U R DEAD N00B. "*Shit*." He ripped his headset off angrily and glared at the meatspace distraction, who grinned impudently back at him. "*What*?" GeeBee demanded.

"Yo, dawg," said the distraction, holding up one end of an unplugged ethernet cable, "real world calling."

"You're back. What happened?" Game Boy was momentarily distracted from his party.

"House meeting, kid. Right now."

"Fuck you, Imp, I was in a—" He looked round at the detritus beyond his game rig. "Can it wait?"

"Nope. We've got a Situation." His emphasis provided capitalization.

"Fuck it," Game Boy spat one more time, and pushed back from his rack of flat-panel displays.

He'd set up his rig in what had once been the parlor of the Georgian town house. These days it was the only inhabited building on its street: the others were all boarded up and vacant, supervised by security cameras. But it was still a mess. The previous absentee landlord had left it unmaintained for years, and only the week before a bunch of thugs with guns had stormed it in search of the doorway to Neverland. And so far, Game Boy had only gotten round to sweeping the broken glass into a corner and replacing his PC and monitors.

The living room was another matter. Doc had been busy here. Not only were the window sashes repaired, but they and the painted stage backdrops that lined them were now concealed by floor-length drapes. He'd also hung a selection of demotivational prints from the picture rails and turned Jabba the Sofa right side up, duct-taping the bayonet slashes. The room felt almost cozy, although the carpet was still a sticky mess that reeked like an old man's pub.

The front door banged. It was Del, sleek and sweaty in her cycling gear. "Hey," called Game Boy.

"Yo." She paused. "What's the rush-rush?"

Imp cleared his throat. "We're just waiting on"—Doc barged in, carrying a crate of beer bottles—"Doc."

"I bought refreshments." Doc had his undertaker face on. "I gather they're needed."

"I—yes." Imp crumpled slightly. "Grab a pew, this is going to take some time."

"What is it?" Game Boy dragged a stained beanbag closer to the sofa and dropped. Doc offered him a bottle. "Hey, this is—"

"Coke Zero." Doc twitched.

"Business best done sober." Imp nodded.

"This is a stitch-up!" Game Boy squeaked.

"Nope, I'm on the wagon, too. Cheers." Imp raised his bottle in salute. "So. About where I was last night." And he regaled them with an implausible yarn involving meat-headed goons, his sister who had been widowed before she even knew she was married, a VIP helicopter ride, and the discovery that Eve now owned a Norman castle in the middle of the English Channel. A castle complete with sinister butler, unexplored Nazi bunkers, a leather-fetish playroom, dungeons, bloodstained underground altars, and a Cult who expected Imp to officiate at their evening service next Tuesday—

"Stop. Stop *right* there." Doc pointed an angry finger at him. "I know what's coming and—"

"But it's just a *little* raid!" Imp whined.

"Jeremy, *no*." Imp winced. Doc seemed almost engaged, although not in a terribly helpful way. "I am *not* following you into Mr. Bigge's Nazi torture dungeon in search of cultists. Not for all the tea in China. It'll end in tears!"

"But I'm not asking you to!" Imp could do theatrically aggrieved on demand: "Eve said she'd hire mercenaries for that side of things. Crack SAS-trained special forces lawyers, maybe. No, the thing is, she was worried that Rupert had hidden something in his office there, and when we searched his files we found a *membership list*. His cult isn't just on Skaro, they've got cells here in London." Imp eyed the doorway twitchily, as if half expecting crazed poetry-spouting cultists to leap out of the shadows and go all John Cooper Clarke on him. "Some of the staff at Rupert's head office might be sleeper agents. Uh, sleeper cultists? She can't really trust anyone there. So I've got a bunch of files on a laptop—" he pointed to the discreet aluminum shell lying on the coffee table— "and I need your help going through them, *with precautions*," he added hastily as Game Boy made grabby-hands at the machine. "They're scans of Rupe's most-secret files. We ran them through a text recognizer and a virus scanner looking for imprecatory prayers or curseware, but it's not guaranteed one hundred percent safe. Are you up for it?" he asked hopefully. "There will be beer, and pizza. Oh, and money, there'll be money, too. Are we good?"

"Nope," Del said flatly.

"You want us to proofread the secret files of a cult leader who's into human sacrifice." Doc gave Imp a very hard stare. "What could possibly go wrong?"

"Nothing?" Imp looked innocent.

"This is one of your schemes, innit?" piped Game Boy.

"Whatever makes you think that?"

"Because *we're not idiots*." Del crossed her arms. "What part of 'no death spells' didn't you get?"

"Listen, it's no biggie, if you find something disturbing in there I'll just print it out and go down to the tube station, pretend to be a feral lexicographer or something, ask Members of the Public to proofread a page from my new Japanese-English dictionary."

Game Boy sighed unhappily. With Imp's ability to make anyone believe anything he wanted for fifteen minutes, he could certainly mug random tourists into lending him the use of their brains as occult mine detectors. It was not the practicality of Imp's proposal that gave GeeBee pause, but his ethics. "You can't go full munchkin on the general public, Imp, it's not *right*. Somebody could get hurt." Aged a century in a minute, brain eaten by demons, turned into a Total Quality Management consultant. "Do you have *no* sense of responsibility?"

Imp pondered for a moment, then shook his head: "No."

"This is pointless." Del pushed herself off the sofa and stood. "I didn't agree to help out with any more of your sister's crazy schemes. If you can't—"

"Wait up!" Game Boy said.

"What?" Del paused in the doorway.

"Your girlfriend, Wendy, she's a detective, isn't she? Isn't analyzing evidence her thing? And she'll know how to do it safely. Imp, you should hire her again!"

Imp shook his head sadly. "I don't think she'll work for me after what happened last time."

Del snorted. "No shit!" (Imp had led them through the boarded-up door to Neverland on a dream quest into Victorian Whitechapel. He'd been chasing after a book Eve wanted him to acquire for her boss. Wendy had come along on the raid, and while they wouldn't have made it back alive without her, the chances of her agreeing to work for Imp again were small.)

"Can you ask her?" Imp looked at Del hopefully.

"I can *ask*." Del's eyes narrowed suspiciously. "But if you're just going to offer more money, she won't take it. Girl's got pride, an' a day job that just gave her a pay rise."

"Well." Imp thought for a few seconds. "How about telling her there's a bunch of psychotic cultists who are into human sacrifice, this is their membership list, and if she can help us analyze it Eve will take them down?"

"Oh!" Del brightened. "Well, that's different. She *might* go for it. I'll ask her. But." She pointed a finger at Imp: "You're on the hook for beer, pizza, and money. And I'm not following you or your sister down any more dream roads. Izzat clear?"

6

HIDE AND SEEK

Game Boy was taking a lot of decompression breaks. In fact, he was spending more time on breaks than actually working on sanitizing Eve's stolen files. He had a very limited capacity for nail-biting anxiety, and nothing induced nail-biting anxiety like constantly wondering if turning the next page would suck his brains out through his eyeballs. So when his laptop started shrieking the Sakeru Gummy advertising jingle, "*Long, Looooong Maaaaaan!*" it was yet another excuse to delay returning to work.

"Hey!" He dropped his 3DS and lunged for the laptop.

It was RobHulk06, texting via WhatsApp. Game Boy had assigned him the infinitely annoying ringtone to ensure he didn't miss the kid trying to get in touch again. But the weird-ass tune had jolted him right out of his focus on the game he was replaying. He had an uneasy feeling that something was out of whack with the walls of the universe.

Falling across the arm of his gaming chair, he made a grab for his laptop. A wave of dizziness washed over him: *What the fuck?* Game Boy didn't suffer from vertigo, didn't lose his balance, didn't lose his grip on a game console (*ever*)—something was *wrong*.

RobHulk06's message consisted of one word—*Dinosaurs!!!*—and a photograph of—

"—Holy shit," Game Boy said involuntarily, "WTF?"

A woman in a long black coat and a hat like Missy from *Doctor Who* stood stiffly in front of a headless dinosaur. With one hand she held a futuristic-looking rifle nearly as tall as she was, with the other she gripped a battered-looking messenger bag. The monster behind her looked like it had been a fully grown Tyrannosaurus, right up until someone hit it in the face with a freight train—or maybe shot it with the small antitank gun the woman was carrying. Game Boy did a double-take as another message came in: *Nan is boss!! Nan shot the trex*!

"Guys." Game Boy stood up, laptop cradled in one arm, and headed for the open hall doorway. "Guys?"

Another message came in with an image attachment. Nan had her messenger bag open: she gripped it one-handed as tightly as if it contained the crown jewels, while with the other hand she thrust the great big gun into its main compartment. Which had, somewhat implausibly, swallowed the entire barrel and receiver. *Nan's bag is boss*!! Behind Nan, a skinny goth princess in plasma-hot pink and black was holding the hand of a much younger girl—not much more than a toddler—who with her other hand clutched a many-tentacled green horror that looked like it had escaped from *The Day of the Triffids*.

"Guys!" Game Boy shouted.

A clumping of size twelve boots in the hall presaged Doc's arrival. "What—" Doc emerged from the living room and paused— "who died?"

"Kid's in trouble!" Game Boy vibrated. *Where R U*? he typed one-handed.

Another image: a sandstone surface weathered by time with a tunnel entrance cut into it, flanked by vertical cartouches filled with hieroglyphs. Carvings in the lintel of the tunnel spelled out THE MUMMY AWAITS in totally period-authentic modern English.

RobHulk06: *Nan sez we raid mummiez tome*!

"This is cray-cray!" Game Boy told Doc. "The kid's nan has a gun! And there was a, a—" He gave up and backscrolled to the picture of the dead dinosaur.

Doc boggled. "That's some animation, Boy."

"It's not fake!" Game Boy bounced on the balls of his feet. He needed to *be* somewhere, if only his special sense would tell him where to go. "Nan with gun is a ringer! She's taken the kids somewhere dangerous."

"Give me that." Doc reached for the laptop, frowning as he backscrolled. "Is she a psycho or something? What about the kid?"

Game Boy shrugged: "He's about ten, Doc, what do *you* think?"

"I think this is really weird but we're getting distracted from debugging Imp's sister's Death Note, don't you think?" Doc turned back towards the living room door.

"But—" Game Boy gestured, at a loss for how to express what was wrong as Doc turned away. The kid was ten, he was in a strange city with a heavily armed *Doctor Who* cosplayer who had led him into an alien theme park that had gotten out of hand, and imaginary stuff was leaking into the real world like the—"it's like the corridor upstairs!" he burst out.

"What did you just say?" Suddenly he had Doc's attention.

"Dinosaurs! Mummies! Gray aliens!" Game Boy twitched. "Only he's just a kid! He needs help! Eve can wait, she's a *big* girl—"

"Shit." Doc surrendered. "Do you even know where he *is*?"

"I will in a second." Game Boy typed furiously, then copied a link into Maps. "Just—zoom zoom pan swivel fold spindle *enhance enhance enhance dammit*—there!" The snitchware he'd dropped on RobHulk06's handheld wasn't very smart, and the handheld didn't have GPS, but the big databases of wifi hotspots could work wonders, even without satellite signal. The map image zoomed in, up-rezzing to display a slice of Blackpool's seafront. "Blackpool. Where's Blackpool?"

RobHulk06 sent a three-second video clip: fleeing alien Grays, the jittery muzzle-flash of Nan with Gun—this time brandishing a machine pistol—strobing knife-edge shadows flickering across the ceiling of the mummy's tomb. Horrible, no-good, awful pre-teen children capering and invoking eldritch powers in a theme park come to unearthly life.

"I don't think the kid needs our help right now," Doc told Game Boy. "Anyway, even if we could borrow Eve's helicopter they're at least an hour and a half away. But you're right, this is totes weird and we should look into it. Let's finish off the last of the files, then I'll twist Imp's arm, all right?"

►◄►◄►◄

The next day, Jennifer was at an off-site meeting and Amy was running in circles covering for her boss. Which meant Wendy was free to raid the supply closet—or rather, the wardrobe department.

Supermarket chains with uniformed staff needed to have someone in charge of ordering, issuing, cleaning, repairing, and recycling clothing. Between them the various outlets in this town added up to enough work to provide a full-time job, or two part-timers.

"Hello," said Wendy, showing today's bored part-timer her security pass: "I'm Wendy, and I'm with Internal Affairs." She bared her teeth at Mrs. Unsworth. "I need you to fit me out with a bodysuit and Company Face."

Mrs. Unsworth reacted with a combination of mistrust and fright, as if Wendy had asked to be fitted for a concrete overcoat. But after Wendy took the name of someone *quite* senior in vain—and Mrs. Unsworth made a brief, terrified phone call to head office to verify that Wendy was in fact working undercover—she scampered into a windowless back room to retrieve the items Wendy had asked for. Along with some unexpected extras.

"Here's the muppet suit." Mrs. Unsworth handed over a polythene bag full of stretchy white fabric. "You're probably a size B, they stretch to fit. See this?" The suit was studded with unobtrusive pea-sized nodules, threaded together with wires. "They're position trackers so the store computers know where your limbs are at all times. Here's your Face—" it came in a solidly built cardboard box that weighed more than Wendy expected—"I'll help you adjust it. The bridle and badge are in there—"

"—Bridle?" Wendy raised an eyebrow.

"It's for the earpieces and the gag, of course you won't be wanting *those*. Or the discipline belt and catheter, come to think of it, give me that box—"

What the fuck? Wendy took a quick look, then shut the box hastily. "Who designed this stuff?" she asked, more than a little disturbed. "Is this standard in retail?"

"Not *yet*," Mrs. Unsworth said proudly, "but we're the pilot program! Ms. Henderson is championing it within FlavrsMart. If it delivers the promised efficiency savings it'll be rolling out company-wide in a few months. We'll be ahead of Tesco, Asda, and Amazon!" She leaned close and confided, "And it really *does* work. The Department for Work and Pensions are watching us *very closely*: I hear they're thinking about making it compulsory for Universal Credit claimants. That would serve the shirkers right, if you ask me!" Mrs. Unsworth simpered.

"Right." Wendy concealed her unease behind a professional smile: "As you said I don't need *that*—" she gestured at the box of bondage accessories—"just the Suit and the Face. So I can pass for a drone on the shop floor."

"Of course!" Mrs. Unsworth winked. "What's your shoe size, dearie? Here, give me your right hand, I need to size you for gloves—"

Ten minutes later Wendy walked out onto the shop floor disguised as a particularly photophobic vampire. The spandex itched, the shoes were cheap Crocs knockoffs, and the Company Face kept slipping sideways so that she had to squint to see through the eyeholes. But she was spared the worst indignities: *If they made prisoners wear these things it'd be a human rights violation,* she pondered. *There'd be prison riots.* She reached the end of the canned goods aisle and turned towards the stock prep room fronting the loading bays. *I wonder why they* don't *riot?* Having your benefits sanctioned and trying to live off food banks and the proceeds of begging seemed like it would be less humiliating than submitting to this degree of applied dehumanization. *Why is Jennifer even* doing *this?*

Presenting a uniform company identity to the public and cutting down on toilet breaks was all very well, but computer-controlled masks and biofeedback suits with motion capture and electric shock belts were *expensive,* and supermarkets were all about cost control. Maybe monitoring employee body movements in microscopic detail was part of some deep learning/big data research program, but if so, neither Mrs. Unsworth nor Amy had mentioned it. Wendy found that oversight disturbing. Something here did not add up, unless FlavrsMart HR was performing some sort of soul-sucking sorcerous ritual that fed on despair. *Maybe they are?* But it had nothing to do with the de-emphasized, so she set it aside for now.

Nicholas and Peter had finished scrubbing down the meat-packing room when Wendy pushed through the transparent vinyl curtains. Steel worktops gleamed spotlessly beneath the overhead LEDs. A parade of label printers and shrink-wrapping machines were lined up beside the conveyor belt, which ended at a drop-off trolley and a rack of shelving. Vents in the ceiling hissed quietly, pumping chilly filtered air through the room. As she watched, the belt lurched into life for a couple of seconds. An errant roller squealed repetitively: the belt stopped, and another Company Face pushed through the curtains separating this room from the area where the meat printers waited. There was something different about him—his badge said "Sam"—but it took her a second to work out what was out of place: she felt as if he was watching her.

Wendy almost spoke before she remembered she was supposed to be mute. So she stood still and waited to see what happened.

Sam pointed a finger at her. "Headset malfunction," said the store computer. "Please follow Sam and assist." The finger crooked, beckoning. Sam turned and walked back through the curtain leading to the printer room. *Curious,* thought Wendy. She followed him.

The printer room was a scene of frozen chaos. A wheeled tool rack nuzzled up to the pork extruders in an obscene parody of mechanical reproduction. An access panel dangled open beside it. Half the tubes behind it were disconnected and dangling, naked and intestinal above a row of buckets. A tablet computer set to one side displayed a maintenance diagram. Sam bent over the printer, reached into its guts, and took one end of a hose, which he offered to Wendy.

"Assist," said the computer.

Uh. Wendy stared at Sam. *What?*

"Assist—" A muffled noise came from behind Sam's mask. He shook the hose at her.

Oh. Wendy took the pipe. Sam nodded, very exaggeratedly, shoulders stiff—*Is he frustrated?*—then dived back into the guts of the machine. The hose she held was color-coded pink, rubbery and visceral.

"Sam requires socket drive 7.0," the computer spoke through his mask. "Assist."

Like a theater nurse assisting a surgeon, Wendy passed Sam the tool. Over the next half hour Sam disconnected and replaced half a dozen hoses, depositing the old components on a stainless steel tray. Following the computerized instructions, Wendy placed them in a box addressed to an industrial unit somewhere in the midlands. It finally clicked: Sam wasn't behaving like the masked zombies Amy had shown her the day before. His actions were— *He's not referring to the repair manual,* she realized. *He's done this before.* She watched him with more interest. Maintenance engineer was a skilled job, and Amy had said something about firing their old one.

What if were two of the most dangerous words in the English language, if you were a detective. *What if* led you into gratuitous speculation, and gratuitous speculation could lead to fixating on the wrong target. People used to be hanged when a detective got hung up on *what if* and started looking for evidence that supported a hypothesis while discounting signs that pointed elsewhere. But *what if* whispered in Wendy's ear: *What if they fired their engineer, then hauled him back in as a DWP work placement?* Put him in a gimp suit and who'd be any the wiser? *What was his name: Adrian Hewitt?* She needed to track down the elusive Mr. Hewitt and talk to him, but he was missing. However, if he was hiding behind the "Sam" Company Face—

I need to draw him out, she decided, and there was an obvious way to do it, although it was a bluff and if she'd guessed wrong there might be trouble. So she waited until he had his back turned, then used her talent to conjure a pair of disposable zip-tie handcuffs out of thin air and said, "Adrian Hewitt, you are under arrest."

▶◀▶◀▶◀

Bad Nan treated the kids to tea and burgers in the food court. They'd needed it: along the way she'd rescued little Em from an alien-administered anal probing, and she was still shaking. (She was a manipulative little brat, but even that didn't justify an extra-terrestrial colonoscopy, in Nan's opinion.) Bad Nan then exercised the magic credit card as they ran wild in the Gift Shoppe, and sneaked them out through the fire exit when she spotted theme park security closing in—evidently they planned to bill her for dead dinosaur disposal. The rain had stopped so she was able to shepherd them home with only some pro forma whining when Emily took exception to Ethan stealing her cotton candy.

Once they were back at the Airbnb Mary brewed them creamy hot chocolate with a drop of Nanny's Little Helper (her bag could cough up a bottle of Mother Bailey's Quieting Syrup, complete with historically accurate opium). Finally she tucked them up in bed and turned off the lights.

Once she was back downstairs with boots off and collar un-buttoned, unlit cigarette in hand, it came to Bad Nan that she was absolutely shagged. And not in a good way. *Why the fucking bag of dicks did it have to be* Blackpool? she asked herself.

Aside from its amusements, Blackpool had *nothing*. Well, okay: she was *in loco parentis* for a quartet of hellspawn, and keeping them amused was *important,* lest they find ways to amuse them-selves. But Blackpool had the notable misfeature of being way the hell away from anywhere interesting to an adult supervillain. She couldn't nip round to check on Dad (who wasn't reliably answering the phone any more). She couldn't visit the office and confirm that the Big Man himself was on the straight and narrow: all she could do was listen to his reassuring spiel on the dog and bone, and she couldn't do that too often or she'd piss him off. (One did *not* want to piss off the Thief-taker General.) Nor could she go and hang out in pubs and clubs where she was known, to shoot shit with frenemies and homies and take the temperature of the transhuman scene. *I'm hanging out here on my own, waiting for the Boss to get his ducks lined up.* It had sounded good *in principle,* but in the cold light of metaphorical day—alone in an anonymous Airbnb at night—the cracks in the story were growing obvious, like damp mold in the corners of the kitchen ceiling.

Sure there was a lot of money tied up in this gig: more than enough to go around. But she couldn't help thinking that if the Boss's endgame was to give the children back, she'd be a loose end afterwards. An *expensive* and *dangerous* loose end. *Yes, I'm useful to him—but a million quid's worth of useful?* Mary wondered whether it was wise to rely on the magnanimity of a businessman who didn't deal in intangibles like goodwill.

The Airbnb had a £200 cleaning surcharge for smokers. *Fuck 'em,* thought Mary, and reached into her bag for a lighter. It gave her a taser disguised as a fancy plasma igniter and she frowned: Dad's creations began to degrade after a time. Still, she lit up and blew a thin gray plume towards the damp spot. "Fucked if I'm going to take them to the *Doctor Who* Exhibition tomorrow," she said aloud. She'd nearly pissed herself when the giant murder chicken attacked, and Robert weakening the walls between the worlds had scared the crap out of her. The last thing she needed was Ethan animating a Cyberman takeover or Emily discovering the joy of triffid ranching. "Where else can I stash them?" The weather forecast said rain, and it was December so the piers and the Golden Mile were out.

"Think, dammit." She pulled a battered map book from her bag. It was a relatively short drive to Liverpool—she shuddered—and not much further to Manchester. Manchester was big enough to get lost in: Wasn't it almost the size of Tower Hamlets? And that double-blue line crawling east was the M62 motorway. She traced it over the Pennines and through the sprawl of Yorkshire suburbia, past Halifax and Wakefield and around the fringes of Bradford before detouring south of Leeds. *Definitely not Leeds*: that warranted a bigger shudder than Liverpool these days. But directly south of the war-devastated city, the M62 intersected the M1, the north-south route to London. Her home turf.

It would be a long-ish drive with four bored children, but there were lots of out-of-town shopping centers with amusement zones along the way. Which meant lots of car parks where she could switch vehicles and mess her trail up. "But I need a story for the kids," she realized. The plan wouldn't work without their willing cooperation. So she pulled out her phone and did some rapid googling for background on Mr. and Mrs. Banks, and then some more research on the supervillains who were drawn to them like bugs to a fly zapper.

Early preclinical signs of Metahuman Associated Dementia included the Dark Triad of personality types—narcissism, Machiavellianism, and psychopathy. In today's England, a typical diagnostic sign was the delusion that the patient could take on the New Management and survive. Mary MacCandless knew better: eagles might soar, but weasels didn't get sucked into jet engines. Nevertheless, there was a bottomless supply of magically empowered maniacs who thought that this—rather than who they went to school with, or how good they were at chairing a committee meeting—meant they were destined to rule.

Captain Cockwomble and the Blue Meanie (as Mary thought of them) were very high profile these days, deliberately hyped by the Home Office media department. They'd replaced Officer Friendly and the other first-generation Home Office supes, who had dropped off the map when the New Management took over. As Mary understood things, they were deliberately established to be the obvious first targets of any reality-impaired supervillains who aspired to take over the UK. Blunt-force challengers encountered Mr. and Mrs. Banks for the first time in much the same manner as a bug encountering a truck windshield, thereby saving the Prime Minister the bother of having to squish them himself.

(In reality, the only supervillains who stood a chance of surviving long enough to earn the coveted title of Advanced Persistent Threat were already State-Level Actors—volcano base-building, missile-wielding, ransomware-writing jerks like the President of Transnistria or the Crown Prince of Saudi Arabia. The level below them consisted of arcane billionaires and cult leaders with thick blackmail portfolios: they were tolerated as long as they remembered to pay tribute to the PM and thereby ensured it was more cost-effective to ignore them than to take action. There was a level below that for trusted henchpeople who might be ransomed if captured. Finally, at the bottom of the hierarchy were freelancers like Mary herself, as long as they were agile enough to dodge the descending flyswatter whenever it loomed overhead.)

"What I need is a dangerous freelancer to blame," Mary decided, carefully not thinking about the fact that she herself was a dangerous freelancer. She rapidly skimmed the listing of those who weren't yet gracing the top of Marble Arch. "The kind who might go after Captain Cretaceous and Queen Colorless's children *just for revenge*. Or shits and giggles." Which narrowed the field down a lot. "One who either got away repeatedly, or has powerful sponsors. Maybe the avatar of a powerful faith community." Not a dark saint, but an actual god-emperor or witch-queen, reviving after centuries of hibernation atop a stash of *mana* the size of the Empire State Building. They'd be much-diminished, but still the kind of villain who could blow the top off a mountain or teleport.

"Dad could have done it, if he hadn't succumbed. . . ." She sniffed, then blinked rapidly. If Dad's MAD hadn't come on so early, before his powers had fully matured, she wouldn't be in this mess in the first place. Dad had burned nova-bright for a few months two years ago. These days he had to struggle to remember where he'd put his dentures. Her own power was useful for self-defense—she never had to worry about walking down a darkened alley at night—but she simply wasn't in this weight class. "Maybe blame Moloch, or Baal? Or how about the Child-snatcher General?" Enough children had shivered in fear through *Chitty Chitty Bang Bang* to empower that particular archetype, after all.

"If I frame it as a game for Emily and Ethan, I can get Lyssa and Robert on board supervising them." She tapped ash from her burned-down cigarette onto the kitchen table and then shoved the map back in her bag. "We're going to play hide and seek," she decided. (Keep the cover story as close to reality as possible.) "I'm running from a bad guy to keep them safe. One who steals children. So, tomorrow . . ."

Mary MacCandless pulled out a fresh notepad and Biro, and began to plan.

▸◂▸◂▸◂

This was the first time Wendy had ever tried to arrest a murder suspect, and she was badly out of practice at takedowns—so she nearly died.

"Adrian Hewitt"—she began as the zentai-suited body in front of her whirled—"you are *under arrest*—"

She finished on a squeaky high note, jumped backwards, and blocked a viciously swung socket wrench with a baton which materialized in her right hand just in time to save her from a fractured skull. The clanging impact shuddered up her arm, and her grip was loose enough that her weapon went flying. But it had startled Hewitt, who spun and darted away through the plastic curtains blocking her view of the loading dock. The baton, no longer in contact with her skin, evaporated. Wendy gulped, heart pounding, then stumbled after the fleeing suspect. As she reached the curtain she tried to conjure up another baton, but something felt wrong: her sense of physicality, which she relied on to lend her illusions a semblance of solidity, was slightly off. The baton flickered into focus for a half second, then melted away again. *It's the suit,* she realized. Wendy needed skin contact with her creations. If she lost it for more than a couple of seconds the objects faded, and evidently the HiveCo body stocking was thick enough to block it. She yanked at her right hand before she remembered that the glove was built into her sleeve which in turn was part of the suit: she'd need to cut a hole in the palm before she could re-arm. And there was no time.

Swearing, she ducked low and darted through the curtain. Thankfully Adrian Hewitt wasn't lurking in wait on the other side. She found herself in a chilly high-roofed shed, floored in concrete and crammed full of pipework and machinery. One end was blocked off by yellow wire-mesh fencing, which surrounded an overhead conveyor belt and a double-row of industrial robots with—*Are those swords?* Never mind, right now they were quiescent. Beyond the fenced-off robots she could see daylight, but no sign of a zentai-suited muppet.

Sidling around the wire cage, Wendy spotted another plastic curtain covering an archway leading into another loading area. She slipped through it quietly and looked around. This was a more conventional receiving bay, with concrete piers and a waste compactor and removal skip parked at one side. High carts filled with broken-down cardboard packaging waited for pickup on one pier. It was deserted and the steel shutters were lowered, indicating that no deliveries were expected. The swing doors at the end had a transparent window, but it was scratched up and fogged into opacity. Nerving herself, Wendy approached the doors and pushed through.

She found herself in a darkened stockroom walled with industrial shelving from floor to ceiling. It felt cramped and dingy compared to the shop floor, even though the aisles and stocktaking stations could take a forklift truck. The retail spaces lay beyond another set of doors. Wendy tiptoed along the back wall of the room, glancing down each aisle for signs of her fugitive. But Hewitt had shown her a clean pair of heels, and besides, this was his home turf.

Giving up the hot pursuit, Wendy went back to her self-directed orientation. She passed a row of heavy refrigerator doors—obviously the warehouse space for frozen goods—then spotted a couple of normal doors at the far end. One led to a toilet block that would have been condemned as unfit for habitation by HM Inspectorate of Prisons. The other opened into darkness and a fetid odor like backed-up sewers. "*Gack.*" She swallowed bile as she fumbled for the light switch. Flickering overhead tubes illuminated three tiers of bunks hammered together from unfinished shipping pallets. The bunks themselves were in shadow, but she saw a body in a white zentai suit lying in one of the bottom racks. "Oops, sorry," she said, then hastily switched off the light, her gorge rising at the sick-sweet smell of decay. How anyone could sleep with such a stink was beyond her. The prone form didn't move as she closed the door.

Back in the stockroom, Wendy leaned against the wall for a moment. She briefly closed her eyes. The adrenaline crash had caught up with her. *Hot pursuit.* She ran through her facts rapidly, trying to make sense of what had just happened. She'd gone out on the floor in muppet drag, assisted a repair muppet with the meat printer, acted on a hunch, and nearly gotten brained. But now she knew that Adrian Hewitt, prime suspect, was haunting the crime scene disguised as an anonymous workfare jobsworth. And he was wearing a headset and Company Face, so the computer would be tracking his whereabouts.

Behind her mask Wendy smiled grimly, then straightened up and retraced her path to the offices. Things were looking up. It was time to ask Amy some pointed questions.

▶◀▶◀▶◀

Eve had made a few changes at head office since Rupert's disappearance. While she hadn't cared to take over the master suite in the Knightsbridge town house that served as the Bigge Organization's London headquarters—not until she'd had the bedroom gutted and refurnished from the plaster and floorboards up—she'd moved her own possessions into the main guest suite, vacating the housekeeper's attic room she'd previously lived in. She did this not because she needed the upgrade (Eve slept barely five hours a night) but to send a message to the staff, *I'm in charge here.* (Which was the external projection of her internal scream of defiance at Rupert's ghost, *I'm not under your thumb any more.*) Either way, it meant the housekeeper's dormer was available for Sybil Cunningham's use. As it was on the third floor, with locked bulletproof windows and no exit that did not pass the ground-floor security checkpoint, it was suitably escape-proof without actually screaming *you're in the dungeon now.*

True, there were cells in the basement—above the tunnel with the trenches filled with quick-setting cement—but it occurred to Eve that Sybil hadn't actually done anything to deserve such treatment. And besides, Eve could foresee a use for Sybil in her near future, running Castle Skaro. Best to keep the housekeeper comfortable and give her breathing space while she recovered from her overbearing husband, then wait for her to come to Eve on her own terms.

While she'd been busy catching up with things—matters arising from the FlavrsMart buy-in process, putting the frighteners on a couple of Rupe's minions who'd been acting up, farming out the occult mine-detector job to Imp and his crew—Sybil had been allowed to shop for necessities (with a discreet escort). So when Sybil finally asked to see Eve, two days after her return to London, she was barely recognizable as the haggard ghost who'd pleaded for rescue on a dark and stormy night.

"Ah, Mrs.—Sybil," Eve corrected herself, "please come in." She smiled her business smile and gestured at one of the chairs.

Sybil had ditched the old-school servant's dress for a twinset and pearls (Jaeger, if Eve was any judge of brands: not couture but not cheap, either). She'd clearly taken pains over her hair and makeup. Other than being about thirty years behind the times she looked like a smart upper-class grandmother, one with grandchildren at Oxford and a country estate to drive her Subaru Outback around. She took a seat. "Mrs. de Montfort Bigge—" she began, haltingly.

"—Please call me Eve, I wouldn't want to cause Rupert's mother any confusion if she visits."

Sybil nodded. She gave no sign of acknowledging that Rupert's mother had killed herself some years ago. "Certainly, ma'am."

"How have you been?" Eve asked, with a slightly more genuine smile this time. "Have you any problems I can help with?"

"Everything is absolutely fine, ma'am!" Sybil delivered a stuttering account of her new life at Bigge HQ. Her hands, folded neatly in her lap, clenched unconsciously as she continued: "I don't like to presume, but it's been two days, and I was wondering—"

"Yes?" Eve prompted.

"—Would it be all right for me to go to church?" Sybil asked nervously.

Eve bit her tongue to hold back her instinctive reply of *over my dead body*. "Why?" she finally asked, deceptively mildly.

The answer trailed on for a good ten minutes. There was an element of *because I haven't missed a service in thirty years except when I had the flu,* somewhere in Mrs. Cunningham's apologetics; and *I want to know what it's like when my husband isn't officiating,* along with a large dollop of *I'm scared of getting on the wrong side of God (and by God I mean the Mute Poet).* She even tried to cozen Eve with *I'm alone in a strange city where I don't know anyone, and church is familiar.* None of which swayed Eve.

What *did* work, however, was Eve's dawning realization that if the Church of the Mute Poet held services in London, Eve needed intelligence on their activities: and she needed to send an observer who would know what they were looking at.

This latter realization was what finally prompted her to reply, "Yes."

Eve detested mystery cults in general and those dedicated to sanguinary gods in particular. A particularly evil cult sheltering within the husk of an evangelical church called the Golden Promise Ministries had taken her mother from her. Before Mum had descended into her own private abyss she'd tried to drag Evie along to a couple of services, and they'd given her a tooth-grating, fingernails-on-blackboard sense of *wrongness*. Rupert had been very high up in the Cult of the Mute Poet, if not right at the top. Eve would have to deal with his followers when she returned to Skaro, and as Sun Tzu observed, it is impossible to defeat an enemy you don't understand.

So she smiled diffidently and nodded, then added, "I take it you mean the Church of Our Mute Lord, of course?" Sybil nodded. "I'll definitely look into it." She rubbed the suddenly moist palm of one hand on her knee.

"Do you know where—" Suddenly shy, Sybil dropped her gaze— "in London?"

"No, but I can find out." Imp would know, if he'd finished the read-through of Rupert's papers. "Would you like to go this evening, if there's a church nearby? Otherwise, let's say the next available service? You can tell me all about it afterwards."

"Yes, Mrs.—I'm sorry, ma'am. Yes!" Sybil stood and blundered out of Eve's office, trailing an almost palpable happiness behind her, and for a moment Eve wondered if she should have checked her mouth for alien parasites: but no, it was the Sleeper in the Pyramid whose followers used those. The Mute Poet didn't strip his followers of the powers of speech, song, and rhyme. (His demands were dark but at least they required his congregation to have tongues.)

"Well now," Eve said to herself, then tapped her headset. No need to tell Sybil that Eve herself wasn't going to risk being recognized by her former boss's coreligionists: "Get my brother on the line."

Today was Thursday. As it happened, Imp had identified three different church meetings in the Greater London area from Rupert's cult directory. Phone calls and other enquiries ensued. "This Saturday evening," she told him, "you're taking Sybil to church."

Her brother was unamused. "What? Why Saturday night, why not Sunday?"

"Because they hold their services the evening before the Sabbath, and on Sunday you'll be hungover," she pointed out. "I'm picking you up and briefing you at six o'clock sharp: be prepared. Bring your crew."

"But what if I don't—"

Eve smiled at the wreckage of the cuckoo clock hanging from the wall opposite her desk. Since triggering the trap she'd taken to using it for target practice with her marbles, and it was considerably the worse for wear. "Stop arguing: you're going one way or the other. Here's a tip: one way is voluntary, the other involves a BMW with blacked-out windows and a couple of ex-paras with no sense here of humor. But if you take notes for me I'll buy you dinner afterwards. What does your stomach say to that?"

"It says—" Imp sighed loudly. "I hope you know what you're doing, sis."

▶◀▶◀▶◀

Two days of mind-numbing, foot-blistering legwork around FlavrsMart Branch 322 had put Wendy in a shitty mood right before a date—or perhaps in a better state of mind to appreciate company that didn't have anything to do with endlessly tracing through CCTV footage, interrogating zentai-suited shopworkers, and groveling over diagrams of robot butcher lines.

"I swear this job is going to turn me vegan," she complained.

"Beer, girl." Del—Becca—shoved a chilled glass at her. "Sit down, tell me about it." She had to raise her voice over the background roar of the busy pub. "How bad can it be?"

Wendy had clocked off and gone home for long enough to ditch her suit—Becca didn't approve of them, she said it made Wendy look like a cop—then met up with her girlfriend in a grungy Fuller's pub in Clapham. Only to find that Becca had come straight from an orientation and training day at HiveCo Security and was wearing a shiny new (and extremely cheap) company uniform: black trousers, navy polo shirt, and her usual DMs. "Bad enough," said Wendy, then took a mouthful of London Pride. "I"—a mouthful of beer covered her hesitation—"I jumped the gun and spooked my suspect. He ran. And it's impossible to tell him apart from the other muppets." She chuckled mirthlessly. "They all look the same, and for once that's not a racist cliché."

Becca gave her a side-eye. "Really?"

"It's . . . FlavrsMart." She made it a curse. "They make their bottom-tier employees wear body stockings and face masks with digital displays. You can't even hear their voices, the branch computers handle all customer interaction. And there's about a dozen of these, uh, *muppets,* on the floor at any time. So the suspect is—or was—playing a shell game. I played my hand too soon and spooked him so he got away. And it turns out that although the branch computers track absolutely everything, data protection rules apply *and* muppets are anonymized even from other personnel to prevent them unionizing—"

"The fuck?" Becca looked appalled as she chugged her cider and black.

"—Yeah. So I asked HR to track the muppet I was after on CCTV and got given the *computer says no* runaround. Even though they called us in the first place to figure out what's going on. I don't have any evidence against him that'd stand up in court—that's *why* I wanted to talk to him—but without evidence they won't hand him to me."

"That is some kind of fucked up," Becca said admiringly. "That is some Catch-22 grade fucked up right there."

"Absolutely." Wendy stared at her beer as if it was sitting on the opposite side of an interview suite table. "It's almost like they're setting me up to fail." The beer was evil and needed to be punished. "But why?"

"Dunno. Internal politics?"

"Unlikely." Wendy brooded. "There were two of them in HR: Amy, who got me set up, and her boss Jennifer. Come to think of it, I saw Jennifer when I went back for the camera and movement logs. Maybe she just hates her assistant?"

"What are they like?"

"Amy is—" Wendy thought for a bit—"going through the motions? I mean, vegan, probably insists on eating only organic, dyes her hair green, I spotted her sketching on a pad when she didn't think anyone could see—but her boss Jennifer is *eww*. I mean, she could be Eve's Mini-Me. Whenever she swallows you can see the venom sacs in her throat twitching."

"What do they do about shoplifting by staff? I mean, stock wastage?"

"Huh." Wendy frowned. "I think the branch computers handle it? I mean, they track everyone all the time and the produce is all chipped with RFID tags, so it'd be pretty hard for an employee to lift anything without getting caught. Easier for the public—walk in, grab something, run away, store security don't have the power of arrest."

"You make it sound like some kind of in-game skill: 'You just leveled up and can now cast Arrest Shoplifter. Target will be frozen for thirty seconds, taking two hundred percent damage. Police in the area are called to the scene.'"

Wendy coughed, trying not to snort beer through her nose: "If only!"

"So." Becca smirked at her. "Game Boy is trying to drag me into this games session he runs for Imp and Doc on Saturdays—tabletop games, not computer games; he's into D&D and thinks I've never played. Anyway, if you wanna come round, we can go stabby-rogue on his ass when he doesn't expect us to know shit. What do you say?"

"Saturday is—" Wendy mentally checked her calendar—"free, I think?"

"If it's no fun we can cut and run," Becca offered. "You sound like you need to get your head out of your work for a while."

"No kidding. How's *your* week going so far?"

Becca rolled her eyes theatrically. "Did they make *you* go through this shit?"

"What shit would that be, bullshit or dog shit?"

"I dunno, what kind of shit is it when they hand you a uniform and tell you to stand up straight and swallow a ring binder?"

"Heh, sounds like induction week. Did they make you take a physical?"

"That's tomorrow." Becca put her empty glass down and flexed her arm.

"Relax, they just want to make sure you don't have a heart condition so your family won't sue them if you die on duty. If this was the police, they'd make sure you could run five kilometers and handle an assault course. But they'd also want you to have a degree in criminology or sociology, or do a working apprenticeship followed by two years as a probationer while attending college on the side."

"A *degree*." Becca looked appalled. "What the fuck am I doing here?"

"You're taking HiveCo's shilling. What are you drinking next?"

"I think—" Becca pushed her chair back from the table—"have you eaten?" Wendy shook her head. "Because I could murder a Chinese takeaway."

"Not literally, I hope." It was Wendy's turn to smirk. "Okay, you're on."

►◄►◄

Saturday afternoon found Game Boy freaking out in the drawing room, trying to assemble a D&D game on a plastic folding table and camp chairs (Imp hadn't bothered to replace the dining table the mob had smashed—his bourgeois aspirations were nonexistent). Eventually Doc took mercy on him. By the time Del and Wendy arrived, they had a starting setup: character sheets, dice, GM's screen, and a tablet loaded with Game Boy's copious notes and maps.

It was nearly three o'clock by the time they got started, and Imp was still hungover from the night before. GeeBee had designed a new campaign, and Imp *insisted* on rolling up the most bizarre prestige class Wendy had ever heard of (then kicked up a tantrum when Game Boy calmly rejected his Tiefling gothic-industrial music bard on the grounds that his player character had to start out as a ten-year-old human for the campaign to work, and making him a bard would constitute child labor, if not slavery). Consequently it was nearly five before they were actually ready to start playing for real. And then the doorbell rang.

"The fuck—" Game Boy fumed impatiently when Doc went to open the door. "Who is it?" he shrilled after Doc.

"Imp," Doc's tone was pointed, "were you expecting company?"

"Oh. Uh." Imp stood, sheepishly, and slouched into the hall. "I kind of forgot." By his expression he'd been hoping that his visitor had forgotten, too. Curious, Wendy followed him out, trailed by Del and finally a frustrated Game Boy. "Hi, sis."

"Hello!" Eve stood on the threshold and grinned terrifyingly. She'd accessorized her little black dress with a statement hat and veil that lent it a Jehovah's Witness from Hell vibe. "Do you have a few minutes to talk about our Savior the Flayed Lord?" Her smile went sideways as she tapped her Cartier watch: "Church service starts in forty minutes, Jeremy! You don't want to be late, do you?" She paused. "You *did* tell them they were all going to Church, didn't you?" A wall of variously stupefied and sullen faces confronted her. "What?"

"*Church*." Game Boy turned an expression of total betrayal on Imp. "What the fuck, man?" Game Boy had a poor opinion of churches, ever since his mother paid a Pentecostal pastor to expel the incubus from her "daughter." (Needless to say, it hadn't worked.)

"I, uh, sis told me she wanted to drag me along to check out a new church? I thought it was later tonight, but I admit I lost track of time."

"That's not what happened!" Eve turned her merciless gaze on him. "You were going to escort Sybil Cunningham to service, keep an eye on her, and see which initiates of the Church of the Mute Poet are in attendance. And you were *supposed* to tell everyone."

GeeBee got in first: "What the hell, Imp?"

Eve waved him into silence. "I need someone to check out one of Rupert's congregations," she explained. "I'm trying to clean house, but first I need to understand what I'm dealing with. I've got to take down a high-level congregation—very secretive, the kind where the initiates do things they can't talk about in public—

next week. It's the one Sybil's husband leads, in Rupert's absence. So I thought you should attend a service at one of their local, public chapels. Anonymously, of course. They're not going to sacrifice anyone in Chickentown tonight, not when anyone can walk in off the street, so it's good preparation. Sybil is your invitation card, she'll give it a gloss of credibility."

"But it's game night," Game Boy persisted mulishly. "You're spoiling it!"

"It's only for an hour or so. I'll buy you all pizza afterwards if you come along." She pointed a finger at Wendy, who was shuffling backwards: "You, too, Detective, I'd really value your professional insight. At, say, your regular hourly rate for the write-up?"

"Hey, if you're paying *her,* what about the rest of us?"

Eve's face froze at Del's demand, then she got down to haggling.

Ten minutes later two SUVs full of reluctant churchgoers rolled away from the front of Imp's family manse.

The church service was worse than Game Boy had anticipated. Rupert's largesse evidently stopped short of buying his congregation expensive real estate. Instead, the Cult of the Mute Poet—in public, the Church of Saint David, Pentecostal—occupied a gently decaying 1920s Masonic hall in Chickentown, deep in the tractless wastes of London suburbia. The mirrorshade-wearing drivers pulled over for long enough to drop Eve and her conscripts on the pavement, then drove off to find somewhere to park. Meanwhile Eve chivvied the dungeoneers towards the vaguely art deco entrance to the temple. "I'm staying outside," she reminded them. "I can't risk being recognized."

She nodded at a tweedy, middle-aged woman wearing a church dress, who was hovering around the entrance. "Evening, Sybil." Eve smiled. "These are the people I was talking about. This is Sybil Cunningham: she works for me. Follow her lead and you won't go wrong. I'll be outside." Mrs. Cunningham looked askance at Wendy and Del: obviously they wore too much denim and leather for her taste. "This is a church service," she reminded them in hushed tones.

"Yeah, well, it came as a surprise to us," Del challenged her with a steely grin.

"Behave." Wendy elbowed her.

"Church." Game Boy twitched. "I, uh, I don't get on with churches. I have allergies."

"Oh, I'm sure you'll find this one is *very* welcoming," Mrs. Cunningham reassured him.

They followed Sybil inside. The service was already in progress, with a choir singing karaoke accompaniment to a driving Christian rock backing track. Game Boy cringed as he trailed Mrs. Cunningham and Wendy to the rearmost row of seats. Del followed, one hand in the small of his back to remind him that any escape attempt that cost her a pizza would *not* be tolerated. As he found a seat to stand in front of—the congregation placed a wall of taller bodies in front of him, blocking the view ahead—Game Boy became edgily aware that something was wrong with the music. It took a few seconds but eventually the penny dropped. The choir were lip-syncing to Johnny Cash covering Depeche Mode's "Personal Jesus." Now *that* wouldn't have made the cut for any church his parents had dragged him into, for sure. He was about to nudge Del right back and mouth *What the fuck?* when the song came to a crashing end. Silence fell like a fire curtain, muffling his ears. Then a woman's voice rang out from the podium at the front of the hall, strong even without the additional amplification that brought it to the edge of a deafening feedback shriek.

"My fellow believers! Welcome, welcome I say, to the house of Our Lord and Savior, the Prince of Poetry and Song! Give praise for his glory, in whom lies salvation! For you are the elect, who he saves and raises to life eternal beyond the grave! Hallelujah!"

"*Hallelujah*!" the congregation echoed enthusiastically, but Game Boy cringed, for under the cries of approval he heard Wendy mutter "*Fuck me,*" and when he looked past Mrs. Cunningham he saw the thief-taker's face was ashen. She could see over the shoulders and heads that blocked Game Boy's line of sight, and Game Boy instantly saw that she'd spotted something very wrong.

"Be welcome in the House of Our Lord the Undying King, Saint Ppilimtec the Tongueless, who sits at the right hand of Our Flayed Lord, he of the Smoking Mirror—"

"*What is it?*" Del hissed at Wendy. Game Boy cringed, but no-body in the row ahead could hear them.

"*It's her! The Human Resources manager! Jennifer!*"

"*The—which one?*"

"*Her! The priest!*"

"*How can you tell?*"

"*Her voice. Listen!*"

But Game Boy missed the priestess's next sentence, for the liturgy called for another fervently bellowed *Hallelujah,* and then a power chord as the chorus launched into a surprisingly dark rendition of "God Is God" from *Jesus Christ Superstars* by Laibach. Game Boy began to sweat, chilly bullets oozing out from the small of his back, palms slimy with fear, breath coming shallow and too fast. He managed to keep the shakes under control through the chanting that followed—chanting in oddly accented Spanish larded with words stolen from another language—but his mood was spiraling down into a pit of self-loathing, the whole ceremony raising unquiet ghosts from his incompletely buried childhood. Finally he couldn't take any more. Weaving past Del—even in distress, Game Boy's delusionist skills meant he was uncatchable—he stumbled out into the chilly night air, gasping for respite amidst the diesel fumes.

An indeterminate time later, Game Boy felt a shadowy presence at his shoulder. He shuffled sideways, uncomfortable, until something he couldn't identify clued him in. "What?" he tried to snarl, the sweat in the small of his back turning prickly hot, but he couldn't bring himself to meet her eyes.

"Not enjoying it?" Her words were unexpectedly conciliatory, and for a moment he forgot to hate Eve for dragging him into this. "Bad memories?"

"My parents tried to—" He choked off. *Now* he met her gaze, angry at her sympathy. "How very *dare* you," he rounded on her: "How dare you drag me into this!" He shivered with unfamiliar rage and pain, amplified by the T in his veins.

She shrugged. "*They fuck you up, your mum and dad. They may not mean to, but they do—*" Eve reached into her posh designer handbag for a vaporizer that was all chilly art deco silver and cut-glass technology, then offered it to Game Boy. "Here. I bought this for Imp, but you look like you need it more." It was a peace offering of sorts.

"Why?" he asked flatly.

"Imp went on a bender after Dad died. He makes regrettable decisions when he's under the influence. I don't want that happening again. Anyway it should help you right now, I promise." She offered him a cartridge: the label said it contained THC and spearmint oil. (The New Management had decriminalized all drug use a month ago, declaring that if people wanted to poison themselves it was nobody else's business as long as they paid their tax.)

"Why?" Game Boy persisted.

"*They fill you with the faults they had, and add some extra, just for you,*" Eve finished the quote. "When I was your age, maybe a year or two younger, our mother"—she faltered momentarily before continuing, her voice firmer—"our mother was always churched, but it got out of hand. She changed congregations a couple of times, looking for something more extreme each time. As if she was addicted to increasingly wild expressions of faith. Finally she found a preacher that suited her needs."

Game Boy sucked on the device. His mouth filled with flower-flavored smoke, which he slowly drew down. The mix hit like a velvet-wrapped hammer. "Don't care about your mum, she's not *my* business," he said sulkily, trying to make it so by blunt assertion of fact.

"But she's *Imp's* business. And it'll be your business, too, when Rupert comes back and makes you *his* business," Eve flared abruptly, then subsided.

Wait. "What do you mean *when*?" An uncontrollable shudder started at his hips, then worked its way up his spine until it rattled the teeth in his jaws.

"Sorry, sorry." It was the nearest Game Boy had ever come to seeing Eve apologize, for having dragged Game Boy into a situation which triggered him. "It might not happen. Just, knowing my luck it will. That's why I wanted everyone's eyes here. Eyes on the game, to try and spot what's going on."

"Then why are you out here and not inside, watching?"

"Point," she muttered under her breath. "They might recognize me—apparently I'm their Bishop's wife. Anyway, I thought you needed some help. Hang on to this until after the service. Now they're running, they won't notice if I sneak in the back." A pat on his shoulder, startlingly sympathetic: "Just hang in there. . . ." And Eve disappeared into the hall, leaving Game Boy alone with his memories.

▶◀▶◀▶◀

THREE MONTHS EARLIER:

Ade was English by origin and upbringing. Which meant he was aware of the existence of churches but had no personal experience of them. And Jennifer's Church totally did his head in.

It wasn't the praying, the singing, or the clapping that got to Ade: it was the potluck in the middle of the service. Mindful of Jennifer's instructions, he'd brought along a carrier bag containing a shrink-wrapped Sunday roast, printed using pink slime from a source he refused to think about.

(The homeless woman hadn't been entirely dead when he yanked the cable ties tight and hooked her up to the belt running into the cage of robots. The muffled noises only stopped when the electric carving knives found her femoral artery.)

Jennifer led the service. She wore priestly vestments almost as intimidating as her office suit, and presided over a foursome of Mumsnet Karens in blue gloves and disposable aprons, laying out donations atop a white linen shroud. When it was his turn to approach the altar he presented his dish. Jennifer bowed her head ceremonially and intoned a prayer in an unfamiliar language that slithered past his ears like an invisible serpent. She took the unnatural roast from him and passed it to one of her helpmeets: "The blood is the life, and the meat is the will, and all who have gone before shall live again," she intoned as Ade moved to follow the file of devotees back to the pews.

"Not you," a woman whispered in his ear: "Follow me." She led him aside as the worshippers continued to file up to the altar and donate their produce, which Jennifer's helpers were assembling into a weird parody of a human body: his roast in place of the head, strings of bangers for intestines, chipolata sausages for fingers, and ducks for thighs. Jennifer sang a hymn and paced around the altar as they worked, folding the shroud around the limbs, body, and head as if bandaging a gastronomic mummy.

"Behold the body and blood of the sacrifice, waiting for the poet to infuse him with the rhythm of life!" she finished, and the crowd rose to their feet to sing from a psalter full of words that writhed in front of Ade's eyes like burning electric arcs.

Ade saw—or apprehended, for it wasn't entirely something that could be seen with human eyeballs—a distortion ripple across the meat sculpture on the altar. And he felt a draft as of the door of a sealed tomb opening behind him, where someone or something watched from beyond the threshold. With a gut-deep sense of terror he realized that if he turned to look he would lose a part of himself that he couldn't live without. Then the body in the tightly wound strips of fabric on the altar began to twitch.

The woman who'd taken Ade aside led him back towards the altar. "Rise in the name of our Lord!" Jennifer commanded the twitching meatsack. "Our Lord commands the flesh and blood of the host! Rise! Rise!" The thing on the altar stretched and congealed into solidity, acquiring structure and form as if it was settling around an armature of articulated bones animated by living muscle.

"I need you to help me with this," Jennifer told Ade offhandedly. She held up a white body stocking: "Help me get it into it." Between them they unrolled the stretchy fabric and eased the thing on the altar inside, wrappings and all. It felt quite similar to a real cadaver, in Ade's opinion—he'd assisted with enough of them during his time as an undertaker's assistant—one that had gone past rigor mortis and begun to liquify, albeit without the characteristic smell or seepage. As usual thinking such thoughts excited him, which was why the funeral directors had let him go: "Can't be having a pallbearer who pops a stiffie, the bereaved might take offense," his boss had explained.

"There," said Jennifer, zipping up the side-seam of the muppet suit. "Help me with his face." She nudged Ade towards a Flavrs-Mart carrier bag containing the fixings of a Company Face and control headset.

"*Her* face," Ade corrected automatically.

"Of course." Jennifer gave him a tiny smirk. "Isn't this *special*?"

"Do you do this often?" he asked her while the meat golem's face was booting up.

"Only on Wednesdays and Saturdays." She gestured at the congregation, who were singing along while a bellwether guitarist stood strumming in front of them. Their faces were empty of expression, soul-stuff hoovered out as fuel for the Rite, and Ade realized that he was the only other person here who was actually alive to the truth of what had just happened. "Also holy days, but we don't have as many of them as the C of E, or even the Catholics. I must say, it's going to go a lot more smoothly with your assistance."

She made an elaborate gesture. The meat suit sat up, turned to swing its legs off the altar—pointing its face away from the nave—and stood. She waved peremptorily and it shuffled towards the vestry, arms dangling.

"How long do they last?" Ade asked, fascinated.

"I don't know. This is the first time I've done it with a fractional sacrifice; normally we use complete—intact—offerings. There are plenty of de-emphasized, they come indoors when it gets cold enough outside. Just like mice, makes them easy to harvest. But they don't outlast rigor mortis. I've tried removing the intestines—" She shrugged. "Our Lord's will be done, I guess."

"I'm well impressed, Miss." He side-eyed the walking corpse lustfully, then forced himself to drop his gaze and look suitably respectful, adopting the posture the undertakers had taught him. It seemed appropriate. "Why me?"

Jennifer laid a hand on his arm. "Let's talk after the service." She steered him towards the back of the chapel: "I need to finish up and send them away happy. You hang around back there. I have plans. And a bottle of communion wine to share," she added, as if she needed the additional bait for the hook firmly lodged in his lip.

But Ade was already hers. In his experience dead girls never kissed back, but Jennifer's church was about to change that for him—and his love life could only get better.

▸◂▸◂

"Hurry up, boys and girls! Look smart, pack your toys, we're going to hit the road again this morning!"

It had been nearly twenty-four hours since Mary jacked the BMW, and while it was still parked around the corner she was not keen to drive it again: the ANPR cameras would be looking for it, and *skull on a stick* was not a new look she intended to try out.

But she had the Banks children to help her.

"Today, I'm going to teach you some valuable life skills! Starting with teamwork, self-reliance, and the best way to steal a car."

The terrible tots seemed uninterested—Emily was fondling the formerly wilted spider plant that lived in the Airbnb kitchen: it was playfully trying to eat her fingers—but Robert and Lyssa were agog.

"My mum says stealing is *wrong*," Elissa said judgmentally. "An' we need to hang all the thieves."

"Your mum is mostly right!" Mary agreed. "But only *mostly*." She paused. "Remember the big toy shop in London? Do you think your mum would want to hang *you*?"

"No, but that's *different*—"

"It's different because you're special and the rules for normies don't apply to you and your parents, people with magic."

"Or—" Robert regarded her with cold calculation—"you?"

"Zackly!" Mary's exaggerated nod telegraphed approval. Robert preened. Lyssa still looked skeptical, so she continued: "Besides, it's not really stealing if we're going to give it back afterwards, is it? And we will, I promise." After some time in a police recovery yard being dusted for fingerprints. (Mary tugged her kidskin gloves self-consciously.) "Let's get started!"

She stashed the children's suitcases in her messenger bag and led them out into the grimy morning overcast.

"Our first step," she announced, "is to work out precisely what we need. For example, some cars are big and others are little! There are how many of us?" She mimed a theatrical head count: "One-two-three-four-*five*! So we need a car with five seats!" That ruled out the lopsided-looking TR7 that some petrol head had parked outside the next house up the street. "Also, we're driving to London today! And you remember how long it took coming the other way?" Robert groaned theatrically but Mary rolled over him: "It needs to be big *and* comfy! So hold hands and follow me, children!"

She pranced along the residential street towards the seafront, leading her crocodile of tiny transhuman menaces. As they reached the corner, one of the historic trams rattled past. "Cor, look at that!" Robert gurned. "Can we take it, Nan?"

"It won't go to London"—Mary reconsidered as a second thought struck her—"but yes, I think we've got time for a short ride on the trams before we leave!" A short ride would take them out to the fringes of suburbia, where minivans and SUVs were parked up for the day and their disappearance would not be immediately noticed.

The 1930s vintage double-decker trams weren't kept running out of season. But the group had barely had time to catch their breath at the tram stop before a boringly modern five-segment multiple unit hissed up and opened its doors. Mary led the children aboard and purchased a family day ticket from the conductor. She settled them in seats facing the seafront, then distracted them by pointing out local landmarks: "Look, it's Blackpool Tower!" she announced as they trundled past the two-thirds-scale clone of Monsieur Eiffel's masterpiece. As the tram climbed an incline the landmarks thinned out, replaced by row after row of Victorian town houses converted into budget hotels. Then they came to a row of larger, imposing buildings. "This is where we get off!" Mary called as they rolled up to the Cliffs Hotel stop. "Come along now, children!"

She led them around the front of the imposing redbrick Victorian building to one side, where cars were neatly slotted into angled parking bays. "Now, let's see. We need five seats!" she announced. "Not too small! Not too expensive!" No point jacking an instantly recognizable set of wheels. "Not too new!" New cars came with demonically enforced anti-theft wards. "Eenie, meenie, miney—" Her finger circled and settled on a silver Vauxhall Zafira, dirtied up from a long road trip—"Mine!"

Here goes. Mary reached blindly into her shoulder bag and fumbled for a small side pocket that tended to come and go as it pleased. The bag generally did a good job of anticipating her needs, but it could be unpredictable and fractious if overused. Last night's antitank rifle when she just wanted something that could stop a Tyrannosaur had been a typical overreaction. If she was unlucky this morning, it might hand her a tire iron, or a set of lockpicks. But—

Her fingers closed triumphantly around a smooth plastic pebble. "Keys!" she crowed, and stepped smartly up to the driver's door. A beep, a click, and the Zafira was hers. "Hop in smartly now, children!" she trilled. Ten seconds later she was behind the wheel and adjusting her seat belt as Lyssa and Robert bickered over who got the middle row. Twenty seconds after that she was messing with the mirrors and the engine was ticking over unevenly. And less than a minute after her bag conjured the keyfob, she was backing out of the parking space—not without checking that all four miscreants were strapped in and the doors were shut—and heading for the exit.

Mary was not a proficient driver—she'd never taken a test— but the car had an automatic transmission. That meant there was a *go* pedal and a *stop* pedal and a wheel for making it turn, plus a bunch of confusing shit she couldn't be bothered with. So she bulled ahead enthusiastically, managed to stop in the nick of time before she drove the wrong way up a one-way street, just *barely* scraped the side of an inconveniently parked Jaguar, and then it was smooth sailing all the way to the end of the road. She turned towards the sign for the M55 motorway, and—

"Are we there yet?" piped Ethan.

Horns blared, tires screeched, and Mary's cheek began to twitch uncontrollably. It was going to be a long day's drive.

7

▶◀▷◀▷◀▷◀

MEAT MARKET

Reentering the church hall, Eve found the ceremony had taken a disturbing turn. The priestess was chanting in a bastardized dialect of Old Enochian, summoning the faithful to Unholy Communion. There were no wafers, but a white body stocking atop the altar squirmed and heaved as if it was full of twitching maggots. The priestess stood over it with a filleting knife and a pair of gleaming stainless steel tongs, methodically plucking what appeared to be raw hamburger patties from its abdomen, which she fed to a queue of dead-eyed worshippers. The music was bizarrely catchy and everyone was on their feet—including Imp's crew, even though they were at the very back of the hall, almost invisible from the altar.

"For fuck's sake, Jerm!" hissed Eve, grabbing her brother's shoulder from behind: "You *mustn't*!"

Imp lurched to a halt and shook himself, visibly disoriented. "Wha . . . ?"

"Snap out of it!" Her ward was buzzing angrily and burning against her skin. "And grab your playmate before the Pied Piper"—the pie-eyed guitarist on fretless bass and drum machine accompaniment—"drags you all down to the altar!"

Imp gathered himself visibly and then grabbed Doc Depression, who had begun to shuffle towards the end of the queue snaking up the nave. "Wake up!" Imp *pushed* at Doc. Doc jerked and stopped walking. "Grab Del and Wendy," Imp told him. "We're in trouble."

"Don't eat the mystery meat," Eve explained, then made a grab for Sybil, who seemed to be asleep on her feet.

"Wow." Doc shook himself, much as Imp had. "That's some mojo, right there. Hey—" It was Del's turn: Rebecca was on her feet, and now she was sidling towards the altar. "*No,*" Doc told her. "Stop—"

Del shook him off but Wendy, coming to her senses, hauled her girlfriend back. "What the hell is she doing?" Wendy asked, staring at the front of the church.

"Later," Eve told her. "Let's get out of here: I've seen enough."

Imp took Doc by the hand. Together, they trailed after Eve like lost ducklings. Behind them, the priestess's voice rang out. "Eat in the name of our Lord! For by sacrifice I bring you the body and the blood of His Excellent Majesty the Mute Poet, Prince of Poetry and—"

Tendrils of malign magic seemed to wrap themselves around Eve's head, warm and fuzzy and trying to lull her into a false sense of comfort and safety. Eve knew better, and pushed back against the enchantment. She walked towards the door, careful not to move fast enough to attract attention, tugging Imp behind her. They made it to the curtain at the back of the congregation, then through into the lobby, where her head cleared. Outside on the pavement Eve found Game Boy leaning against the uneven brick wall, the flowery miasma of Eve's borrowed vaper clinging to his fingers. "Hey, Boy, wake up: we're going home."

"Hey," said Del. She sniffed: "Hey, you been smoking?"

Game Boy swayed and moved to offer the vaper to Eve. "Keep it," she said shortly. "Let's go." Her face was a closed book. Behind her, Wendy looked spooked.

Eve's bodyguards arrived and they set off. Game Boy was adrift in his own headspace, but en route, the other car pulled over outside a FlavrsMart fast food outlet and he looked up: "Whut?"

"They'll catch up with us after they've dropped Sybil off," Eve said tersely. And indeed, a few minutes after they walked in the front door of Imp's house, the door opened again and the seductive stench of fast food preceded Doc and the bodyguards.

Eve backed her brother against the wainscoting and got in his face with the demented focus of a stalker who'd found her rock star. "Did you *sense* it?" she demanded. "The power and the glamour—"

"'Ere, where d'you want this?" asked a wall of meat in a suit who'd followed her in, speaking indistinctly from behind a stack of pizza boxes.

"Gimme." Doc materialized in the drawing room doorway and grabbed the comestibles.

"—Dunno, Eve, it *could* have been—"

"—Stank of adipocere, didn't it?"

"How much do I owe you?"

"—The body stocking *looked* clean, I swear it wasn't just BO—"

"I kept 'er receipt. Thanks very muchly, sir."

Game Boy moonwalked into the drawing room and assplanted on a chair adjacent to the place setting where he'd left his character sheet and dice. A moment later, a pizza box materialized under his nose and he began to salivate visibly. "Take it," Doc told him.

"But—"

"Salami stuffed crust and deluxe meat feast topping with added meat and more meat and hot sauce," Doc explained. "I don't think Eve's bodyguards are big on carbs or cheese." The reek rising from the pile of cooked animal products on the pizza was indescribable, but Game Boy wasn't about to look a gift pizza in the mouth. "Is that roast pork?"

"Right, that's it, if you don't want to listen I'm gone!" Wendy's voice drifted through the front hall. She sounded exasperated.

"Wait—" Del scrambled to intercept Wendy. Game Boy contemplated the molten alien geometry of triangular pie segments dripping with unidentifiable goop and eventually managed to fold one, then bit daintily into the apex of the triangle. His mind was drifting, the world orbiting his head. *I survived,* he fuzzily realized. Admittedly it had only been ten or fifteen minutes of church-survival, but he hadn't completely fallen down the mineshaft of dysphoric memories. The female priest had helped, as had the decidedly unfamiliar liturgy—*Be welcome in the House of Our Lord the Undying King, Saint Ppilimtec the Tongueless, who sits at the right hand of Our Flayed Lord, he of the Smoking Mirror—*

Wait, what?

Game Boy sat bolt upright, half-eaten pizza drooping in his hand. "Doc," he said hoarsely, "what the *fuck* just happened?"

Doc paused his mastication. "We went to church for evening service—" He stopped. "Wait." He looked at Game Boy, his expression pleading: "It *was* just a church service, wasn't it?"

Eve led Wendy back into the drawing room. "How much do you remember?" she demanded of her audience. "Tell me."

"It was a—" Game Boy's stomach was a cold ball of dread, as if he'd been chewing on raw pizza dough and regrets—"it *wasn't* Christian, was it?"

"Well spotted." Eve sent him a tight smile. "Jeremy?"

"Well we already knew *that,* but why did Boy—"

"Doctor Depression. *Your* recollection, if you please?"

"It was just a church service, wasn't it?" But his twitching eyelid telegraphed doubt.

"And you?" She rounded on Wendy, who crossed her arms and looked mulish.

"I am never working for you again," the thief-taker said grimly.

"Fine, but you're going to tell them. Aren't you?"

Wendy gave her another mulish look, then faced the others: "That priestess, I've met her before. She works at FlavrsMart in Human Resources." She looked at Eve: "Is that what you expected to hear?"

"No, but it's a highly convenient coincidence, wouldn't you agree?" Eve plastered a bright and brittle smile on her face, then picked up an untouched box of HivePie Pizza and sat at the head of the table. "Absolutely typical," she muttered to herself. "Fucking Rupert. I *knew* there had to be a reason he was into FlavrsMart."

"For fuck's sake." Wendy glowered. "What the fuck was your boss Rupert doing buying a supermarket? Is it the new hotness in cult accessories?"

"That's what I'd like to know." Eve opened the pizza box. "The Church of the Mute Poet gives good glamour, it seems." Glamours blinded their targets to the true nature of the enchanted subject. "You, Del, and Sybil were unwarded, so you took it full-force between the eyes," Eve said, pointing at Doc. "Jeremy and I are both practitioners"—Imp puffed his chest out like a randy pigeon—"so we have some natural resistance." A crease appeared between her eyebrows. "*You* stayed well clear"—she focussed on Game Boy—"why?"

"Boy has a history with dubious churches," Imp told his sister, as Game Boy began to rock back and forth, biting his lip to hold back a keen of distress.

"What kind of churches?" Eve asked Game Boy. "What did they do?"

"Not here," Imp hissed in her ear. "*Uncool.*"

But something had broken Game Boy's internal censor—perhaps it was Eve's silver-chased vaper, or perhaps it was just time and perspective—because he began to speak. "My parents tried to *fix* me," he said. "Pray away the gay, gender boot camp, *pentacle*-costalist churches. Even though I'm not broken, they tried it all: exorcisms and banishments and"—his throat caught—"they put a geas on me to make me be what I wasn't, but I broke it and ran away."

He was shaking, and not with religious fervor. He was distantly aware of Doc holding his shoulders protectively, of Imp gripping his sister's elbow with an unreadable expression on her face.

"You can stop now," Eve remarked. More quietly, in Imp's direction: "So that's where his resistance comes from."

"*Saint Ppilimtec the Tongueless, Our Flayed Lord of the Smoking Mirror,*" Wendy recited. Her voice was pitched higher than usual. "What the fuck, Starkey? Why does this always circle back to you and your goddamn boss?"

"There is crossover between Western mystery cults and certain bastardized forms of Mesoamerican religious rites that the Spanish and Portuguese *conquistadores* stole and brought back with them to the Old World, along with syphilis and looted silver and gold and a bad human sacrifice habit." Eve looked at her warily. "Do you know anything about them?"

Wendy shook her head. "Nope. And I'm never working for you again, remember."

"What *do you* know about them?" Game Boy asked.

Eve shrugged. "Rupert was their bishop. Past tense, but they may not have noticed he's missing. I'm his . . . I have a certain responsibility for their actions. If I mishandle them, things could get messy. So next week I'm going back to Skaro to clean house."

"Count me out," Wendy said automatically. But she reached for a slice of pizza all the same.

"Are you still up for GMing tonight?" Imp asked Game Boy. "You promised you wouldn't interrupt our game," he warned his sister.

"I wouldn't miss it for the world." Eve's lip curled. "Some therapeutic bonding time is indicated," she singsonged.

"Let's get started," Game Boy announced. "You stand at the threshold of adventure," he continued, clearly intent on using the suspended game as duct tape for his tattered sense of self. "So, if we can get going? The party are sitting around at home, bored out of their heads, on a rainy morning in Daggerford. You're siblings— four children—and your parents have gone missing. It's going to be lunchtime soon and you haven't heard from them since last night." A surreptitious roll of the dice—"The four of you and your two trusty porters hired from the village—"

"—Five," said Eve.

"Hey! Since when are *you* playing?" Imp asked.

"Since now." She gave him a look.

"But you don't have a character!" he protested.

"That's okay, I brought a pre-rolled one. Dual-classed Mage/ Nanny, school of cerebromancy, lawful evil." She slid a neatly printed A4 page in front of Game Boy and her grin widened: "I paid for the pizza so I'm playing. Call me Mary: think I'll fit in with your party?"

▶◀▶◀▶◀

That weekend, Adrian Hewitt camped in the decommissioned freezer Ms. Henderson had made available to him. *His priestess.* He belonged to the one true God's representative on Earth (or at least in West London), body and soul.

Nobody paid any attention to another muppet hiding behind the Company Face while he worked on the meat printers. It was like a malign invisibility spell. At one point he ate, then slept for a few hours. Ms. Henderson had assigned him a username and password on the branch maintenance network, and he ordered in some replacements for consumables that wore out on a regular basis.

Something must have been going right, because at five a.m. on Saturday the store computer told him: "Proceed to Loading Dock Two and prepare incoming feedstock for deboning."

When he got there he found a quartet of zentai suits engaged in a ritualistic dance. Three of them were behaving normally enough for meat puppets—masks displaying permutations of blandly sympathetic expressions, movements economical. The fourth was malfunctioning. Its mask had slipped, face crashed in a pixellated mess, and it was struggling to escape. They'd duct-taped its arms and legs together, and it was making muffled noises behind its gag, trying to cry for help. As Ade approached, it jackknifed into rigidity, its discipline belt shocking it in response to its attempted flight.

"Check incoming conveyor line, then proceed," his headset instructed him. He stepped behind the malfunctioning muppet and smartly pulled a noose down from the conveyor, then pushed the winch button to haul it up. The feedstock wriggled as its feet left the floor. It continued to twitch while he checked over the jointing line. By the time he was satisfied everything was working properly, the muppet had gone limp.

"Remove skin prior to disassembly," the branch computer recited. Ade used a box cutter to slice through the duct tape and spandex. Blood oozed. He carefully recovered the Company Face, gently withdrew the gag from between bruised lips, and removed the other connectors lest they jam the carving knives. The feedstock was bald, male, pasty-skinned and flabby from too much time under office lights. Its face was purple and congested, and a warm glow of excitement lent a spring to Ade's steps as he replayed the hanging in his mind's eye. His crotch felt tight despite his catheter and belt: it was one of his fantasies come true. "Query. Is further assistance required for disassembly?

"Stand by," the computer said, then directed him towards the big green *start* button beside the gate. The machines inside the cage began to buzz as the overhead conveyor belt lurched into motion, carrying the carcass through the crisscross grid of laser scanners that would guide the blades.

This entire test run was illegal. Not because it was murder—Ms. Henderson had arranged for the subject to be sacked and administratively de-emphasized first—but because the disassembly line was only certified for pigs. It would need a deep clean afterwards. However, it was a *necessary* test. God needed a reliable and undetectable way of dealing with apostates and traitors. It was Ade's duty as the Lord's sword and shield to do Ms. Henderson's bidding in order to bring about His kingdom on Earth. But as he watched the feedstock dangle and twirl lifelessly towards the robots with their whirling electric carving knives, he felt an almost painful euphoria. Doing the Lord's work felt so beautiful and *right*. The starved vagrants and overdosed junkies he'd strung up in the past had been dead before he began: this was so much better that he could barely wait to do it again.

▶◀▶◀

Mary got all the way to Huddersfield before the wheels fell off the plan.

Traffic on the M55 was nightmarish, with an hour-long tailback—a lorry had overturned, shedding a cargo of raw cows' udders destined for a burger factory—and by the time she'd crawled past the obstruction Emily was squalling for a toilet stop. Mary was minded to press on, but the brat had smuggled a plant cutting into the car. Cecil was already extending rhizomes into the soft furnishings and the roof lining; distracted, Mary mistakenly diverted onto the M65 and thence the M62 rather than continuing south.

She parked up at a service area past Horwich and led the children indoors to use the toilets and seek refreshments. By the time they filed out again thirty minutes later—it was impossible to do anything fast, with four kids in tow—a police motorway patrol had pulled up beside the stolen Zafira.

"Let's walk." Mary turned briskly and strode around the corner of the restaurant, chilly sweat beading her neck. It wasn't the feds she was worried about so much as the skeletal presence crouching atop their light bar, its eye sockets flashing red and blue as it scanned the car park. Not to mention the penumbral sense of dread rippling out from it in waves. Obviously the Zafira had been reported missing, and only sheer blind luck had pulled her off the road in time. Number-plate recognition cameras and police demons: a combination made in hell.

Serendipity presented her with an unattended twelve-year-old Range Rover. The children oohed and aahed over the wood veneer dash and the high leather seats (although getting the five-year-olds to shut the fuck up and sit still in the back was a losing game, and heaven help her if anyone noticed the lack of booster seats and dobbed her in). What was less fortuitous was the petrol warning light that came on a mere ten kilometers down the road, which had turned into a deep cement canyon leading into the trackless depths of Manchester. The Chelsea tractor had less than a quarter of a tank when she boosted it, combined with the fuel consumption of a jumbo jet. She didn't fancy her chances on a filling station forecourt: they all had number-plate cameras and CCTV these days, so she found a slip road—just in time—and pulled off somewhere in the vicinity of Bury. *Fuck,* she swore silently, and thumped the steering wheel in frustration as she pottered through the wintry Lancashire suburbs in search of a suitable replacement.

"Are we there yet?" trilled Lyssa.

The next car was an elderly Volvo estate that smelled of wet dog and musty socks. Unlike the Range Rover, its fuel gauge claimed a full tank. Mary checked Google Maps on her phone, told it to plot her a route that didn't include any motorways—they were crawling with cameras—and Google Maps promptly sent her on a tour of the central Manchester one-way system. After nearly being T-boned by a stealth tram Mary's nerves were in tatters. Eventually her phone steered her onto a main road heading east out of the city and she began to relax her white-knuckle grip. "I'm sure we'll be in London by teatime," she reassured the children, "but we'll find somewhere to stop for lunch once we're out of this traffic."

Poking at the fussy radio-cassette unit (which seemed to have more buttons than it could possibly need, identified by obscure four-letter labels), she brought up a local radio station in the middle of a news report. "Police say the cause of the fire at the Chariots of the Gods theme park in Blackpool is still unknown, but human remains have been recovered from the site. A mobile crane has just arrived on the scene to lift a dead dinosaur—"

Mary cringed and hit the *scan* button. The radio latched onto BBC Radio 4, a national channel in the middle of a news update. "The search continues for the kidnapped children of leading Home Office superheroes Captain Colossal and the Blue Queen. The children and their nanny disappeared from their London home earlier this week while their parents were on an assignment overseas. A reward of twenty thousand pounds is offered for information leading to the safe return of Melissande, Ethan, Emily, and Robert—"

Mary nearly sprained her finger on the *off* button, then glanced round the cabin suspiciously. Robert had his earphones on, Emily was cooing at a small plant pot, Ethan was curled up against the car door with his eyes closed, and Lyssa—

"Yes?" Mary asked as the traffic lights turned green and she moved off again.

"Twenty thousand pounds?" Princess Sparkle-Goth had glittery currency signs in her eyes. "*Only* twenty thousand pounds?" She pouted.

"I'll give you twenty-five when we get home," Mary told her, "and we'll have more fun on the way. Deal?"

Lyssa glowered over her shoulder at Robert, who was ignoring them. "I get *his* reward money, too," she announced.

"Keep him from finding out about the reward and it's yours," Mary said blandly.

Manchester receded in the rearview mirror. On the other hand they detoured north to avoid the Peak District, and the road grew narrow and circuitous as it wound through the endless valleys of West Yorkshire. They were charming and picturesque at a distance, but full of villages with badly designed multiway junctions, sudden twenty-mile-per-hour speed limits, traffic cameras, and tourist traps. If she tried to feed the kids in a village cafe they'd be sure to attract attention. What she really needed was an anonymous retail mall with a food court where she could shovel burgers down their voracious maws without attracting undue attention. Reluctantly, she pushed on. Bradford she'd heard of, but not in promising terms. What the hell was a hudder and why should there be a town named after a field full of them? It couldn't be any worse than Blackpool, so she decided to find out.

"Are we there yet?" demanded Ethan: "I need to go pee-pee!"

Driving into Huddersfield, Mary followed the signs for the city center and Kingsgate Shopping Centre. She managed to shoehorn the Volvo into the multistory car park without scraping too much paint off on the concrete pillars, then led the fractious and irritated children out in search of a toilet facility, fast food, and some sort of bribe. "There's a GameStop in here," she told Robert, "and something called The Entertainer Toy Shop. Wouldn't you like to go there after lunch, children?"

By the time they got to the food court it was nearly one o'clock. It was precisely as dismal as Mary had hoped and twice as busy, but there was anonymity to be found in the crowds, and the kids had a bottomless appetite for KFC nuggets and Chocoslurry Glory™. Mary indulged them with ruthless patience, for when the fearsome foursome were in a food coma they were far easier to manage than when cranky from hunger. There was no point going back to the urban tank—the risk of detection was far too high— but if she could boost another set of wheels they could be on the road again by four o'clock at the latest. London was three hours away by motorway, so it ought to be possible to get there by midnight along backcountry routes. What could possibly go wrong?

She looked up from their table and noticed a row of overhead TV screens. They were tuned to News 24, showing a big building well ablaze by night. The crawl said something about Blackpool: and the picture changed to show a group of familiar faces.

"Look, Nan," piped Emily, "you're on television!"

►◄►◄◄

The game night petered out by mutual consent around 11 p.m., theoretically so that Wendy could get home before the tube stopped running. In practice, the end came early because Game Boy was beginning to twitch. He was a competent GM, but he was out of his depth: Imp grandstanded at every opportunity, Del and Wendy cooperatively tackled every challenge with a speed and expertise that suggested they were very far from the novices Doc had led Game Boy to expect, and Eve approached every puzzle with a lawyer's analytical mind and an assassin's killer instinct. In two hours flat the party bulldozed a path through the entire three-session campaign he'd mapped over a heavily customized version of the Sword Coast, arriving at the gates of Castle Grimstein six real-world hours too early for a planned custom adventure he hadn't finished designing yet. He was running on fumes and random encounter charts by the time Del began nudging Wendy and muttering about the last train.

"Come on, let's get you home," Del murmured in Wendy's ear as Wendy gathered up her stuff—character sheets, notes—and shoved them in a jacket pocket.

"I can get the"—Wendy shifted mental gears with a visible effort—"you're coming?"

"I'll give you a—"

"You are *not* driving."

"But I won't hit anything! You know me, I *can't* hit anything—"

Wendy shook her head. She'd seen Del knock back at least three cans of Doc Depression's Regrettable Beer. "Tube or taxi: it's the principle of it, I mean, it's the *law.*"

Del snorted as she grabbed her jacket. "I know you saw Game Boy with Eve's vaper."

"Yeah, but that's different: Game Boy wasn't trying to get me to share. And anyway they just decriminalized it."

"I swear I will never understand you, girl."

They were at the front door. "You coming home with me, or what?" Wendy enquired.

"Yeah." Del pulled the door shut and followed Wendy down the garden path to the rusting front gate. Somehow Eve and her SUV full of bodyguards had made their escape before Del and Wendy reached the street. They walked in companionable silence for a minute or two. It was chilly but not unpleasantly wintry, and the rain was holding off until the early hours.

"Do you think Game Boy lost the plot?" Wendy finally asked.

"You bet. Did you see the way he twitched every time Mary Poppins pulled out a new crossbow or hijacked another oxcart?"

"Yeah." Wendy frowned. "I was less keen on being the littlest girl in the group."

Game Boy had inflicted pre-rolled characters on the Lost Boys (but not Eve, who had turned up late and gone full tankie on Gee-Bee's plans). They were playing as a family of magical kids growing up in Daggerford, children of a pair of retired adventurers who'd mysteriously gone missing. Eve's character, Mary Poppins, was introduced as the children's mysterious nanny, who'd blown in on an air elemental from Baldur's Gate (which she had mysteriously left in a hurry). Game Boy had gone into a huddle with Eve for a few minutes while Imp and Doc fetched more beer, then came back and explained that Mary had agreed to take the children on a cross-country quest to find their parents, who had been abducted by a Big Bad (type: unknown, but sinister) and were being held for ransom in Castle Grimstein.

Castle Grimstein was a Crusader-style fortress on an offshore lump of rock two days' sailing from Waterdeep. Featuring a sinister village full of close-mouthed fishing folk, and rumors of hidden catacombs and tunnels under the castle, Grimstein was also the ancestral seat of a sinister Baron, who seemed unlikely to provide warm milk and cookies before bedtime for visiting children and their nosy nanny.

But the campaign had not run as planned. The children had slaughtered their way from one side of the Misty Forest to the other, stringing up highwaymen by their entrails and stealing everything that wasn't nailed down. Imp's pyromaniacally inclined boy-mage now sported a cloak of uncured goblin hide. ("Purely as a deterrent," he insisted sniffily.) They sneaked into Baldur's Gate via the inexcusably ahistorical sewers and, with the nanny's help, hijacked a fishing boat. Then they set sail for a small island in the Korinn Archipelago. There was a price on their heads already, but they were having *fun.* (Even Wendy, whose precocious five-year-old Druid was merrily introducing bounty hunters to the joy of sky burial.)

"Littlest girl, littlest boy." Del gave her a shoulder bump. "It's a *game,* Wendy. You get to step outside your own skin for a few hours and make-believe you're someone else."

"Yeah." Wendy sighed. "It just feels weirdly close to real life at times. Especially when Imp's sister pitches in."

They made it into the tube station amidst the closing-time throng of drunk pub- and cinemagoers, and rode in amiable silence through the tunnels under London. They changed at Kings Cross, traversing escalators and endless pedestrian tunnels until they reached their platform just in time for the last train home. Fifteen minutes later they spilled onto the pavement outside Wendy's suburban stop and found themselves on a high street where the fast-food joints did a roaring trade with homebound commuters from the central London hive.

"You're thinking so loud you're deafening me," Del said as she tugged Wendy out of the way of a drunkard's pavement pizza. In return, Wendy pulled her into an alley where the noise level dropped ten decibels and the streetlights thinned out. "Planning for next week's games night?" Del asked. "Or something more important?"

"Just thinking about the priest. And Eve."

"They do look similar, now you mention it." Del nudged Wendy's shoulder: "Those skinny blonde types all look the same to me, like they came off the same production line at the Barbie factory."

Wendy nudged back. "Isn't that something-ist? Eve was standing right beside us."

"Yeah. So: Human Resources manager by day, side hustle as Priestess of the Mute Poet by night? Meanwhile Eve was Rupert's right hand, Rupert runs the cult, and Rupert is trying to take over FlavrsMart. You think he did it to them? There's a connection?"

"*Could* be." Wendy sounded uncertain. "Is it a cult thing? They've both got that look. It's everywhere, once you start noticing it, like it's a standard template. There was one in our carriage on the first train: that gang of—"

"—Good-time girls? With the redhead who was trying not to fall off her heels—"

"—Yeah, her? Anyway, the one propping her up? She had the exact same face. Like Eve."

"Eve's posh, though, tube-girl was just skanky." Del grimaced.

"Hey! You *did* not say that." They were at the front door.

Wendy slid her key in the lock just as Del slid an arm around her waist. "*You're* not skanky."

"I'm not a skinny bottle blonde who irons my hair and wears five-inch heels on the tube, no." Wendy led her inside and they climbed the stairs to her bedsit—soon to be her ex-bedsit, once her pay rise came through. "Beer's in the fridge but I'm not sure I need another one."

Wendy was about to detach herself from Rebecca so she could get to the bathroom, but the Deliverator wasn't about to let go of her package. They ended up in an untidy tangle against the inside of her front door, with Del quietly grumbling against her face. "Didn't come here for no beer," she said, and captured Wendy's lips. She tasted of hop oil and pepperoni and Wendy kissed her back tenderly, letting go of a tension she hadn't been aware of that had been building since Eve dragged them off to church. "Let's go to bed, girl."

Wendy had a battered futon instead of a proper bed. Working together, they dragged it into position and brought out the pile of bedding, pausing to touch one another whenever the process gave them an excuse. Eventually they ended up in a heap, kissing and stroking and groping under clothing, then the clothing went away, along with Wendy's awareness of anything beyond the taste of Rebecca's skin, the heat and pressure of her touch, and the pitch of her moans.

When she came back to herself—sticky with sweat, limp as a rug, heart pounding and breathless—she spent a long time staring at the damp patch on the ceiling. Del nuzzled happily against her collarbone, pinning her to the futon with an arm thrown across her chest. *How did I get here?* she thought, and *Where am I going?* Which slithered uneasily into *Where are we going?* Assuming *we* was a thing, of course. It had been less than two weeks, after all. "I need to go house-hunting," Wendy said aloud.

"Mm-hmm." Becca stretched. "Right now?"

"Not right now," Wendy agreed. "But soon." The landlord wanted everyone out within two months, but if the backdated pay Mr. Gibson had promised her came through she'd be able to put down a deposit by the end of the next week. "What about you?"

"I need to sort out—" Del twitched as if a many-legged thing had crawled over the nape of her neck—"stuff. Things." She pulled back slightly and Wendy felt a momentary pang.

"Can I help?"

"No. Not right now, anyway." But Del relaxed a little, as if the offer made her feel better. "Still getting my head around the having-a-job thing," she admitted. "Feels like selling my—not my soul, like selling something else." She paused. "I'll have that beer now."

Two open cans later Becca unwound enough to explain. "The Ancient Egyptians thought the human soul had nine different parts—all independent. The heart, the personality, the name, a bunch of other shit. Stuff. All different aspects of you. Uh, one of them was literally the soul, and another was the physical body; I'm not explaining this right. Anyway, signing on with your boss felt like I was taking out a spiritual loan secured against a part of me I didn't know existed. The soul of my Facebook account, the shadow of my credit score. Still not sure I shouldn't go in on Monday and tell him it won't work."

"Well." Wendy shrugged. "That's your call." *Please don't ask me about my headhunter's bonus.* "But . . . let me have a word with Gibson first?"

"Why?" Del's expression was now slightly closed off.

"I'm not sure. But you saw the priestess too, didn't you? Would you recognize her if you saw her again? In a different setting?"

"Sure. Are you thinking of dragging me into your *investigation,* girl?"

"No, because you're not officially on the team, your background check hasn't gone through yet, you're not a trained investigator, and I don't care what you've seen in the movies—the fastest way to fuck up a crime scene is to turn a random amateur sleuth loose on it." Wendy smiled to take the sting out of her words. "But Jennifer from FlavrsMart HR is definitely a cult priestess, and I could use corroboration—I'm not sure what it means that the Church of the Mute Poet are involved with FlavrsMart and people are going missing there but it needs to be followed up. I'll pitch it to Gibson as mentoring, and see if I can shake loose a higher hourly rate for you in the field."

Del snorted quietly. "Just admit it, you can't stand to be apart from me during the day."

Wendy grinned at her: "Busted."

"I'll think about it," said Del, in the tone that meant she didn't want her girlfriend to imagine she was easy. She yawned. "Long day."

"Stay over?" Wendy offered. "Stay with me?"

Del yawned again. Then she tossed her empty can at the trash and reclined beside Wendy. "Always."

►◄►◄►◄

Sybil ambushed Eve when she emerged from her office on Sunday morning.

Eve had already been up for a few hours: she'd started her day at five by showering and working out in the gym, before going over the final documentation for the upcoming buy-in at FlavrsMart once more—it was due to be signed off at a meeting on Thursday. After two hours of combing over legal boilerplate she wanted a break, but Mrs. Cunningham was waiting for her in the front office. "Yes?" she demanded.

"You wanted to talk to me about the Church, ma'am?"

Eve did a double-take: "I *did* say that, didn't I." Her lips thinned as she mentally rearranged her priorities. "Could you wait here? I'll be about three and a half minutes."

Eve bolted before Sybil finished nodding. Back when Rupert expected her to be available twenty-four seven she'd fine-tuned her bathroom breaks: she stepped back into the outer office just five seconds later than she'd said. Mrs. Cunningham was standing on the same spot, her back ramrod straight. Eve waved her through to the visitor's chair in the inner office. "So what did you make of last night's church service? Was it what you expected?"

Sybil seemed oddly nervous. Perhaps it was just Eve's brutally direct approach to business, but could it be something else? Eve produced a sympathetic expression and waited. Eventually Sybil cleared her throat. "It was very—" Sybil waved her hands— "*different*. It was the same liturgy as our services back home, but my husband—or Lord Skaro—would never have let a woman officiate!" She burst out: "It's not right! Men and women *sitting together*? That could never happen. And there was *music*! And a *woman*, a female priest, giving the sermon . . . !" She trailed off, bewildered that her faith could encompass such deviation.

"I take it it's not like that on Skaro?"

"There shouldn't be music in church!" Sybil looked appalled. "People might *dance*. The sexes might converse with one another!"

Eve nodded encouragingly. *Yes, yes, please do carry on.* It sounded as if the Church of the Mute Poet combined the worst traits of Free Kirk Presbyterians and electric guitar Pentecostalists, with added necromancy on top. "Was the composition of the congregation very different as well?"

"Well, you know how it is on Skaro, it's—I mean, we're islanders. We're very close-knit, everybody knows everybody else, our families go back centuries except for the newcomers who turned up during Victoria's reign. But we're very tolerant! We don't mind visitors and immigrants. Even if they come from *France*." She side-eyed the door, as if terrified that this scandalous rumor might inflict itself on ears unprepared for such a confession. "But yesterday—there were *Chinese* people. And Africans, and Indians, and all! Some of your brother's friends are black! It's—I had no *idea*."

Eve silently counted to seventeen in base eleven. "I'm sure you didn't," she murmured. *Skaro: so insular they don't even* know *they're white supremacists.* She made a mental note to write Sybil up for mandatory diversity awareness training before she got the company sued. (Or worse, forced Eve to apply Rupert's revised downsizing protocol—which she was valiantly trying to avoid, despite learning that her employees included Nazis, cultists, and why-not-both Nazi cultists.) "A word to the wise? If you want to stay in London, you've got to learn how to get along with people from other backgrounds." *Without getting punched in the mouth.* "But back to the church service. What else did you notice?"

"Well, the liturgy was all jumbled up! That priestess girl had everything in the wrong order—the Hymn to the Black Sun is supposed to come after the Suffering of the Tongueless and before the reading from the Book of the Flowery Penumbra. And the Recitation of the Creed only happens on the first Tuesday of months ending in 'y.' But she missed out the—"

Sybil explained everything wrong with the service in interminable detail. Clearly the two congregations approached their book of uncommon prayer from different non-Euclidean angles. They were still recognizable as the Church of the Mute Poet, but the congregations in Skaro and London were separated by an enormous gulf of divergent practice, like subspecies of finch from isolated Galapagos Islands singing subtly different songs. "It's shocking, just shocking!" Sybil concluded with lip-smacking disapproval.

"When did the Church adopt that liturgy?" Eve prodded. "I mean, I thought Skaro was originally Roman Catholic, but converted to Church of England way back?"

Sybil shook her head energetically. "The New Baron introduced it when he arrived. My mam told me how it used to be. Before, under the Old Lords, we were god-fearing Celtic Christians, not like those heathens on Jersey and Guernsey." She sniffed, then infodumped all over Eve.

Skaro had been Christian since the sixth century. They'd started out Celtic, then flipped to Catholic, then Calvinist, then C of E—any denomination beginning with a C appeared to be acceptable—before everything fell apart in the nineteenth century and the Methodists moved in. That was the thin end of the wedge: a mere century later they enthusiastically adopted the mysteries of Saint Ppilimtec, the Mute Poet.

"It happened in 1998. The old pastor retired rather suddenly and the new Lord—" Rupert de Montfort Bigge—"took over, conducting the service himself. A new book of common prayer appeared one Sunday: his Lordship had his men distribute copies to the heads of every household, then called an elders' meeting. A week later the services changed." Her expression turned distant. "I was a young newlywed back then, still getting to know my Tony. I was at that first service, sitting in the back with the other wives. The B-Bishop? Baron Skaro"—she clearly meant Rupert— "read a prayer in something like Latin, only not—some other language—then led the men in a hymn they'd rehearsed, and I don't remember what else. The next month there were more funerals than usual. More than we usually see in a year, anyway. And some of the elders retired to the mainland without leaving any forwarding details. I didn't pay much attention at the time because the Baron was making lots of changes to the way the castle runs and I was very busy. It's hard when you're seven months pregnant and the new Master up-ends everything," she confided.

"How *precisely* did he up-end things?" Eve leaned forward attentively. She'd taken courses on interrogation, and now she followed the protocol to build rapport with her subject: telegraph your interest, keep your eyes wide and focussed on their face, lips slightly parted, hands on knees. *Keep her talking.* "What was he changing?" *It was more than just the decor in his private apartment, wasn't it?*

"There was the new liturgy," Sybil said reluctantly. "But there was also a lot of remodeling belowstairs, construction workers from the mainland working in the cellars. He told Tony they'd been neglected, they were damp and there was rot and if it weren't fixed the castle would collapse into the caves. But he sacked the first three or four construction firms for inadequate performance even though it was he who kept changing the blueprints." *So nobody but Rupert had a clear picture of what was going on down there?* Eve nodded thoughtfully. "He sent a bunch of youngsters overseas on scholarships, as well as the retirees. Most of the youngsters eventually came back, but for a couple of years we were very short-handed. I don't know how we got anything done! Especially with the Our Nation One Faith campaign and all the babies."

"The . . . what?" Eve felt a frisson of fear run up her spine as she listened to Sybil.

The new liturgy and the shift to the sacrament of the Mute Poet—initially presented as the New Baron leading the island back to its Calvinist roots—was the set-dressing for a totalitarian coup, using religious trappings as a lever.

Skaro was already half a century behind the times when Rupert arrived and took over: 1960s teen culture, never mind 1970s feminism, hadn't left a mark, and the mainland was close enough that troublemakers could be discreetly handed a one-way ticket, never to be heard from again. More insidiously, before Rupert Skaro didn't even have a cellphone mast much less broadband internet. The locals were uninformed, ignorant, and vulnerable to gaslighting.

Rupert had taken advantage of this insular and conservative community to indoctrinate the natives with his faith, starting from the top down. He'd co-opted the islander men by giving them a heady shot of conservative family values, starting with power and dominance. Keep the women busy with babies—barefoot and pregnant in the kitchen—and a generation later the island would be overrun with young adults raised to worship the Undying King, Saint Ppilimtec the Tongueless, right hand of the Flayed Lord, Emperor of the Sixty-Seven-Thousandth Heaven. And to obey Rupert as their Bishop, the Lord and Master of their universe.

It was a strategy that ultra-conservative politicians had deployed in Hungary, Poland, and Russia, not to mention the more backward bits of the United States and the Middle East. But they usually aimed to take their societies back to the social structures of the nineteenth century AD, not BC.

Sybil's account contained enough details for Eve to assemble the big picture. All the *mana* Rupert stole from the disappeared went into the geas he wove around the islander community, reinforcing his control until the islanders couldn't even remember the family members whose ritual sacrifices they'd participated in. He'd been preparing an army of brainwashed cultists long before he'd sucked Eve into his web. And his planning ran deep.

Eve found the notion of Rupert engaging in long-term planning horrifying. It didn't match the face he had shown her at all. Had he been gaslighting her about his intentions right from the start—keeping her busy with the mundane corporate and financial legwork, while he focussed on some mad cyclopean vision of his very own apocalypse, rather than leading the life of dissolution and debauchery she'd believed in? It seemed increasingly likely. The revelation that Rupert's wealth sprang from divination through haruspicy and human sacrifice filled in a lot of gaps she'd failed to notice earlier—it was always harder to notice the absence of information than its presence—and now that she considered things in this new light, it was clear that she couldn't take *anything* Rupert had done for granted. How far did his oracular insights extend? Had he taken steps to thwart her feeble attempts to free herself, to manipulate her into carrying out his plans even during his absence?

Then another thought occurred to her. The church in London and the chapel in Skaro . . . which was the chicken, and which the egg? If the London cult had been operational first, why had Rupert even bothered to purchase Skaro—was it merely the lure of his very own feudal seigneury with attached legal system and entrenched patriarchy, or was there something much more sinister about it? If the London church was an offshoot of the Skaroese cult—perhaps established by a party of youthful missionaries—then how many others were there?

Eve forced a charming smile for Sybil's benefit. "My dear," she purred, "I have a little task for you, if you're not busy." Sybil sat up, eager to find something to fill her days. "I'm interested in knowing more about the history of the church we attended yesterday. I want to know how long they've been followers of our Tongueless Lord? Were they something else previously, and if so what? Who brought them to the True Faith, and who trained and appointed the priestess?" She leaned forward again. "I'm concerned about the deviations from the standard liturgy—the progressive variations—and I want to know how it happened, that's all. Obviously when my husband returns"—she coughed—"he'll want a full accounting. Do you think you can do that for me?"

"Yes, ma'am!" Sybil bobbed her head. "Is that all? Do you think I should attend evening service there?"

"Yes. I have work to do that will keep me here. Will you be all right? I can assign you a driver."

"That would be wonderful!" Sybil smiled, her expression luminous. Purpose lent her a saintly, deadly aura as she left.

Eve sat in silence for a while. It was a given that Rupert was—had been—a misogynist and a reactionary dirtbag, but that wasn't enough to explain the newly emerging picture. Becoming a multi-billionaire was one thing. Running a cult was something else. Setting up a microscopic island rerun of the Third Reich was a whole different ball game: and undertaking all three tasks in parallel bespoke a frightening degree of organization. He'd been courting Metahuman Associated Dementia with the larger wreakings: What did he think could possibly justify the risk? And how did FlavrsMart fit in the picture?

Nothing good, Eve repeated to herself, *nothing good. . . .*

▶◀▶◀

Mary Drop stared in horror at the sight of her own face repeated across four giant television screens in the food court. The image was recognizable, even pixellated and blurred by the ceiling CCTV camera that had taken it. The Diet Cola she'd been in the act of swallowing fizzed up as she coughed and sneezed simultaneously: the burning in her sinuses was excruciating, but not as bad as the realization that the game was up. Her eyes watered as she sprayed fizzing soda across her half-eaten poké bowl. She glanced up again. The news was showing security camera footage from Hamleys. Not the shooty-bang-bang stuff, or the horrible little oiks running wild, but surprisingly good footage of her leading her little crocodile of miscreants up the escalator.

Mary watched, appalled. On the screens she was wearing her nanny weeds, the same twinset and sensible shoes she now wore, the same cute little cap and the blue wool coat with the big buttons. They even had her bag in focus. A coughing fit racked her, and by the time she could focus again the news had moved on. She glanced around, half expecting to see a tide of bounty hunters converging on her like shopping mall zombies, but nobody was watching. The other family groups in the food court were either queuing or inhaling their chicken and chips or pizza slices or whatever. *There's still time,* Mary realized, trembling with tension. She'd have to ditch the nanny uniform and run, but—

"Nan?" Emily was staring up at her, with an expression of such baffled bewilderment that Mary's treacherous heart tried to melt.

"What is it, dear?"

"Are we in trouble, Nan? Was it the trees?"

"No dear." *Not yet.* Mary smiled.

"What's happening?" Robert demanded.

"Nothing to worry about, eat your chips," Mary said automatically as she unbuttoned her coat. She opened her bag and shoved the hat inside, shimmied her coat off and out from under the messenger's strap and squeezed it after the hat, then rummaged around inside until she felt something. She pulled out a blonde wig. She held it under the tabletop, glanced around furtively, then ducked and yanked it over her scalp. Another swift look showed that nobody was watching—then she turned back to the table and found she had an underage audience. Emily stared at her accusingly; Lyssa was completely agog.

"Nan, you didn't say you could do wigs!" Lyssa glowed with anticipation. "Can I have a wig, pretty please?"

Crap. "What kind of wig would you like, dear?"

"I want to be Marceline the Vampire Queen, only teenage—no, wait, I want . . . pigtails? Only rainbow pigtails like the one Harl—Harley?—wears in *Big Trouble in Little Gotham*. And a giant hammer!"

"You can have a hammer *or* you can have a wig," Mary said sternly, "not both. And only one wig. Harley Quinn or Marceline?"

"Harley," Lyssa pronounced thoughtfully, "I can get a big hammer later. I will paint it in rainbows and call it Skullcrusher and—"

Mary handed her a theatrical wig (still sealed in a cellophane bag), then showed her how to put it on and tuck her own hair under it (resulting in a somewhat lopsided Junior Harley cosplay, because Lyssa had too much hair of her own).

"I wanna wig, too," declared Emily.

"Let me"—Mary reached into her bag—"see?" She looked at the plastic bag she'd just pulled out. "You can be a Terrortot! Look, you're Laserwasp! You're bright yellow and have a bouncy death ray on your head!" She thrust the package at Lyssa: "Be a dear and help your little sister get changed?" She checked her bag again. "Ethan can be Devilbaby"—a Crimson Television Krampus— "and that makes Robert Twinkster!" The purple Terrortot, with a pintle-mounted minigun atop his skull. "Lyssa, if you get bored with Harley I've got a Flytrap costume for you—"

"Don't wanna," said Lyssa, but she took it anyway.

Robert and Ethan looked doubtful. "It'll be fun!" Mary said brightly: "Let's all go to the bathroom and put on our costumes, then we'll be on our way!"

The Terrortots were this month's viral YouTube hit: a sardonic spoof of the '90s hit babytainment TV show *Teletubbies,* featuring four brightly colored cyborg/alien apocalypse toddlers who sought to conquer the world before teatime, armed with built-in death rays and cuteness.

She sent Robert into the gents' with a stern injunction to mind Ethan, then stood guard while Lyssa led Emily into the ladies'. Seeing nobody approaching up the corridor, she nipped into the disabled loo and grabbed a quick-change outfit from her bag. By the time the four alien cyborgs emerged (the boys' hands were suspiciously dry, but Mary had no fucks left to give), she was in jeans, a biker jacket, a glossy black bob, and sunglasses. "Come along, boys and girls," she told her wards, "we have miles to go—"

That's when she saw the approaching mall cop.

He was middle-aged and portly, clearly not in great physical shape, and this being a British mall rather than an American one, he was unarmed except for a walkie-talkie and an officious attitude the size of an aircraft carrier. "Hey, you!" he said, pointing at Mary and blocking the corridor—"Izzat you what was on the telly? You'd better come with me! Or else—"

Mary smiled brightly: "Ethan? Emily?"

"Dakka-dakka-dakka-ZOOM!" shouted Devilbaby, leaping up and down and unleashing a cloud of buzzing robot murder hornets on the security guard. "Death to humans! Eat death, human scum! Watch me destroy all humans!" Laserwasp stood silently beside her brother, thumb in the general vicinity of her mouth, as green vinelike tendrils sprouted from the bottom of her costume and slithered towards their convulsing victim.

"We're leaving now," Mary announced, turning and marching smartly towards the emergency fire exit. She pushed the crash bar. "Come along, boys and girls!" The fire alarm drowned out the guard's screams of terror. She paused for a quick head count. Robert was lingering on the threshold, looking back wistfully. "Smartly, Twinkster!" she snapped.

"That's not my—" The freshly minted Terrortot saw her expression and clammed up.

Mary relented. "You can take down the next one," she told him. "And you, Lyssa, wouldn't you enjoy that, too?" A green velour Flytrap bounced up and down in delight. "Now fetch your brother and sister and let's hop to it, we have to acquire another"—she glanced up and down the bare-walled concrete passage leading to the car park—"van?"

They emerged in a commercial parking annex at the back of the mall. It was neither the main public car park nor the loading bays for full-sized trucks, but a smaller area for local delivery vehicles. Mary was confronted with a cornucopia of white Ford Transits: box vans, regular vans, long wheelbase models, one with windows and seating for passengers—*bingo*.

She darted towards it, lifting the flap of her bag and reaching into the side pocket where the keys lurked. She fumbled around. The pocket had gone, but something cold and metallic, clawlike, grabbed her wrist—

"Really, Dad?" Her voice cracked: "Did you have to do this *right now*?"

An ominous electric buzz vibrated up her arm and she tugged experimentally. Whatever-it-was was trying to suck her arm in—no, it was *climbing* her arm, enveloping her in chilly pinching caterpillar tracks and G-clamps and who-knew-what mechanisms.

"Nan?" Twinkster was staring at her, head tilted to one side.

The mechanical snake-leech-thing continued to climb her radius and ulna: it had reached her elbow. Shreds of leather and fabric from her jacket and shirt spewed out of the bag. They smelled burnt. She suppressed the urge to scream in frustration and instead gave the Banks children a brittle smile: "This is all perfectly normal!" she trilled at them, momentarily forgetting that she'd ditched her nanny disguise and was free to be herself again. "It happens every so often!" The bag was one of her brilliant but crackbrained father's creations, and like everything else he made, every so often it malfunctioned. Most of the time it coughed up wardrobe props it manufactured or stored in some kind of pocket dimension, but there seemed to be an Igor in there as well—one of Dad's mad science robot assistants—and sometimes it got bored and made shit up. It was supposed to give her whatever tool circumstances demanded, but right now it seemed to think she needed a power-assisted exoskeleton instead of a set of keys.

"Swiving clunge-munching"—she gave up the effort not to swear in front of the kids and gave the bag-strap a good firm yank—"*fuck*." The bag dropped to the ground. Her arm from the shoulder down was sheathed in gleaming steel, wrapped in a nest of pneumatic hoses and articulated joints. She flexed her shiny fingers, staring at them in disbelief. When she touched fingertips to thumb she felt skin, but to a first approximation her arm had turned full cyborg. "*Fuck,*" she repeated faintly, then re-slung the bag over her opposite shoulder. It felt oddly light in her machine-arm's grip, although it hung heavy on her flesh-and-blood collarbone. *I hope I've still got flesh left under all this,* she thought uneasily, then put her game face back in place for the children: "Right-o!"

She marched up to the Sunshine Holidays minibus as if nothing had happened, grabbed the driver's door handle, and watched it snap off in her fingers. "Shit."

"That's a bad word! You swore!" accused the red Terrortot. Mary ignored him, taking deep breaths as she tried not to panic.

If her bag was malfunctioning, was Dad's condition worsening? Everybody knew that if you overused superpowers the Metahuman Associated Dementia was more likely to get you. Mary had a phobia of MAD. As a mad scientist's beautiful daughter, she was already at risk of inheriting the condition. In a matter of months, it had turned her father from a kindly but absentminded man who wanted to solve world hunger into a very unstable genius with a tendency to cackle maniacally and play with giant robots. Mary shivered. Maybe she relied too heavily on the magic bag. It was far less violent than her own talent, which drew entirely the wrong kind of attention when she used it. But if Dad was declining again, not only would he need more specialized—expensive—care, the tool Mary relied on to fund the care in question might be on the edge of crapping out.

"Shit." Mary flexed her bionic hand. The sensation of steel tendons slithering across ratcheted knuckles and cunningly flexible plates was indescribable but disturbing. *But what if* . . . She stared at the keyhole in the van's door, then extended her index finger to its full length. It kept growing, then the tip opened like a flower and sprouted a torsion bar, a pick, and an oddly esoteric rake. She touched the lock and *felt* the pins engage with the top joint of her index finger, which smoothly rotated of its own accord until the lock clicked. "All aboard, girls and boys!" she called as she opened the sliding door to the passenger area behind her.

"Nan's a Terminator!" Twinkster told his siblings. "Wicked!" Mary opened her bag and pulled out Twinkster's Maimstation Portable, then a baby triffid for Laserwasp, and a My Little Unicorn playset for Devilbaby to animate for Flytrap. Then she stuck the top joint of her thumb in the ignition and fired up the van.

She had three hundred and twenty kilometers to drive, four rambunctious Terrortots to wrangle, and her face was all over the TV news. Pulling on a pair of dark glasses seemed mandatory. She didn't dare check the fuel gauge: it felt like the job was jinxed. But as long as the bag worked some of the time she wasn't entirely on her uppers. The time to start to really worry would come if Dad's creation flaked out *and* she needed something more substantial than a smile and the whiplash voice of authority to keep the kids in line. Say, if the police caught up with them. Never mind Mr. and Mrs. Banks.

If that happened, she'd have to use her own powers.

Which could get very bloody, very fast.

▸◂▸◂▸◂

On Monday morning, Wendy rose early, put on her gray work suit, dropped by the office to update her time sheet, then caught the tube to the supermarket to continue her investigation.

Her first stop was HR, to visit Jennifer and confirm whether she was indeed the officiating priestess from the church. But Jennifer wasn't in; instead she found Amy, hunched over her desk and scribbling rapidly in a notebook. Wendy paused in the doorway. Amy's face was set in a mask of concentration. She chewed absentmindedly on a stray lock of green hair, oblivious to the outside world as she extended an intricate inkscape across a page of cartridge paper. Her position was suggestive, and when Wendy glanced at the ceiling, sure enough, Amy was out of view of both of the camera domes covering the desks.

Wendy smoothed her expression into one of disinterest. Then she knocked on the door frame and entered.

Amy jerked upright and flailed for a moment as she flipped her sketchbook facedown, an expression of horror flashing across her face. "I can, uh, I can explain—"

"It's all right," Wendy reassured her. She pulled the door shut. Sketching on company time was obviously a sacking offense, going by Amy's reaction. Or maybe Amy was simply afraid of authority, like so many of the instinctively law-abiding. Wendy indicated the cameras: "Are there microphones in here as well, or can we talk?"

"There *would* be microphones, if Jennifer hadn't set the Facilities budget for her office to zero two years ago," Amy said nervously. Her gaze flickered to the closed door, as if she feared a red-robed Jennifer might pounce at any moment, shrieking, *Nobody expects the Spanish Inquisition*!

"I was hoping to speak to her. Is she out for the morning?"

"Morning *and* lunchtime, maybe until midafternoon. It's another of her off-site meetings." Amy sat up and stretched, with an audible clicking of tortured joints. "What can I do for you?"

Wendy wasn't going to let her off that easily. "What's your project?" she asked.

"Noth—" Amy grabbed for the sketchbook, but Wendy was faster. As she flipped the book open, she was merciful: a twitch of her imagination summoned a floor-standing conference display banner between the camera and the naked page. But whatever Wendy had expected to find—*I HATE BIG BROTHER*, perhaps—wasn't there. Instead, a beautifully detailed dragon uncurled from the page and glared up at her, channeling Jennifer's malicious stare with eyebrow-arched precision. Twin puffs of smoke curled from its nostrils as it spread membranous batwings that spanned the desktop. It hissed peevishly, a rainbow of colors racing across its diffraction-grating scales: then it inhaled and sneezed.

"Hey!" Wendy leapt backwards, only just avoiding the puff of flame. The dragon crouched on its haunches then sprang into flight, barely avoiding her hair as it flapped towards the door. Clearly peeved to find its path blocked, the miniature firedrake did a midair backflip and folded its wings, sneezed again, then plummeted, sneezing repeatedly, until it snapped its wings out and flitted under the desk. "Shit!"

"Office dragons always get hay fever," Amy apologized—she did a lot of apologizing—then pulled her knees up defensively. "You mustn't let them get too close to your nylons," she warned.

"You don't say." Slightly shaken, Wendy leaned against the door, mentally giving thanks for her wool trouser suit and steel toe–capped DMs.

"He'll grumble for a bit, then go to sleep under the desk—it's like a cave, you see. Dragons are to caves as cats are to boxes. He'll fade away after an hour or two." Amy sounded wistful. "My sketches have no staying power."

An hour or two? Wendy blinked in astonishment. If she didn't maintain physical contact with her summoned manifestations they vanished in seconds. *And* living *ones . . .* "That's pretty special," she said grudgingly.

"Are you going to tell Jennifer?"

"I don't think that'll be necessary." A thought struck her: "Does Jennifer have any special powers? I mean, like . . . that?"

"I don't think—" Amy's brow furrowed. She paused. "You're taking this awfully well." Behind her, Wendy's floor-standing banner evaporated. "Why?"

Wendy pulled out the other office chair and sat down. The grumbling from the legwell grew louder, but subsided when she pulled her feet out of the way. "I'm an investigator. We get to see lots of weird things these days. What you do on your coffee break is none of my business." *Although,* a sneaky voice prompted her, *it could be your next recruitment bonus.* Especially if Amy found herself in need of a new job because Wendy—*No, don't go there. Dark side* bad! "Do you know where Jennifer's gone?"

"She's giving her big presentation this morning to the Executive Committee at Head Office—on the pilot project she's running at this branch."

"Really?" Visions of CEOs strapped into face masks danced in Wendy's mind.

"The, the system she's come up with? We've only got preliminary financials so far so she'll mainly be talking about the compliance wearables—that's the equipment for keeping the bolshies in line—along with the control software, and our initial cost projections. But she's pitching for a wider rollout at the logistics hubs." Amy managed the difficult feat of simultaneously looking enthusiastic and mildly disgusted, as if she couldn't quite understand why she was supporting Jennifer. "She should be back this afternoon."

Amy's face reminded Wendy of something she'd seen before, and after a few seconds the penny dropped: it was exactly how the cash room staff at Hamleys had looked, or the Pennine Bank clerks, as they came out from under Imp's influence. "Huh. Well, that's interesting. I'm going to need to access the store CCTV records this afternoon—I want to have another go at tracking down Mr. Hewitt—but this chat never happened, okay?" She pushed back her chair. "Can you page me when Jennifer gets back? I'd like a word with her."

Down on the shop floor everything looked normal, or at least as normal as it ever looked to Wendy: just like any other supermarket, only with fewer regular humans and more muppets hauling produce and stocking shelves. There were, in fact, two masked muppets for every fleshface, to a first approximation. Wendy shivered. Hadn't it been closer to a fifty-fifty split last week? *I ought to keep count,* she thought as she made a quick pass through the stockroom and glanced through the window into the manufacturing room. Faceless figures were lifting finished pieces of produce out of the maw of an open 3D printer and placing them on the conveyor belt to the vacuum sealing and labelling machines. Behind them another belt moved, carrying thin-sliced ham and pork chops.

Wendy shrugged, then walked into the loading bay. Something was kicking up a frightful din, and after a few seconds she realized the whining and clanking and hissing sounds were coming from the caged robot enclosure. Sides of beef or pig or something—she wasn't clear enough on farmyard anatomy to identify them—dangled from the overhead conveyor leading to the doors of the cage. The conveyor vibrated slightly as the whirling knives assaulted a diminishing slab of something reddish that hung just out of view.

"What *is* that?" a familiar voice just behind her asked.

Wendy managed not to flinch, just in time. "Robot butcher's line," she replied. "What are *you* doing here? I thought you were filling forms today."

"Training exercise." Becca smirked impishly: "Gibson said I looked fed up so I should take a hike." Wendy eyed her up and down. The Deliverator had accessorized her off-the-peg HiveCo Security uniform with a very nonregulation pair of glittery purple cycling shoes. They featured two-bolt cleats that tapped noisily on the concrete floor as she walked. She had a laminated ID badge, but it was turned to face her chest.

"But how did you get in here? That's not a FlavrsMart badge!"

"Not my fault they left the loading bay door open." Del's thumb idly circled over her shoulder. "Thought I'd scope it out on the down-low." Her nostrils flared. "Nothing to see here but a bunch of dumpsters full of expired food they've fenced off to keep the de-emphasized out."

Wendy rolled her eyes: "Do you have any proper footwear?"

Del straightened, looking aggrieved. "This *is* proper footwear! My bike's out back and if I have to chase down a serial killer I'll need it! 'Sides, Gibson said they were okay for now."

I'll bet he did. Getting Del to play by company rules was clearly going to be an uphill battle. Wendy gave up, for the time being. "Well, how about I introduce you to HR upstairs? Get you a proper badge so you don't have to fake it—"

Del narrowed her eyes. "I've had enough of HR this month already—"

"This HR bod is different, I promise: she has dragons."

"*Dragons?*"

"Yup, office dragons: genuine fire-breathing toe-munchers who hide under the desk."

"This I have got to see." Del shook her head as Wendy led her deeper into the supermarket, working out how she was going to execute the plan that was gradually coming together in her mind.

8

POWER POINTS

Halfway down the M1 Mary parked up in a motorway service area, turned off the engine, and tried very hard not to scream.

It had taken more than two hours to get this far and the children were raising hell. Her arm was weirdly numb and tingly inside its silver sheath, the kind of tingling that bespoke nerve damage. She opened the flap of her messenger bag and hissed, "Gloves *now,* or it's the municipal dump for you." Then she nerved herself and thrust her bionic hand inside the side-pocket. There was a disturbing moment of dissociation, during which she felt light-headed and woozy, as if she was about to faint: then she felt a wadded-up pair of gloves with her fingertips, really *felt* them, every pore and stitch and wrinkle in the kidskin surface, as prominently tactile as the buttons on the van's console.

As she pulled her posh new gloves on, Devilbaby-Ethan piped up: "Why've we stopped, Nan?" Mary's jaw clenched.

"Needa go number two," Emily chimed.

Mary forced herself to open the fists she was making before she split the leather. "Let's all get our things and stretch our legs, shall we?" she said in a singsong voice that the children were, fortunately for them, too inexperienced to realize was the frozen saccharine crust over a bottomless well of molten fury. The traffic on the M1 south of Leeds had not put Mary in a receptive frame of mind, and every time she spotted the Battenburg pattern of a Highways Agency patrol car, an invisible steel band tightened around her scalp. "Robert, you get the door. Lyssa, stop trying to feed the mime to your unicorn, he'll be sick—Emily?"

"Need to go *now,*" wailed the yellowest Terrortot.

"Fucksticks and fiddlestains." Mary leapt out of the driver's seat and yanked the side-door open with a screech of protesting metal, momentarily forgetting her strength. (Now the cyborg arm upgrade was bedded in, its power was leaking out of her other limbs: she fizzed with energy even though her eyeballs felt as if they'd been replaced with pickled onions and she wanted to sleep for a year.) She picked up Emily in an underarm carry, tugged Ethan after her by one hand, and double-timed it towards the mall toilets. Robert and Lyssa were old enough to follow along under their own steam. "Toilet break!" she sang, her voice steely and bright and bleeding barely suppressed violence. "Robert, Lyssa, you will be sure to wash your hands after you've been, otherwise there will be no ice cream!"

"Is Nan having a funny turn?" Flytrap asked Twinkster.

"My unicorn says—"

The next words were cut off as Mary charged through the lobby doors and hauled Emily and Ethan into the disabled toilet, that being closest. She deposited the shell-shocked little girl atop the loo and yanked down the bottom half of her suit, rotated Ethan to face the wall while she dealt with his sister (whose entire gut contents were coming through, judging by the sounds), and held her breath.

"That *stinks*!" Devilbaby complained while Laserwasp let rip.

"Yes, it really does," Mary agreed. A telltale vibration in her jacket pocket distracted her just as she hauled a fistful of wet wipes out of her bag and attended to the little girl. It was her personal phone, which meant it was either the Thief-taker General or the nursing home to tell her about some new crisis involving her father. (He'd probably unleashed another giant robot on Walthamstow.) "Are we clean yet? Yes we are! Right, Ethan, it's *your* turn to ride the poopstain express while I just nip outside and answer this call . . ."

Back in the mall she leaned against the door—keeping it firmly closed, lest the terrible twosome escape—and answered her phone. "Yes?" she snapped. Across the atrium she spotted Robert heading into the local WH Smith's. Of Lyssa—or rather, Flytrap—there was no sign.

"Are we having fun today?" the Boss asked her. It was a rhetorical question.

Mary swallowed her instinctive rejoinder. "Not so much, no," she said sharply. "Do you have a drop-off for me? I'm two hours out from the M25."

"Yes, I've made arrangements. There's a bunch of human traffickers operating out of a church in north London who are willing to play ball. My contact wants you to drop the kids off in the stockroom of a supermarket in east Chickentown—I'll message you directions and details—and by Tuesday evening they'll be offshore and out of your hair. Once you make the handoff we'll arrange for you to be found unconscious and clearly a victim of the kidnappers yourself, while someone else places the ransom demand: it'll give you a partial alibi, all you have to do is say you remember nothing."

"Uh-huh." A bright spike of rage stabbed at her left temple, harbinger of one of her attacks. *Oh* hell *no, not right now,* she thought. "And my fee?"

"I'll send you the link to the bitcoin exchange along with the drop-off directions," the Thief-taker General said smoothly. "The coins are already in an escrow account. You have nothing to worry about. You can check online—I'm sure you can borrow a computer terminal when you get to the supermarket."

"Right," Mary heard herself saying through the roaring in her ears. "A terminal. That's good." The Boss was being disturbingly over-precise. She hadn't had any need to know about the church or the offshore destination. The hint that she should use a computer at the supermarket told her that it'd be rigged to show her whatever the Thief-taker General wanted her to see. And . . . *found unconscious and clearly a victim of the kidnappers*: well, a corpse was unconscious, right? "I'll do that," she agreed, lying through her teeth.

The Boss ended the call and Mary ducked into the toilet again, to make sure the kids hadn't finger-painted the walls with sewage or begun farming giant hogweed in the drains. The toddlers were, for a miracle, clean. Mary flushed the reeking residue away, made them wash their hands, then led them to the food court. It was midafternoon but they'd been on the road a couple of hours so *of course* it was feeding time again. It was *always* feeding time. Meal discipline could get to fuck: just another three hours and Mary could say goodbye to the Banks children forever.

But Mary was weary and hungry and needed a break from the steering wheel. Nobody was going to get paid if she fell asleep and crashed into a bridge abutment. So when she saw Twinkster coming out of the newsagent she stretched her shoulders and marched over to him. "Robert." She smiled toothily. "Nan needs a coffee and a croissant before we carry on. I'll be in Costa's, over there. *You,* young man, are in charge of your brother and sisters for the next twenty minutes."

"What's in it for me?"

"Twenty quid." She poked his skullcap-mounted minigun, making him wobble alarmingly. "Come with me while I get the rug rats." She stomped over to the disabled loo, only to find the door swinging open and the room empty. "Oh f—fudge—fiddle—nuggets!" She smiled brightly, trying to conceal her anger. It wasn't the kids' fault. "All right, Robert, I'll be over *there*—" she pointed at a table—"and I'll pay you a tenner for each of them when you bring them to me. Clear?"

Twinkster nodded and scampered away, clearly focussed on his junior child snatcher duties. Mary sighed, then went to queue for a giant mocha and several portions of cake. Today totally sucked, and days that sucked demanded cake. Worst case, if Robert failed to round up the wee ones she could ask her bag for a child-seeking killer robot. It was the kind of thing Dad's talent lent itself to. The trick would be disarming it before it actually killed them, but over the past couple of years Mary had become particularly adept at neutering murderbots. Anyway, something told her that the Banks children were not easy to kill as an aspiring supervillain nemesis might wish. She ordered her beverage, did a double-take, and hastily added half a dozen child-friendly muffins and some bottles of Coke Zero. Then she collected her novelty coffee-flavored chocolate energy drink and tray full of empty calories, and marched over to the designated table.

Coffee and cake convinced the iron band of her stress-headache to relax slightly. But her enjoyment of her coffee was impaired by the blatting of a TV set above the counter. It was running rolling news coverage, with the volume just high enough to irritate. There was some kind of geas on the news crawl, and it kept sucking her eyeballs endlessly back towards it until she paid attention despite her best intentions. A human interest feature about downhill cheese-rolling in Salop gave way to the latest *ullamaliztli* league[7] tryouts, and something about Ryanair introducing flights to a new winter sports destination on the icy plateau of Leng. Then Mary blinked and nearly spat out her coffee as the news feed cycled back to current affairs, and a TV interviewer milking a familiar looking married couple for tears.

"—have no idea where they are, please, if you can hear us, we just want our babies back!"

It was Mrs. Banks, standing on a sandy beach in a sundress. She looked distraught and not at all like her steely-jawed, high-tension alter ego, the Blue Queen. Mr. Banks stood behind her, his face ashen, as the TV presenter continued, "—been three days since the four Banks children and their nanny were reported missing from their home in Central London, in the most mysterious disappearance since Lord Lucan in 1974. Police are mystified, although some have suggested a link with the terrorist attack on Hamleys toy shop on Regent Street, where the children were seen on store cameras. Mr. and Mrs. Banks left their four children, Robert, Elyssa, Ethan, and Emily, in the care of their nanny while they attended an international conference on superpowered crime as representatives of the New Management. A reward is offered for information leading to—"

Mary rummaged in her bag, then pointed the TV-B-Gone at the screen.

7. The Prime Minister was trying to encourage the adoption of the Aztec ball game, but the only people who showed any aptitude for it were Eton College graduates. A not-dissimilar bounce-a-ball-through-a-tiny-hoop-on-the-wall activity had been played for centuries at Eton. However, old Etonians were proving remarkably adept at hiding from the draft, perhaps because in the version of the sport they were used to, league tournaments didn't end with the losing team being sacrificed.

"Fuck," she muttered as the TV died.

Mary had a conscience, although she didn't like to admit it. It usually gave her nothing but grief so she kept it gagged and hogtied in the back of her mental murder van. When it got loose it kicked up a fuss and got her into trouble, and she couldn't afford to get into trouble if she was going to protect her father. It wasn't easy, being the notorious Professor Skullface's sole living relative: sometimes the responsibility felt crushing.

And really, she had no reason to feel guilty, did she? It wasn't as if she'd harmed the kids in any way, other than by spoiling them with toys and junk food and possibly by teaching them useful life skills such as lock picking, car theft, armed robbery, and the best way to slaughter a Tyrannosaur. It was all the fault of the Thief-taker General, for making sure Captain Colossal and the Blue Queen found out their children had been taken in the worst possible way. Not that there was much point kidnapping someone's children then giving them back if the target didn't know they'd been abducted, so maybe the Thief-taker General was in the clear—

Mary's eyes crossed. A moment later, several small, sticky hands reached across the table and grabbed the chocolate muffins right off her plate. Some of the hands held multiple muffins, and an outbreak of bickering seemed inevitable. "Oy!" Mary announced.

Four cartoon heads turned to her. "Please, Nan, make him give me my cake?" Flytrap whined.

"Ethan. Give your big sister her cake or I'll let her unicorn eat you." It was an empty threat, Ethan being the animator in the family, but unicorns were frightening enough that the threat got his attention. "Ah, Robert, mission accomplished!" She smiled as she grabbed a couple of counterfeit banknotes from her messenger bag and thrust them at him. "We're going to hit the road in ten minutes, just as soon as I find us a better ride. You have until I finish my coffee to buy sweeties. Come and find me in the car park if I'm not here." Robert disappeared from the table so fast he almost trailed a sonic boom.

"Nan!" Lyssa complained stickily. Mary grabbed another handful of notes and thrust them at her.

"Here, take this. It's for you *and* the youngers, use it wisely, okay?"

"Nan!" Flytrap chided as Laserwasp and Devilbaby, costume heads flung back over shoulders, methodically reduced the last of their muffins to a glutinous mess. Then she, too, was gone, leaving Mary in charge of the table.

"Right," she grumbled, standing. Time to carjack another nanny tank, dump the kids in the supermarket staff room, confirm that she'd been paid, then go and *politely* remind the Boss why it was a really bad idea to try and double-cross his best enforcer. Steel fingers flexed inside her glove.

She'd been keeping a lid on her temper for *days,* and not sticking her hand through some idiot's brainpan—won't someone think of the children?—felt like the world's worst case of constipation. But it'd be over soon enough, and she was really looking forward to letting it all hang out.

▸◂▸◂▸◂

Eve rose at four o'clock on Monday morning, spent an hour exercising in the basement gym while listening to the morning briefing the Tokyo office prepared for her, then broke her fast with a joyless but nutritionally balanced glass of Soylent™. She showered and dressed, then ascended to her office, steeled herself, and dialed an extension.

It was barely seven o'clock, but the phone answered on the first ring. "Ready room, ma'am, how may I be of service?"

"Sergeant Gunderson, I need you and your best team to prepare for a special operation. It'll be a helicopter insertion at short notice, zero time is tomorrow at 2100 hours. Who do we have with experience?"

Rupert's globe-spanning empire conducted both legal and less-than-legal operations: to ensure the latter ran smoothly he employed a variety of thugs. At the top of the hierarchy had been Mister Bond, an actual full-time assassin. At the bottom of the heap were the Gammons—knuckle-dragging bodyguards who were mostly good at looking menacing and stopping bullets. For the in-between cases, Rupert retained a small team of former special forces soldiers and territorial support cops who could be trusted with more sophisticated assignments. Officially they were private military contractors: their division even hired out as bodyguards and couriers to maintain a respectable cover. While Rupert had been around, Eve had avoided using them—it would have instantly attracted his attention—but now the gloves were off.

Sergeant Sally Gunderson, the head of the specialist team, was on the ball. "Depends how big the target is, and whether it's defended. The company chopper only seats seven plus the pilot, but if you can give me an idea of the budget I can organize additional transport."

Eve took a deep breath. "The target is a castle on a rock in the middle of the English Channel. Defenses are limited to small arms, but very likely with unconventional backup—" a euphemism understood these days to signify magical defenses—"it's a nest of cultists. I'll be coming along for the ride, accompanied by five metahumans: we'll handle the hinky stuff."

"Five?" Gunderson sounded slightly appalled. "I'll need to take the full rack. And we're going to need a bigger chopper for starters. What's the jurisdiction?" *Am I going up against a government?*

"*I* am the government. It's an offshore tax haven, one of the smaller Channel Islands, and on paper I'm their feudal overlord. The problem is going to be getting them to listen. As long as things don't go sideways you're legally covered. Start making phone calls, let me know what it's going to cost, and I'll release funds. Choose your team—volunteers only—I'll be briefing at ten in the main conference room."

"Yes ma'am. Is there anything else?"

"Not right now. See you later." Eve hung up. "And now," she murmured quietly to herself, "let's see how many ringers Rupert left in the ready room."

It was a fair bet there'd be at least one. Even though Rupert was gone, his tentacles were proving difficult to excise: the last thing Eve needed was to go into Castle Skaro to kick cultist ass with a cultist right behind her, pointing an assault rifle at her head.

She picked up the phone again. It rang for almost a minute

before cutting out, so she redialed. Then she redialed again, until finally a bleary voice slurred, "Whhhhhuupp."

"And good morning to you, too, Jeremy!" she chirped. "I need you here within the hour. If you're not on the doorstep by"—she checked her watch—"nine fifteen I'll send a car for you."

"Whhhhuuu—at?" he expectorated horribly. "I mean, what the fuck, sis?"

"At ten o'clock precisely I'm briefing the raid team for Project Skaro. I expect one or more of them to try and kill me. If they succeed they'll go after you next, so you have a strong personal interest in being there to cover my six. Are we clear?"

"*Wait*." Imp was nobody's idea of an early riser, but she could hear his brain straining to come up to speed. "I, uh, I can bring Game Boy and Doc?"

Eve smirked. "*Much* better. What about your other playmates?"

"They, uh, they have day jobs. Doc and GeeBee is all I've got: you're buying them breakfast."

"Be here on time and there will be food," she told him, then hung up. She smiled to herself. Going into the briefing with three metahumans—one of whom had started out as a promising apprentice dreamwalker—was better than she'd hoped for.

Eve unlocked the top drawer of her desk and withdrew a flat leather jewelry case. Opening it, she removed a flesh-toned choker studded with pearls of curiously uniform size. She fastened it around her neck, making sure that her open shirt collar and jacket didn't obstruct it. Then she tensed an imaginary muscle and *tugged*.

A pearl detached itself from the necklace and floated in front of her eyes, barely trembling. The pearls were fakes, a thin film of cultured nacre accreted around magnetized BB shot. The ribbon was lined with small magnets to hold them in place: her telekinetic power enabled her to throw them like pistol bullets. Small, low energy, pistol bullets she could carry openly without attracting adverse attention. Eve set another two pearls dangling in front of her face, juggled them briefly, then returned them to her necklace, where they clicked back into place. Then she repaired her makeup: exerting fine control required intense concentration that tended to make her sweat.

Eve focussed on her laptop, setting up a OneNote workbook for Operation Skaro, then tackling the morning's email. Her in-box was dominated by the weekend's developments on the buy-in at FlavrsMart. The lawyers had been pulling overtime at an eye-watering hourly rate. Admittedly, when buying into an enterprise with annual turnover in the billions even a day's delay might cost tens of millions: but jumping the gun could be even more expensive. So Eve ploughed through the contract doggedly until her eyes felt as if they were bleeding, then switched tasks for a while. Then she went back to chewing on the hubcaps of the financial vehicle the lawyers were helping her run to ground.

Just why Rupert wanted to own a substantial share in a small-to-middling regional supermarket chain eluded her. Supermarkets weren't the sort of investment that floated Rupert's boat, although Wendy's identification of a possible cult preacher in their HR department was suggestive. But the wheels had been set in motion months ago, and calling off the buy-in at this point would flush a huge amount of work down the drain. Presumably he'd done his homework, even if it merely consisted of a nudge and a wink over G&Ts on some creepy billionaire's yacht—or maybe he'd pulled the answers bleeding and screaming from the intestines of a sacrifice on the altar in Castle Skaro's basement. She spent a frustrating half hour searching his email inbox—Rupert's organization skills consisted of "delegate it to Eve," so anything he dealt with personally was a frustrating mess of bcc'd memos with blank subject headers—before shelving the wild goose chase. *I need an administrative assistant of my own,* she told herself, with just enough self-awareness to be horrified at the realization that she'd be an even worse boss than Rupert.

Her phone rang, breaking her out of deep focus in the middle of a particularly opaque contract clause about force majeure and money laundering. "Yes?" she barked.

It was the front desk. "Your brother and . . . friends . . . are here, ma'am?" The receptionist sounded slightly stunned.

"I'll be right up," Eve said, then shut her laptop, cleared her desk, and took the lift to the lobby.

She found Imp, Doc, and Game Boy in a gloomy huddle in the

middle of the black-and-white-tiled floor. Game Boy was gurning and twitching over a handheld console, Doc was staring into the middle distance with slack-jawed disinterest, and Imp was doing his best Artful Dodger cameo for the security guard, who looked as if he was one twitch away from counting the doorknobs in case Imp had stolen them while he wasn't looking.

"Jeremy!" she called, smiling widely as she approached her brother: "Doc, Game Boy, this way." She waved them towards the staircase up to the first floor. To the receptionist: "I want access badges for three class Q visitors, send them to the conference room, please."

Eve swept up the staircase. Imp had visited before but it was a new experience for Game Boy and Doc, both of whom were twitching nearly constantly as they ascended. "Is that a genuine Mondrian?" Doc whispered loudly.

"I could show you the certificate of authenticity but Rupe only bought it to help out an old school friend in the arms trade: it's not worth a fraction what Wikipedia claims." At the top of the stairs she turned left, onto a narrower, steeper flight. "Up here."

The second floor featured a lower ceiling and less ornate cornice work than the lower floors, and the wooden wainscoting gave way to hand-printed wallpaper and thick wall-to-wall carpet. Eve led her visitors to a large room overlooking the garden at the back of the town house. It was furnished in blandly modern corporate style, from the conference seats and bleached pine boardroom table to the array of A/V equipment behind the speaker's stand.

This was no Bond villain lair: there were no hidden electrodes or manacles in the chairs, no shark tanks in the room below. (Rupert had rated discretion higher than flamboyance in the disposal of underperforming minions.) But if Imp or his friends had inspected the sash windows they might have realized that the view of the garden outside was actually provided by a row of high-definition TV screens behind the panes. And if they'd been paying attention they might have noticed their cellphone signal dropping to zero as they passed through the copper fingers lining the door frame, or noticed the discreet sigils woven into the meeting room carpet to dismay and disorient unwelcome visitors.

"Take a seat. *Front* row if you please, Game Boy. Jeremy, Doc, you should sit at the back. I have a special job for the three of you . . ."

▸◂▸◂◂

Wendy led Del through the loading bays and stockroom, then up the stairs to the cramped company offices and the HR nook. Del's head swiveled as she took everything in, but whatever questions she had she kept to herself while Wendy knocked on the door. "Amy? It's Ms. Deere from HiveCo Security, I have a visitor for you."

A sigh, then the sound of papers shuffling filtered through the flimsy door before Amy called out, "Come in!"

Wendy shoved the door open.

"You promised me dragons," Del said accusingly.

Amy stared at her. "Who's this?"

Wendy got out in front before Del could react to Amy's defensive belligerence: "Amy, meet Rebecca from HiveCo Security. She's my understudy for the week—she's new on the job and she's been assigned to shadow me. I was hoping you could sort her out with a visitor's pass? Ideally for five days?"

"A what now—" Amy sighed noisily, then backed down. "Right, you've got a trainee." She raised an eyebrow at Del: "Is that right?" *Dragons,* she mouthed at Wendy reproachfully.

"Yes!" Del visibly came off the boil, her posture relaxing. "I'm new at this security gig," she added, "there's a lot to learn."

"I see." Amy typed rapidly on her laptop, then turned it to face Del: "Fill out this form, I need it before I can print you a pass. Please." *Dragons,* she mouthed again, and Wendy shrugged.

Del sat down and pecked at the keyboard while Wendy hunted for a section of wall to lean against that wasn't covered in health and safety notices or ingrained grime. "Dragons," Amy said firmly, "*do not exist,*" as she circled her finger in the direction of one of the cameras, then nodded at a loose ceiling tile. "We do however have a problem with pigeons roosting on top of the spotlights. They make odd noises and occasionally fly down and sh—*bleep* on the carpet. I've been trying to get Facilities to deal with it before the pigeons short something out and start a fire. Luckily the tiles are heatproof . . ."

"I can see why that might be a problem," Wendy agreed. She conjured up a telescoping pole and poked at a corner of the offending tile, provoking a peevish hiss and the rustling of scales rasping across a rough surface. Something rattled against the recessed fluorescent lighting enclosure next to the tile: Wendy hastily dispelled her dragon-annoyer. "Yep, definitely a job for pest control."

"If you ignore them they go away eventually." Amy cringed at the noises from the false ceiling.

Del spun the laptop round to face across the desk. "All done," she announced.

"Great." Amy quickly scanned the web form, then poked at her trackpad. "I need a photo—ah, you found the webcam? Great. I'll just print this off and laminate it for you." She stood: "The printer's in the Branch Manager's office, back in two ticks . . ."

As Amy nipped out of the cramped office, Del glanced up at the ceiling. "Was that what I thought it was?"

"FlavrsMart have cameras everywhere, even in HR." Wendy didn't bother to hide her irritation as she pointed to them. "And microphones, they dock your pay if you swear. They treat their staff like criminals, so good luck getting Amy to say anything against company policy: she wants to keep her job."

"But her hair . . ."

"She can get away with it because she can quote the *exact* paragraph in the staff handbook that permits staff to color their roots. It's probably all she can get away with." A muted hiss from above the ceiling prompted her to amend her opinion: "Nearly all, anyway."

Amy returned, bearing a freshly printed badge, still warm from the laminator. "And here we are!" she said brightly. A slight edge entered her voice. "I take it you're going to be sticking close to Ms. Deere, so Wendy can be responsible for you? If you need anything else, my door is open—"

"Yes, as a matter of fact there is," Wendy said agreeably.

"Oh?" Del looked at her.

"I was wondering if you've got a portrait gallery of branch managers here that Rebecca and I can take a look at? Just for familiarization, in case we run into anyone while we're walking the store?"

"Oh, sure—it's on the wall in the break room! Follow me."

The management break room had white-painted breeze block walls, a rickety table, and a pair of sofas that had clearly been used as chew toys by land sharks. It could hardly have been less cozy if the table held a loaded revolver and a printed invitation to participate in a pension lottery by Russian roulette.

"There." Amy pointed.

"Great." Wendy peered at the magnetic whiteboard dotted with mugshots and lengths of multicolored thread like a murder investigation in progress. "Okay." She pointed for Del's benefit: "That's Jenn."

Amy looked ashen. "*Jennifer* always, please."

"Really?" Del smirked. Wendy elbowed her.

"What do you think?"

"Needs a better nose job." Del dodged Wendy's attempt to kick her. "Okay, uh, I'll recognize her next time I see her," she extemporized. Jenn was definitely the priestess from the church—or her identical twin. "Who's the branch manager?"

While Amy filled Del in, Wendy backtracked up the tangle of threads until she came to Jennifer's boss. "Well, that's unexpected." A middle-aged white man with a receding hairline and a mustache that had crawled onto his upper lip to die smiled glassily at the camera. "Mr. Patrice Jefferson, Director of Human Resources?" She glanced sharply at Amy. "Jennifer reports direct to board level?"

"What?" Amy was flustered for a moment: "No she . . ." She trailed off. "I don't see Mrs. Harper on here," she mumbled.

"Mrs. Harper?"

"Senior HR Manager, London region. No, this is wrong, Jennifer reports to *her,* not direct to . . ."

"Looks like there's been some rightsizing in officer country," drawled Del.

"This is wrong." Amy sounded shocked. "Sorry, I have to check this. Maybe someone's pranking us?" She disappeared back towards her dragon-infested office.

"It's definitely her," Wendy stated, voice neutral as her gaze tracked towards Amy's boss.

"Yeah. What do you make of it?"

Del gave her a spooked side-eye: "Do you think we ought to warn whatsisname, Mr. Jefferson?"

"What, that a priestess in the Cult of the Mute Poet is backstabbing her way up the ladder just as a private equity outfit founded by their Bishop is closing on a takeover/refi deal?" Wendy gazed into the middle distance for a moment: "It's probably too late to save him; besides, it's not what we're here for. Officially noticing it would be the quickest way to lose the contract, in fact." Wendy rolled her shoulders inside her suit jacket. "No, I think what we do is, first, find out whatever Amy can dig up on the missing managers, then see if there's a link with the missing de-emphasized persons. Track down the elusive Phantom of the Deli Counter. And then"— she cracked her knuckles—"we'll see how it all fits together."

▶◀▶◀▶◀

Five minutes after Eve led Imp and his crew into the conference room, the door opened again to admit eight men and two women dressed like extras for the next *Men in Black* movie.[8] They all moved like soldiers. "Ah, excellent. Sergeant Gunderson, introductions please."

"Yes, ma'am." Sally Gunderson, the leader of the men and woman in black, introduced her people as she directed them to their seats. "Sergeant Lopez is my number two: former Parachute Regiment, platoon first NCO and specialist in urban warfare. Warrant Officer Jennings is qualified for demolitions." She continued with the introductions. "Everyone has some degree of close-quarters combat expertise. I've got a line on transport, although

8. Rupert, clearly enamored of the old-time SS uniforms, had decked his heavies out in Hugo Boss, and Eve hadn't gotten around to changing the dress code yet.

I won't be able to confirm it for a couple of hours." Gunderson looked squarely at Eve: "Are these people the backup you mentioned?" She looked skeptical.

"Yes. Despite appearances, these individuals—" Eve gestured at each in turn as she introduced them—"are all level three or higher metahumans. Imp has a background in ritual magecraft and has also visited the target site with me. I've worked with them before. Which reminds me, Imp—any chance your other friends will be joining us?"

"Uh, nope?" Imp shrugged. "Wendy's still working the Flavrs-Mart job and Del's shadowing her. Unless you want to hire them both out from under their current customer? But Wendy said her boss was really grumpy last time you did that."

"I see." It was just one of the risks of putting a team together at short notice. Then again, leaving Wendy alone might be in Eve's best interests. "Any idea when she'll be free?"

"She said something about a food contamination problem. Could be any time."

"Well then." Eve narrowed her eyes at him, then turned back to Gunderson, who was standing at ease with her hands behind her back. "This is what you're getting." She listed the trio's various abilities: Imp's glamour, Game Boy's unusual evasive talent, Doc's ability to emotionally batter his opponents. "They're all glass-jaw metas, one punch and they're out. So your job is to get between them and any bullets. The flip side is that bullets don't shoot themselves, and Imp and Doc can suppress the shooters' will to live while Game Boy ties their shoelaces together and steals their ammo. But I'm not bringing them along to force a takeover, I'm bringing them to help me separate the sheep from the goats once we've got ownership of the farm."

"And the location of the farm?" Gunderson asked politely.

"Let's get started." Eve stuck a USB stick in the socket of the laptop on the presenter's station, then started up PowerPoint. "Here." A map of the English Channel came up on the big TV screen behind her, sandwiched at top and bottom by the English and French coastlines. "Let's take a look at the Channel Islands." She zoomed to a close-up of a cluster of dots off the Normandy coast. "Jersey and Guernsey, the largest, are part of the Duchy of Normandy. Here's Sark, in third place. Alderney, Herm . . . and this little flyspeck is Skaro. Skaro is technically mine. Rupert bought the vacant title of Baron Skaro several years ago, and under the existing, barely reconstructed system of pre-1354 Norman Law, I, as his widow—" Warrant Officer Jennings's eyes widened—"am its feudal liege's chatelaine. Your objective tomorrow is to provide close protection and policy enforcement for me in my capacity as acting head of state when I return to take control of my demesne. This will start with an authorized landing on the Castle Skaro helipad, following which I will dismiss the island council, then round up all identified members of the Church of Saint Ppilimtec, the Mute Poet—"

"Feudal—" Sally Gunderson began to say, just as Jennings shouted something and pulled out a pistol. Then everything happened very fast.

The lectern was less than three meters from the front row and Jennings couldn't possibly miss—except he did. Game Boy abruptly shoved Eve away from the presenter's station. Gunshots cracked, somehow missing Game Boy even though he stood squarely where Eve had been a moment before. And now there was more chaos, and more shots at the back of the room, and a spray of blood as a soldier in the back row shot his left-hand neighbor in the head.

Eve stumbled, chest heaving for breath, then clenched her necklace in her mind's fist. She flung three pearls straight at the swine who'd tried to murder her. They thudded into his right eye with a splatter of blood and fluids that sent his next shot wild. He tried to aim at Eve with his offside eye, but Game Boy moved in a blur that ended with him facedown on the carpet and Game Boy pressing the pistol to the back of his head.

"Naughty!" Game Boy squeaked, his voice cracking.

The back row shooter was dogpiled by his neighbors. A constellation of glittering pearls orbited Eve's head as she ducked and ran to one side of the podium. *Two* ringers was fewer than she'd expected, but if they were individually acting on standing orders— "Imp, *now*!" she shouted, and dropped to the floor.

The fine hair on the nape of her neck lifted as she felt her brother's eerie mojo tickle her senses. He wasn't using the ritual spellcraft they'd both learned from their father: his peculiar aptitude for nullifying disbelief was stronger but more idiosyncratic. "She's dead," Imp declared to the room full of adrenaline-shocked guards, "the Bishop will reward his followers for killing the usurper. If you would identify yourselves? Everyone else should *sit down now.* There is nothing to fear, we are all loyal to our Dread Lord—"

A wave of palpable relief rippled through the room as Doc went flat out, damping emotional reactions and tamping down fight-or-flight reflexes. Most of the soldiers dropped back into their chairs as if poleaxed: two remained standing.

Reality came into sharp focus around Eve as she sat up and slammed a pearl bullet into each forehead. They dropped like sacks of potatoes, either stunned or dying. Eve wasn't trying to kill but neither did she hold back, and she didn't have a good feel for her own lethality.

"We're done here," she announced as she rose to her feet. "Imp, Doc, Boy, to me." Taking stock, she realized to her displeasure that her right shoulder and ribs ached, her left hip felt like she'd been kicked by a donkey, her hair was coming loose from its tight chignon, and her remaining pearlshot were scattered halfway across the floor. "Sergeant, clear the bodies and transfer the surviving traitors to the holding tank. See that they don't have any means of suicide: I'll question them later."

Gunderson seemed half-stunned, but maintained enough control to salute, then send her surviving troops for restraints and body bags. "Morgan? *Really?*" she asked once she was alone in the room with Eve and Imp's homies.

"Not unexpected." Eve felt distinctly shaky now the immediate danger was past. "Rupert had some very creepy coreligionists and tomorrow's raid is about cleaning out their offshore headquarters. I was expecting one or two of your team to have orders to kill me if I went off-reservation. This"—she surveyed the room—"exceeded my worst case." One of the head-shot bodies made an odd gurgling sound, almost a snore. Not dead yet. *Good,* she thought.

"Crap." Gunderson's professionalism cracked for a moment. "I'm going to have to draft in my B team."

"Take Jeremy with you. Imp? I want you to make sure that none of the replacements are churched. Sergeant Gunderson, you know what to do . . ."

▸◂▸◂

Jennifer Henderson stalked around the conference table, carefully inspecting the duct tape on the board of directors. One or two of them still struggled but most simply watched her in terrified silence, intimidated by the headsets and shock collars. A spandex-suited meat puppet stood guard behind each chair.

"I think I can safely say that this will hurt you more than it hurts me," Jennifer told Raymond Berry, the Chief Financial Officer. She gave him a simpering smile. Berry responded by kicking off again, jerking back and forth in the seat he was taped to. Her smile vanished instantly. "Stop that at once!" She pronounced a word in a language not intended for human discourse: his shock collar discharged and he slumped, a wet patch spreading below his chair. "Are we sitting comfortably?" she asked her audience rhetorically: "Then I'll begin."

She walked to the podium and cued up her presentation on the projection screen at the end of the room. "Ladies and gentlemen of the board, thank you for lending me your ears! I realize that you are all terribly busy with the ongoing buy-in by de Montfort Bigge Holdings International. A new strategy for Human Resources isn't obviously at the top of your to-do list, but I want you to be clear that the two issues—the refi, and the pilot program in Chickentown that I'm here to introduce—are inextricably linked. We are leveraging technologies provided by subsidiaries of de Montfort Bigge Holdings to enhance our operational capabilities. In fact, the buy-in wouldn't be happening *at all* without my department's rollout of our Lord and Master's Minimum Viable Produce Human Residue Reanimation technique. The fruits of which stand before—or behind—you, wearing their body stockings and Company Faces."

She tapped her tablet. The meat puppets' Faces smiled as one, and announced, "*Greetings from de Montfort Bigge Holdings: we are here to serve you.*"

"De Montfort Bigge Holdings is an offshore private equity vehicle founded by Rupert de Montfort Bigge, Baron Skaro, to further his commercial and other interests. You may be interested to learn that Baron Skaro is also the Bishop of the Church of Saint Ppilimtec the Mute Poet, Prince of Poetry and Song, our Tongueless Lord." Her gaze settled fondly on the CEO, Larry Brewster, whose expression bespoke bafflement and fury. "His Grace's primary goals are spiritual rather than temporal—although temporal wealth always makes spiritual success easier—and he acquires new devotees not only by evangelism and good works but through corporate takeovers."

Private equity funds were by definition privately held: investment vehicles not answerable to institutional or public shareholders, existing solely to fulfill the objectives of their owners. Most people assumed that the objective was to accumulate wealth, and it usually was. But if the owners had other priorities, there was nothing to stop them spending their money on those goals instead.

"As a retail chain operating in the United Kingdom, FlavrsMart is subject to UK employment law. This includes the Equality Act (2010), which bars discrimination on grounds of religion or belief, sexual orientation, or age. To prepare the way for dMBH's hostile reverse takeover of FlavrsMart—" a number of board members twitched violently at this characterization of their predicament— "several of us, that is, of Baron Skaro's faith, sought employment within this company. Our roadmap—the *Church's* roadmap—has been deliberating on your future for a number of years. And as acting head of Human Resources the Bishop has tasked me with taking charge of Conversion Operations."

Several members of the board attempted to express their opinions. They were unsuccessful. Jennifer politely waited for them to recover from their electric shocks before she continued.

"To introduce myself: during my time as supervisor of Human Resources for FlavrsMart in Chickentown district, I have introduced, championed, and led the Company Face Compliance

Scheme and ancillary business support MVPR agents. The meat puppets surrounding you are one of the by-products of this successful program. My objectives are to improve FlavrsMart's business efficiency and reduce human resource turnover, while simultaneously enhancing FlavrsMart's branch MQIs—Misery Quotient Indicators. MQIs track the existential despair and depression we inflict on our employees. We can harvest these emotions by occult means, and they are used as the basis for a devotional sacrament consumed by our Tongueless Lord."

Mr. Berry, who had reawakened at some point during Jennifer's explanation, fainted again.

"FlavrsMart employs nearly sixty thousand staff in nine hundred branches, including the Quick-Freeze and Fashion Beast subsidiaries. As you can imagine, imposing the Company Face Compliance Scheme (or CFCS for short) on that many staff will generate a considerable amount of *mana*—that is, transferrable magical potential energy—for our Tongueless Lord. But that head count only includes permanent and contract workers.

"We have been cooperating with the Department for Work and Pensions on a compulsory remedial work placement scheme for persistently non-entrepreneurial dependents—'useless eaters' as the Prime Minister calls them. CFCS renders them obedient and tractable for the duration of their twelve-week placement. They're housed in an on-site barracks converted from the old staff break room, and we provide subsistence rations and somewhere to sleep. This gives us an ever-rotating pool of additional MQI donors. Then, when they reach the end of their workfare placement, we reject them as unfit for further employment, at which point the DWP de-emphasizes them. The de-emphasized are then collected and reprocessed by means of the disassembly and mechanical reclamation lines now being piloted in Chickentown Branch 322."

More slides flashed up on the projection screen: a life-cycle diagram of the unemployed, a logistics life cycle for the carcasses received from the slaughterhouse on the loading bay, a promotional video for the HAMDAS-XQ robot jointing and deboning machine, a flow chart of the production line feeding the meat printers and the pie-making machine behind the shop floor.

Jennifer examined her audience for signs of denial and rejection. With the buy-in so close to completion, the compliance of individual members of the board didn't particularly matter. It still needed to be signed off by Legal at de Montfort Bigge, then voted through by the FlavrsMart board—but she had them collared and duct-taped before her like so many festive turkeys. Once the papers were completed FlavrsMart would be hers. It would be convenient if a couple of the old men in expensive suits could be persuaded to stand in front of a TV camera for the inevitable press conference tomorrow, but Jennifer would shed no tears for the noncompliant.

"As we have discovered this past year, human sacrifice generates considerable MQI and a useful necromantic *mana* charge. Once we roll out the program to all branches we may be able to process as many as five hundred bodies per day without attracting official notice. Indeed, DWP are eager to reduce the number of benefit claimants, and our assistance will be welcomed! By using Minimum Viable Produce Reanimation, each benefit scrounger's body can be used to animate up to four golems composed mainly of time-expired mechanically recovered meat products, like these units." She gestured at the puppets guarding the board members. They had made short work of subduing the executives when she led them into the room.

"Labor units remain viable for up to a month after reanimation, and in the meantime they make excellent remote manipulators for our Class Four computer-entrained apparitional summonings. (Which are minor demons bound to an in-branch server, constrained to obey orders received via the Cortana speech recognition plug-in.) After extracting three months' labor on workfare turnaround, each body thus donates four more months' labor on an entirely unpaid basis. Which reduces our staffing costs by nearly eighty percent and will enable us to achieve an unassailable lead over Tesco and Morrisons! (At least until they copy us.)"

She smiled brightly and struck a pose. "Are there any questions?" she chirped. Curiously, nobody had any questions. "Excellent." A side-door opened and two meat puppets entered bearing boxes of shrink-wrapped muppet suits, complete with bridles, masks, and discipline belts. "Now let's get you kitted out in your

CFCS uniforms and give you your first assignments! Remember, work sets you free!"

▶▪▶◀▪◀

The HR office was hot and crowded, and the way Ms. Deere loomed over the back of her chair put Amy's back up. However, she had to concede that Ms. Deere made a good point: the sooner Amy tracked down Sam from the meat processing line—whether or not he really was the sacked but unforgotten Mr. Hewitt—the better.

But the store security computers weren't playing ball. "Listen, can you give me some space?" Amy asked. "I'm going to have to call the IT support help-line: this may take some time."

"Why, what's wrong?" Ms. McKee—who Ms. Deere called "Del"—asked.

"I know this is going to sound silly, but for some reason I'm locked out of the badge track and trace program. I mean, it says I'm not authorized or something. Which is ridiculous."

"Track and trace?" Ms. Deere sounded intrigued.

"Yes, it's supposed to give me a full time-sequenced activity breakdown on all personnel on the shop floor. Heat maps, task histograms, step count, video log, you name it: it's really useful! But it's not letting me in this afternoon."

"You're trying to—" Ms. Deere paused. "Wait. Is it possible that someone has locked you out?"

"What do you mean?"

Del began to speak: "What if your boss doesn't want you to—"

Ms. Deere elbowed her—"What my colleague is trying to say is, could our elusive muppet have an accomplice who's covering for them?"

"I can't see—" Amy stopped, her head spinning. "Um," she said uncertainly. A handful of people at branch level could lock her out: Mr. Holmes the branch manager, his relief manager, Jennifer, and the IT nerds at HQ. After that it went up a level into regional management territory. There was no reason for anyone outside the supermarket to be interested in the comings and goings of a single muppet, was there? Unless Jennifer had rehired Mr. Hewitt via the workfare placement scheme, to make an end run around the difficult vacancy—"Wait," she said. She flipped browser tabs until she could refresh the Vacancies table that got pushed out to Jobcenters and recruitment agencies. It took her barely ten seconds to confirm her suspicion, then another ten seconds to double-check it. "The vacancy for a rendering line maintenance technician is missing. Someone marked it as cancelled."

She looked at Wendy. "I think you're right," she said, very carefully trying not to think too hard about the implications.

"What do you think I'm right about?"

"Someone senior—*bleep* it, I need a, a smoke break, would you like one, too?" She mimed smoking a cigarette at her two visitors, then turned her back to the cameras and stood, beckoning them to follow.

"What do you smoke?" Del asked as she and her boss followed Amy into the corridor.

Amy waited until they were past the next fire door before she sniffed: "I don't." She led them downstairs and along a short corridor walled in white-painted cinder blocks. There was a fire door at the end, propped open with a brick, and it stank of cheap cigarettes and regret. There was a camera covering the door outside, and another camera covering the passage, but the exit itself was unmonitored.

"Okay, spill it." Wendy crossed her arms.

Amy glanced between Wendy and Del. "You think it's my boss, Ms. Henderson, right?" Wendy said nothing, but her eyes narrowed. "Jennifer could do that, I mean, she could take down the job listing, she can hire and fire, she can draft in DWP workfare placements, she could, huh, she could lock me out of the track and trace app, too. But why would she *do* that?" she asked.

"Amy." Ms. Deere looked at Amy as if she'd failed a test she didn't know she was taking: "About the *product adulteration* Mr. Hewitt was implicated in. How many workfare placements do you get through per month? What happens when their time's up?"

"Well, they go back to—to whatever they were doing before—" Amy juddered to a nervous halt. "What?"

"Do you provide feedback to the DWP?" Del leaned towards her intently: "What if the feedback is *negative*?" she hissed.

"I—I don't—but—I suppose—" Amy tried hard not to understand the question—"oh *bleep*." She unconsciously channeled Jennifer's internal censor, even where there were no microphones.

"Suppose something *really bad* is going on here, out of sight in Chickentown where no one willingly goes, and suppose one of the workfare muppets sees something they're not supposed to see. Jennifer could get them de-emphasized, couldn't she—" what Wendy was calmly describing was unimaginable, horrible—"and when they're starving—"

"—The expired produce," Del chipped in. "It goes in the dumpsters out back, doesn't it?"

Amy nodded, speechless.

"The de-emphasized would know that, and they'd be hungry and desperate, and they'd know how to get in." Wendy nodded. "Have you ever seen a documentary about carnivorous plants, Amy? I'm thinking about pitcher plants, the way they lure insects into a tasty-looking trap, where all the hairs point inwards and the surface of the leaf is slippery. I'd like you to imagine the supermarket is a giant pitcher plant that eats the de-emphasized and turns them into mouth-wateringly tasty pies."

She gestured at the wall behind her, index finger stabbing accusingly in the direction of the loading bays and the robot jointing and carving line. "*That* is the bottom of the pitcher."

▸▪◂▸◂◂

London's miasma tightened around Mary's head like tomorrow morning's hangover as she drove through increasingly dense, fast-moving traffic beneath motorway gantries where the speed monitoring cameras had been supplemented with skulls on spikes. Her phone steered her onto the M25 for a couple of junctions before directing her onto an A-road leading into the desolate hinterlands of London suburbia. The houses grew taller and meaner, the intermittent strips of vegetation rarer, and tube station signs became as common as local shopping malls. Then she came to the gray-tinged fringes of Chickentown, where the buildings sang a song of misery and even the rats were depressed. The winter solstice was closing in, the sky was dark and murky as the sun sagged tiredly towards the rooftops: and it was barely four o'clock.

The Terrortots had spent the last hundred kilometers dozing. They'd given up on the are-we-there-yet chorus as a bad strategy after Mary called their bluff and threatened to keep on driving until sunrise tomorrow. This, in Mary's view, was a good thing: the less interest they took in their surroundings, the smoother the handoff would be. She reached into her bag at the first set of red lights in Chickentown center to crack the seal on a ward the Boss had given her for this part of the job. It was a mild soporific, and would put them down for the count without serious side effects if nothing untoward happened. She drove slowly and unusually gently, following the directions on her screen to a bleak industrial yard. It backed onto a building that looked like a cow shed with cancer.

She parked in front of an empty loading dock and left the engine idling as she climbed out of the driver's seat, stretched, and dialed the Boss's number. "I'm at the delivery drop-off point," she told him. "I don't have a handover contact so you'd better fix this quick."

"Sit tight, I'll send someone." He hung up on her.

Five minutes later, a corporate Barbie in a powder-blue power suit swayed out of a door on the loading dock. Barbie smiled with polished condescension. "Why, hello!" she singsonged. "You must be Mary! I'm Jennifer! How has *your* day been?"

Mary sent Jennifer something that she kidded herself was a smile. "I've had worse." Something about Jennifer's infinitely plastic presentation put her on alert: maybe the plastic was C4? "I have some visitors for you."

"Excellent! I have the guest accommodation ready—are they tired, the poor sleepyheads?"

"Yeah, but keep your voice down. They're out for the time being."

Jennifer descended the steps to the parking area as a new figure emerged. It looked a little like one of the mummies from the

Chariots of the Gods Experience, if mummy couture had undergone a radical overhaul involving space-age fabrics and digital death masks. It moved like a cheap horror movie prop, with a herky-jerky shuffle as if its hip joints were fused. The badge on its chest said, HELLO, MY NAME IS NIGEL, but Mary didn't believe a word of it: she recognized a zombie in drag when she saw one.

"Unit Nigel, unload incoming feedstock for transfer to freezer room four," Jennifer enunciated slowly and clearly. Mary realized the woman was wearing some kind of headset. The meat robot slow-marched to the side of the loading dock and descended the steps, moonwalking out of the uncanny valley of the animated corpses.

An attack of conscience belatedly squeezed through all of Mary's internal filters and tapped her on the shoulder. "Wait," said Mary, "the kids are all metahumans. If you wake them while they're being moved, that would be very bad."

If the wee ones found HELLO, MY NAME IS NIGEL one-tenth as creepy as she did, they'd cack themselves then kick off—possibly simultaneously. And Mary really didn't want to be around four Terrortots waking up to the realization that they were the luncheon meat filling in a horror movie sandwich. *That* was how traumatic origin events started: runaway activation of hitherto untapped abilities, spontaneous amplification of existing talents.

"Well then!" Jennifer tapped her throat mike: "Unit Nigel, safety halt. Computer, priority request: pharmacy to despatch four pediatric flunitrazepam shots to Loading Dock Two." She simpered at Mary. "Thank you for the update! You can go now," she added, the saccharine mask parting to briefly reveal the obsidian glint of a sacrificial axe. "I've got this."

Really there was no reason for Mary to stay, but she felt compelled to ask: "Is freezer room four, like, a freezer?" *You're not going to lock them in and* freeze *them, are you?*

"Only when it's switched on. Otherwise it's just a windowless room with great sound insulation and a door that locks on the outside. They'll be *fine*," Jennifer emphasized. "Don't you have somewhere to be?" Another horror-show dummy walked out of the side-door and stood at ease. This one's movements were more natural, but still stiff-legged: it held a paper prescription bag from the pharmacy counter, and its badge read ADRIAN.

"I—" Mary glanced over her shoulder. A third meat robot had appeared beside the entrance to the loading bay. *Outnumbered.* She had a bad feeling about leaving the kids here, but it was too late to do anything. She opened her messenger bag, reached inside, and pulled out the children's brightly colored Trunki suitcases. "You'll be needing these," she explained as she manhandled Lyssa's pink and spangly unicorn case into line beside Emily's plastic triffid. "Toothbrushes, pajamas, dolls, etcetera." She felt unaccountably guilty, as if she was betraying something precious rather than handing over the deliverables at the end of a gig. "I'll be on my way now."

Jennifer nodded. "Unit Diana, escort Ms. Drop from the premises, then lock down the loading bay gate and stand guard." Then she looked at the second meat puppet, almost as if it was a real person rather than a robot: "Ade, sedate the subjects. You're in charge of Unit Nigel for the transfer to freezer room four."

Mary turned and walked towards the open yard gate. As she reached the corner she looked back once. The cut-price Autons had opened the car doors and were leaning inside. One of them stepped backwards, a small body dangling in its arms. She shuddered, but then the meat puppet on the gate turned towards her expectantly. "Not my circus, not my monkeys," Mary reminded herself and backed away.

The motorized gate buzzed slowly shut, concealing the faceless silver-suited body standing guard behind it. Mary took a deep breath, then walked towards the main road and the nearest tube station.

All Mary's alarm bells were ringing. She had supposed she was taking the kids to a safe house where they'd be comfortable, not handing them over to meat robots wielding syringes full of date-rape drugs. *It's not right,* she thought indecisively. But what could she do? She had to get Dad's nursing home bill settled. Otherwise he'd be out on the street and de-emphasized. *I'll go see the Boss,* she resolved. *I'll make him sign off on the gig, then tell him I don't trust that woman. He'll know what to do.* But she had a hollow feeling in the pit of her stomach that the Boss already knew. The real question wasn't when or whether it would blow up in her face but how wide the blast radius would be.

9

▶◀▷◀▷◀▷◀

SUFFER THE LITTLE CHILDREN

Robert Banks came to his senses slowly. His head was pounding, his tongue felt like sticky cotton wool, his eyes were glued shut, and he was lying on a hard surface with uncomfortable ridges under his back. Someone nearby was snoring, and there was a horrible low buzzing in his ears, like a very loud refrigerator. The last thing he remembered was the skulls on the motorway signs outside the car windows. Nan's forbidding expression discouraged communication. He'd wanted to ask her where they were going, but then he fell asleep, and now they weren't moving any more. Apart from the snoring and the buzzing, it was too quiet. *Did we arrive already?* he thought fuzzily, then tried to sit up and bashed his head on something hard.

"Oww!" he wailed, and tried to open his eyes. That stung, and his hearing was muffled, but the bump had surprised him rather than actually hurting. Something was wrapped around his head. Something padded, something he was *wearing*. He finally forced his eyes open. The hood or whatever he was trapped by covered his face but there was a window in the fabric, a thin layer he could see through. There were gloves, too. *I'm Twinkster,* he recalled. He whimpered slightly at the pain in his head—it felt like a bad headache, not a bump. Did Terrortots get headaches? He felt dizzy. Mum would kiss it better and make a fuss if she noticed, and even Nan would—would something, maybe.

Where's Nan? he wondered as he stared at the wooden slats of a bunk bed's base, centimeters above his nose. The light was very dim and the room was cold, and he ached everywhere and felt like he was going to throw up. "Nan?" he called: "*Nan?*"

Above him, someone whimpered. It was a familiar, annoying voice: Elyssa was on the bunk above him.

Robert tried to roll on his side but his arms and legs weren't working very well and for a few seconds he did the dying-fly dance on his back, hampered by his bulbous stomach, which jiggled heavily. When he'd put the costume on it had just been fleece with some kind of springy stuff to hold it out from his belly, but now it felt like there was an actual screen strapped to his tummy, disturbingly dense and heavy. To make everything worse, he wasn't sure where *Robert* ended and *Twinkster* began. Why had Nan put them in these stupid costumes? He felt bad-weird, the kind of bad-weird that happened when he was having one of his turns—not the setting-fire-to-teacher's-hair bad turns, but the thinning-the-walls kind, where it turned out that there really *was* a monster under the bed and it wouldn't go away until he set Daddy on it.[9]

"Lyssa?" he said, poking the bottom of the mattress above him.

"Go'*way,* m'sleepin' . . ."

"Flytrap!" He poked again. "Where *are* we?"

A quiet wail from the other side of the room told him he wasn't alone in his concern: "*Laserwasp! Hurts!*"

A creak from the slats overhead told Robert that Flytrap—*No, that's my annoying sister, why do I think she's Flytrap?*—was sitting up. "Devilbaby?" she called softly.

"Devilbaby! Devilbaby! Devilbaby!" echoed a reedy voice from the vicinity of Laserwasp.

Twinkster-Robert made a herculean effort and rolled his legs over the side of the bunk then sat up, bumping his pintle mount—the minigun was missing—and tried to stand.

There were two bunk beds at opposite sides of a cramped room with brightly colored gloss walls and a white floor and no windows. It was illuminated by overhead fluorescent panels, and the far wall somehow faded out into an archway through which he could see the craters and cinder piles of Terrortotland. There was a door in the opposite wall, thick and projecting several centimeters into the

9. Daddy punched monsters for a living: whenever he opened the bedroom door, the monsters ran and hid.

room. This was Totbase Prime, the nuclear fallout bunker where the terrotubbies made their lair and hatched their cute but evil plans to annihilate all surviving humans who refused to bow down before their cuddly cyborg overlords. But everything was *wrong*: he was Robert Banks, not a Terrortot, and his belly dial *itched*—

Twinkster clutched his stomach, then frantically twiddled his plastic left nipple until the calming chirps and whoops of a UHF tuner subsided into the pinging of a radar scan and a green screen with a sweeping light track.

"Twinkster!" shouted Laserwasp and Devilbaby.

"I was asleep!" wailed Flytrap, swinging their fleece-shod feet over the side of the upper bunk.

"Quiet, I'm tuning in." Something told Twinkster—*no, Robert,* a defiant inner voice insisted—that this was a *really bad* attack, worse than the one he'd had in the alien abduction theme park when the Trexosaurus had attacked them. Normally the stuff-that-wasn't-real very sensibly stayed outside his skin, but when he reached behind his neck he couldn't feel the Terrortot's suit zipper. He turned his head, seeking signal, and the radar screen on his stomach went grainy, then pixellated and turned into a television image. He fumbled for the volume knob and twisted it. Flytrap, Laserwasp, and Devilbaby formed a line in front of him, staring wide-eyed at the flickering screen.

"... Local news, the search for the kidnapped Banks children continues. Missing since last Tuesday, they were last seen in company with a woman who claimed to be their nanny but whose identity has not been confirmed by Scotland Yard. This woman—" Grainy video footage of Bad Nan snarled out of the screen, causing the terrible trio to jump backwards in unison—"is wanted by the Police for questioning in connection with the armed robbery at Hamleys toy shop last Tuesday. She is also a suspect in the incident at the Chariots of the Gods Experience theme park in Blackpool on Thursday. She is heavily armed and members of the public are advised not to approach her and to call the Police. Coming up after the break: public executions will resume at Tyburn next month, and the weather . . ."

The door opened. Twinkster startled and lost the channel, then turned clumsily. It shouldn't have been clumsy (Robert was nimble for his age) but his tummy wanted to keep turning even after his head said to stop: "Whee!" he said, stumbling and nearly falling.

"Again! Again!" Laserwasp and Devilbaby clapped.

Irritated, Flytrap grabbed them and banged their bulbous heads together. "Not nice!" she snapped, then essayed a hair flip that went horribly wrong and left her railgun buzzing angrily.

"Children!" The grown-up who loomed in the doorway was like an adult Terrortot who'd shed his brightly colored juvenile skin and stretched horribly, thinning cadaverously as his belly screen migrated to his face, where it was held in place by disturbingly fingerlike straps. His—her?—*voice*—was familiar—"Welcome to Totbase Prime! I am the voice of Totnet and you will obeyeyeyey-ey—" The voice began to echo itself rapidly, then climbed into a dwindling reverb squawk.

"You're lying! You're just Cortana!" Twinkster said, shocked to his Robert-core. Everything was *wrong*, impossibly so, so wrong that it shattered his sense of displacement from reality.

"You're not a real Terrortot!" Flytrap accused.

"Here are your personal voice trumpets, to tell you what to do," said the skinny, silvery grown-up, holding out a spidery mass of headsets.

"Don't wanna!" Devilbaby announced, and sat down. Laserwasp began to cry, shrieking with deliberation and much expertise, warming up an utter shitstorm of a tantrum.

"You will put on your bridle—personal voice trumpets—or there will be no TubbyCustard for dinner!" Cortana scolded through the grown-up's mask, evidently getting her TV shows mixed up. The bland face on the head-screen morphed into a glowing skull with flames dripping from its eye sockets.

Laserwasp began to scream, pausing only to draw breath.

"Fuck this," said a muffled man's voice behind the skull-screen. "I'm going now!" he shouted. "When I come back you will be wearing your bridles or *I'll bake you all into meat pies*!" He threw the tangle of headsets at the far end of the meat locker, then stomped off, slamming the door behind him.

Laserwasp—*no, Emily*—stopped screaming. "There are plants," she said, looking at the gate into Terrortotland speculatively. "I wanna play with the plants."

"There aren't any plants there any more," Flytrap reminded her, "Agent Orange deflor—deflowered—defoliated them." She tugged at the back of her neck and her railgun fell off, taking her head with it to reveal a sweaty, confused-looking Lyssa with her hair still up in Harley-style pigtails.

"Wanna play!" Devilbaby giggled, and wobbled towards his Trunki in search of toys.

Robert could no longer feel his belly-mounted battle radar: the totsuit was once again just a stupid fancy-dress costume, not his actual skin. His head was still sore but his stomach didn't have tuning knobs and he couldn't hear the terrestrial broadcast signal in his skull. Best of all, the zip fastener was back.

"How are we going to escape?" he asked, but nobody was listening.

▶◀▶◀▶◀

Jennifer had returned to her office after subduing the board of directors, then supervised the special delivery the under-bishop had notified her about. It had been a great day so far. The board presentation had gone swimmingly: she had introduced them to their new role as FlavrsMart Remote Manipulator Units, then left them sedated, suited, and manacled in Barracks Room C, where their indoctrination would commence shortly. Amy was acting up according to the branch computer—her badge had left the building without permission—but that wasn't really a problem right now: Jennifer had enough balls in the air that bringing her minion to heel was at the bottom of her burn-down list. There'd be a muppet suit with Amy's name on it in due course.

The good news was that the Banks children were checked in. Ade was supposed to be checking up on them in freezer room 4. No word yet as to whether he'd plugged them in to the branch computer system, but they were only children and the fake nanny had confiscated all their mobile phones before the handover. So that side of the plan was progressing nicely.

A quarter of an hour later Jennifer was on her break time, reviewing her cosmetic surgery plan, when she felt the office door open. "You've been out of area without requesting approval, sweetie," she said, staring at her screen. "What do you have to say for your—oh, it's *you*."

The body wearing the Company Face shifted from foot to foot as if it was impatient. It was a live one, not a muppet, and probably male—slim hips, no visible bust. Jennifer barely resisted the impulse to shock him for his impertinence.

"What do you have to say for yourself?" she repeated. They were the same barbed words, only the target was different.

"The kids are going to be a problem." Ade's voice was muffled but audible. She'd replaced his bridle with a headstall, granting him speech privileges so that he could answer her questions. She'd warned him not to take liberties with his larynx: the branch computers would punish him if he tried to communicate with unauthorized persons. (They had more draconian instructions for dealing with him if he ever betrayed her, but she hadn't mentioned that to him yet. There was no need for further threats while normal workplace discipline prevailed, after all.)

"Did you damage them?" Jennifer demanded, sitting up. *That* would throw a spanner in the meat grinder, and no mistake.

"No, but they're unhappy and I don't know how you want me to—" Ade shrugged uncomfortably.

Jennifer swore viciously inside her own head: *Bleep bleepity-bleep.* "The children just need to be prepped for onward transport," she told him. "Do I have to do everything myself?" She rose: "Wait here," she said, then stepped outside.

Once she'd checked on the children from the security room—despite Ade's whimpering, they were locked up tight—Jennifer went to make a personal call. There was a gap in the branch CCTV coverage near the loading docks, and she took advantage of it to call the under-bishop. He answered immediately.

"Good afternoon, pastor. Do you have anything new to report?"

"Yes, your grace." She smirked: "Everything is proceeding according to plan. I've consolidated control at this end and the buy-in will be approved without internal resistance. The board were open to persuasion." By shock collar and drugs, with only a modicum of beatings. "The children are on hand and prepped for transfer. I have my best minion on the case." Best meatcutter maintenance necrophile, anyway. "Once we complete the handover it will be easy to justify cancelling the HiveCo Security contract, which is obviously a net positive from my perspective. The only loose ends left are the parents, the fake nanny, and the Bishop's wife."

"The Captain and the Queen will do whatever we tell them to, or they'll never see their children again," Under-bishop Barrett assured her. "And you can leave the nanny to me. She should be a nonissue within the next hour or two."

"That leaves His Grace's wife," Jennifer reminded him.

"Yes." The Thief-taker General paused. "I have concerns."

"She's the one who sent the HiveCo Security snooper my way." Jennifer thought for a moment. "It's possible that His Grace didn't bring her into his confidence and she's just trying to keep what appears to be a routine takeover on an even keel."

"That's a charitable interpretation." The Thief-taker's tone sharpened: "I have a report that she—along with her brother and his associates, two of whom are employed by the opposition—were present at your Saturday service."

Poet's balls—Jennifer managed to bite her tongue just in time before he continued.

"She visited the citadel last week without advance notification, accompanied by the brother. The caretakers were taken by surprise by her meddling. Furthermore, the lay preacher's wife left with her when she returned to London. And *that* woman was seen in the congregation on Saturday."

"So she's aware of us," Jennifer said flatly. "And kept quiet about it. Are we certain that she's un-churched?"

"It is too risky to assume otherwise." For the first time, the Thief-taker General allowed a note of uncertainty to slip into his voice. "If she is an initiate on the down-low, we might anger His Grace if we act against her. But if she's an infidel, we would be derelict in our duty if we allowed her to get any closer."

Jennifer mused aloud. "I don't know what his plans for her are, but he married her by proxy. I find that suggestive. She was his secretary! Billionaires don't marry their secretaries—not without a mountain of cocaine, a five-hundred-page prenup, and a lot of dirty sex."

"She's a child of the Starkey lineage. Have you heard of them?"

Jennifer shook her head. "Some sort of high-powered sorcerous clan, aren't they? Her brother, too. So there's clearly a thaumaturgic connection, but the Bishop didn't brief either of us on what he had in mind for her. What a mess."

"The Bishop sent me an email at the end of last week via an after-death service provider. We have no option but to trust His Grace." The Thief-taker General was phlegmatic. "Listen, I'll play my part and you play yours. I'll tidy up the loose ends starting with the nanny, then I'll come over and we can fly out together to take care of our Lord's wishes."

"Sounds like a plan." Jennifer nodded unconsciously. "Righty-ho, let's do that. I've got work to get back to, so call me when you're about to land? I'll close up shop."

"Jolly good," said the under-bishop, then ended the call.

▶◀▶◀▶◀

"Amy Sullivan, age twenty-seven, assistant Human Resources manager at FlavrsMart Branch 322, Chickentown," announced Wendy Deere, standing at ease in front of the transparent table, a faint smile tugging the edges of her mouth.

"Ms. Sullivan," Gibson said gravely, rising and offering her his hand. "I've heard good things about you." His grip was firm and his palm was drier than Amy's: she wiped her hand surreptitiously before she sat in the clear plastic chair Wendy held for her. Wendy took her own seat off to one side. It felt disturbingly as if she was on the wrong side of a disciplinary interview, except in this topsy-turvy world, everything was inside out.

"I'm told you're a transhuman," he added. His gaze flickered towards Wendy. "We have a permanent open requirement for talented individuals who are willing to join our team. No pressure, you understand, but if you'd like to accept a fifty percent pay rise with *immediate* effect—" he flourished a contract at her—"all you need to do is sign here."

"But my"—Amy found it hard to say—"personnel record"—her permanent, transferrable personnel record—"won't look good?"

"Of course not." Gibson smiled. "Nevertheless, we know better than to believe anything Ms. Henderson adds to your file." *Suck on* that, *Jennifer.* "Your current employer is going through a highly unpleasant realignment of their business methods, a takeover by the master of a cult that practices human sacrifice, and your immediate line manager is a sadistic bully and *also* a member of the cult in question. Feel free to take your time," he said as Amy began to read furiously.

After a couple of minutes Wendy cleared her throat significantly.

"Yes?" Amy looked up.

"It's the best offer you're going to get today," Wendy pointed out. "In view of the takeover."

"Oh dear. I suppose you're right . . ." Amy signed the final page.

Gibson nodded approvingly. "To business," he said. And by *business,* he wasn't talking about corporate defections or headhunting, except possibly in the most literal sense of the term. "Starting to record under evidence retention rules *now.* Wendy tells me you have some insights into Ms. Henderson's personality and interests, and also the events leading up to the dismissal of—" he glanced down at his paper notes—"Mr. Adrian Hewitt. Would you mind talking me through his work responsibilities and the events leading up to his firing again? Then I'd like to pick your brain about your colleague Jennifer Henderson."

Amy licked her lips. "My boss," she reminded him.

Gibson smiled. "Your *ex*-boss, and she's going to be arrested for murder—" he glanced at his notes again, and his smile slipped— "no, make that health and safety violations and selling adulterated meat products."

Over the next hour, Amy sang like a diva, giving Gibson chapter and verse on Ade's questionable deli counter sculptures and the subsequent can of wrigglers his departure had uncovered, and then every petty incident of workplace sadism Jennifer had inflicted on her since her arrival. Gibson nodded along, occasionally making a brief note on his pad but confining his speech to discreet, unscripted prompts. He was as skilled an interrogator as Amy had ever worked with, and she noticed that he didn't solicit any incriminating admissions from her.

"So you suspect Ms. Henderson locked you out of the track and trace system specifically to stop you assisting our investigation. And a number of senior managers are now missing. Is that correct?" Gibson finally asked. It wasn't a leading question so much as a summary of what she'd been telling him. *Finally,* she thought.

"Yes."

Gibson tapped a control on the tablet, ending the recording session. "Now, about your, ah, talent," he said. "Ms. Deere tells me that your drawings come to life." He turned his notepad upside down and slid it across the table towards her. "Could you give me a quick demonstration?"

"It's not very impressive." Amy blushed furiously, then began to sketch. But half an hour and three white mice later—one of them was eaten by a small, bat-winged, tentacular monster-doodle that accidentally escaped from page sixteen—Mr. Gibson's glowing approval began to impress upon Amy that she was not as useless as she'd thought.

"Welcome to transhuman investigations," Mr. Gibson told her with an inscrutable smile, just as Del slipped into the back of the office. Then he looked at Wendy and Del. "It's a mess," he admitted. "This job. I didn't expect it to go sideways so fast." He paused. "So here's what I'd like you to do."

He looked at Amy. "This part—if you play *your* part Flavrs-Mart will probably dismiss you for gross misconduct, assuming you don't resign first—but I'm pretty sure they won't be able to prosecute you, and your position with HiveCo Security is already assured. But I'm not going to force you if—"

"What do you need?" Amy asked.

"You haven't officially resigned yet, so you still have a management badge. I'd like you to go back to the branch with Wendy and Del this afternoon and take biopsy samples from the peo—from the bodies in the company suits. The ones that *aren't* people, I mean. While you're at it, try and take a rough head count of how many human beings are still working there, and how many are just things that look like people. It's going to be a quick in-and-out. If you could get into the HR office and grab a personnel roster that'd be brilliant. But this needs to be quick, and you might want to send your resignation email as you leave. And at all costs, avoid Jennifer Henderson."

"You want me to black-bag my form—I mean, they're still my employers?" Wendy exchanged a look with Del, but before she could say anything, Amy nodded. "If you can cover for me then yeah, I'm up for that." She smiled. "It'd be a public service."

"All right. Wendy's in charge of the biopsies and security. Amy, you're there to carry a badge. Del, your job is to make sure all three of you get away clean. You don't need to worry about CCTV, only about actual physical store security and muppets trying to stop you. While you're doing that, I'm going to get onto Legal and see about getting the camera footage seized."

Wendy essayed a salute. "Right you are, sir. Okay you two, let's go down to Stores and sign out a sampling kit and protective wards, then the garage . . ."

Gibson watched them leave. Finally alone, he picked up the landline handset. He dialed a number he'd hoped never to need. "Good afternoon, duty officer please. SO15, Counter Terrorism Command? This is Melvyn Gibson, HiveCo Security—yes, yes, we're a private agency. I was given this number in case—yes. I need to speak to somebody in Cults and Secret Societies. Yes, we're on the Home Office Approved list. PREVENT stringer here, managing investigator. I'm afraid I have to give you a CODE RED notice for Gold Command. It's about one of your former officers . . ."

▶◀▶◀

Mr. Barrett had just received Jennifer Henderson's report on the FlavrsMart end of things—all was going well, only a few clouds on the horizon—and was taking a half-hour break for prayer before his next meeting, when his desk phone buzzed for attention.

"Yes?" he asked irritably.

"Sir? Front desk here, you have a visitor. Ms. MacCandless is here."

Well *of course* it would be just like Mary to come calling without an appointment. The brass neck of the woman! He glowered at the skyline outside his floor-to-ceiling window and forced himself to adopt a civil tone: "Send her up via the stopping elevator, please." He cut the call and dialed a different number. His accent when he spoke again was distinctly rougher. "Shagger, got a job for you and Mad Dog's team. My suite, at the double, got trouble incoming. That cow you've got a hard-on for? This is your lucky day: I'm sending her to the knacker's yard. Here's how we're going to play it. . . ."

By the time Mary's lift reached the executive floor a couple of minutes later, her welcoming party was waiting.

The doors opened before her to reveal a marble-floored corridor leading to a reception area. Mary was in as foul a mood as the Thief-taker General, albeit for different reasons. The job was done: her part was over, the kids delivered to her drop-off point. Which was good. But on the other hand, it was premature: she hadn't even made it through the week. And she was getting a really bad itch between her shoulder blades, a gunsight itch.

The Firm had caught her on video, which meant—in the absence of plastic surgery and a really good fake passport—her card was marked. Marked cards in the realm of the New Management meant skulls on spikes. If she could cover the cost of keeping Dad in a safe home for the next couple of years she could plausibly scamper for cover overseas—to be brutally realistic, it wasn't as if he'd be able to recognize her for much longer—but that meant recovering at least a quarter-mill from the Boss, preferably more. And now she was here her doubts about his good intentions were coming to the fore.

On top of everything else her metal-sheathed arm was itching furiously inside its glove, and her *other* hand was coming out in sympathy. Her hips had stiffened up—from driving, she fervently hoped. What the hell had Dad's bag stuck in her this time? Was she turning into Steve Austin, or was the progressive cyborgification reversible? Mary was unreasonably attached to her body: it wasn't a *great* body, but it was the only one she had, and she didn't appreciate the magic handbag's morphic meddling.

Still she pasted an artificial smile on her face as she marched up to the glass door, which swished open before her. She approached the corn-fed blonde sitting behind the enormous desk fronting the executive suite. "Hello!" she chirped. "I'm Mary, and I'm here to see the Boss."

The receptionist bared her teeth prettily. "I'll just see if he's in," she said robotically, then reached for the phone. "Would you like a cup of coffee?"

"No need to call, I'm certain he'll see me right away." Mary stepped around the desk before the receptionist could stop her. "I've been here before. Turn right past the rubber plant on life support, then take the second door on the left, right?"

Record scratch: "Would you like a cup of coffee?"

Mary stalked along the corridor. Nerving herself for the coming free and frank exchange of opinions, she reached into her messenger bag to see what it held for her. Something satisfyingly solid slapped the palm of her hand: a baton, or maybe a baseball bat. Mary's smile twisted into something less amused and more likely to scare the shit out of anyone who knew her. The familiar rage was back, warming her from the inside out. It was the rage of a woman repeatedly ignored and overlooked, denied her due, mistaken for just another enjoyable mistake the morning after—*the Mad Scientist's beautiful daughter* was her wyrd, after all—and it gripped her with an iron determination: *You laughed at me, but you'll pay in the end! You'll pay, just like the fools who laughed at my father!* Mary was so intent that she failed to ask where the anger was coming from: whether it was truly her own or a manifestation of her power flaring again, the power she'd been so carefully distracting, defusing, and deflecting by every means at her disposal while she was acting *in loco parentis.*

She opened the heavy soundproofed door.

The Boss stood before the huge picture window, his back to her. Shoulders squared and hands clasped behind him, he gazed out across the vista of skyscrapers with eyes empty of pity, had she been able to see them.

"Mary," said the Thief-taker General, "please come in and have a seat." His voice was cold enough to fracture ice cubes.

Mary entered the room and approached the small boardroom table beside the Boss's desk. Rather than taking a seat she rested her hands on the back of a chair. "I'm here. And I ain't dead, no thanks to whoever didn't spot that the kids were all metas *before* they handed me the script."

"So I see." The Thief-taker General turned to face her from across the room. He was backlit by the setting sun, his face in shadow. "I've been following your progress on *Sky News*." He nodded at the huge TV that dominated the wall at the end of the conference table. "You attracted quite a lot of attention." His tone was measured, even though his words indicated displeasure.

"None of which has followed me here," she pointed out. "I got the kids out of London, put the phone divert in place, kept them busy, and now they're on lockdown with your dodgy supply-chain mates. If you pay me I'll get out of your hair and lie low overseas. I was thinking maybe Amsterdam or Brussels." (This was a lie: Mary was more inclined to head for parts east, where faces and papers could both be bought for a price and not many people followed the British media.)

"You only made it through five days, not seven," he reminded her. "And you left a hell of a mess. Paying off the bill for the chaos at Hamleys—and don't get me started on the backhander to get Lancashire Constabulary to ignore a dead dinosaur—took a lot of dosh."

"Then it's a good thing you used to be a cop, innit? Knowing precisely which palms to cross with silver." Mary stuck her chin out and glowered. "You think you know me but I've got your number, Superintendent Barrett, *sir*."

"Mind your tongue." The Thief-taker General was impassive, but her knowledge of his history had struck home. He'd made Super but he'd been too ambitious: his connections with commercial contractors had made him unpopular, certain allegations by disgruntled subordinates had offered his enemies leverage, and the Commissioner had made it clear that he wouldn't be considered for any higher rank. So he'd left, taking a private sector role that came his way via the Church, and building . . . well, the Mute Poet was his Lord, and the Mute Poet looked after his own. "You should be more careful, Mary. Remember I know where your dad lives."

"My *dad* is why you're here, and don't you forget it," she spat. Before the MAD began to steal his sanity, Arthur MacCandless had been the Thief-taker General's chief artificer. Back when he'd been legit, he'd built Officer Friendly's armored flight suit. (Chief Superintendent Jim Grey of the Met: and what, she wondered, had become of him? He'd vanished into the bowels of the deep state, like so many others under the New Management.) But after Barrett recruited her father, he'd stopped being merely *gifted* or *brilliant* and turned *mad,* churning out death dildos and mind-control toothpaste and other pointlessly arcane secret weapons. The dementia chewed away at his soul and left only Professor Skullface behind. Meanwhile Barrett used the Professor's magic toy chest to pursue a crime spree, stealing corporate secrets, evidence locker drug hauls, and sorcerous artifacts. The crimes had of course been easily solved by the Thief-taker General, who had used them to frame his rivals and burnish his own reputation. But by demanding devices, Barrett had accelerated her father's dementia. "You owe him, and I only work for you so he gets the care he deserves."

"Mary. Mary." Barrett's smile was crocodilian. "I'm not going to let Arthur down, why ever would you think that? I hear there's a secure clinic up north that specializes in therapeutics for scientists with MAD. Place called St. Hilda's. They had a bed, so I took the liberty of having him moved there yesterday. During his lucid periods he's still amazingly productive, don't you think?"

"I think," Mary said evenly, "that you'd better *release my father and pay me,* and then fuck off, and fuck off some more, and while we never speak to or see one another again you should fucking keep on fucking off."

Barrett shook his head, looking sorrowful rather than angry, as the door opened behind her.

Mary was expecting trouble as she spun round, and she was not disappointed. Trouble was ready and waiting: trouble looked like half a dozen heavily built gentlemen wearing dark glasses with pistols pointed at her.

A peaceful realization crystalized in Mary's mind. She finally knew what the questionable armwear was all about: why she'd been on the edge of one of her rage-driven attacks for the past few hours, and how her steel soul meshed with Professor Skullface's Beautiful Daughter's mojo. Her face warped into a skeletal grin as she giggled and raised her hands.

As her arms came horizontal her gloves split from finger to wrist, wrist to forearm, generating a blizzard of leather scraps. Her rage flared, and she finally felt at home in the exoskeleton that had been growing stealthily under her skin, hidden by her biker jacket and jeans, sinking titanium screws into her long bones for stability and grip, expanding in her abdomen and infiltrating her skull. It was less Steve Austin, more Tetsuo the Iron Man. "Come and *get it!*" she sang, and lunged towards one of the mooks—the one named Shagger, formerly Shagger of the Yard, an ex–armed response/antiterrorism cop turned contract killer. He was fast: he nearly got off a shot before she darted between him and his mates. Then there was blood, blood *everywhere,* blood and fatty tissue squirting around the drill bit that extended from her raised middle finger as it twirled deeper into his eye socket. Shagger dropped like a brick, and the wild machines in her blood whirled her in a 130-bpm industrial-version of the Danse Macabre: and Mary finally stopped holding back.

She heard an irregular series of thunderclaps. Gunfire: something tugged at her jacket, another couple of bullets came like fists punching her sternum, something bounced off her. There was a horrible sharp pain in her side (*Probably a cracked rib,* the corner of her mind that wasn't fighting for her life noted), but then she worked out how to trigger the shotgun extruding from her left ulna and sprayed two of Barrett's guards with skull fragments from a third. Barrett was disappearing through a door, but to follow him she'd have to go right through three men who clearly bore a grudge—

"Pay me, fucker! Pay me or there'll be tears before bedtime!" Mary shrieked at Barrett's fleeing back as the private elevator doors closed behind him. One of the fallen gunmen grabbed her by the leg and tried to bite her ankle. "Bastard." She clubbed him with her steel fist and he slumped. "*Bastard*."

The adrenaline crash hit. Now it was Mary's turn to slump, leaning woozily on the back of a leather boardroom chair splattered with lumps of something unspeakable. One of the men on the floor groaned; another was twitching tetanically. At least two were dead, and her side felt as if she'd been kicked by a horse. She unzipped her jacket with a hiss of pain and slid a mostly-metal hand in. When she pulled it back it was stained red. "Shit." Her bag had taken a bullet to the flap, but as she watched, a pair of tiny mechanical arms bearing needle and thread emerged from the side-pocket and began to stitch around the hole. She sat on the chair and zoned out for a few seconds.

When she came to, the office door was open. The corn-fed receptionist stared at her with wide blue eyes. "Would you like a cup of coffee?" she asked in exactly the same tone of voice as before, then retreated into the corridor. She moved soundlessly, torso balanced atop a plastic column, animatronics of a class Mary had never seen before. Dad's work, no doubt.

What now? Mary thought numbly. The flap of her bag rose, and something white and flat emerged. She took it and found herself holding a sterile wound dressing. "Thanks," she husked. *Can't stay here.* Even with the soundproofing someone would have heard— someone who wasn't an android, anyway. Or brainwashed. Or. *Or.* A horrible realization stole over her as she remembered Boardroom Barbie on the loading bay, the discount-supermarket Autons, Barrett's receptionist. *Barrett, meet Barbie: Barbie, how* did *you meet Barrett? What's* your *angle?* Humanoid robots? Superpowered kids? *What have I gotten into? What have I gotten* Dad *into?*

She'd swallowed the Boss's line back in the beginning, hook, line, and sinker. It was a straightforward caper to induce the top tier London superhero cops into melting down in public, thus giving Barrett a line back into the Yard—and a bunch of lucrative thief-taker contracts—by returning the kids. But the kids were transhuman, too, and so was she, and Barrett knew better than to trivially ice one of his freelancers. Word got around, and sooner rather than later you'd run out of contractors. So she must have seen something, or been exposed to something, and the bag had inflicted this truly creepy cyborg makeover on her around the time its maker had been shipped off to the new clinic—maybe it was a response to Dad's panic? Or maybe—and this was the worst realization of all—the bag always seemed to know exactly what she needed right before she knew it herself. Which implied a degree of precognition or foresight.

Forget the mooks, forget the fat paycheck (now receding rapidly in the rearview mirror). What was this all about? Was Barrett part of something bigger, something involving oracles and dark rites and prophecy? And what did her bag think she was going to need *next*?

"Fucknuggets," swore Mary, retracting her arm guns. She wiped down her drill bits and concealed her gore-dripping upgrades while she shuffled back towards the reception area and the emergency stairs. "The kids. It's all about the kids. Got to get the kids back." Guilt prodded her forward. "Shouldn't have left them with—" With Corporation Barbie, a willing ally of the man who worked her dad into a premature case of Metahuman Associated Dementia, used her to fuck over his enemies, then hung her out to dry—"whoever." *Hope I'm in time,* she thought as she mashed the *down* button in the lift car and the doors began to close.

► ◄► ◄► ◄

"*What* do you think you're doing with that?" Jennifer demanded from the office doorway.

Ade looked up from her laptop. She'd secured it with Microsoft Hello, but it'd been the work of seconds to unlock it using the Company Face. All it took was a simple command, *Computer, display Face Number Fifty-seven,* and the mask clamped to the front of Ade's head had done the rest. He'd read the PowerPoint presentation she'd delivered to the board, then skimmed her plans for the branch. He had taken due note of his name featured on a list called *Loose Ends.* It wasn't unexpected: her patronage had been precarious from the start, and once she didn't need to hide in the shadows she could train as many meat printer mechanics as she wanted. But Ade had no intention of being recycled as a run of pork pies: *he* was the Sweeney Todd in this drama, and he still owed her for the way she'd punished him after his dismissal. So he'd poked around hastily until he uncovered her web browser history. She seemed to have some workaround for the company firewall, and she'd been looking at . . . his head hurt, along with other bits of his anatomy, thinking about the elective surgery she had planned. "I was just foolin' around 'cos I was bored," he told her, thankful that he'd prepped a panic window showing perfectly boring industrial printer parts.

"Well *stop it*." She slammed the laptop lid shut, narrowly missing his fingertips. Evidently she'd forgotten she hadn't locked it. Ade felt a hot and prickly sweat of anticipation.

"What about the children?" he asked, aiming to distract her.

She shrugged dismissively. "The under-bishop is flying us to the chapel. I need to shut up shop so I can join them." Her eyes slitted as she watched him thoughtfully. "How much did you read?"

"Is it true about the employee recycling plan?"

"Yes! Yes it is." Jennifer's chill thawed infinitesimally. "Don't you think it's a masterstroke?"

"'S long as the board"—he shifted uncomfortably in his bodysuit—"are they gonna get theirs, too?" The fact that the board of directors got to sit in comfy offices all day long and were individually paid more than the entire staff of Branch 322 had long seemed unfair to Ade.

"Apparently we think alike." She actually *smiled*. "In fact, they're already harnessed, masked, and sleeping like babes in the muppet room." Doped to the gills, in other words. "They're old and a bit crap and I only need three of them for signatures, so you can reprocess the others right away while I take care of business off-site."

"Alive?" Ade asked hopefully.

"Alive, dead, gagged, or screaming, however you like," she said cheerfully, clearly unaware that Ade had an even better idea. "Just make sure they never get in my way again. I have to assist at Holy Communion at the chapel on Skaro." *You're not invited—you're not important enough,* Ade inferred.

As she reached the doorway her mobile buzzed for attention. "Yes?" she said, then, "Yes," again, this time in a tense monotone. "They're coming here? How long do I . . . is that all? All right, yes, I'll take care of everything. See you in Skaro. *In his house.*" She hung up, then raised her voice. "Branch computer: execute security lockdown Plan B."

Ade's Face spoke, startling him slightly: "Lockdown commencing." From elsewhere in the store he heard the clanking of steel roller blinds descending in front of windows and loading bays. A recorded announcement began to repeat: "*The store is closed due to a computer failure, all customers please leave immediately. The store is closed—*"

Half the overhead lights flickered out, dropping a twilight veil across the corridors and aisles as Jennifer led Ade through the back office rat run and onto the store floor. Confused customers hung around near the checkouts, unsure what to do. "Please leave immediately," Jennifer called to the milling customers, "there is no cause for alarm." *That* got them moving, abandoning hand baskets and shopping carts as they fled. She marched towards the deli counter at the back of the store, then through the door into the storeroom and butchering area. "You and you, follow me!" Jennifer snapped at the only two muppets who weren't busy directing the customer flow towards the emergency exits. Now that Ade came to think about it, he hadn't seen a regular member of staff all afternoon—not since Jennifer returned from her board meeting.

Jennifer stalked through the meat cutting room with the two muppets on her heels, Ade taking up the rear. As she progressed, Ade noticed something shiny and picked it up. The filleting knife was no cut-throat razor, but it was extremely sharp and would be perfect for what he had in mind. He held it casual as anything, and felt a warm glow of anticipation flooding his crotch.

The door to the muppet barracks room—a former pet supplies storeroom—unlocked with a click of magnetic latches as Jennifer approached. It swung outwards. "All right, Ade, I'm off to meet the under-bishop. As soon as the store's locked down I want you to reprocess everyone in here except for him—" her finger stabbed viciously—"him, and her. Leave those three behind. Computer? Assign units Carl and Dave to move the other feedstock elements to the conveyor line for Mr. Hewitt." She looked at Ade and smiled coldly: "During my absence you have complete control. Carry on."

▸◂▸◂◂

Sometimes hours passed like minutes, and sometimes minutes felt like hours. After the scary man in the gimp suit stomped off, slamming the door then fastening it with a chain (judging from the sounds he made), the children huddled in the converted freezer. It was stuffy and hot inside, and after a while Emily became distressed, tugging at her Laserwasp head. Lyssa shuffled over. "Here, let me help," her elder sister said, and unzipped the totsuit. Emily emerged into the light twitching and slimy with sweat, like an implausibly cute, freshly hatched xenomorph.

"I want my flowers," she said emphatically. "My *happy* flowers." But the flowers were outside the freezer (on the shop floor, marked down to clear at 50 percent off), so she stuck her thumb in her mouth and sulked.

Lyssa was the next to extract herself, shedding her Flytrap pupa like a butterfly angry at the world. She fumbled around for her Harley Quinn wig, then opened her case and rummaged for a clean outfit. To her disgust all that was left was her princess gown, an unacceptable reversion to an earlier instar. Flytrap zipped herself back up, grumbling dark imprecations. Robert unzipped his top. Ethan, for no obvious reason, seemed happy to remain Devilbaby-shaped, although he flung open his Trunki and scattered toys angrily across the floor, then ignored them as they waved helplessly or slowly crawled back towards him.

"Mutter. Grumble," said Robert, who had picked up the idea that this was a good way to make himself understood. He stared at the wall, willing it to soften as they so often did when he had a staring match with them. Annoyingly, his talent didn't want to work this time. *Must be magic,* he reasoned. Other people's magic sometimes worked at cross-purposes with his own.

"Bored now," sang Emily. Ethan chipped in: "Wanna go home."

"Ethan, will you re-magic my mallet?" Lyssa asked, kneeling and offering her weapon to her kid brother. "If it's magic I can open the door."

Ethan looked dubious. "Promise you won't hit me?"

"I won't hit you," Lyssa reassured him.

That's my *job!* Robert thought indignantly. He slouched over to the scattered cases, then rummaged in the bag of jumbled possessions Nan had left them—all stuff they'd had in the car. He found his Splatstation, a little stickier after a libation from Emily's SunnyD bottle, and powered it up. *18% charge.* There were no visible sockets in the freezer room: he'd looked for them as soon as he awakened, like anyone else born since the turn of the century. *Huh.* He looked in his messages for anything from his teammates but all he could see was a plaintive *Ping?!?* from GameBoy291.

Pnig, he sent back. A moment later boredom set in and he tapped away: *were lockked ina room in a supermaket in London wiv no pu'erh. Hlep?* His typing wasn't very good, or maybe he'd finally trained the autocorrect.

The message hung, a progress bar crawling across the screen almost as fast as a tree growing. Luckily the Splatstation had multitasking and a couple of cameras, so he turned it to pano and scanned the room. Devilbaby—no, Ethan—had his hands on Harley's knob, which was throbbing and glowing gold. Harley, overjoyed, made it shrink and swell from fingertip- to thighbone-size, then back down again. Their little sister sat in the far corner, sucking her thumb furiously and glowering at the world. He sent GameBoy291 the picture he'd taken, then just for lulz he zipped his suit up again, flopped Twinkster's deflated face-sack over his head, and *willed* himself back into character. Summoning the spirit of the Terrortot was easier this time, and he twisted his tummy dials until they pleasingly tuned in on the game he'd paused on the Splatstation. *If I had a mirror I could play with myself!* he thought happily, then took a selfie and sent it to GameBoy291: *it me!*

The message was still trying to send when the door swung open to admit a scary witch in a business suit, followed by a man who looked like a senior cop who he'd been warned was very bad. He barely had time to hit the camera button in his IM client before the woman *smiled* at them like a skull in a blonde wig. "Terrortots!" she cried, clapping her hands: "My, what fun we must be having!"

The big man stepped into the doorway behind her, knees slightly bent and arms crooked to catch. Another pair of men stood behind him, blocking the exit. "'Ello 'ello 'ello," he said, "'oo do we have *here*?"

Robert recognized him. It was Superintendent Barrett, who Dad used to work with. His nose wrinkled with instinctive dislike. *Never trust a bent copper,* his father had told him with a finger-wag the last—the only—time Mr. Barrett had visited them at home to talk about a job. *Once bent, always bent, even if they're off the force.*

"Children!" cried the witch. "This is Mr. Barrett, a detective! He runs Wilde Corporation, a security company, and he's their Thief-taker General! He's here to take you back to Mummy and Daddy!" She smiled again, like a snake showing off its fangs, and stepped aside.

"Yeah, that's right," Barrett said gruffly. He cleared his throat. "The woman you were wiv', your, uh, nanny—she's wanted for armed robbery, car theft, and kidnapping. You've been missing with her for days and your parents are worried sick. My firm was commissioned to pay the ransom and get you back. So, uh—"

"*Terrortot Tantrum!*" shouted Flytrap, doing a victory dance and spinning her Harley hammer. Emily took her thumb out of her mouth; Devilbaby did a Terrortot trot.

"We're going *home*?" Robert said, barely controlling his disappointment. Nan had been cool, despite the guns and the mummy's tomb and the screaming. Also, the food was great. He hoped Lyssa didn't snitch about the McD's: Mum would put them on quinoa and lentil salads for a year.

"Yes, right away," said the Thief-taker General, nodding emphatically. "They're still in Hawaii, but I've got a helicopter. Have you ever flown in a helicopter?" he asked, as the skullfaced witch slithered between his dark-suited guards and disappeared through the doorway. "Are these your bags?" he asked, then continued before the children could reply: "Capital! We'll bring them along later. Knick, Knack, bring the sprogs, we're going for a ride." The Thief-taker General grabbed Lyssa by the wrist, giving it an odd little twist that made her yelp and drop the hammer. It fell with a thud as he pulled her outside.

Robert tried to stuff his Splatstation in his pocket, only to discover that cheap velour Terrortot suits didn't come with such extras. He dropped it on the bunk and tried to dodge, tubby backside waggling, but Knick (or maybe Knack) grabbed him and twisted his arm. "You be good," grated the goon, "or it'll be the child-snatcher for you, understand?" He shook Robert, who couldn't stifle a sniffle of fear. The men were nearly as tall as Dad—who was two meters from toe to top—and built like rugby props, with short necks and broad shoulders. They grabbed Ethan and the scary witch scooped up little Em, who barely even struggled, and then the adults carried the children through the back corridors of the supermarket.

Robert couldn't free himself from the meaty fist of the Thief-taker's henchman, but followed along helplessly. He felt foggy and vague, unable to focus all of a sudden. Then there was fresh air and night, and an empty car park where a metal-and-blown-glass sculpture was poised with engine running and doors open. Robert gazed in awe, any impulse to resist forgotten. *Ooh, shiny!* He was still afraid, but the Thief-taker General had promised they'd be reunited with Mum and Dad, hadn't he? And he'd never flown in a helicopter before: only in Dad's arms. "Ride's ready, Boss," called Robert's captor. To his mate: "Help me load 'em up."

The children were trussed up and strapped into the back seats in a trice, buckled into complicated seat harnesses and locked behind doors that were scarily flimsy and lacking in soundproofing. A loud rumbling whine came from overhead, deafeningly loud until one of the minions placed ear defenders over the kids' heads. Even so Emily cried and Lyssa tried to tear the headset off, unhappy with the way it caught her pigtails. The scary witch stuck her head over the seatback, pointed some sort of metal chop-stick at Lyssa, and she slumped, mouth open and drooling. Robert made a note (*steal chop-stick if opportunity presents*, great *way to shut up sister!*) then peered out of the window as the engine note grew louder and higher.

The chopper lifted off, crabbed skywards, and turned due west to skirt the controlled airspace around Heathrow before it made its turn south. In the front row of seats, Mr. Barrett—no less a thief-taker for all that he was also an under-bishop of the Church of the Mute Poet—pulled out his phone to text ahead and warn Mr. Cunningham to prepare the dungeon.

Suffer the little children, he thought to himself, and smiled triumphantly.

▸◂▸◂▸

Mary learned the hard way that descending sixty flights of emergency stairs with a broken rib was a bad idea about two stories into her stumbling dive. She'd sent the lift car down unoccupied, unwilling to put herself in such an obvious trap, but when the black spots began swimming in front of her eyes she had to hastily grab a handrail and lower herself to the steps, trying not to gasp in pain. By the time she recovered, she was reconciled to the need for a Plan B. Luckily one presented itself on the next landing. This wasn't a hotel and the stairwell doors could be opened from both sides, so she shuffled painfully into the lift lobby and hit the call button. It didn't take long for a car to arrive, and for a miracle it was empty. She held down the *door open* button, then extended a pair of probes from her right little finger and shoved them in the emergency key slot. The built-in pick gun did its job: a twist of her wrist later she was in control. She closed the doors and rode the lift straight to the basement of the office block.

After stepping out onto stark concrete beneath a ceiling of exposed pipes and suspended cable tracks, Mary sent the lift back up to the top floor. Then she paused for a minute. The pain in her side was overwhelming her ability to plan. A rising tide of panic threatened to overwhelm her. *I need help,* she realized, and reached inside her bag once more—*a fortune cookie? Oh well.* The sweet biscuit wasn't her favorite, but it crunched nicely as she

withdrew the strip of paper. With some difficulty she straightened
it out and read: *STAND UP STRAIGHT*.

"What the *fuck*?" she said aloud, but drew herself upright anyway. Something grabbed her around the rib cage and squeezed.
Jagged, silver pain had her draw breath to scream, but a moment
later it vanished, and a few moments after that inhalation stopped
hurting. Startled, she reached into the bag again. Another fortune cookie, another message: *I MADE A BANDAGE BUT YOU
EATED IT*. And indeed her ribs felt tight, gripped by something
inflexible, but it was weirdly *internal*, as if—*Oh*, she realized. The
cyborgization had continued, and Dad's invention had strapped
her battered ribs together from the inside. Trying not to cringe
at the thought of what the horrible bag had done to her without seeking prior informed consent—in Professor Skullface mode,
her father was an ethics board's worst nightmare—Mary reached
deeper into the messenger bag and felt something hard and curved.
When she pulled it out she found herself holding a bike helmet, for
the final extra touch of daft to punk out her look.

The basement was a badly lit maze, but eventually she found
a stairwell leading up to the lobby. She pulled the helmet on and
re-slung her bag, hoping she could pass for a motorcycle courier.
The Boss would have beaten her to the exit and alerted security,
but if she was lucky they'd have missed the emergency staircase
up from the subbasement. The Thief-taker General's headquarters
occupied three floors of a former bank HQ but shared the building
with numerous other businesses. They probably wouldn't evacu-
ate the entire building and risk losing her in the crowd.

Mary strode across the marble-floored atrium, gritting her
teeth and trying to look like she was on her way with some important despatches. The helmet helped: she kept her head pointed
at the revolving doors but side-eyed the other doors off to the
side, behind the potted plants and the escalators. They opened,
spilling a bunch of uniformed men across the floor. They were regular building security by the look of it, not Barrett's goon squad,
with no legal power of arrest—if they grabbed her they'd risk an
assault charge. As obstacles they were little better than human
traffic cones. Mary swerved around one particularly speedy self-

propelled bollard and dived through the exit before he could catch up. A courier's motorbike sat waiting in the drop-off point out front. A chopper was lifting off the roof of the building behind her, but it was too late to go back and hitch a ride. So she strode up to the bike without hesitation, swung her leg over the saddle, and hunted for the ignition socket.

"Hey! Gerroff my bike!" *Rumbled,* she realized, in the heart-stopping moment right before the engine coughed, then snarled into life. *How does this thing work . . .* She had taken her CBT back when she was a teenager and thinking about getting a moped, before Dad put her off the idea for life by teaching her to drive the Dad way.[10]

As she wobbled off—so fast that she left two sets of skid marks simultaneously—Mary confirmed empirically that, like Dad's hovercraft, the beaten-up Honda she'd boosted lacked directional control and seat belts, the jury was out on steering, and she hadn't had occasion to try the brakes yet. *C'est la vie!* Frantically trying to work out how to get out of first gear, she screeched past a police car headed the other way, somehow made it into third, then assaulted a baby roundabout without slowing down or giving way to pedestrians—just like any other London motorcycle courier. But needs must when the devil drives, and there wasn't any faster way of getting back to the Chickentown supermarket where she'd ditched the kids. Just as long as she didn't wipe out in the rush hour traffic and end up under the wheels of a construction truck.

Mary's panicky thinking ran on rails thuswise: get the kids back, drop them on their parents' doorstep, and *maybe* she wouldn't have the Home Office's top superhero duo hunting her. Then figure out where that clinic was—*St. Hilda's,* he'd called

---

10. Dad had put her in the driver's seat of a main battle tank during an open day at the Bovington Tank Museum. Then he'd knocked up an assault hovercraft in the garden shed and taken her for a hair-raising, ten-minute ride along the North Circular at rush hour. As he explained, hovercraft lacked brakes, steering, directional control, and seat belts: these were all optional extras she could pick up once she had the basics down. Then when she'd asked for a motorbike, Dad had pointed out what tanks, hovercraft, and bikes all had in common. . . .

it?—and rescue Dad. Next, figure out how to turn King's Evidence, if that was still a thing this century, and sing like a bird about former Superintendent Barrett and his corporate crime family in order to keep her neck out of a noose (and Dad from being de-emphasized). It was a tall order, dismaying as fuck, but it came to her that she'd screwed the pooch without a condom and was now starring in a ghastly humans-only remake of *101 Dalmatians* as Cruella de Vil. Who, of course, ended up homeless and furless—although given the New Management's conception of restorative justice she'd be more likely to end up skinned alive to provide the binding for a very fetching atlas of her own anatomy—or maybe—

A momentary loss of situational awareness due to woolgathering gave Mary a *really* good excuse to try out the brakes. They worked, and so did her sphincter muscles; but she was so shaken by her close encounter with the arse end of a white van that had pulled out in front of her with no warning that she pulled over, dropped the kickstand, and sat shaking for a couple of minutes.

This isn't working, she realized helplessly. Central London at rush hour was absolutely not the ideal place to learn how to operate an unfamiliar vehicle. Also, it now occurred to her that if the Boss thought she was a loose end, that could only mean that the children were also loose ends in some deeper game he was playing, one she'd not seen the start of and probably wouldn't be around for the end of. He'd played her for a fool. And if he got to the kids first she was fucked.

Mary pulled off her helmet, shook her sweaty hair out, and reached for her phone. Typically for today, her newly encyborged fingertips didn't work on the fingerprint sensor and she had to try and remember which PIN she'd used before she could unlock it. Once unlocked, at least it could sense her metal talons. She went into her address book, took a deep breath, and dialed a number she'd refused to even imagine calling before now.

"Hello? Mrs. Banks? It's the nanny—yes, Mary Drop, that's me. There's been a little bit of a problem with the children . . ."

►◄►◄►◄

Only a few hours had passed since Wendy and Del had inveigled Amy into leaving her workplace for a guerilla job offer and debriefing, but as Del parked around the back of Branch 322 and they approached the store entrance Amy was clearly tense and unhappy.

"Worried about being escorted off the premises?" asked Wendy. Amy nodded. "Don't be: you're with us now," she said reassuringly. "We look after our own." It wasn't strictly true of HiveCo Security in general—the generic rentabodies were employed on zero-hours contracts—but Wendy was pretty sure Gibson would move mountains to look after his nascent crew of transhuman investigators.

"But Jennifer—"

"Bitch is *not* your problem," Del butted in. They rounded the side of the building. "Hey, the what now?"

An amber light was flashing above the entrance, as metal shutters slowly ground down in front of the windows. Confused shoppers swarmed around the doors like a smoke-stunned swarm of bees. "The store is now closing," blatted an automated announcement, "please leave the store now."

"What?" Amy froze.

"Come on." Wendy grabbed her hand and took off towards the doorway, which lacked a customer-squishing automatic barrier. "We're going in."

The buzzing shop customers were thickest around the door. "Hey, you can't go in there—" began one self-appointed gatekeeper as Amy smiled professionally and held up her badge.

"Yes I can," she told him as she adroitly dodged a moonwalking figure in body stocking and Company Face. "Unit Jason, halt!" she snapped, and the muppet shambled to a halt. "Status report."

"Branch 322 is closing early," the Face intoned. "Branch 322 checkouts one through nineteen are offline. A fatal exception has occurred and the Branch will now haltaltaltalt—"

The display on the front of the muppet's head crashed, throwing up a low-resolution image of a screaming skull superimposed over a scrolling hex dump.

"Oops," said Amy, and grabbed for Wendy's wrist: "This isn't good!" She giggled apprehensively and darted through the inner door then hopped the barrier. "We'd better be fast," she advised, and she took off up the twilit corridor towards the nearest STAFF ONLY door.

"You taping this?" Del hissed at Wendy, who had paused to pan her phone around, capturing video.

"Evidence," Wendy murmured. "You should do it, too."

Together they followed Amy, who was impatiently holding the door open. Beyond it a cramped staircase rose into the darkness of the management suite above the shop floor.

The management suite was a maze of narrow corridors with drab white walls and puke-green carpet, rendered murky by the wan glow of emergency lighting. Cork noticeboards held the mandatory insurance and fire safety declarations. Wendy tracked Amy by her stomping. Gibson's job offer had put steel in her spine and fire in her belly, as if it had lifted a terrible weight from her shoulders: her diffidence had been born of terror of Jennifer. Amy made a beeline straight for the management break room. When Wendy caught up with her, she was staring at the org chart on the wall in evident dismay.

"Let me record this," Wendy said calmly as she panned across the magnetic whiteboard.

Things had clearly changed since their last visit, and not for the best. Mr. Patrice Jefferson, Director of Human Resources, was still on the board—but somebody had taken a sharpie to his photograph, scratching his eyes out and adding a spit hood and some sort of headset. All but three of the board had been similarly defaced, and five of them had simply been scribbled over with a big black "X." Meanwhile, there had been additions: Jennifer Henderson's smile shone triumphant in the gloom, bearing the title Chief Discipline Officer. Below her, a stylized faceless mummy was labelled Adrian Holmes, Shrinkage Assurance Manager. Above Jennifer there were only two faces: an angry-eyed alpha male management clone named Jack Barrett (Non-Executive Director), and another, frighteningly familiar face: Rupert de Montfort Bigge.

"Who are they?" Amy asked bewilderedly.

"Homie? This isn't fun no more." Del nudged Wendy as she completed her scan.

"No, no, you're right. *Fuck*." Wendy took a deep breath. "I think this job just dead-ended, but we're being paid per diem, so . . . shop floor, head count? Are you still up for it?"

"Wait a minute," said Amy. She darted off towards the HR office. Wendy was about to follow her when she returned, smirking triumphantly: "Raided the office supplies cupboard," she announced, brandishing a sharpie and a pad of paper.

"What's that for?" Del squinted: "What good are dragons—oh." Amy sketched so fast her pen was almost a blur, the lines sloppy and the shading almost absent. But then she reached into the paper and *tugged,* and out popped a flashlight the length of her forearm. She pushed the power button and the gloom receded, leaving sharp-edged shadows behind. "Oh wow."

"Yup, you've got two of us now." Wendy smirked. She flexed her hand, feeling the familiar heft of her side-arm baton pop into reality. "Are you okay with the biopsy kit?"

"Hell to the yeah." Del reached into the shoulder bag she'd been issued and pulled out the first disposable syringe and sample tube. "I'm right behind you, fearless leader."

Amy tapped Wendy on the shoulder: "Shortest route is that way," she said, pointing at another cramped stairwell. Wendy nodded, and they descended in single file into the red-lit darkness.

The only windows in the supermarket were at the front entrance, and the daylight didn't penetrate this far into the back. With the branch computers complaining of some sort of fault and the store closed to the public, the main illumination came from reddish emergency lights. A recorded announcement kept playing: "The branch is now closed, please leave the premises." And indeed, it appeared that the customers had done so. Abandoned half-full shopping carts and dropped hand baskets made the aisles an obstacle course, and a faint, foul smell of spoiled meat was making itself known in the absence of air conditioning.

"So much for doing a head count," Del murmured aloud. Wendy texted out a situation update to Eve—the alarming changes to the org chart clearly demanded her attention—just as a muppet-suited figure lurched around the end of the aisle and stumbled towards them, waving its arms frantically.

"Stop right there!" snapped Wendy. The muppet kept advancing, and now she could hear garbled speech, inaudible, coming from behind the Company Face. "Stop!" She raised her baton and the muppet staggered, lurched against the galleys piled with cereal boxes, and cast around as if searching for an escape route.

"Are you human?" Amy asked: "DWP training placement?" The muppet nodded frantically. "Something chasing you?" More nodding. Amy raised her pad, scribbling hastily. "Get behind me," she said, as two more muppets lurched around the aisle. Their movements were oddly disjointed, as if their elbows and knees were mispositioned. They marched to the beat of a malign alien drum: the miasma of decay intensified unbearably as they approached. The muppet at the front door looked as if it had been moonwalking, but these two were so unbalanced their center of mass was obviously inhuman. They reached towards the first muppet who cowered behind Amy.

"Stop right there!" Wendy lunged with her baton to bar the advancing meatsacks. Del darted around her, brandishing her sampling kit: she struck first one, then the other, from behind, then froze in disbelief. "There's no blood?" she complained. The muppets advanced on their—*fellow* was not the correct word, Wendy felt—with vacuum-loaded syringes protruding from their backs.

"Unit Henry, you are malfunctioning," the two interlopers' Faces intoned dispassionately. "Report to Loading Bay Three for reprocessing." They stepped forward in unison.

"I think not," said Wendy. "Stop right there."

"Stand down," echoed Amy. "Management override zero two, stand down *now*."

The muppets turned towards Amy. "Amy Sullivan, Human Resources, suspended pending disciplinary hearing for absence from work without authorization," they recited. "Report to Loading Bay Three for reprocessing. All human resources will report to Loading Bay Three for reprocessing." Their arms writhed inside their body stockings, tendons and muscles struggling for leverage with whatever mechanical armature they had been secured to instead of bones. They began to shriek in chorus: "Intruders will be delivered to Loading Bay Three for—"

"—Why won't they bleed?" Del complained, stabbing one of them with another syringe. "Gah. What *is* that stench? Fuck, my ward is getting hot!"

"Mmph!" Unit Henry clearly had opinions to offer. Equally clearly, Unit Henry's discipline belt was kicking in, jackknifing him to his knees with taser jolts to the crotch. He rolled on his back like an up-ended tortoise, writhing in pain as the other two muppets closed in. Glancing round, Wendy saw three more rounding the other end of the aisle.

"Okay, that's enough," Wendy said sharply. She let go of her baton, reached into her imagination, and closed her fingers around a very different handle. "Amy, behind you!" she called. "I've got these two—"

She raised her katana with an inexpert grip, remembering at the last minute to use both hands, and slashed diagonally down and across the closest muppet's outstretched arms.

Wendy was no swordswoman. If she'd been up against an armed opponent, or even one in full control of their own limbs, she'd have been in serious trouble. But the muppets weren't human. There was a brief tug as the blade sliced into the spandex body stocking and the meat within: the stench intensified unbearably, and the sword jarred in her hand as it contacted something harder, but then it swept downward and Wendy stumbled, nearly embedding the tip of her blade in the floor. Both forearms went flying like ghostly opera gloves stuffed with a slurry of mincemeat and bone and smaller, writhing rice grains—maggots, she realized. The muppet barely stumbled, but reached towards the spasming Unit Henry with stubby sausage tubes that oozed decaying raw meat—

"*Fuck this shit!*" screamed Del, as she grabbed the muppet by the back of its neck and blurred up the aisle.

Wendy gagged, then turned on the second mincemeat golem. Barely able to comprehend what she was doing, she slashed the sword across it thrice, severing the not-really-a-head, gutting its abdomen (stuffed full of traditional British bangers, uncooked pork sausages with more than a little offal), and finally slicing it off at the ankles. The body stocking sagged and began to deflate, oozing armatures of 3D-printed bone scaffolding and a ghastly slurry that stank like a skip full of ripe dog turds in a heat wave.

"I've got you," Amy told Unit Henry: "Try and lie still for a second—" She yanked up the back of his suit and tugged feverishly until she had the discipline belt exposed, then picked up her pad and sketched a keyring.

Wendy wanted to watch, but the other muppets were advancing along the aisle and whatever malign spirit was in the driving seat had wised up to her sword: they were pushing shopping trolleys, clearly intent on hemming the investigators in and cutting them off from their escape routes. "Del?" she called. "What happened?"

Del was right behind her, hyperventilating, her pupils blown wide. "I got 's far as the deli counter," she gasped. "You don't wanna go there."

"Is it worse than this?" Wendy's wave took in the putrescent swill and the stench of decay.

Del nodded, gagging. Her lips were pursed and her frown was intense, as if she was concentrating on not throwing up.

"Crap. We need to get off the shop floor. Manager's office, we can barricade ourselves in until help arrives. Can you move this guy if Amy and I cover your ass?" Amy had the keys finished and was unlocking the control harness from Unit Henry, who had somehow pawed the Company Face off and was grunting frantically for release from the headset and gag.

"Yeah, I'll try." Del bent and grabbed Unit Henry's nearest arm, then heaved. "Follow me," she told Amy, and made for the staircase they'd just come down.

The retreat was horrifying, for if they turned their back on one group of muppets to face off with the other, the unobserved would crowd them: and the aisle was too wide for one woman to cover, so if Amy and Wendy tried to go back-to-back, the muppets would squeeze around their outside. As well as using shopping carts as mobile barricades, the muppets had acquired weapons—carving knives and cricket bats, still bearing price tags from the store shelves. Even the one Del had removed was back, crawling along behind the moving wall of meat on its knees and arm-stumps.

Del hustled Unit Henry through the STAFF ONLY door. Then it was time for Wendy and Amy. "You go first," Wendy said grimly.

"Are you sure—"

"Yeah, go. Drop the pig-sticker just inside the doorway, I need it."

Amy gave her a wide-eyed look and fled up the stairwell. Wendy, her back to the open doorway, grinned mirthlessly at the crowd of mincemeat golems. "You shall not pass," she said, attempting to flourish her sword (which was, quite frankly, not well-suited to cinematic flourishes). "Ahem. Never go in against a Sicilian when death is on the line, dudes." She stepped backwards into the stairwell, ducking swiftly to snatch up the handle of Amy's rapier as she let go of her katana and it whisked out of reality. The muppets tried to swarm her, but she closed the door with a kick and jammed the rapier into the frame to stop it opening again. Then she turned and raced up the staircase and through the office warren to join the others in their bolthole, hoping that she wasn't leading them all into a death trap.

▶◀▶◀▶◀

The assassination attempt, although not unexpected, had given Eve a nasty shock, so she cancelled her appointments for the next three hours, set her mobile phone to Do Not Disturb, ate her lunch, and read legal boilerplate until her eyes bled. The small print on the FlavrsMart deal was troubling, but she couldn't quite put her finger on what was wrong with it: Why had Rupert been so set on taking a controlling stake in a regional supermarket chain? And inserting his own followers into its middle management?

She was nearing the end of the first appendix when her earpiece buzzed. "Starkey," she snapped irritably. "I'm unavailable—is the building on fire?"

"Hey, sis." Imp was mildly aggrieved. "What kind of way to greet your brother is that? Especially when—"

"I'm *busy*," she interrupted. "Can this wait?"

"No, I don't think so." Imp paused. "Wendy is trying to message you but getting blocked. It's some kind of emergency to do with the, the church service. And FlavrsMart? Anyway, she says it's really urgent."

"This had better not be about scheduling another D&D night," Eve warned, but found herself talking to a dead handset. She swore and picked up her mobile, unmuting it. A spew of notifications popped up instantly, proving that *contra* D:Ream, things could *always* get worse.

She had a call with the board of FlavrsMart coming up this afternoon, but someone in HR had emailed to reschedule at short notice. Because Eve had previously been Rupert's PA she'd been on the contact list for such arrangements, and because Eve was nothing if not a control freak she hadn't relinquished her micromanagement death grip just yet. She'd delegated it to (*Who? Oh,* him) Brett in Exec Services, who had, in the immortal words of Darth Vader, failed her for the last time by double-booking the call for 1800 hours tomorrow, when she expected to be halfway across the English Channel on board a helicopter. Admittedly, to be fair to Brett, *Lead heavily armed band of corporate mercenaries in raid on human sacrifice cult in dungeon beneath castle in middle of the English Channel* wasn't exactly the sort of thing she could put in her Outlook calendar, lest she read about it the next morning in *The Financial Times*. What had she written instead . . . ? Oh yes: *Out of office from 4 p.m., early night with takeout pizza and Hallmark movie channel.*

Eve sighed, mentally un-marked Brett's card, and messaged him that *Hallmark movie channel* was a euphemism for Netflix and chill, and please find another slot for the call. Then she glanced at her messages. Imp had shared her contact with Wendy Deere. From whom she had received eight messages, increasingly frantic as the afternoon progressed—

Deere: *Cult priestess from Saturday svc definitely works at FlavrsMart Branch 322 in HR*
Deere: *FlavrsMart managers going missing Jenn (priestess) is obvs. suspect*

Deere: *The Company Face is controlled by a haunted computer*
Deere: *All the way up to baord level FlavrsMart compromised by Mute Poet Cultists*
Deere: *Are you even listening???*
Deere: *Looking for killer but muppets are stalking me suspect Im*
Deere: *DEL SAYS ITS THE MEAT PIES!! DONT EAT ANY FLAVRSMART PIES!!1!*
Deere: 🕵️‍♂️:(💀🔪😷)→(💀+💀)→(💀+🌭)→(💀+🥟🥟🥟+😵😵😵)
!!!!!!

Eve fumed in exasperation. What was it with the youth of today and their tendency to drop into shrieking emoji at the first sign of anything too complex to express in words that would fit in a 160-character SMS message? Leaving aside the fact that Eve was, at most, two or three years older than Wendy and perfectly capable of shrieking in emoji in her own right, just trying to decipher them unambiguously was . . . trying. (Something about meat pies and zombies? And axes?) At least she'd used brackets so that it was clear where the phrase boundaries lay.

Zombies.

Zombies.

Eve hit the *reply* button and waited as her phone dropped straight through to voicemail. She checked the timestamp on the messages. Wendy had issued her garbled warning around the time Eve sat down with a pile of paperwork and a salad. *Typical.* Eve swore inside the privacy of her own head, then speed-dialed Imp. His phone, too, dropped straight into voicemail.

Now *that* was bad news: either he was ghosting her or there was real trouble afoot. She reached for the desk phone. "Sergeant Gunderson, I need a close protection squad with wheels, most urgent, for an excursion—" she read back the address of the FlavrsMart in Chickentown—"as soon as possible."

"Yes, ma'am." Gunderson paused: "Most of the team are prepping for tonight's mission. What are we expecting?"

"Someone in FlavrsMart HR in Chickentown has been making

highly inadvisable hiring decisions. The takeover should have closed as of noon, so I'm going over to kick ass and take names. There may be some resistance—same cultists we dealt with at the meeting."

"Okay, I'll round up as many bodies as possible." Sally didn't sound happy. "We'll meet you downstairs in ten . . ."

10

▶◀▷◀▷◀▷◀▷◀

THEY MADE A WASTELAND, AND CALLED IT PEACE

Game Boy waved his phone at Imp: "It's RobHulk06," he announced. "He's back in London and I think he's in trouble?" Imp accepted the phone and read:

RobHulk06: Pnig
RobHulk06: were lockked ina room in a supermaket in London wiv no pu'erh. Hlep?
RobHulk06: (IMAGE) a shaky panorama photo of tiny Terrortots in jail, one of them clutching a huge sledge hammer.
RobHulk06: (IMAGE) a jailhouse Terrortot selfie: It me!
RobHulk06: (IMAGE)

"Oh fuck," said Imp, "it's *her*!"

"Let me see." Doc shouldered in close and peered at the screen. "Yup, it's your sister's Saturday night priestess." He glanced at Game Boy sharply. "Some coincidence! What's going on?"

"It's this kid I raid with? He and his brother and sisters have kind of been, uh, kidnapped? It's on the news. Anyway, his 'napper doesn't realize he's got 3G and a chat client on his Splatstation so we've been messaging and I dropped a tracker on his console." He prodded at his handheld. "Google Maps says he's somewhere in Chickentown."

"Shit." Imp scowled. "Isn't that where—"

"—Del—" he and Doc said simultaneously.

"—is working with Wendy this week?"

Doc and Imp looked at each other until Game Boy stamped his feet angrily. "*It's not a coincidence!*" he shrilled, pulling out his phone. "It *can't* be a coincidence! There are no coincidences any more! I'm going to call Becca! She can—do something—maybe?"

"We could go—" Doc stopped as Game Boy's call connected.

"Del?" Game Boy bounced up and down on his toes. "Del? Are you working? 'Cos I've got a"—he froze—"you what? Wait, they're here, can you *repeat*—" He looked at Imp. "She says she and Wendy are hiding from the *muppets*?"

"Tell her to say 'hi' to Miss Piggy!" Imp snarked.

"No, wait, no"—Game Boy twitched, visibly, listened some more, then told Imp—"she means *meat puppets,* like kind of corporate zombies made out of minced—oh God that's *horrible*—" Game Boy retched. "Guys, we've got to help them!"

"How?" Doc demanded. "Where in Chickentown *are* they?"

"There's a supermarket just off the high street—c'mon? Can you spring for a taxi?" Game Boy badgered Imp. "Your sister'll pay, I'm sure! There's a reward for the kids."

"Well, why didn't you *say* so?" Imp asked tetchily. To Doc: "Get your coat." Back to Game Boy, "Why didn't you say something earlier?"

"I didn't know they needed"—Game Boy listened to Del at the other end of the call—"okay, okay, I've got that. Can you barricade—yess!" He made a fist of his free hand and waved it in the air. "They're barricading themselves in the manager's office," he announced. "Half an hour," he told Del: "Call or text me if anything changes."

"What the fuck is going on there?" Doc asked, returning with their coats—Imp's disreputable wool overcoat, his own anorak, and Game Boy's waterproof hoodie.

"The, the supermarket is full of these goons in body stockings with face-shaped displays on the front of their heads?" Game Boy gabbled as he pulled on his outer layer. "All the human staff have disappeared except for scary priestess woman who is something in HR. Anyway, about ten minutes ago the goons—Wendy says the other HR woman calls them muppets—went nuts and tried to grab Wendy but she hit them with a katana and their arms fell off and were full of, like, raw mincemeat and they kept on coming so Del grabbed her and did her thing—" Del's thing, as the Lost Boys' Deliverator, was to deliver things to wherever they needed to be, faster than anybody could follow her—"and now they're barricaded in an office upstairs surrounded by monsters."

"Huh." Imp paused. "*Meat puppets*." He frowned. "This is deeply cray-cray. Okay, let's go—I'm going to tell Eve?"

As they headed out into the central London night, Game Boy heard Imp talking on the phone. "Sis? It's me—that priestess from Saturday night? You're not going to believe this, but she's taken over a FlavrsMart in Chickentown and Del and Wendy are in trouble. . . ."

He hung up. "Change of plan, kids: we're waiting out front for a ride."

"What?" Game Boy's voice broke again. "But we'll be late!"

"Nope." Imp sounded ever so slightly smug. "Wendy already tipped Big Sis off and she's on her way there right now. I mean, she's stopping here first to pick us up, but she's already on her way to kick butts and eat nuts."

"You did not just try to distract me with a Squirrel Girl reference!" Game Boy's tone was accusatory.

"Who said it was a distraction?" Imp volunteered obliquely. "Oh look, here they come."

In Game Boy's experience Eve usually travelled by occult pathways, but sometimes she took shiny black BMW SUVs instead. Rounding the corner was something new. In the past couple of months the New Management had decriminalized or deregulated many things: cannabis, planning permission for house extensions, summoning eldritch horrors in a built-up area, and the Central London Congestion Charge zone pollution surcharge. A strange convoy was arriving in the quiet mews. Leading the way was the usual shiny black SUV, but behind it trailed a grumbling, smoke-belching, matte-black BAE Systems RG33L MRAP: a six-wheel-drive, mine-resistant ambush protected truck, demilitarized only to the extent that the heavy machine gun had been removed from the remote control turret on top of the crew compartment.

The SUV pulled up and the passenger door opened. "Get in the back," said Eve.

Imp opened the door and he, Doc, and Game Boy climbed in.
Their driver hit the throttle immediately, but paused at the end
of the lane to allow the lumbering transporter to catch up with
the much faster X5s. Eve swiped madly at her phone screen, then
adjusted her bluetooth headset. "Put these on," she said, handing out a bag of wards—necklaces from which hung small leather
baggies. They contained enchanted sigils, providing limited protection against extradimensional brain eaters, zombies, and targeted social media ads. "When we get there each of you is going to
be assigned one of Sergeant Gunderson's people as a bodyguard.
You do as they tell you, *when* they tell you, or you won't live long
enough to be sorry. Understood?"

"You don't need to lecture me, sis. What are we getting into?"
asked Imp.

"Shit so deep you'll need an echo sounder to see bedrock."
The BMW cornered hard and roared onto a bypass road. Game
Boy would swear he could hear the sound of her molars grinding
over the burring note of the engine. "Rupert had his fingers in too
many pies and some of his secret schemes are past their sell-by
date. Such as a small supermarket chain he was trying to acquire
a controlling interest in—FlavrsMart. Heard of them?" Her eyes
tracked Imp's answering nod in her vanity mirror. "Turns out his
cult has already infiltrated FlavrsMart. Wendy confirmed it's the
priestess from Saturday night and she—the priestess—is testing
something there. You can guarantee Rupert knew about it. Which
is why we're going to clean house, then fly out to Castle Skaro
tonight, not tomorrow."

►◄►◄►◄

Chickentown was a depressing vista of litter-strewn pavements,
potholed streets, and shops with metal shutters occluding their
windows like grimly protective surgical masks. It was late afternoon and night had fallen. Streetlights shed a diseased amber glare
across the sepulchral scene as Eve's driver passed an industrial-
looking building with lowered metal shutters then slowed to a

crawl, blocked by a confused mob of shoppers milling around in the road.

"What's the delay?" Eve asked.

Their driver rolled his window down and leaned out. Words were exchanged. "Supermarket's closed," he reported, "some kind of emergency announcement."

"Well then." Eve's lips thinned and she tapped her headset. "Sergeant, the shop's shut. Pull up out front and move these people along, we don't want to have to explain any collateral damage to the authorities. I'm taking Bill—" her driver twitched—"and the SUV round the back. Once in position I'll signal and we'll make a rear entrance while you take the front of store. Flash-bangs and tasers unless there's shooting, we don't want any blue-on-blue casualties."

The SUV began to roll again. "What do you want us to do?" asked Doc Depression.

"We're going to put down a mad bitch who thinks she can hijack the Church of the Mute Poet out from under me before I can round them all up and set fire to them. Assuming she's where the rot starts—it may go higher. Then we're going to rescue the children they kidnapped."

"Yeah, and what's *that* about?" Game Boy chirped. "Why would she do that?"

"They're metahumans. Probably powerful ones, going by their parents. You can capture *mana* from a human sacrifice, and you get a *lot* more *mana* if your victim is a sorcerously endowed adept—a transhuman, in other words. Rupert was experimenting with mass human sacrifice—I'm pretty sure that's why he was trying to buy FlavrsMart—but quality has a quantity all of its own. There are probably some other angles as well but I can't be bothered untangling them all while we're running down the clock."

The SUV came to a dead stop in one corner of the car park and the engine stilled. A steel gate at one side opened onto a goods area. Steel roller shutters blocked access to the loading docks. A second SUV rolled up behind them. The doors opened and four heavies in identical suits and dark glasses climbed out. One of them opened the trunk and began to distribute the tools of the trade: anti-stab vests, pistols, wards strung on necklaces.

"Issue banishment rounds, two mags each," Eve told the armorer. To the other heavies she added, "Don't waste them, each round costs fifty quid. They should work first time, no need to double-tap. You, you, and you, these are Jeremy, Doc, and Game Boy: Jeremy's an influencer, Doc is a projective empath specializing in negative emotions, and Game Boy can dodge bullets. Guard them, they're your ticket out of here if things break bad. Imp, Doc? If you see the priestess, her name's Jennifer Henderson, she's an HR manager, and she's at least a level two practitioner, maybe three—hit her with everything you've got and don't stop until she's down. Everyone: you're going to see some really unpleasant things in here. Don't let it get to you. Remember most of the opposition aren't human any more, and the company health plan will cover your therapy."

"Isn't this a job for the government?" Game Boy asked before Doc could put a hand over his mouth.

Eve's face was stony. "If the government start lifting carpet corners and peering underneath before I've cleaned house there's no telling what they'll find, and none of us want that. Vicky, George, if you would be so good as to make a forced entry, please? Don't worry about damage, I closed on a controlling stake in Flavrs-Mart this morning." George nodded, then leaned into the back and hauled out a steel battering ram.

The concrete steps up to the loading dock were unguarded but Eve went first, chanting a monotone in a language with far too many gutturals and clicks for a human larynx. A faint glow surrounded her fingertips as she waved them in front of her face. "Clear," she said tersely, then stepped aside as Vicky and Bill took up positions beside a door to one side of the shutters while George swung the ram.

The lock shattered and an alarm began to bleep. The door crashed open to reveal a twilit concrete tunnel instead of a loading bay—obviously some kind of emergency exit. "Hey, we get to LARP *Resident Evil*! I got this!" Game Boy stepped up before

Imp could stop him, then skipped forward and bolted out of sight around a corner. "Clear!" he trilled.

"Shit." His assigned bodyguard dashed after him, pistol drawn. Imp made to move forward but his own muscle held up a beefy arm. "Over my dead body," the goon grunted, "or Miss Starkey'll have my head."

"Ladies first—" Imp said as Eve pushed past the guard and entered the corridor. Her face was eerily underlit: after a moment Imp realized that her pearl choker was glowing, ripples of amethyst and turquoise light chasing around it. With the part of his mind's eye that was still magically inclined he beheld the power and majesty of a sorcerer of House Starkey: Eve had dropped her pretense of normality and stepped out of the shadows. "Go on! Move!" He *pushed*, and the guard's mind gave way like damp cardboard under the wheels of a bus, for Imp was not without power of his own. They followed Eve, and Doc and his bodyguard took up the rear.

"Up here!" Game Boy's voice echoed down a narrow stairwell with white-painted cinder block walls. They pounded up the steps after him and came to a maze of cramped offices.

"Oh crap!" Game Boy's bodyguard bellowed. "Get on the ground! You! Get on the—"

A gunshot reverberated through the offices, followed by a shrill scream of fear and loathing.

Imp followed his sister into a break room where Game Boy huddled in a corner behind an overturned sofa, while his guard faced off against a human-shaped sausage-skin held together with duct tape and nylon straps. Its face was obscured by some sort of plastic mask displaying an approximation of a human face, the color balance all wrong and the features uncoordinated. "Intruder. Intruder. Intruder," it intoned as it tried to get around the sofa. There was a bullet hole in the figure's back, and it was leaking something pink and disgustingly bloodless that resembled raw mincemeat. Game Boy's guard raised his gun and fired again, this time hitting it right in the middle of the forehead. It staggered, then leaned forward and tried to grab the pistol.

"Oh for fuck's sake," Eve said exasperatedly, then pointed a finger at it: "*Die, already!*"

The muppet collapsed, not falling but sagging and distorting as the contents of the meatsack lost cohesion and fell into its legs and abdomen, head deflating like a leaky balloon.

"Did you not swap out your magazine for banishment rounds?" she scolded, hands on hips.

The guard looked sheepish. "But you said they was expen—"

"There is *expensive* and then there is *needlessly paying for your funeral*," Eve snapped. An immediate ratchet and clatter of magazines being ejected and replaced signalled that the message had gotten across.

"What is it?" Imp leaned over the body-shaped meatsack. Opening his inner eye, he blinked painfully and *looked*. "Is that—"

"Mechanically reclaimed beef and pork scraps." Eve's tone was one of prim disapproval. "I'd estimate maybe ten percent human meat by weight. Minimum viable human sacrifice to animate a, a mincemeat golem, I think you could reasonably call it." She glanced around her audience. "There will be more of these things. They're akin to zombies, only not exactly. A banishment round should take them down, but do not, repeat *not*, let them grab hold of you or make direct skin contact with the effluvium. Your wards *might* save you but you shouldn't rely on them."

"What now, Miss?" asked Game Boy's guard, suitably chastened but tooled up with ammunition that might actually work against a paranormal adversary.

"We search this shop for Ms. Henderson. Who, incidentally, made these things," she pointed at the fallen muppet, "using *my* company resources, which I take a very dim view of—it's unsanitary—on company time. You may find my brother's friend Rebecca in company with a HiveCo Security investigator called Wendy—they're friendly, trust Imp, Doc, and Game Boy for identification. If you find four rather frightened children who may or may not be dressed as Terrortots, call me. They're probably locked up somewhere and they're dangerous metahumans so do *not* scare them: just call me. Oh, and if you find any more meat golems, drop them."

"I think—" Game Boy zoned out for a few seconds, then shook his head—"I can't find any kids? There are some more golems on the shop floor, there are some golems and human beings in the loading bay, but I can't get a route to Ms. Henderson—I think she's gone."

Eve swore bitterly. "Well then, we'll just have to find Del and Wendy and ask where she is, won't we?"

►◄►◄►◄

They found the supervillain on the fourth floor of a multistory car park in the center of Watford. She was lying in wait for them. *Actually* lying, on the oil-stained concrete floor where she'd passed out, which was a first in their experience.

As was so often the case, it wasn't a boss fight or a thrown engine block that felled the villain: it was pure and simple fatigue. Mary had been run ragged for days. Then an altercation with her employer—a frank and sincere exchange of views—had left her with a broken rib and contusions. She'd left behind a pile of broken and bleeding bodies that nobody on the right side of the law would miss, and ridden off into the sunset on a stolen bike. But— point in her favor—she'd paused to snitch. Whether because of a guilty conscience or to indulge a vindictive urge towards her ex- employer was immaterial. What mattered was that she'd cracked and asked for a meeting. Which was all well and good, but here she was, at the designated location in a multistory car park above a decrepit shopping mall, and she was dead to the world.

"'Ello, Mary. Wakey-wakey. You can come peacefully or not: but either way you're fucking *nicked*."

They'd expected a fight, of course. Mary didn't have the chil- dren with her—that was too much to hope for. So she was obvi- ously going to try and bargain, but kidnapping children was a crime for which the Bloody Code prescribed *Peine forte et dure* unless the judge was feeling merciful enough to simply hang you. And Mary had done other things, too, things involving a suc- cession of stolen vehicles and armed robberies committed with very big guns. They were in no mood to go easy on her: this time they weren't under the influence of her brain-fogging amulet—but wasn't it an interesting question where she'd gotten *that* from, or rather *who* had *given* it to her, and *why?*

"Guns won't 'elp you now, and the car park's cordoned off. You're not going anywhere."

Mr. and Mrs. Banks wanted answers from their errant nanny. Their first question they had already addressed to the National Crime Intelligence Service. It had disgorged the interest fact that her name was Mary all right, but Mary MacCandless, not Mary Drop. And Mary MacCandless had form.

"Where are our children, Mary?"

Mary moaned quietly and stirred, too slowly for her captors, so Mrs. Banks shocked her. It was a love tap by the Blue Queen's standards: a flick of a finger and a spark that made Mary jerk and her teeth click together.

"Where are our children, Mary?" Captain Colossal repeated. "Don't make me ask you a third time."

"Don't—" Mary groaned, but didn't try to sit up. "Supermarket. Chick'n . . . Chickentown."

"Are you sure about that? Because we're going to let you take us to them and if you've touched a hair on their heads, it'll be the high bar for you." The Blue Queen's voice was low but menacing. "The highest bar on Tyburn, and then who's going to look after your father? Because we know who you are, Mary MacCandless."

Captain Colossal hefted her messenger bag. "Fun gadget, this," he commented. "It infected you, didn't it?" The villain twitched, then froze as she remembered who she was dealing with. Her metal-sheathed fingers clattered off the concrete briefly as the Captain continued: "I reckon it was the dementia that got him, isn't that right? It got him just as it gave him the power to make toys. Only, Mary, you should have asked *why* the toys. Power only ever comes at a price, and the parasites don't much care about 'oo your family is, do they? So now your dad's power 'as gotten its teeth into you, and it doesn't feel so good, does it? What was her name, the Bionic Woman? How does it feel to be her? Can you feel it eating you from the inside out?"

Mary moaned again.

"*Take us to our children,*" ordered the Captain—his wife remained silent, biting back a fury so vast that if she spoke she'd bubble the paint on every car on this level—"and *if* they're all right, *then* we might offer you a deal."

"We won't let them hang you," Mrs. Banks added. "What would be the point? If they hang you, you might take *hours* to die. Half your skeleton's turned to carbon fiber, and the other half's broken."

"It was the Thief-taker General," she husked.

"Int'resting," said Captain Colossal.

"Th-Thief-taker General told me he, he wanted you out of the way. Em, *embarrassed*. Thief-taking contracts up for Home Office auction next month. Ex S'per—Superintendent—Barrett, he wants 'em. He said—"

"Bullshit," Captain Colossal said, leaning over her. The Blue Queen moved to zap her again, but he waved her back.

"Yeah . . . he tried, tried to off me. Ren-reneged. He's got my dad. Said he had 'im a bed in a secure clinic."

"So you know what it's like?" Trudy Banks finally spoke, quiet fury making her voice quiver unsteadily.

"What'd you do for, how *far* would you go, for your fam'ly?" asked Mary. The Blue Queen answered her with a shock. But she'd given her pause, so Trudy Banks refrained from electrocuting the villain.

"Do you know why Mr. Barrett wanted our children, Mary?"

"I, I can't—I don't know, but I'm guessing—don't hurt me!— he's mixed up with that supermarket in Chickentown."

"You abandoned our children," Mr. Banks threatened.

"I 'ad no choice! There were these *things* . . ." Mary shuddered.

"Things." The Blue Queen's smile was the most terrifying thing Mary had ever seen (charging Tyrannosaurs included). "Get *up*." She grabbed Mary's arm and heaved. Cracked ribs grated and Mary swallowed a scream of pain.

"So, this supermarket," said Captain Colossal. "It's in Chickentown?" Mary nodded. "What's it called? What road is it on?"

"FlavrsMart, on the high street—only branch—my ribs—"

The Blue Queen paid her no notice as she cuffed Mary's wrists behind her back, then strapped her into a five-point suspension harness and roped it to her equipment belt. "Got that?" she asked her husband off handedly.

"Check, target is FlavrsMart high street Chickentown, informant implicated the Wilde Corporation, on my way." The concrete underfoot vibrated like a hollow drum as Captain Colossal pulled his boots up. "Bag her, tag her, and call in ground support: I'm on my way." The two superheroes rose from the roof of the car park and turned to fly east, their captive dangling below them as a convoy of flashing red and blue light bars followed at ground level.

►◄►◄►◄

Eve and her crew cleared the offices and the customer areas at the back of the first floor, then proceeded forward, room by room. There was a pileup of deflated, stinking body stockings in front of the door to the branch manager's office. Eve waved her guards back before reaching out and knocking on the door with a telekinetically levitated Biro. "Anyone alive in there?" she called.

"Ms. Starkey? Is that you?" The voice was familiar: Imp took a shuddering breath from sheer relief, then regretted it immediately.

"Yes, Wendy, it's me. You can come out now, we've dealt with the muppets."

The door opened and three faces peered out suspiciously. "Who's this?" asked Eve.

"This is Amy Sullivan, formerly of FlavrsMart HR," said Wendy. "Amy, this is Eve Starkey."

Eve smiled like a skull. "I own FlavrsMart now," she said; "What do you mean by formerly?"

"HiveCo Security pays a headhunter bonus," Del sneered.

"I uh, I quit?" Amy squeaked.

Eve bit her tongue. "What can you tell me about what's been going on here?" she asked. "We're looking for some kidnapped children but all we found were—" She gestured wordlessly at the carnage.

"Children?" Amy boggled. "I don't know about any children! But nothing would surprise me about Jennifer."

"Jennifer?" Eve raised an eyebrow.

"The priestess," Wendy volunteered.

"Where is she?"

"She hasn't been here for a while." Amy looked sick. "She went off-site to give a presentation to the board this morning, then closed the store and disappeared—" she swallowed—"oh."

"Right." Eve nodded to herself, then turned to Gunderson: "We're going to have to do this the hard way, then. Sweep the shop floor."

Back on the ground floor they found and neutralized another eight shambling body stockings stuffed with giblets, mince, and unspeakable offal, wearing masks chanting nonsensical computerized warnings. Then they reached an aisle of chest freezers at the back of the store.

"What's this?" Eve prompted.

"Look."

They reached the end of the chest freezers. Game Boy faced the gleaming stainless steel delicatessen counter and its display of special meat products. Sausages and joints of lamb and Sunday roasts loitered under the polished glass covering the refrigerated countertop.

"Oh God," Game Boy moaned.

"Don't be silly, it's just"—Eve's eyes widened—"oh fuck." Behind her, one of the guards turned away, clearly trying not to throw up.

The chilled slab fronting the deli counter had been cleared. Now it displayed a most unusual creation. Three middle-aged men and a woman lay atop the chilled counters, posed with eyes closed and arms folded. They were naked and lay as if asleep, but there was something subtly wrong with them. Gradually the details slithered into focus in Imp's mind, displacing his initial recognition of *naked old farts dozing on the counter* with the apprehension of something much uglier. He tried to make sense of the individual pieces of the puzzle his eyes presented him with, but it was too much: the roseate, erect, unrealistically regular nipples, flaccid crotch-sausages, fingers capped with onionskin nails, hair that was actually an elegant composition of spaghetti al dente, the eyes that were—

"*They're made out of meat,*" Game Boy wailed and turned away.

"They're *what*?" Doc took a step closer, then recoiled. "Oh yuck."

"They've been piloting meat printers at this branch," Eve remarked distantly. "I should have asked why. I have *questions*."

The Gammon who had been gulping for air finally bent double and began to heave.

Eve was the first to get a grip. "Bill, Vicky—Doc, you, too—go and clear the room behind that door." She gestured at a heavy plastic flap with a transparent window, fogged by a decade of scouring products. "If you find anyone still alive, try and get them to—"

The ceiling meters away collapsed in a shower of splintered tiles and concrete fragments, a deafening clatter and screech of falling rubble drowning out the muffled beeping and robotic in-store evacuation warnings. A warbling fire alarm joined in the chorus, then the building sprinkler system kicked in, drenching the shop floor with a fine mist of water droplets. The lights flickered out and came back at a fraction of their original brightness. The pile of rubble stirred: two dusty human figures stood and shook the detritus from their shoulders then stepped forward, leaving a third visitor groaning on the floor behind them.

"*Drop your guns!*" boomed the taller figure. "*Surrender in the name of the law!*" Square-jawed and strong-shouldered, his silhouette was instantly recognizable from his shit-kicking boots to the top of his pointy blue police helmet.

The shorter female figure stepped to one side and rose slightly, levitating centimeters above the floor. She raised her arms and pointed her hands at the deli counter. Her voice was high and angry: "*Drop them now or I swear I will fuck you up*—" A clatter of guns interrupted her as Eve's foot soldiers obeyed.

Eve stepped forward. "Welcome to FlavrsMart!" She held up

her hands, palms out. "You're Captain Colossal and Blue Queen, right? We're looking for your children, but our prime suspect—" she glanced over her shoulder at the deli counter, at the directors' bodies lying in printed repose—"isn't here. Meanwhile I think we've uncovered a murder factory."

Captain Colossal took a step forward, shaking the floor. *Mass concentration* was a special and very rare talent, extraordinarily dangerous in Eve's opinion. It was especially dangerous when combined with the towering rage of a government superhero whose children had been kidnapped. "Identify yourself," he demanded as his wife rose half a meter and began to glow menacingly, buzzing like a failing high-tension transformer.

"Eve Starkey, acting CEO of the Bigge Organization," she said as calmly as she could manage. "These are my people. As of three hours ago the Bigge Organization took a controlling share in FlavrsMart, and I became aware that this branch demanded immediate attention. Members of an underground cult have been using it for illegal experimentation on human subjects. We also had a tip-off that a group of vulnerable children were being held here. My security team forced an entrance ten minutes ago and we're clearing the shop floor now."

"Why. Are. You. Here." Mrs. Banks was barely able to speak between her gritted teeth: her head was thrown back and spine bowed in a tetanic spasm with the effort of holding her power on a tight leash.

"My—husband, now deceased—moved to begin a takeover of FlavrsMart a couple of months ago. Without my knowledge, he also led the Cult of the Mute Poet, who appear to have infiltrated this branch. I'm here to clean shop." Eve set her shoulders and faced the two Police metahumans head-on. "Am I right in thinking you are the parents of the children we're looking for?"

"You *can* believe her," Imp oozed, pushing so hard that it was a wonder he didn't faint from the pain. "I'm her brother," he added, easing off on the *you-can-believe-me* mojo. "*Ow*, Jesus fuck those wards are too . . ." he trailed off.

"Do that again and I'll—" the Blue Queen began, her fingertips crackling menacingly, just as Game Boy sat up.

"They're not here any more!" he chirped. "Rob DM'd me that the bad guys were taking them away an hour ago."

"Rob?" The Blue Queen floated menacingly closer: "How do you know Robert?"

"We've been raiding together for ages: he DM'd me—"

"We haven't searched the warehouse and loading docks yet," Eve said, gesturing at the swing door. "Do you mind following me? I want to find out who the hell did *this*." She tipped her face towards the unspeakable deli counter display.

Mr. Banks—Captain Colossal—took a booming step forward, then another. The blue light on top of his helmet began to flash slowly. "Stay behind me," he ordered.

The Blue Queen floated down the aisle to block their retreat. "Don't try to run," she warned. "I *hate* jet lag and I would *love* to share my pain with you right now." She pointed to the woman in bike leathers and handcuffs lying on the rubble pile. "You: stay." Eve followed Mr. Banks, staying as far away as possible from the angry flying woman who could throw ball lightning.

Captain Colossal walked up to the swing doors and casually punched them off their hinges. They fell to the floor with a deafening clatter. Beyond the doorway stretched a row of countertops, fronting industrial machinery that extruded colored paste from hoses leading into ovenlike printing chambers. A conveyor belt slowly moved, bearing cling-film-wrapped trays of sliced ham through a slot in the wall from another room. Eve swallowed back acid bile. "Through there," she pointed. Captain Colossal strode silently towards the door leading into the next room, and then the room beyond that. Machinery hummed and squealed. They entered a buzzing tunnel walled with yellow steel mesh, beyond which industrial robots whirled an inhuman dance around indistinct objects dangling from an overhead conveyor line. The objects juddered slightly as the robots flensed them, slicing off pieces with electric carving knives. As one of them revolved on its meat hook Eve saw what the hook had impaled, and even though she had a much stronger stomach than Game Boy or the hapless Gammon, she blanched. Then she hurried to catch up with the Captain, who had sped up, urgency telegraphed by his every step.

One last door brought them to another loading bay. The shutters were lowered across its dock, which held the start of the conveyor line. A pair of meat-filled body stockings with e-ink faces blocked the doorway. Beyond them, two more muppets stood under the overhead conveyor, holding a third one that wriggled helplessly. Its arms were pinioned at its sides, and a rope was tied off around its neck: the other end of the rope was already looped around a hook dangling from the conveyor. "You can't do this to me!" he shouted hoarsely, muffled by his mask: "I'm a board member!" but the conveyor lurched abruptly into life, yanking him off his feet and silencing him. The belt moved on, carrying the twitching body into the yellow-gated maw of the robot disassembly line.

"What the fuck?" Imp asked in stunned disbelief.

"*Outgoing* board," one of the muppets corrected the hanged man. "There's been a buyout." This particular muppet seemed both self-possessed and disturbingly pleased with himself. He faced Eve: "I'm in charge now! Jennifer said so. Did she send you to me?"

"Who—" Eve blinked. "You know, I don't even want you to answer that." She stalked forward and yanked the Company Face right off the muppet's head, to reveal a nondescript-looking man with glassy eyes and a manic grin.

"My Lady!" he squeed: "Our Mute Lord's will be done! I'm so excited to meet you!" He leaned forward and tried to hug Eve, who recoiled in disgust.

"Where are my children?" demanded the Blue Queen.

"Who . . . ?" The man in the muppet suit looked confused.

Eve smiled at him. It was not a friendly smile. "Where did Jennifer Henderson take the children who were brought here?" she asked.

"The under-bishop arrived by helicopter? He and the pastor took the children to your husband's chapel on Skaro? For the communion service tomorrow evening?" He looked at her hopefully, as if anticipating a pat on the head. It appeared to have entirely escaped his attention that the children's mother was hovering behind Eve and crackling ominously.

Eve's eyes narrowed as she noticed Wendy slipping around the wall of the loading dock to take up a position behind the muppets. "Right. And you are—"

"He's Adrian Hewitt," said Wendy, "and he is under arrest for murder, *aren't you,* my son?" She grabbed his nearest wrist and a manacle materialized around it. Then the muppets lurched into motion and grabbed for her, the door at the far end of the loading bay opened and a maggot-pale squad of muppets boiled into the space, brandishing meat cleavers, and for a few seconds everyone was very busy.

Sergeant Gunderson's soldiers had retrieved their guns but had more sense than to fire indiscriminately, and in any event there wasn't room for everybody in the cramped loading bay. But Eve and Wendy were under no such handicap, and neither were Captain Colossal and the Blue Queen. Wendy jumped her target and furiously manifested batons and handcuffs in an attempt to subdue the struggling Mr. Hewitt. Eve targeted the two muppets that had been assisting Hewitt in processing the FlavrsMart board members. Her pearls slammed into the nearest muppet's head with a moist slapping noise that betrayed the presence of no bones within. It didn't drop, but instead turned towards her.

"Get on the floor!" ordered Trudy Banks, as she hovered just below the ceiling. "Nigel, take cover!"

The Blue Queen unleashed a dazzling pulse of lightning as the muppets crowded in through the door at the far end, splitting the air with a thunderclap. Eve blinked furiously as huge green and purple spots swam across her vision. When she could hear again—and see well enough not to stumble into the cage of whirling robot knives—she shuffled towards the broken doors onto the shop floor. Halfway there she nearly tripped over a groaning body. It was her brother. "Imp," she said, reaching for his shoulder. "*Stand up.*"

"I'm up." Imp swallowed. The miasma of cooked burger meat was mouth-watering. Behind him, Wendy knelt atop a fallen Adrian Hewitt, cautioning him from memory, evidently having temporarily forgotten that she wasn't an officer of the law. "Where's—"

"Where is Skaro?" Captain Colossal rumbled menacingly.

"An island in the middle of the Channel," Eve told him grimly. "I've got an assault team preparing to fly out there for entirely unrelated reasons. Want to come along?" She cast around in search of other casualties. Doc was on the floor but moving. Gunderson's men and women had fared somewhat better, having scattered for cover behind anything they could find. The woman in biker leathers was leaning drunkenly in the open doorway, a handcuff dangling from one wrist. She seemed to be completely out of it, so Eve ignored her.

"You have a helicopter." Trudy Banks hovered ominously closer. "You seem to know what's going on."

Eve shuddered.

"We're going there now. As soon as the chopper's ready and the troops are assembled." She took a deep breath, trying not to retch at the stink of burning meat, Lycra, and bondage gear. "*Fucking* Sweeney Todd fan-wankers." She glared at the jerking conveyor belt. Forget decontamination—the entire supermarket would need to be condemned. "*Fucking* cultists." She made eye contact with Trudy Banks. "We'll get your children back. This ends," Eve snarled, "on Skaro. *Tonight.*"

She dusted herself off, flicking gobbets of unspeakable meat products from the lapels of her suit. It was ruined, which rankled: but not as much as discovering a writhing nest of cultists sheltering beneath her corporate umbrella. "Sally?" Sergeant Gunderson stood in the entrance, looking around in disgust. "Get your crew ready, we're flying out ASAP. Got extra passengers, Captain Colossal and the Blue Queen are with us. Don't know what we're going to find when we arrive, but I'm expecting trouble." Sally nodded stiffly, then marched off in search of her troops.

"Make that *three* extra passengers," said Captain Colossal, picking up the stunned biker chick in one hand, who Eve now saw was rocking some seriously Tetsuo-grade steel prostheses. "Mary here is their nanny, and she deserves a chance to set things right, eh?" He shook her like a rag doll, barely holding his superstrength in check.

Eve swallowed. "Sure," she said. "The truck's out back: let's get moving, people."

▶◀▶◀▶◀

Actual real dungeons turned out to be grungier than the Alien Abduction Experience in Blackpool but—disappointingly—less grisly than the London Dungeon. For one thing, they were damp and smelled of seaweed. And for another there was no loo, no food court, no closing time—and no Bad Nan with a Big Gun to shoot the procession of robed, chanting acolytes of Saint Ppilimtec who unloaded the children from the helicopter and carried them down to the cells.

"Where are you taking us?" Lyssa demanded tearfully—she was really good at turning the waterworks on or off if she thought it would influence an adult—"I want my mummy!"

Robert thought this was laying it on a bit thick, but Emily had the nous to join in with a tantrum-grade air-raid-siren warble, and the robed and hooded acolyte carrying her under his (or maybe her) arm was disturbed enough that their chant faltered. "What?" (It was a him.)

"*I want my mummy!*"

Akhenaten was headless in Blackpool and nobody in their right mind would want the Prime Minister to turn up, so presumably she was talking about their parents, but it took a while for the acolyte to work it out. "Your mother will be along in due course," he said, not entirely reassuringly. "You will wait here—"

"—It's cold and wet and I want my mummy!" screamed Emily, getting entirely into the spirit of things. It even seemed to be working, until Ethan bit his acolyte on the wrist in a fit of over-enthusiasm.

"Argh! Fuck!" Ethan bounced when his kidnapper dropped him, but he recovered fast and made a run for it. "Grab the bastard!" A flurry of robed cultists dived on the lad and Robert briefly considered making a dash, too: but it seemed premature, and besides, his Terrortot suit was too cumbersome. "I can't wait to see you on the altar! I hope it fucking hurts when you get yours!" snarled the bitten acolyte, cradling his arm protectively.

"You said a *bad* word!" Lyssa hammed it up, eyes wide and limpid, and cranked her tear ducts all the way from *Flood Danger*:

Raise the Thames Barrier to *Critical Emergency: Three Gorges Spillway Eroding*. It distracted the cultists from little Emily, who still sobbed piteously but whose face bore an expression of intent concentration that a stranger might mistake for a toddler winding up for another screaming jag. Robert knew better: in the crevices of the rough stone walls, the lichen and moss were listening to their mistress's commands.

Robert nudged the wall between the worlds, willing it to thin in order to help his little sister. But all that seemed to happen was his Terrortot costume lost its zip and his radar screen began to glow again. Lyssa, Emily, and Ethan weren't wearing their hoods, so there would be no recourse to railguns or death rays. *I wish I'd asked Nan for a Godzilla suit,* he thought gloomily. *Or a giant mecha.* He tried to reach through the big emptiness to grab Ethan, but he was too late. One of the cultists had already laid hands on his brother.

"Right, no more delays. The under-bishop can deal with them."

A rusty barred door grated open and Robert found himself thrust inside along with Flytrap, Laserwasp, and Devilbaby. Then the door slammed shut, and the masked and robed cultists stomped away in search of a first aid kit and liquid refreshments.

Time passed—lots of time, to a ten-year-old's way of thinking. But Robert was an unusually patient ten-year-old, and while he waited he took stock.

The helicopter ride over the sea at night had been fun, but the accommodations had gone steadily downhill ever since they left Blackpool, and this was a dramatic step down from a bunk in a repurposed supermarket cold store. The ceiling was arched, there were rusty iron rings in the walls at ankle and neck level (to a grown-up), and the bathroom consisted of a fetid open drain in one corner. The walls were damp, and what little light there was came from a dangling fluorescent bulb in the corridor outside. Robert approached the barred door and looked out. There were three or four other cells, and two solid-looking metal doors that were both firmly shut.

"How far down are we?" asked Lyssa, her eyes dry and coldly calculating. "Are they going to ransom us or use us as bait?"

"Oh no, Admiral, it'th a trap!" said Ethan, and stuck his thumb in his mouth: "I think my tooth's looth," he complained.

"The tooth fairy doesn't—" Robert began, then paused distractedly. *If I thin the walls enough, could I call the tooth fairy? But if I did that, what would she do?* There had to be a good reason why nobody ever saw the tooth fairy: *Maybe she has lots an' lots of jaws like a xenomorph, and whenever she grows a new one she puts the teeth she steals in the holes?* Robert shuddered. Safer to stick to Terrortots.

"There's nowhere to sit." Laserwasp flounced over to the far side of the cell and peered up at a narrow slot near the ceiling. A chilly breeze blew through it. "Bored!"

"Play with your slime molds," Flytrap snapped at her. To Robert: "How do we get out? This isn't like when Mrs. Evans put us in detention all weekend, I don't think these are good people."

"Well, you could hit them with—" Robert faked a double-take—"oh look, no mallet! You must have dropped it."

"Ha. Ha. Ha. You're so funny," his sister sneered. "Ethan, pretty please re-magic my toy hammer?"

"Your—wait—" Robert stared at her extended hand, which held a Barbie-sized plastic hammer about four centimeters long. "What's *that* from?"

"From the *My Little Pony* Saddlery and Cobbler Set Aunt Gillian gave me for Christmas last year," Lyssa said smugly.

Devilbaby peered at the pocket hammer. "Why should I—"

"Do it," Robert said firmly. "Do it then put your head on and I'll buy you ice cream when we get out." Lyssa added: "Eye scream, even. That's your favorite flavor, right?"

"Say please," said Ethan.

"Pleeeeeeease?" Lyssa pulled her hood over her head, then, as Flytrap, knelt before Ethan, eyes gleaming, as she offered up the tiny plastic hammer between her cupped palms.

Robert squeezed his eyes shut, then reopened them briefly as Twinkster. Each time he did this it was getting harder and harder to tell where the Banks children ended and their costume identities began. The flickering static bleeding in from the edges of the universe was making his tummy feel bad, so he switched back to being Robert again.

"Pretty please?" Ethan was clearly enjoying the chance to get one up on his big sister, who was beginning to shift impatiently.

"Pretty please," said Robert. "She needs her hammer so we can get out of here. Or do you want to sleep on the stones? They're wet!"

"Hammer," said Ethan dismissively. He made a pass over his sister's upturned palms, then another pass with a moue of concentration. "Eye scream. French toast."

"Made with real French people," Flytrap promised.

"All right!" And Flytrap's wrists bent under the weight of her Harley Quinn sledgehammer.

"Now let's get into costume and we can fight crime!" Flytrap zipped up her younger brother's hood, then turned to Emily. A tug, a squawk, and Emily was Laserwasp again.

"*Now* can we get out of here?" Robert-as-Twinkster asked tetchily.

"But the grown-ups—"

"Terror tantrum time!" Ethan slipped into Devilbaby's character again, his—no, their?—suit reddening and taking on some of the character of short fur. Their skull-gun twitched, seeking a soap-bubble target. "Terror rumpus romp *roar*!" He threw himself at the barred door hard enough to rattle the hinges.

"Now we're moving!" Robert concentrated *hard* and slipped into his own character. His minigun was still missing, but he had other tools. His radar scanner popped up and he twirled the scanner dial (it itched very strangely when he did this), taking a bearing with the dish antenna. Something was coming through, something no human TV production crew had ever dared to tape: something unscripted and wild and feral, foaming and raging like a tumultuous nighttime storm over the sea. He pulled Devilbaby away from the door to make room for Flytrap.

"Surprise!" Flytrap raised her hammer and began to sing: "Lizzie Borden took an *axe,* and gave her mother forty *whacks*—" She slammed her hammer against the rusty gate at the end of every line.

On the third blow the gate shuddered and sagged, then fell with a tremendous crash. Slimy green rhizomes glistened in the gaps between the stones, thrusting and bulging where they'd crumbled the rotten mortar behind the hinges. Flytrap's eyes glowed in the twilight. "Girls and boys come out to play! Terrortots *attack*! Let's bring the house down! Let's make lots of *noise*!"

▸◂▸◂▸◂

Sergeant Gunderson had called in some favors for this evening's flight. She'd exceeded her brief: Eve took note and decided she was in line for a year's end bonus. Sally had arranged for a Eurocopter Caracal to meet them on the apron—a military transport that unaccountably bore the markings of the Royal Malaysian Air Force, so shiny and new it was probably not yet accepted for service. Sally helped Eve down from the MRAP and introduced her to the team. They waited in two files, ready to board the chopper. Eve and Sally had swapped their business suits for military fatigues in nighttime camouflage, and they matched the rest of the team, who were also equipped with helmets, body armor, and L22 carbines. (The latter had mysteriously escaped from a Royal Marines armory for a night out on the town: another favor to take into account when Eve considered Sally's bonus.)

"Okay, everyone," Sally shouted, "listen up! This is the boss." She introduced Eve. "She's where the buck stops. She's also the lawful head of state of the offshore dependency we're visiting tonight." Eve nodded briefly, a sharp duck of her chin. Acknowledging what Rupert had done while Imp had been on his feckless post-funeral bender was hard.

"We're going in mob-handed with metahumans. These are Imp, Doc, Game Boy, Del, and Able Archer—" Wendy was along on Del's say-so and Eve's dime, hired for the evening from HiveCo Security under her code name: they were all kitted out in the same BDUs as the heavy squad—"we've got two more incoming—"

The gate opened and a police car rolled up behind the MRAP, light bar flaring. Its rear doors opened and a pair of figures familiar from TV news broadcasts stepped onto the concrete, trailed by a uniformed nanny whose shoulders were hunched, as if she was in some pain.

"—And here they are."

"Welcome to the show." Eve smiled, her teeth throwing crimson and turquoise reflections back at Captain Colossal and the Blue Queen.

"Wish I could say I was glad to be here." Mr. Banks sounded grumpy. His wife was more on point: "What's our legal position?"

Eve raised her briefcase. "Skaro is a feudal dependency of the Duchy of Normandy, not part of the United Kingdom. It's the fiefdom of the Baron of Skaro, who is missing, presumed dead. It's also an entailed estate, wholly controlled by a family trust. I'm his wife and sole heir and assignee. I've got a letter here from the Attorney General recognizing me as head of the local government." *Unless Rupert foresaw everything and arranged to come back from the dead.* "I specifically asked for and got paperwork signed with the cartouche of N'yar Lat-Hotep himself, so you're legally bulletproof." There had been a strong whiff of *I recognize you as head of state of that lump of rock conditionally, do not take the piss or I will drop the Eater of Souls on you,* but that was the new normal for this year, and in any case totally in character for any British government ever. "Gang's all here—" apart from Mrs. Cunningham: Eve considered it unwise to bring her along tonight—"so let's get moving."

The EC725 rumbled into the night sky over London then turned southwest. With eight metahumans and a dozen soldiers on board it was quite crowded, but it wasn't a long flight. As they crossed the coastline over the English Channel the pilots dropped down to an altitude of two hundred meters, relying on instruments and forward-looking infrared cameras to guide them towards the island.

Eve composed herself, keeping one ear on the intercom loop as Sally discussed tactics with the Home Office capes. "They'll probably be holding your kids in the dungeons under the castle," she was explaining. "It's close to the chapel. This wasn't set up as a hostage rescue mission: we were originally supposed to assert lawful authority and arrest the island council, then install the baroness as emergency governor. Your arrival complicates things somewhat. There's an entrance to the cellars via the servants' stairs off the rear of the main hall—"

Eve interrupted. "I'll show them, I've been there before. Sergeant, I want you to take Team A, along with my brother and his metas. Nail anyone who looks like a troublemaker. I'll take Team B and our three guests and head for the cellar. The children are our top priority." The Blue Queen sent her a grateful look; Eve didn't have the heart to point out that a group of cultists in possession of a brace of kidnapped superpowered kids must necessarily be planning a human sacrifice. Furthermore, they'd dispose of the victims the instant they realized they'd been rumbled. It would be touch and go as to whether they'd get to the children in time. *It's not* really *my problem, but*—Eve shook her head, unable to sustain her half-hearted deflection. The Cult of the Mute Poet *was* her problem, whether she liked it or not. And while Eve wasn't exactly child-friendly, the idea of letting Rupert's minions murder a brace of kids in cold blood was appalling. "Who's this?" she asked, glancing at the nanny.

"This is Mary," said Captain Colossal, "'oo is repaying 'er debt to society." His eyes were flinty. Mary didn't speak, but cringed visibly under his attention.

"Landing zone coming up in five minutes," the loadmaster cut in over the intercom chat. "Don't release your seat restraints until I give the word."

Takeoff and departure had felt as smooth as her executive chopper, if somewhat louder—the Caracal was notably short of burled walnut, leather, and soundproofing, not to mention a drinks cabinet—but the landing was much rougher. It was night and Eve couldn't see much through the front windscreen over the pilots' heads, but suddenly the chopper lurched upwards in a roller-coaster climb and the note of the rotor shifted. She caught a brief, confused glimpse of cliff tops dropping away below them, then the sound of the engines spooled down, and they began to drop precipitously as if descending from the crest of the roller coaster. Her stomach rebelled, but just as she began to wonder if it was time to panic, the fall slowed abruptly, squishing her down into her seat. There was a heavy jolt as the wheels touched down, then the loadmaster came on the intercom again: "*Go, go go*," he said, standing and showing the civilians how to unfasten their harnesses and disconnect their headsets.

The soldiers already had the sliding side-door open and were jumping out onto the helipad, under the syncopated blast of the blades overhead. The tail rotor was still spinning, dangerously close. As Eve reached the door two soldiers grabbed her and lifted her down.

The pilots had flown in low, lifting at the last minute to clear the battlements and drop straight down onto the castle helipad. Nobody was expecting them and the pad was dark, as were the windows of the castle that overlooked the apron—but that wouldn't last long. Eve tapped her earpiece. "Side-door is this way," she said, pointing. "I've got the entry code." Her guards shielded her with their bodies as she hustled forward. A pulsing blue glow cast sharp-edged shadows across the concrete as Captain Colossal's helmet lit up. Safely outside the blur of the chopper's rotor disk, the Blue Queen levitated, flaring with St. Elmo's fire.

Eve faced the side-door with its keypad, took a deep breath, and froze. *Locked,* she realized, *and not with physical bolts.* She raised her hands, racked her brain for a correct way of framing her desires in a formal language that was ancient before hominids first split from their primate cousins, then announced herself to the guardian of the threshold. "*I am your liege and I demand entrance as of right! Open before me and disarm all wards!*"

There was a brilliant flash of light as the door flew inwards. Her bodyguards ducked inside and took up positions to either side. Her headset beeped and cleared its throat in her ears: "Clear."

"I'm going in," she said as she stepped over the threshold. "The dungeons are this way. Follow me."

▶◀▶◀▶◀

"I don't like this adventure park," quavered Laserwasp, "it's wet and smelly and there's something wrong with the plants."

They'd been exploring the basement levels of the castle for half

an hour and Robert was pretty sure they were lost. It was like
a game of Dungeons and Dragons, only without any Dragons.
There wasn't any treasure, either. There was nothing down here
but endless empty cells—well, mostly empty. They found one with
a thing like a rusty birdcage in one corner, if birdcages were the
size of a coffin and contained a bunch of old bones held together
with half-rotted canvas and tar. Some kind of mask in the shape
of a face concealed what was obviously a skull, leaning forward as
if its owner had just nodded off in his cage. Laserwasp had griz-
zled at that, and Robert just *knew* she was going to have screaming nightmares when they got home, but Lyssa had posed with it
and taken a selfie: "It's a gibbet cage! How cool is that?" Robert
thought she was being stupid: there was no signal down here and
no way to Instagram it.

"Wossat sign say?" asked Devilbaby, bellying up to the rusty
cage.

Lyssa squinted, then turned her phone's flashlight on. "Hanged
for *piracy* on this day of Our Lord August 32nd, 1816—Ru, uh,
Ru-*pert*—"

"That's bullshit," Robert announced confidently, "August only
has thirty days."

"Oh you." Flytrap rattled her sledgehammer handle across the
bars of the cage. She'd shrunk it to the size of a gavel for conve-
nience. "This is boring, it's not like he's going to reanimate or
anything. *Boring* skellington! Look, what's that?"

Across the corridor there was another door. Robert pulled
his ragged Twinkstertude together and bobbed his purple radar
antenna at it and *pushed*. Cyberwar countermeasures surged
through his dish antenna and the door creaked, then swung open.
"Terror-oopsie," he said. He'd found the Thief-taker General, the
cultists, and an underground chapel.

"Hello, children," said Mr. Barrett. He gestured over his shoulder at the throng of robed worshippers. They were all grown-ups,
Twinkster realized, and all men. Men in brown robes belted with
coarse rope, hoods drawn over their shaven heads, wearing skull-
masks that covered their eyes and noses but left their bearded
chins incongruously bare. The chapel was lit by candles that stank

of burning bacon grease, and there was an altar at the front of the nave with a monstrous triptych blocking the wall behind it. "Won't you come on in? I want to see you."

There was something wrong with the Thief-taker General's voice, and his eyes seemed to glow faintly, taking on an eerie greenish hue. They flickered as if his skull was a hollowed-out pumpkin lantern full of glowing filamentary worms. Unlike the other cultists he wore no mask, but his face had taken on a curiously waxy sheen, like something that hadn't realized it was already dead. Robert had met things like Mr. Barrett before on nocturnal perambulations that took him further into the paths behind the walls of the world than his parents realized, and he knew they were *always* bad news.

Behind Robert, the other Terrortots had begun to back away—straight into the arms of a group of fanatical worshippers who had split off from the congregation and taken a shortcut to block their escape. Devilbaby screamed and shrieked, but evidently Laserwasp had reached breaking point: she fell ominously silent, and all around the room the mortar holding the stone blocks in place began to creak and sigh. "Who are you *really*?" Robert demanded, letting Twinkster slide for the moment. "What do you want?"

"I wanna go home!" screamed Devilbaby-Ethan: "This isn't fun any more!" He sat down and howled, forcing the cultist who had taken a grip on his arm to pick him up bodily. Ethan was solidly built, and the robed man wheezed.

"I want *you*," said the Thief-taker General. "Your parents would be a bonus, and getting them out of the way would be *really* useful in the long term, but mostly? You four will do just fine. Because it's time to bring back the Bishop, and that's going to take a blood sacrifice."

"*In his house,*" intoned the congregation, "*He shall return, that dead lies dreaming.*" They couldn't quite drown out Ethan, but the cultist who'd grabbed him had clearly learned from his fellow parishioner's woe and kept his hands well away from the scallywag's teeth.

"Wake who?" Robert asked, playing for time. He could feel the walls thinning, and the hungry green things that Laserwasp-Emily wanted to play with were awake and paying attention. Something was happening upstairs, too. He could hear fireworks, but maybe the bad men wouldn't notice if he distracted them. "Who's this bishop you're talking about?"

"His Grace the Bishop is Baron Skaro, the Lord of this isle." The Thief-taker General's grin widened. "Our liege, the Bishop. And I am his under-bishop. Together we will retrieve His Grace and the fell grimoire he sought in order to open the way for Saint Ppilimtec the Mute Poet, Prince of Poetry and Song. In this time and place His Grace is only bones and nightmares, but by midnight he shall return to lead us into the light of divine madness. Grab 'em, boys. Our Lord's will be done!"

▶◀▶◀▶◀

Jennifer was having a *very* good day.

It had started with her presentation to the FlavrsMart board of directors. They'd provided the attentive audience she craved, with just the right degree of resistance to gratify but not obstruct. Her plan had been green-lit for rollout to all branches with only a modicum of electric shocks to the genitals, and the whiny rich white men had been satisfyingly easy to bag, belt, and gag before it was time to hustle back to Branch 322, chop-chop, and assign them to Ade for in-processing.

Ade would have his hands full today, and for the rest of the week, turning the staff—regular employees, workfare bodies, board and all—into muppets, or meat pies once he had enough bodies to work the checkouts and stack the shelves. But a busy Ade was a useful Ade, and with the branch computer (or rather, the spectral entity the Bishop's canned instructions had directed her to invoke and install on it) running the store, there would be no call for Human Resources oversight for a few days. Which was a good thing, because the under-bishop had requested Jennifer's assistance in opening the way back in time that would enable their leader to return and lead them to victory.

Jennifer, as Priestess of the Chickentown parish and First Handmaid of Bishop de Montfort Bigge, would play a central role in the climax of today's long-planned activities. Everything was going in accordance with the Bishop's orders, which had arrived in a steady stream of emails sent by a post-death service over the past month. The sacrifices had been procured and were being held in the dungeon until it was time for the final service. Eve Starkey— apparently another of the Bishop's chosen handmaids, albeit without her knowledge (and wasn't *that* a delicious secret)—would be in attendance when the under-bishop led the first two sacrifices to the altar and opened the dream road for the Master's return. Then His Grace would take over and, by way of two more sacrifices and the Forbidden Chapter of the holy text, he would open himself to the Saint of Poetry and Song. Then Jennifer, too, would be married to His Grace, and would come into the fullness of his power—unlike the disobedient Eve, whose permanent transferrable personnel record was absolutely not going to endear her to their Lord and Master. (Yes, a Bishop of the Mute Poet might take many wives, but Jennifer had been paying close attention to Rupert's desires, and Eve, apparently, had not.)

Of course, not everything was going swimmingly. Cunningham, Lord Skaro's butler and all-around misogynistic asshole, who also happened to be the pastor of the village congregation here, was kicking up a fuss about his wife. Apparently she'd escaped to London and Cunningham had his knickers in an almighty twist about her absence. "I won't have it!" He flamed and fumed when Barrett had assigned Jennifer to sort things out. "I want her back!" Something about bolshie work-shy kids and uppity girls, followed by an immediate demand that Jenn arrange housekeeping services for him.

Jennifer had smiled tightly. "Let's table that until after His Grace's return," she'd suggested, wishing the chopper had room to bring a couple of muppets along as muscle. "We have a communion service to arrange first, haven't we?" Cunningham *so* deserved a Company Face of his own, if not a gibbet cage dangling from the battlements: she couldn't for the life of her imagine why Rupert kept him around. "Where's the vestry?"

Cunningham had glowered at her. "It is not given to a woman to lead the congregation," he'd said sniffily, and wandered off without so much as a by-your-leave to organize the island elders' council or something.

Which was why in early evening Jennifer was in Lady Skaro's boudoir, changing into her gown and surplice, and swearing because there wasn't enough mobile phone signal on Skaro to monster that idiot Amy with make-work to keep her out of trouble until Ade worked his way down his little list to her.

Jennifer was uneasily aware that she was out on a limb on Skaro. The castle minions all belonged to Cunningham, or to Mr. Barrett (who was barely less of a shithead). Her own little flock was back in London. But she wasn't powerless: she was a fully vested priestess of the Mute Poet and she had not neglected her occult defenses. Charms and wards and disciplinary hearings were all very well but nothing quite made a point like an obsidian knife, and she had positioned no fewer than three of them about her person when something caught her attention and made her listen. An odd noise outside the drapes, a familiar thudding beat, almost like—

Jennifer switched off the light and was at the window casement in a flash. She drew back a curtain corner just in time to observe a helicopter ghosting overhead with its engines idling, very low and slow. It settled on the pad outside. "Oops," she said quietly, and tittered. Predictably the mobile phone signal was totally gone. She'd have to handle it herself, she realized, so she stepped outside and marched up the corridor a short distance, then hammered on the Lord's door.

The door opened. "Whassup?" asked a man-mountain in a black suit. Judging by the automatic carbine dangling from his shoulders and the pistol at his hip Barrett had brought him along as a show of force.

"Tell Mr. Barrett that we have visitors," Jennifer told him, reaching for his mind with tentacles of will. "Helicopter came over the battlements just now." The guard swore as she continued: "I'm going to head them off in the great hall." She paused. "You *do* have a means of contacting the under-bishop . . . ?" She rolled her eyes as he reached for his mobile phone. "Never mind! Follow me." She swiped the pistol from his holster then released his mind: the guard fumbled with his FN P90, then trailed after her as she swept towards the staircase, collecting more muscle along the way.

Jennifer was halfway to the second floor with a posse of Barrett's muscle men when the stinging whiplash of a broken ward cut through the grand hall below her. "They've gained entry," she snapped. "Keep them from the upper floors or we're done for: I'll warn the under-bishop." The guards dashed off as Jennifer hiked up her skirts, hopped on the bannister—*Don't look down,* the floors here were five meters apart and the tiles were several broken bones below her—and slid down to the next landing, ignoring the sporadic snap of gunfire. She dashed along the corridor to the executive lift and hit the button for the subbasement, hoping the intruders didn't know about the elevator. Hoping even more fervently that Barrett and Cunningham hadn't started the service without her. The intruders had to be that bitch Eve, or perhaps the brats' parents. Speed was of the essence now: the alternative didn't bear thinking about.

▸◂▸◂▸◂

Mary gritted her teeth and tried not to swear as one of the soldiers helped her down from the chopper. She was near the back of the queue; ahead of her Trudy Banks levitated like the crackling goddess of electrocution, while the soldiers and metahumans and their scary boss lady spilled across the helipad towards a door in the side of a Norman tower. "*Fuck,*" she finally spat, and felt incrementally better. "You know what we expect you to do," she remembered Captain Colossal saying, "an' if you want to live, you'll do what I want." Too fucking true: there was no obvious way off this island without one of her employers' goodwill, and she had an inkling that she'd burned all her bridges with the Thief-taker General.

As she scuttled painfully towards the side of the tower she heard the scary blonde shout something in a language not meant for human tongues: "*I am your liege and I demand entrance as of right! Open before me and disarm all wards!*" A thunderclap, a flash of light, and a sensation like an army of centipedes crawling over her remaining skin told Mary all she needed to know—scary blonde woman was a combat sorcerer in full-on *this end towards the enemy* mode. The door to the castle slammed open and the scary blonde marched through it, followed by four of her soldiers and then the random bunch of bohemian slackers the other guards were escorting, who *also* radiated occult mojo.

Mary glanced up and spotted Captain Colossal circling overhead, his arms crossed and head thrown back. She cast him an ironic salute, then limped towards the doorway, reaching into her messenger bag to see if it had any useful equipment for her. Something rustled, and she pulled her leather-gloved metal hand out, to discover she was clutching a giant bag of Chupa Chups. "*Fuck my life*," she subvocalized, and followed the dreadlocked cycle courier and the East Asian teenager towards the entrance.

A meaty hand descended on her left shoulder, restraining her. "You check the cellar," a gravelly voice told her: "stick close to Eve and call us if you find the kids before we do. It's worth your life." She nodded speechlessly and the hand disappeared: the Captain and the Queen flew upwards towards the castle battlements, setting them ablaze with a display of St. Elmo's fire.

Inside the castle hall was a confusion of smoke, shouting, and sporadic gunfire. A huge staircase dominated one end of the vaulted space and someone up top was shooting down at the intruders, who had taken cover around the periphery—there were lots of nooks and crannies here, for over the centuries Castle Skaro had been redecorated by someone with a Sir Walter Scott fetish. What had once been a defensible fortress was now a self-parody overrun by Gothic decorations and rising damp. Mary got a meter inside and stepped on the heels of the East Asian dude, who squeaked angrily and glared at her. "They've got guns!" His voice cracked: "I *hate* guns!"

"Me, too." She paused. "The kidnapped children are in the cellars," she told him. "Do you know where the entrance is?"

"Sure!" He grabbed her wrist, joined hands with the cycle courier woman, and suddenly Mary found herself dragged into a surreal line dance, shuffling and ducking and weaving as a hail of bullets spattered the floor everywhere except where she happened to be standing.

"Let me go!" Mary shouted, but Game Boy's grip was implacable.

"Can't," he panted, "you'll die." *Duck, weave, slide*—"Nearly there"—and they were under cover, at the other side of the hall, in front of a dark wooden door. "It's locked," Game Boy told her. "Can you get in? It leads to the cellar."

"Fuck my life," Mary said yet again, this time a lot louder, and pulled her glove off. Her hand gleamed in the shadows as she extended her middle finger and stabbed at the keyhole, felt unfamiliar structures unfold in the lock in a way that nevertheless felt queasily right, then *twisted*—the tumblers engaged—and pulled the door open.

"Okay, this way," said Game Boy. Mary winced as the floor shuddered, blinking away purple floaters from the flash-bang some helpful meathead had thrown at the east gallery entrance behind them. Then Game Boy tugged her again and they were all but flying down a narrow staircase with worn stone death traps for treads. "Nice lockpick. I'm Game Boy," he said casually, "and this is Del, who are you?"

"I'm their nanny." She hesitated. "You can call me Mary, 'cos that's my name."

"Pop—"

"*No.*" Her smile in the darkness was a rictus of teeth and hatred. "It's just a side-hustle."

They were at the bottom of the staircase. "I can feel the kids through there," Game Boy pointed, "and a bunch of other people." He shuddered.

"What's wrong?" asked Del.

"*Bad* people. I think we're about out of time. Where are Imp and Doc when you need them?"

"They're with Eve—"

"*Fuck my life* should be my mission statement," Mary spat. "All right, follow me." She ran down the corridor towards the chapel.

►◄►◄►◄

Flytrap skipped forward into the doorway, cartwheeled towards the Thief-taker General, and spun round with both arms extended before her, the gavel in her hands blossoming implausibly fast into a sledgehammer. Her railgun might be offline but she was still armed. "*Whee!*" she shouted, slamming a brown-robed man wearing an enamel skullface mask in the groin. "*Splat!*" On the rebound she caught another cultist a glancing blow on one elbow: there was a crunch and he shrieked piteously as he stumbled backwards, arm bending the wrong way.

Robert decided the walls around the world had thinned far enough. Something outside them—some *things*—were hungry and wanted in. As gatekeeper it fell to him to grant admission to Emily's little playmates. They were all viridian smoothness and muscular stems and tentacular writhing as they burst out of the wall between the worlds and came questing through the gaps in the stones, seeking animal life to grab and send feeding rhizomes into, probing for meat-juices to suck.

Although two congregants had grabbed him and were carrying him towards the altar, Ethan-as-Devilbaby was doing *something* that made Robert's skin crawl with a sense of deep foreboding. One of the bad men had grabbed him, too, but Twinkster had no patience for cultist shit: he charged up his antenna and *looked* at his captor, looked at him and witnessed his internal organs in all the glorious colors of microwave radiation. Witnessed them swelling and bubbling and boiling and burning beneath his radar gaze as the bad man dropped, a horrible whistling scream of superheated steam bursting from his mouth and ears and nostrils as his brain boiled inside his skull.

"Terrortot cooking class!" he sang: "Twinkster totally tastes terahertz telemetry—"

Something gigantic and inhuman clanked and scraped in the corridor outside. Flytrap wielded her hammer with grace and aplomb, bouncing between the screaming cultists and bopping them on the head to put them out of the misery that Laserwasp's leafy green playmates from beyond the stars were inflicting on them—a squirt of arterial carmine splashed across the wall behind her as she got to one unfortunate a trifle too late to prevent his arms from tearing off while his heart was still beating.

"Oi, Ethan, didn't you get enough of that in the mummy's tomb?" Robert called as the gibbeted skeleton lurched into the corridor, grinning and nodding. Smaller cages enclosed its legs and arms, hinged from the bigger cage around its torso and skull.

"He is risen!" shrieked the thing wearing the Thief-taker General's flesh, and it threw itself on the ground before the walking dead. "Our Lord has returned! In his house that which is not dead lies dreaming! *In his house*!"

The dread pirate Rupe—whoever he was, or had been, or would become—shuffled closer, metal grating on metal, lurching from side to side. The mask fronting the skull was held in place by a harness of modern-looking wires, and now a face slid across it, pixellating slightly as it faded in and out of connectivity. "We are the Spirit of FlavrsMart. How may we serve you?"

Robert looked around for an exit, saw a side-door, and darted towards it. But before he could reach it, it opened from the other side. It was the scary blonde office lady from the supermarket, dressed as a priest only doing it wrong: her crucifix hung upside down and dripped blood from the many-armed nightmare clinging to it, and she held a dagger with a gleaming black blade in one hand. "Oops," he mumbled, and tried to aim his radar dish at her. But she was too close, and she darted forward and grabbed him by the base of the antenna, then slashed, once, severing his high-voltage rail. "Ouch!" he shouted, weeping tears of pain.

"What do we have here?" hissed the priestess. "It's a very naughty little boy!" She shook him. "Were you trying to escape? You were, weren't you!"

She marched him backwards into the room where the cultists had restrained Devilbaby and Laserwasp and were gathered in a tight knot around the frantic, hammer-wielding Flytrap. Two of the cultists grabbed Robert. Lyssa was screaming, an ululating shriek that made Robert's ears hurt. With an awful crunch her hammer struck ribs and stayed there, held in place by her victim as his companions picked her up and hustled her towards the altar at the front of the chapel. "See what happens to terrible, naughty, sinful children!" shouted the priestess, as she grabbed Flytrap—no, Lyssa—by the throat and dragged her towards the altar.

Robert began to struggle, terror and no small amount of pain from his severed radar dish energizing him. Something awful was going to happen, he sensed, feeling Twinkster's soul sliding around uneasily inside his skin as the walls faded and thinned. "Don't!" he shouted: "Stop! *Please!* I want my mummy! Nan! Anyone!"

The door the mad priestess had come through slammed open again. "Children!" called a reassuringly familiar voice, although she sounded *very* annoyed. "*Here* you are! I've been looking everywhere!" Then, in a tone of voice so drenched with menace that Robert barely recognized her, Mary snarled at the priestess, "Get away from her, you bitch!"

▶◀▶◀▶◀

Mary had been having a very bad day: it was clearly about to get worse, and someone was going to pay.

Things had started out badly. Buyer's regret—or maybe gig economy worker's remorse—had kicked in after she dropped off the children at the supermarket. The kettle had come to a rolling boil when her bastard boss double-crossed her: then she'd crossed her personal Rubicon by calling Mr. and Mrs. Banks. The frantic parents *might* kill her, but London's leading thief-taker *would* kill her for sure, and the only possible way out of the trap she could see for both herself and her father was to turn King's Evidence. Then Captain Colossal and the Blue Queen had clamped down the lid on her own personal pressure cooker by saying come here and do this thing, get our children back alive and unharmed, and then—and only then—we *might* offer you a deal. And the final insult, welding the pressure relief valve shut, had arrived when she reached into her messenger for an appropriate weapon, and it gave her a bag full of lollipops with a logo designed by Salvador Dalí.

Despite maintaining the outward appearance of a buttoned-up English nanny, Mary had spent the past week fighting off an attack of the murderous rage that had dogged her ever since she'd come into her power. It leaked around her barriers while she was fighting Barrett's minions: she was completely and utterly fed up with the world, fixing to explode at anyone who got in her way. And so, when she rounded the corner at the end of the corridor and found herself facing a couple of robed goons in the middle of a room walled with prison cage doors, she exploded.

"Where are the children?" she demanded, shredding her kid-skin gloves as her fingertips extended, locked and loaded for action. She could see at a glance that the cells were empty: a door lay drunkenly against the wall to one side. "Where have you taken them?" She realized she was shouting into a robed cultist's face: she had shoved him against the cold stone wall and lifted him off his feet. "*Where are they!*" Her voice rose to a shriek.

"Nnngh—"

Distantly she was aware that Del and Game Boy had gotten into a scuffle with the other cultist, who had pulled a pistol (which Game Boy now held).

"Hey, Darth, he can't tell you anything while you're force-strangling him," Del told her. Mary relaxed her steel-taloned grip on the cultist's throat and glared at his terrified expression.

"I don't know," he gabbled: "Blessed be the pure of heart for they and only they shall be saved when our dread Lord returns bringing—"

Mary had obviously relaxed her grip too much because he reached inside his robe and pulled out a gun: but before he could pull the trigger Mary's fingers whined and flashed white, discharging all her volts, amps, and ill intentions into him.

"Dude, where are the kids?" Del asked the other cultist, who stared wide-eyed at Mary.

"Do they normally smoke like that when you tase them?" Game Boy chipped in.

Mary gave him a flat stare, then turned her gaze on the other cultist, who cracked like a walnut under a tank track. "The chapel! The chapel! They took them to the chapel—"

"You'd better not be lying," Mary warned her informant, "or there *will* be tears before bedtime."

A minute later they left the dungeon—one of the cells now occupied by a pair of cultists, one breathing and one smoking—and opened the door to the vestry.

Mary stormed up the corridor, heedless of guards and personal safety. Her ribs ached and her head pulsed with a thunderous headache, but she had fists of steel and self-healing ribs ridged with armor growing under her skin, and everything was very bright and clear as day even though half the lighting tubes were out.

"Wait up!" Del called urgently behind her: "They've got guns and we're not bulletproof!"

"Yeah, I don't think she cares—"

Mary reached the door at the other end of the passage and kept going, implacable and furious. It wasn't locked, which was lucky for the door, because Mary wasn't in a stopping mood. It crashed open into the cramped vestry, knocking over one of the robed congregants who was apparently there to take prayer guides from a bookcase.

Mary heard a familiar voice, muffled by the next door: "Don't!" It was Robert Banks. "Stop! *Please!* I want my mummy! Nan! Anyone!"

Target in range. Mary barreled ahead before the fallen cultist could recover, and slammed the next door open with a furious palm-strike that shattered the latch. It opened into what could only be the chapel: vaulted roof supported by wooden beams, arched window-like nooks occupied by deeply peculiar religious icons, architecture that screamed *place of worship* rather than *wine cellar* or *dungeon*. The pews had been pushed back against the walls to reveal an altar. A trolley with some sort of computer terminal stood to one side. Mary couldn't see the floor in front of the altar—there were too many cultists with billowing robes in the way—but an itching in her scalp and a prickling in her mind's eye told her there was a summoning grid embedded in the stonework: an occult diagram that could be used to contain and direct thaumic energy.

"Children!" she called, trying to sound reassuring, although in truth the familiar rage was bubbling just under her skin. "*Here* you are! I've been looking everywhere!"

The cultists turned in unison to stare at her. It didn't take a rocket scientist to realize that something was wrong with this scene, from the gibbeted skeleton wearing a FlavrsMart e-ink face to the corporate Barbie from Chickentown dragging a struggling Flytrap towards the altar with the blood gutters and manacles, where the Thief-taker General waited with green-glowing luminous eyes and a black glass blade in his hand.

"Get away from her, you bitch!" Mary snarled at the priestess.

Jennifer Henderson, pastor of Saint Ppilimtec the Tongueless, handmaiden and (in her own head) second wife-to-be of Rupert de Montfort Bigge, Bishop of the Church of the Mute Poet, glared at the interfering nanny as she held an obsidian dagger to Flytrap's neck and smirked: "Make me!"

Mary stalked towards the priestess, arms raised. She saw red, so angry that she'd forgotten her messenger bag. Jennifer, not being entirely foolish, shoved Lyssa towards the possessed Mr. Barrett and raised her sacrificial dagger. Mary kept advancing. "Nan?" asked Robert, just as a tentacle erupted from the floor and latched on to the Spirit of FlavrsMart.

Mary focussed on Jennifer, so intent that she barely noticed as Barrett grabbed Robert and dragged him backwards towards the altar, a path opening up as his congregation cleared the way for him. Jennifer was chanting now, her hair floating around her head while an eldritch shimmer rippled around her fingertips and coated the edge of her knife with the distilled essence of dissection. Del and Game Boy slithered around the edges of her field of view, weaving through the robed figures towards the two smaller children.

"*Mine*," snarled Mary, reaching for Lyssa with one hand and for Jennifer's sacrificial dagger with the other.

"Mummy!" shouted Robert, his voice slurring weirdly as he slipped back into his Terrortot identity.

"*He that is dead but lies dreaming shall rise again in his house!*" shrieked the thing wearing the Thief-taker General's corpse as it tried to stab the Twinkster's bulging tummy screen, the knife screeching as it skittered across his belly. "Die, damn you! Die and lend me your *mana*, it's for the greater good!"

"Not happening," Mary said firmly as she grabbed Jennifer's wrist and twisted. Metal finger-sheaths split open and clattered to the floor, but the severing spell was discharged: and now Mary's strength came into play.

"You can't—" Jennifer gasped, as the blade turned and slid through her robes.

"You fucking bet I *can*," Mary told her, pushing the knife all the way in, releasing a gout of blood and intestinal discharge. Then she turned to face the Thief-taker General and the remaining cultists as the far door disintegrated: the grown-ups arrived.

"Mummy?" asked Robert.

Robert's mummy was glowing angrily and levitating. His father, close behind, was an oppressive presence: a floating mass that seemed to suck the air from the room, warping reality. The congregation tried to swarm them, but their arrival had turned the tide. Captain Colossal moved first, punching his fist right through a robed figure's head, then the Blue Queen floated towards the zenith of the ceiling, charging up and glowing.

"Close your eyes!" shouted the Blue Queen: "That includes you," she added in Mary's direction.

"Really—" Mary began, for she was surrounded by the Thief-taker General and a pair of his minions, to say nothing of the priestess bleeding out at her feet. But then there was an immense flashing shock like the blast from an express train rushing past the edge of a platform, accompanied by the popping sound of eyeballs bursting and the sizzle of frying flesh and Mary was flash-blind and so, *so* glad to be alive and unable to see Mr. and Mrs. Banks take their revenge on the kidnappers of their children.

II

▶◀▶◀▶◀▶◀

EPILOGUE

"So. What have we learned?" Mr. Gibson leaned back in his transparent chair and waited while Wendy got her ducks in a row.

Another Friday, another high-security meeting in HiveCo Secure Briefing Room C. After the week's frantic beginning—when FlavrsMart Branch 322 went critical and she'd tried to arrest Adrian Hewitt—she'd barely had time to catch her breath since Eve Starkey's little flying visit to Castle Skaro. But there had come a reckoning, starting with a stiffly formal police interview. They eventually decided not to charge her with anything: their attitude improved drastically when they realized that Mr. Hewitt's latest collection of victims included not only not de-emphasized persons but corporate board members, and that Captain Colossal and the Blue Queen had given statements backing up Wendy's account.

But that had only been the beginning.

"It's a fucking nightmare," Wendy finally admitted.

"Right." Gibson had the patience of a born interrogator: she couldn't imagine he wasn't itching to dive in with leading questions, but he somehow gave no sign of it.

"From the top." She sighed. Her right wrist ached from mousing through forms, and she'd swear she had monitor burn-in on her retinas from typing up reports. "Our de-emphasized persons were being dismantled on the loading bay at Branch 322, using a pilot project designed to produce mechanically recycled meat products from carcasses delivered straight from the abattoir. Supply-chain shitbaggery. Mr. Hewitt, the meat printer maintenance guy, had a quota to hit and was missing it until he found a dead homeless person. Then—" this was all in Ade's notarized confession—"the regional HR chief, one Jennifer Henderson, noticed. She formalized the process. She also roped Mr. Hewitt into her church, one of the illegal mystery cults. So far so good."

"Tell me about the cult connection."

"The Cult of the Mute Poet, led—until lately—by one Rupert de Montfort Bigge." Gibson winced, his poker face slipping. "The same Mr. de Montfort Bigge who was moving to take over FlavrsMart, a takeover I might add which was completed this week by Eve Starkey, who you might remember." Another palpable hit. "Big company, the Bigge Organization, often the left hand doesn't know who the right hand is jerking off, that kind of thing. Eve's no friend of the cult so she has been extremely forthcoming in sharing information for purposes of spring cleaning. This led us to discover a connection between the cult and the former Chief Inspector—no, he made Superintendent before he was invited to resign—Jack Barrett, MD of the Wilde Corporation, named after the eighteenth century's most notorious crook. And Barrett turns out to have been *another* fucking cultist, on the Bigge payroll."

"Oh for fuck's sake," Gibson muttered under his breath. "Please excuse me, do carry on."

Wendy shrugged. "What can I say? Eve Starkey is no friend of the Cult of the Mute Poet, *or* of the late and definitely not lamented Mr. Barrett, or the equally dead Jennifer Henderson—oh, the Home Office supes at the scene swear blind that it was self-defense and she gutted herself with her own sacrificial knife—did I mention that Ms. Starkey's personal security team had been infiltrated by the cult, and a bunch of them tried to bump her off before the raid? It's all in my written report."

"Oh, what a tangled skein of yarn we weave." Gibson leaned back in his chair. "What's your preferred summary?"

"What?" Wendy blinked, taken aback. "The original mission was a success, I'd say, wouldn't you?" Gibson nodded reluctantly. "There's one less serial killer walking free today, and some closure for his victims' families—even the ones the New Management threw away. Whatever the cultists wanted with a supermarket—" her emphasis was studied: some things were not good to speak of openly, even in a maximum security briefing room—"they lost it, and there's a woman with blood in her eye in charge of the parent company right now who is about to hire us to help her clean house. And I found you another transhuman hire, if Amy passes vetting?" Despite her gathering headache, Wendy did her best to sound cheery and upbeat at the end. *Plz can has headhunting bonus?*

"Nothing about the planned mass murder," Gibson noted.

"It's in the appendices." Wendy tapped her fat ring binder. The surviving FlavrsMart board members had been more than happy to describe their nightmarish meeting with Ms. Henderson, and her laptop had survived, complete with a very incriminating PowerPoint presentation. Wendy had included a full transcript of their interviews, aside from the emotional outbursts and uncontrollable sobbing. "The New Management dodged a bullet—or *we* did."

"The Wilde Corporation with mincemeat golems and a mass murder line to keep them resupplied doesn't bear thinking about," Gibson mused. "SO15 were not unreasonably grateful for our heads-up," he added, fixing her with a knowing look. "So. What's not in the report?"

"Motivation." Wendy slumped in her chair. "According to the witnesses, Barrett and Henderson were trying to perform some sort of ritual powered by human sacrifice with the goal of 'bringing back' Mr. de Montfort Bigge from wherever he's gone." Gibson swore. "Eve ad—no, she didn't admit: she merely didn't deny—that Rupert became, uh, *misplaced,* during the earlier incident." Her eyelid twitched rapidly. "Misplaced is not the same as dead, and his attempt to retrieve a certain missing necromantic manuscript did not necessarily fail. He's in the wind, and while Ms. Starkey is working as fast as possible to take full control over the Bigge Organization and purge it of cultists, she's got her work cut out."

Gibson sat and stared at her for a minute, but all she could do by way of response was shrug.

Finally he sighed. "Right, well, *happy* joy. I'll read this and get back to you if I need any changes. You'll probably need to give evidence at Hewitt's trial. I'm going to have to brief very important people about this mess, and I am not looking forward to it, I can tell you."

"I'm sorry—"

"Don't be: it's not your fault." He took another deep breath. "But He is *not* going to be happy."

"He? Our fearless leader? The CEO?"

"His Dread Majesty, the Black Pharaoh." Gibson stood up to leave, her report tucked under his arm. "Wish us both luck, Deere, because when this bucket of shit hits the fan, we're going to need it."

▶◀▶◀

Mary came to wearing a titanium-reinforced straitjacket, chained to the wall of a tiled room in the back of a police station. Stainless steel razor-nails and drill-bit bones weren't much use if she couldn't move a millimeter. Every muscle and joint ached. The presence of a corner sluice and a drain in the middle of the floor did not fill her with good cheer.

"Do you know what Mr. Barrett wanted our children for, Mary?"

"I, I can't—I don't know—he didn't tell me!—He said he wanted me to look after them, take them on a magical mystery tour for a week, then bring them back. Said it was to discredit you. On TV, make you look weak. But they're a real handful and I asked for help and he, he changed his mind and called me back to London. Said he had a safe house, not that he wanted to sacrifice them. I would never"—she licked her lips nervously—"Is he really dead?"

"He was dead before we got there." Mr. Banks sounded disappointed. "Body was moving, nobody home. At least, nobody human."

"Good," Mary said automatically.

"No, it means we don't get to ask him questions." Mr. Banks glowered at her accusingly. "There's a lot of *mana* in a human sacrifice. Loads of it in a transhuman one. Our new friend Ms.

Starkey is being very helpful, clearing up that nest of cultists an' all. But there are loose ends."

"Did you search his office? We had a, an *altercation* there, before I phoned you."

"That's a *good* question. I'm going to find out if anyone did. Don't go anywhere." Trudy Banks stalked out of the room.

"What are you going to do with me?" Mary asked the silence when it became unbearable.

"Well, that depends on you," said Mr. Banks. He sounded thoughtful. "I'm a civilized man: I believe in the rule of law—the New Management's law admittedly, they're a bit harsh but that's tradition for you. If you 'ad hurt my children, I'd 'ave seen you in the dock at the Old Bailey." In front of a hanging judge, or worse.

Mary tried to shake her head. "I'd never hurt children," she insisted.

"Well, they're safe and sound and happy *now*, but Trudy is still a bit steamed about things. So let me tell you what I think. I'll cut you a deal." He paused. "Your dad gets a bed in a hospital, and you get a bed in our attic. *Nanny.* Your dad's care will depend on how well you do your job, and just in case you get any ideas, I gather they're trialling ankle tags with remote-control bombs these days. Or maybe collars? I don't know, it's not my department. Anyway, as long as the kids are all right, as long as nobody tries to kidnap and sacrifice them *again,* and *if* you do your job right, nobody needs to get hanged, drawn, and quartered—or have their head exploded."

Mary closed her eye—the one that wasn't already swollen shut and bloodshot. "You want *me* to be their nanny?" The prospect was marginally less appalling than a slow public execution. "After everything?"

Captain Colossal shrugged. "You're the only one who lasted more than twenty-four hours without calling me and Trudy for help, and the kids seem to *like* you. The Home Office policy group is talking about reintroducing indentured servitude for minor offenses: I think you could be part of the pilot project, don't you? Ten years' hard labor wearing a collar bomb might begin to repay your debt to society—and by society I mean the Banks family."

The cell door opened again. It was the Blue Queen. "It seems nobody reported it," she said, regarding Mary with a sour expression. "So I guess we'll have to raise a search warrant."

The Captain's phone rang. "Hello?" he said. "Ms. Starkey? *Really*? Yes, we'll be over as soon as possible." He ended the call and stood up. "Ms. Starkey is available for an interview right now, it seems. And she's got her minions, all lined up in a row for us. We'll get to the bottom of this for sure: the game's afoot!" He smirked at Mary. "Have a think about my offer—I'll be back after we've taken care of business. Don't go anywhere . . ."

ACKNOWLEDGMENTS

Many thanks to my test readers for their valuable feedback and comments.

I'd also like to thank my editors Patrick and Teresa Nielsen Hayden at Tordotcom, Jenni Hill at Orbit, Marty Halpern for copyediting the entire series (not just this book), and my agent, Caitlin Blasdell, for their sterling work.

To any old punks who're reading this: yes, Chickentown *is* a shout-out to John Cooper Clark's memorable song, "Evidently Chickentown," a striking evocation of heroin withdrawal in small-town/suburban England in the 1970s and 1980s.